R.A. Salvatore's
WAR OF THE SPIDER QUEEN BOOK II

Insurrection

THOMAS M. REID

R . A . S A L V A T O R E ' S
War of the Spider Queen Book II: Insurrection

Distributed in the United States by Holtzbrinck Publishing.
Distributed in Canada by Fenn Ltd.

Distributed to the hobby, toy, and comic trade in the United States and Canada
by regional distributors.

Distributed worldwide by Wizards of the Coast, Inc. and regional distributors.

Made in the U.S.A.

Cover art by Brom
First Printing: December 2002
Library of Congress Catalog Card Number: 2001097183

9 8 7 6 5 4 3 2 1

US ISBN: 0-7869-2786-0
UK ISBN: 0-7869-2787-9
620-88613-001-EN

U.S., CANADA,
ASIA, PACIFIC, & LATIN AMERICA
Wizards of the Coast, Inc.
P.O. Box 707
Renton, WA 98057-0707
+1-800-324-6496

EUROPEAN HEADQUARTERS
Wizards of the Coast, Belgium
P.B. 2031
2600 Berchem
Belgium
+32-70-23-32-77

Visit our website at **www.wizards.com**

R.A. Salvatore's

War of the Spider Queen

BOOK I
Dissolution
RICHARD LEE BYERS

BOOK II
Insurrection
THOMAS M. REID

BOOK III
Condemnation
RICHARD BAKER

MAY, 2003

BOOK IV
Extinction
LISA SMEDMAN

JANUARY, 2004

BOOK V
Annihilation
PHILIP ATHANS

JULY, 2004

BOOK VI
Resurrection
MEL ODOM

JANUARY, 2005

ALSO BY
THOMAS M. REID

FORGOTTEN REALMS®
The Scions of Arrabar Trilogy

The Sapphire Crescent
NOVEMBER, 2003

The Ruby Guardian
NOVEMBER, 2004

The Emerald Scepter
AUGUST, 2005

GREYHAWK®
*The Temple of
Elemental Evil*

STAR•DRIVE®
Gridrunner

To Quinton Riley
You, like a good book,
are a Wondrous treasure
in a small package.

Acknowledgments

*A very special thanks to my editors, Philip Athans
and R. A. Salvatore; this book is so much better
for your tireless efforts.
Also, thanks to Richard Lee Byers and Richard Baker;
one's a new friendship and one's an old one,
but both of you were there "guarding my flanks."*

She felt as if a bit of herself was sliding from her womb, and for a moment she felt diminished, as if she were giving too much away.

The regret was fleeting.

For in chaos, the one would become many, and the many would travel along diverse roads and to goals that seemed equally diverse but were, in effect, one and the same. In the end there would be one again, and it would be as it had been. This was rebirth more than birth; this was growth more than diminishment or separation.

This was as it had been through the millennia and how it must be for her to persevere through the ages to come.

She was vulnerable now—she knew that—and so many enemies would strike at her, given the chance. So many of her own minions would deign to replace her, given the chance.

But they, all of them, held their weapons in defense, she knew, or in aspirations of conquests that seemed grand but were, in the vast scale of time and space, tiny and inconsequential.

More than anything else, it was the understanding and appreciation of time and space, the foresight to view events as they might be seen a hundred years hence, a thousand years hence, that truly separated the deities from the mortals, the gods from the chattel. A moment of weakness in exchange for a millennium of surging power. . . .

So, in spite of her vulnerability, in spite of her weakness (which she hated above all else), she was filled with joy as another egg slid from her arachnid torso.

For the growing essence in the egg was her.

ONE

"And why should my aunt trust anyone who sends a male to do her work for her?" Eliss'pra said, staring disdainfully down her nose at Zammzt.

The drow priestess reclined imperiously upon an overstuffed couch that had been further padded with an assortment of plush fabrics, as much for decoration as comfort. Quorlana thought the slender dark elf should have looked oddly out of place in the richly appointed private lounge, dressed as she was in her finely crafted chain shirt and with her mace close at hand. Yet Eliss'pra somehow managed to appear as though she was counted among House Unnamed's most exclusive clientele. Quorlana wrinkled her nose in distaste; she knew well which House Eliss'pra represented, and she found that the haughty drow reclining opposite her exhibited a little bit too much of her aunt's superior affectations.

Zammzt inclined his head slightly, acknowledging the other dark elf's concern.

"My mistress has given me certain . . . gifts that she hopes express her complete and enthusiastic sincerity in this matter," he said. "She also wishes me to inform you that there will be many more of them once the agreement is sealed. Perhaps that will assuage your own fears, as well," he added with what he must have intended as a deferential smile, though Quorlana found it to be more feral than anything. Zammzt was not a handsome male at all.

"Your 'mistress,'" Eliss'pra replied, avoiding both appellations and names, as the five of them gathered there had agreed at the outset, "is asking for a great deal from my aunt, indeed from each of the Houses represented here. Gifts are not nearly a generous enough token of trust. You must do better than that."

"Yes," Nadal chimed in, sitting just to Quorlana's right. "My grandmother will not even consider this alliance without some serious proof that House—" The drow male, dressed in a rather plain *piwafwi,* snapped his mouth shut in mid-word. His insignia proclaimed him as wizard member of the Disciples of Phelthong. He caught his breath and continued, "I mean your mistress—that your mistress is actually committing these funds you speak of."

He seemed chagrinned that he had nearly divulged a name, but the male maintained his firm expression.

"He's right," Dylsinae added from Quorlana's other side, her smooth, beautiful skin nearly glowing from the scented oils that she habitually slathered on herself. Her gauzy, hugging dress contrasted sharply with Eliss'pra's armor, reflecting her propensity for partaking in hedonistic pleasures. Her sister, the matron mother, was perhaps even more decadent. "None of those whom we represent will lift a finger until you give us some evidence that we aren't all putting our own heads on pikes. There are far more . . . interesting . . . pastimes to indulge in than rebellion," Dylsinae finished, stretching languidly.

Quorlana wished she were not sitting quite so close to the harlot. The perfume of her oils was sickly sweet.

Despite her general distaste for the other four drow, Quorlana agreed with them on this matter, and she admitted as much to the group.

"If my mother were to ally our own House with you other four lesser Houses against our common enemies, she would need certain assurances that we would not be left by the rest of you to dangle as scapegoats the moment events turned difficult. I'm not at all certain such a thing exists."

"Believe me," Zammzt responded, circling to make eye contact with each of them in turn, "I understand your concerns and your reluctance. As I said, these gifts I have been ordered to bestow upon your Houses are but a small token of my mistress's commitment to this alliance."

He reached inside his *piwafwi* and produced a scroll tube, and a rather ornate one, at that. After slipping a fat roll of parchment from the tube, he unfurled the scroll. Quorlana sat forward in her own chair, suddenly curious as to what the dark elf male might have.

Scanning the contents of his stack of curled parchment, Zammzt sorted them and began to circle the gathering, removing a set of pages and handing them to each co-conspirator in turn. When he handed Quorlana her sheaf, she took it from him gingerly, uncertain what kind of magical trap might be inlaid in the pages. She eyed them carefully, but her suspicions were dispelled; they were spells, not curses. He was offering them scrolls as gifts!

Quorlana felt elation rise up into her. Such a treasure was priceless in days of such uncertainty and unease. The Dark Mother's absence had put a strain on every priestess who worshiped her. Quorlana herself had not been able to weave her own divine magic in four tendays, and she broke out into a sweat every time she thought on it. But with scrolls, the fear, the anxiety, the sense of hopelessness might be staved off, at least for a time.

It was only with the utmost effort that the drow priestess resisted the urge to read through the scrolls there and then. Forcing herself to remember whom she served, at least for the moment, she instead pocketed the parchment sheets inside her *piwafwi* and turned her attention back to the clandestine gathering in front of her.

"The only other proof strong enough to convince you of our sincerity would be moving forward with hiring the mercenaries," Zammzt said, though none of the other dark elves seemed to be paying the least bit of attention to him.

Eliss'pra and Dylsinae were both wide-eyed with the same excitement Quorlana felt. Nadal, though not as personally thrilled—the spells were worthless to him as a wizard—could still recognize the value of the gifts.

"It should be obvious to each of you," Zammzt continued, "that once our House approaches outsiders, there is no turning back. We would be completely committed, with or without your pledge of alliance. That, my charming companions, is putting the cart before the lizard."

"Nonetheless," Eliss'pra answered, still smiling as she gazed on the scrolls in her hands, "that is precisely what you must do if you wish to count my aunt among your allies."

"Yes," Dylsinae agreed.

Nadal nodded his concurrence.

"I think my mother would be willing to accept those terms. Especially after she sees these," Quorlana voiced her assent, then gestured at the scrolls tucked away in her *piwafwi*. "Most definitely if there are more where these came from."

How in the Underdark do they have precious scrolls to spare? she wondered.

Zammzt frowned and said, "I am not promising anything. I very much doubt that I can convince her to agree to this, but if she is willing, I will procure the services of the mercenaries and bring you the proof."

No one spoke. They were all one step away from the point of no return, and despite the fact that none of them were actually in a position to make the decision, they felt the weight of that decision just as heavily.

"Then we will meet again after you have hired the army," Eliss'pra said, rising from her couch. "Until then, I don't wish to see any of you near me, not even on the same web street."

Gripping her mace tightly, the drow priestess stalked out of the private lounge.

One by one, the others also departed, even Zammzt, until Quorlana was alone in the room.

Our time has come, the drow insisted silently. *Lolth has issued a* challenge. The great Houses of Ched Nasad will fall, and ours will rise up to take their place. Our time has come at last.

※　　※　　※

Aliisza was so used to the tanarukks' constant grunting, snarling, and slavering that she rarely heard it anymore, so the quiet that surrounded her as she strode alone along the dwarven thoroughfare was noticeable. Being out and about in ancient Ammarindar without an escort of the half-fiend, half-orc hordes was a refreshing change. Kaanyr rarely asked her to—she refused to say "let"—do anything without an armed escort anymore, so she had almost forgotten how pleasant solitude really was. Still, as much as she was enjoying her privacy, however brief it might be, she had a purpose, and it quickened her steps.

She moved to the end of a long and broad boulevard, which had been hewn by long-dead dwarves from the unmarred bedrock of the Underdark itself eons ago. Though she barely noticed it, the craftsmanship of the wide passageway was exquisite. Every angle was perfect, every column and cornice was thick and finely decorated with runes and stylized images of the stout folk. At the terminus of the boulevard, Aliisza entered a large chamber, which itself was large enough to have engulfed a small surface town. She turned into a side tunnel that would allow her to cut across several main passages and reach the avenue that would take her directly to Kaanyr's palace, deep in the center of the old city. It still surprised her how empty the city could be, even with all of the Sceptered One's Scourged Legions roaming around. She crossed the avenues and found the path she wanted, then hurried toward the palace.

A pair of tanarukk guards flanked the doorway into the throne room. The stocky, gray-green humanoids were hunched over as usual, their prominent tusks jutting forward defiantly from overly large lower jaws as they peered at her with their squinty red eyes. To Aliisza, it almost appeared that the two beasts were preparing to charge forward and ram her with their low, sloping foreheads. Aliisza knew that with her magic the scalelike ridges protruding from atop those foreheads were no threat to her, but still the creatures seemed uncertain of who she was, for they kept their battle-axes crossed before the opening as she approached. Finally, just before it seemed that she was actually going to have to slow her pace and say something—which would have made her very cross—the two coarse-haired, nearly naked beasts stepped aside and allowed her to enter without breaking her stride. She smiled to herself, wondering how much fun it would have been to flay them alive.

Passing through several outer chambers, Aliisza crossed the threshold into the throne room itself and spied the marquis cambion lounging on his throne, a great, hideous chair constructed of the bones of his enemies. Every time she saw the thing, she was reminded of how crass it was. She knew too many fiends who considered sitting atop a pile of bones to be some sort of symbol of power and glory, but in her opinion, it exhibited no class, no subtlety. It was Kaanyr Vhok's single biggest lack of vision.

Kaanyr had thrown one leg over the armrest of the throne and sat with his chin resting in his cupped hand, elbow against his knee. He was staring off into the upper reaches of the chamber, obviously thinking and oblivious to her.

Aliisza almost unconsciously began to saunter provocatively as she closed the distance between them, and yet she found that she was admiring his form as much as she hoped he was appreciating hers. His graying hair was roguishly disheveled and, combined with his swept-back ears, gave him the appearance of a maturing, if somewhat devil-may-care, half-elf. Aliisza crooked her mouth in a sly smile, thinking of him engaging in the many subterfuges he was so fond of, passing himself off on the surface world as a member of that fair race.

Kaanyr finally heard his consort's footsteps and looked up at her, his features brightening, though whether it was simply for the sight of her or the news she bore, she was not sure. She reached the first steps of the dais and climbed to where he sat, allowing just a hint of a pout to creep into her visage.

"Ah, my delectable one, you've come, and with news, I hope?" Kaanyr asked, straightening himself and patting his thigh.

Aliisza stuck out her tongue at him and sashayed the remaining distance to plop herself down atop his lap.

"You never just ravish me anymore, Kaanyr," she pretended to complain, wriggling her backside as she settled. "You only love me for the work I do for you."

"Oh, that's not fair, little one," Vhok replied, running his hand lovingly down one of her black, shiny leather wings. "Nor is it particularly true."

With that, he reached up with his other hand, and placing it behind her lustrous black curls, crushed her to him, engaging her mouth with his own in a deep, spine-tingling kiss. For the briefest of moments she considered resisting him, playing one of the infinite variations of the games the two of them seemed to love so much, but the thought was short-lived. His hand strayed down her throat to the hollow of her neck, and it continued lower still. She practically buzzed at his touch, and she knew that with the news she brought him, such flirtations would only break the spell.

As it was, Kaanyr still pulled away after a moment's heated embrace and said, "Enough. Tell me what you found out."

This time, Aliisza really did pout. His caresses on her wings and elsewhere left her panting slightly, and important news or not, she was not ready to be cast aside so quickly. She considered withholding the information for a time, sending a subtle message that she was not to be trifled with. He might rule this place, but she was not his servant. She was consort, she was advisor, and she was free to find another lover, should he cease to satisfy her. Satisfying an alu—the daughter of a succubus and a human mate—was a challenge few were up to. Kaanyr was one of those few. She decided to tell him her news.

"They haven't veered from their course, though it's apparent they know we're closing in. Their scouts have spotted our skirmishers and have continued to avoid contact. We will have them pinned against the Araumycos, soon."

"You're certain they're not here to spy or to wage war? No quick strikes before vanishing into the wilds?"

Kaanyr was absently stroking one of her wings as he asked this, and the alu-fiend shivered in delight. He seemed not to notice her reaction.

"Fairly certain. They are apparently headed southeast, toward Ched Nasad. Each time we cut off their route, they seek out another. They seem intent on keeping to that path."

"Yet, they are not a caravan," he said. "They don't have goods or pack animals. In fact, they travel unreasonably lightly armed for drow. They are definitely up to something. The question is, what?"

Aliisza shivered again, though this time it was as much from the anticipation of the next bit of news as from Kaanyr's absentminded petting.

"Oh, definitely not a caravan," she told him. "It's the strangest drow entourage I think I've seen wandering around the wilds. They have a draegloth with them."

Kaanyr straightened, staring straight into Aliisza's eyes, and asked, "A draegloth? Are you sure?"

When the alu nodded, he pursed his lips.

"Interesting. This just gets more and more intriguing. First, we haven't seen a drow caravan of any sort in the last few tendays. Finally, when a party of drow *do* venture out, they come straight through here, something they would normally avoid like the stink on a dretch, and lastly, they have a draegloth accompanying them, which means drow noble Houses are somehow personally involved. What in the Nine Hells are they up to?"

Vhok resumed staring off into the dark distance, again absently caressing his consort, this time letting his fingers trail gently down her ribs, which were exposed through the lacing of her shiny black leather corset. She sighed in delight but forced herself to stay focused.

"There's more. I listened in on a conversation when they stopped to rest. One of them, definitely a mage of some sort, was taunting another, who looked like a priestess."

"One of the males giving lip to a female? That can't last long."

"Not just any female. He referred to her as 'the Mistress of the Academy.' "

Kaanyr sat upright, his stare deeply penetrating her own.

"Oh, really," he said in a tone so intrigued, he never noticed that his move nearly made Aliisza fall to the floor at his feet.

She managed to maintain her balance, but she was forced to stand to avoid looking silly. She glared at the cambion.

He went on, oblivious, "Oh, this is just too good. One of the highest drow priestesses in all of Menzoberranzan is trying to sneak incognito through my tiny little domain. And she's letting a wizard run his mouth at her. No caravans for more than a month, and now this. This is too much fun!"

Kaanyr turned to face Aliisza once more, and upon seeing her glare, he cocked his head in confusion.

"What? What's wrong?"

The alu fumed, "You have no idea, do you?"

Kaanyr spread his hands helplessly and shook his head.

"Well, then I'm not going to tell you!" she snapped, and turned away from him.

"Aliisza." Vhok's voice was deep and commanding, and it sent shivers down her spine. He was angry, just as she'd hoped. "Aliisza, look at me."

She glanced back at him over her shoulder, letting one arched eyebrow rise questioningly. He had risen from the throne and was standing with his hands on his hips.

"Aliisza, I don't have time for this. Look at me!"

She shivered in spite of herself and turned fully around to face her lover. His eyes smoldered and made her melt. She pouted just a little, to let him know that she didn't like being chastised, but she was finished playing the game.

Vhok nodded slightly in satisfaction.

His visage softened a bit, and he said, "Whatever I did, I'll make it up to you later. Right now, though, you have to get back over there and find out what's going on. See if you can get face to face with them and 'invite' them to pay us a visit. But be careful. I don't want this to explode in my face. If a high priestess and a draegloth are part of this group, then the rest of them are dangerous, too. Keep the Scourged close, to hem them in, but don't waste too many bodies on an all-out attack. But also don't make it too obvious that you're holding them back. Also, don't—"

Aliisza rolled her eyes, feeling a little insulted.

"I've done this a time or two before, you know," she interrupted, her voice thick with sarcasm. "I think I know what to do. But . . ."

She stepped closer to Kaanyr—into him, really—rising up on her tiptoes and wrapping her arms around his waist and curling one smooth, bare leg around the back of his calf. She drew herself close, let her body press against his, and continued.

"When I'm done with this little task," she said, her voice smoky with desire, "you're going to tend to *my* needs for a while." She leaned up and nibbled on his ear, then whispered, "Your teasing is working too well, love."

Triel didn't like brooding, but she caught herself doing it frequently of late. This time, when she realized she was at it again, she was suddenly aware of the faces of the other seven matrons, looking at her expectantly. She blinked and stared back at them for a moment, trying to recall the words of the conversation that had droned in the background of her thoughts. She could remember voices but nothing more.

"I asked," Matron Miz'ri Mizzrym said, "what thoughts have you given to other courses of action, should your sister fail to return?"

When Triel still did not respond, the hard-faced matron mother added, "There *are* thoughts floating around somewhere in there today, aren't there, Mother?"

Triel blinked again, jolted fully back to the conversation at hand by the Mizzrym's biting words, focusing her attention where it ought to be instead of on the empty sensation she felt where the goddess's presence should have been. Other courses of action . . .

"Of course," she replied at last. "I've been giving that considerable thought, but before we delve too deeply into alternatives, I think we must exercise some patience."

Matron Mez'Barris Armgo snorted. "Have you been listening to a word we've said in the last five minutes, Mother? Patience is a luxury we no longer have. We exhausted so much of our reserves of magic quelling the uprising we might—*might,* I say—be able to withstand another major insurrection, should one occur. As much as I love a good battle, putting down another slave rebellion would be wasteful, when it's only a matter of time before Gracklstugh or the survivors of Blingdenstone determine that we are powerless, without . . ."

The hulking, brutish matron mother faltered, unwilling, even as forward and tactless as she usually was, to put words to the crisis they all faced.

"If they aren't already aware," Zeerith Q'Xorlarrin interjected, glossing over Mez'Barris's unfinished thought. "Even now, one or more of the other nations could be amassing an army to drive to our gates. New voices could be whispering poison into the ears of the lesser creatures down in the Braeryn or the Bazaar, voices belonging to those clever enough to mask their true identities, their true intent. It's something we must consider and discuss."

"Oh, yes," Yasraena Dyrr said contemptuously. "Yes, let's sit here and discuss; not act, never act. We are afraid to venture forth into our own city!"

"Bite your tongue!" Triel snapped, growing more and more incensed.

She was angry not only at the direction of the conversation—suggestions of cowardice from the High Council!—but also at the ridicule, the unusually open vitriolic nature, of the other matrons' words. Ridicule directed at her.

"If there is one among us afraid to walk our own streets, she need no longer sit on this Council. Are you one such, Yasraena?"

The matron mother from House Agrach Dyrr grimaced at the chastisement she was receiving, and Triel realized it was not merely because Yasraena knew she had overstepped herself. It was the matron of House Baenre, supposedly an ally to Yasraena's house, that was administering this stern lecture. Triel intended it as such. It was time to send a message, to remind the other matron mothers that she still sat at the top of the power structure and she would not tolerate such insubordination from any of those sitting around her, ally or not.

"Perhaps Matron Q'Xorlarrin is right," Miz'ri Mizzrym said quietly, in an obvious attempt to steer the conversation in a new direction. "Perhaps we should consider not just who knows, not just who moves against us—covertly or otherwise—but who might be allying

together against us. If even two or three of the other nations come together as our enemies . . ."

She let the thought trail off, and the other drow in the chamber looked uncomfortable, considering its obvious conclusion.

"We need to know what's going on," she continued, "at the very
least. Our spy network among the duergar, the illithids, and other
deep races has not been best used of late or perhaps isn't as strong as
we would like. But what's in place should be funneling more information back to us about the intentions of potential threats."

"Oh, it should be doing more than that," Byrtyn Fey said. Triel
raised her eyebrow in slight surprise, for the voluptuous matron
mother of House Fey-Branche did not often find interest in discussions so far removed from her own hedonistic pleasures.

"It should be looking for possible weaknesses among our enemies. It should be exploiting those weaknesses, setting potential allies
against one another, and perhaps, it should be on the lookout for
dissatisfied elements of those traditional enemies, elements that
might even consider a new alliance."

"What, are you mad?" Mez'Barris snapped. "Allying with outsiders? Who is there to trust? No matter how we approach such an alliance, the moment we reveal that we cannot receive blessings from
our own goddess, potential allies will either laugh uproariously or trip
over themselves running to spread the news."

"Don't be dense," Byrtyn snapped right back. "I know how
fond you are of the straightforward, brutal-truth method for everything, but there are better, more subtle ways of luring an ally into
your bed. Potential suitors need not know about your shortcomings
until after you have partaken of their charms."

"Not being able to defend our own city from attack would be
too obvious a shortcoming to try to hide," Zeerith said, frowning.
"Our own charms will have to be most convincing to blind such potential suitors from the truth. Still, the idea has merit."

"It is impossible," Matron Mez'Barris said, folding her thick arms
and leaning back as though dismissing the discussion. "The risk of
discovery by our enemies would only be magnified, and the rewards
are certainly not worth it."

"Spoken like a hag with few to share her bed," Byrtyn said smugly, stretching languidly to make certain her own well-rounded figure was plainly visible through the sheer fabric of her shimmering dress. "And one who's always trying to convince herself that she's better off without them, anyway."

Several of the other high priestesses gasped at the insult, but Mez'Barris only narrowed her piercing red eyes, staring daggers at Byrtyn.

"Enough!" Triel said finally, interrupting the glaring contest between the two matron mothers. "This bickering is pointless, and it's beneath us all."

She looked pointedly at both Mez'Barris and Byrtyn until both of them ceased their glowering and turned their attention back to her.

If only Jeggred were here, the matron mother of House Baenre thought.

Triel wondered briefly if she should be disturbed that she was once again wishing for the draegloth's soothing presence in the face of such adversity. It was something else she had caught herself doing often of late, and she feared what it symbolized. Perhaps she had grown to rely too much on external protection rather than her own abilities. She feared that it was a weakness, and weakness was definitely something she could ill afford in the current climate.

No, she corrected herself, not just now, not ever.

But the need for allies, however brief and volatile such alliances tended to be, were a necessary part of her life.

Maybe Byrtyn is right, she thought. Maybe that's what Menzoberranzan needs: an ally. Another nation, a race from the Underdark, to aid the noble Houses until this crisis has passed.

Triel tightened her jaw and shook her head softly, determined to banish such silly notions from her mind.

Nonsense, she told herself firmly. Menzoberranzan is the strongest city in the Underdark. We need no one. We will prevail as we always have, through cunning, and guile, and the favor of the goddess. Wherever she is. . . .

"I know very well the state of things in Menzoberranzan," Triel said, looking eye to eye with each matron mother present. "The crisis we face tests us—tests us more severely than any ever confronted by the ruling Houses in all the city's history—but we cannot let it get in the way of resolute administration of the city. The moment we begin to squabble, the moment we do not show a united front to the other Houses, to Tier Breche or Bregan D'aerthe, is the moment we show it to the rest of the world, and by then all is already lost.

"For the time being, we continue to show patience. Discussion of ways to deal with the crisis is welcome—calm, respectful discussion—" and Triel once again inclined her head toward the two matron mothers—"or suggestions for new ways to explore what has happened to Lolth, but there is to be no more of this talk of fear or cowardice, and no more of these insults. That is the behavior of foolish males or the lesser races. We conduct the business of our Houses and our council as we have always done."

Triel made certain to catch each and every matron mother with her own gaze this time, staring intently into each pair of red eyes in turn, wanting to ensure that everyone present got her message—that and to ensure that she was showing a strong face.

Slowly, one by one, the other matron mothers nodded, willing, at least for the time being, to acquiesce to the Baenre's demands.

Wielding power always requires such a delicate touch Triel reminded herself as the group broke apart and the other high priestesses went their separate ways, returning to their homes. Like a supple switch, if you swing it about too vigorously, you just end up breaking it on the slave you are trying to goad.

TWO

"I told you coming this way was a mistake," Pharaun panted as he pulled up from his headlong run.

The passage before the drow wizard ended abruptly, blocked by a great gray mass of spongy material that completely filled the tunnel. Turning back to face the direction from which he'd come, the dark elf quickly sloughed off his finely crafted knapsack, lowered it to the rocky floor, and scooted it out of the way with his foot.

"Don't gloat, Mizzrym," Quenthel said, her scowl heavy, stumbling up beside him.

The five snake heads that dangled, writhing, from the whip at the Baenre high priestess's hip rose up and hissed their own displeasure at the wizard, duplicating their mistress's mood, as usual. Quenthel yanked the scourge free of her belt and took up a position beside Pharaun, waiting.

The draegloth was right on the haughty drow's heels. Jeggred bore not one but two heavy bundles, and when the four-armed fiend reached the pair of dark elves, he tossed the supplies to the floor, apparently not the least bit winded from bearing them. He flashed a savage, twisted smile that exposed his yellowish fangs and turned around, advancing a few steps to position himself between Quenthel and anything that might come from the other direction, a low growl rumbling deep in his demonic throat.

The Master of Sorcere was in no mood for putting up with the high priestess's foul temper, and he grimaced as he considered several spells. Settling on one, he fished around in his *piwafwi,* fetching from a pocket inside the extravagant cloak the reagents he would need to weave the chosen magic. Eventually, he produced a bit of squid tentacle. He had warned them they would be trapped if they came this way, and so had Valas, but Quenthel had insisted. As usual, it was up to Pharaun to extricate them all.

Faeryl Zauvirr was the next to stumble into view, her breathing labored. The ambassador from Ched Nasad spotted the blockage in the passage and groaned, sliding her pack from her back and tossing it with a thud to the rocky floor next to the others'. She wearily produced a small crossbow from her own *piwafwi* and placed herself on the wizard's other side.

"They're right behind us," Ryld Argith announced as he and the last member of the drow contingent, Valas Hune, sprinted from around the curve of the passage.

Past the burly warrior and the diminutive scout, Pharaun could see the red glow of multiple pairs of eyes advancing on the group's position. The creatures peered forward eagerly, and the wizard estimated nearly two dozen tanarukks.

Stooped forward as though afflicted with a hunched back, the creatures were reminiscent of orcs, though their features were decidedly more demonic, with their scaled, sloping foreheads and their prominent tusks. They wore little armor, for their hides were scaly and tough, but the battle-axes many of them brandished were heavy and vicious-looking.

Pharaun shook his head in resignation and prepared to weave a spell.

The tanarukks howled in delight and lunged forward, eager, it seemed, to take the battle to their cornered prey. Several swarmed at

Jeggred, and the fiend bellowed his own war cry, crouching and slashing wildly. He tossed one of the tanarukks aside effortlessly, slamming it against the far wall, near Ryld's position.

Pharaun gaped for a moment at the unbridled might and ferocity the draegloth displayed, even as two more of the humanoid attackers went down before the precision slashing of Splitter, the enchanted greatsword wielded with greater skill by Ryld Argith. Faeryl fired her crossbow from beside Pharaun then stooped to reload it. Quenthel, in the meantime, seemed content to watch her subordinates at work. More of the tanarukks swarmed in, though, and the wizard almost didn't react in time to one that slipped through the line of defense that Jeggred and Ryld had formed.

The slavering, green-skinned tanarukk leaped toward the wizard, its axe cocked back for a savage blow. Pharaun was just able to back-pedal enough to avoid the slashing blade as it swooshed through the air where his face had been a heartbeat before. He considered calling the magical rapier from the enchanted ring that held it, tiny and out of the way until needed, but he knew the effort would be futile. The thin blade would never withstand the force of the axe, and besides, he couldn't get enough room between himself and the beast to use the more nimble weapon effectively. He was quickly running out of space to maneuver.

When the tanarukk arched its back and howled in pain and fury, Pharaun saw that Quenthel was behind it, already drawing her arm back for another swipe with her dreaded whip. The tanarukk whirled around, still screaming in anger. It raised its axe high for a killing blow, but before either it or the high priestess could finish their attacks, a flash of shadow materialized at the edge of Pharaun's field of vision—and the shadow became Valas Hune.

The mercenary scout darted in low behind the green-skinned creature and pulled one of his kukris harshly across the tanarukk's hamstring, crippling it with the oddly curved knife. Black blood spurted everywhere from the deep wound as the beast sank to one knee, flailing feebly with its hands, trying to find the source of its torment. As quickly as Valas had appeared, he was gone, vanished again in the shadows.

Quenthel took the opportunity to bring the whip down on the tanarukk again, and Pharaun saw the fangs of the snake heads sink deeply into the flesh of the creature's face and neck. Already, it was beginning to cough and choke, its face and tongue bloating, poisoned by the lashes from the whip. It dropped its axe and crumpled to the floor, spasming and crying out in anguish.

Pharaun realized he was holding his breath and exhaled sharply, regaining his wits. Disgusted with himself for being so undisciplined, he remembered the tiny piece of squid tentacle that he had in his hand. Righting himself, he made a rapid inspection of the battlefield in order to determine where best to place the spell he had in mind.

A host of dead tanarukks had piled up around Jeggred and Ryld, but still the remaining creatures fought their way to get nearer the pair, snarling and leaping about, looking for an opening where they could use their axes. The wizard decided he could easily position the magic behind those few savage humanoids that remained, but then he paused, startled.

A face had caught the drow mage's eye at the far back of the passage. He blinked and peered more carefully, not trusting his assumption. Lurking in the darkness, watching the battle, was a beautiful woman. Pharaun found her attractive, despite the fact that she was not a drow but appeared human. Black curly hair framed her face, and she was dressed in a tight, shiny leather corset that hugged her curves like a second skin. She seemed to be saying something to the last rank of humanoids, giving them orders and gesturing, but when she noticed Pharaun staring at her, she smiled, her highly arched eyebrows raising even farther in a bemused grin. That was when the wizard also noticed the black, leathery wings sprouting from her back. She wasn't human after all.

Pharaun shook his head in wonder. Such a gorgeous creature commanding a company of foul-smelling, enraged half-fiends somehow didn't seem right to the wizard. But, beautiful or not, she was on the other side of the fight. Sooner or later, he supposed, she would have to be dealt with.

Not here, though; not now.

Snapping back to the task at hand, Pharaun finished casting the dweomer he had chosen, and a collection of black tentacles sprang up, situated between the contingent of drow and the remaining tanarukks. Each of the slimy, writhing things was as thick as his thigh and squirming around, trying to locate anything to entangle. Too late, Pharaun noticed that Ryld had felled the remaining enemies that had challenged him directly and was stepping forward, ready to confront the handful that hung back.

Pharaun opened his mouth to shout a warning to the weapons master, but before the words were out he saw Jeggred reach over and grasp the Master of Melee-Magthere by the collar of his breastplate and yank him back, out of harm's way. An instant later, one of the tentacles wrapped itself around the lifeless body of a tanarukk that had been at Ryld's feet and quickly coiled more tightly, constricting the corpse. If the weapons master had still been there, it would have been his leg instead.

Numerous other tentacles squirmed and lashed out, grasping the surprised tanarukks and coiling around them. The creatures bellowed and screamed, thrashing and biting as the tentacles began to crush the life out of them. The she-demon on the far side merely arched one eyebrow at the appearance of the spell, taking a single step back so that she was clearly beyond the reach of the writhing black appendages. She seemed oddly content to watch as one by one, her troops began to grow silent, their breath lost, their ribs cracked.

Pharaun didn't waste time waiting for the spell to end and allow either the beautiful fiend or any of her remaining minions to reach his team. Not wanting to reveal the extent of his magic any more than necessary, the wizard stooped quickly and slapped at the ground before him. He took one last look at the beautiful fiend opposite him as darkness welled up between them. The moment that spell was finished, he began another, producing a pinch of gem dust from another pocket and weaving a spell that placed an invisible wall between the drow and the tanarukks.

The magical barrier was impervious to any normal attack, would withstand most magical assaults, and would buy the expedition time to find another way out. The wall of energy would not hold indefinitely, but it would last long enough for them to figure out how to escape unseen. Pharaun dusted his hands as he stepped back from the casting.

"Well, a fine solution that is," Quenthel sniped, "sealing us in here. We'd be better off facing those filthy beasts on the other side than just sitting here."

Ryld hunched down nearby, breathing heavily, cleaning his blade with a piece of cloth. Faeryl slumped, exhausted, against the far wall, trying to catch her breath. Only Jeggred and Valas seemed unwinded, both of them standing easy. The scout moved to study the blockage, while the draegloth hovered near Quenthel.

"As I tried to tell you," Pharaun retorted, running his hand along the surface of the damp, gray substance that prevented their passing, "this is the Araumycos. It could go on for miles."

The drow wizard knew his scolding tone was unmistakable, but he didn't care. Quenthel let out an exasperated sigh as she leaned against the wall of the passage. A massive fungus, the Araumycos resembled nothing so much as the exterior of a brain. It completely filled the passage.

"At least we can stop running for a while," Quenthel said. "I'm sick of carrying this damned thing."

She growled, kicking at the knapsack at her feet. She began rubbing her shoulders.

Pharaun shook his head, amazed at the high priestess's stubbornness. The mage had tried to be as deferential as possible, to let her see the folly of heading in this direction, but despite his warnings—and Valas's—the Mistress of Arach-Tinilith had, with her usual haughty demeanor, browbeat them into obeying her wishes anyway. Now they were pinned against the bloated growth, just as he had predicted, and she was simply going to ignore that fact.

Pharaun pursed his lips in vexation as he watched her out of the corner of his eye. She labored to work the stiffness out of her shoulders. He could only imagine the discomfort she must be feeling, but he had no pity for her plight. Despite the fact that his own haversack was magically lightened, Pharaun's shoulders ached, too. They had gone far beyond sore and were, he was certain, chaffed raw.

"Ah, yes," he said, continuing to examine the spongy growth, "you've made it quite clear how far beneath a Baenre—the Mistress of the Academy no less—it is to . . . how did you say it? . . . 'demean herself like a common slave lugging rothé dung through the moss beds.' But, I would respectfully point out—*again*—that it was *your* masterful tactical decision to leave our thralls and pack lizards behind, tethered and bleeding, in order to facilitate our escape from those cloakers."

The wizard knew full well that his cutting remarks would further sour her already unpleasant mood, but he truly didn't care. Getting under Quenthel's skin gave him no end of delight, even during trying circumstances such as these.

"You presume much, *boy*," the high priestess snapped as she stood straight again, glaring balefully at him. "Perhaps too much. . . ."

Still not looking at her, Pharaun rolled his eyes where she could not see.

"A thousand times a thousand pardons, Mistress," he said, sensing the time was ripe to change the subject. "So I suppose you no longer intend to bother with the goods you think are stored in the Black Claw Mercantile storehouses in Ched Nasad. Even if they do rightfully belong to House Baenre, how are we going to get them back to Menzoberranzan? *You* certainly won't carry them, and once word gets around that you like to use your pack animals and drovers as bait, no one else will, either."

Pharaun stole a sidelong glance at the high priestess, mostly for the simple pleasure of observing her disgruntled state. Quenthel's scowl was particularly severe, drawing out fully the vertical line that ran between her brows and giving her that pinched look that the mage was beginning to find unduly comical. The wizard stifled a chuckle.

That managed to get under her skin, he thought, grinning, but then he noticed Jeggred moving to stand between the two of them.

The beast loomed over the wizard, and Pharaun's grin vanished. He held his breath as the draegloth smiled balefully. The fiend's fetid panting cascaded over him, making his stomach turn.

The demon served Quenthel unswervingly, and at a word from her, he would gladly attempt to rip the wizard—or anyone else in the group, for that matter—limb from limb with malice-laden glee. Thus far, that word had not come, but Pharaun did not relish the possibility of having to defend himself from the fiend's assault, especially in such close quarters where he would have a hard time getting clear to exercise his own allotment of spells. He would prefer a large cavern to make his stand against Jeggred, but unfortunately, there was only this cramped passage, with no room to stay clear of the brute's claws.

Despite her current foul humor and the very ungainly way she had recently been bearing the load on her back, Quenthel somehow managed to look regal as she pushed herself away from the wall and stalked across the corridor toward Pharaun, her *piwafwi* swishing about her. He understood that she wasn't merely ignoring his jibes. She had waited until her faithful servant had moved into position to back her up before confronting the mage.

"I know very well what I said and did, and I do not need you mimicking my words back to me like some idiot savant, displayed in a gilded cage for all to look upon and laugh at." She focused her stare on him and held it there. "We are on a *diplomatic* mission, wizard, but those goods do belong to my House, and they will be returned there. I'll see to that. If I can't hire a caravan to carry them back, then you'll do it for me. Jeggred will make certain of it."

She held his gaze imperiously for a moment as Jeggred smiled carnally beside her. Finally, she straightened, made a subtle motion to the draegloth, and the fiend moved off to lick the gore from his claws.

"Find us a way around this . . . thing," Quenthel said, jabbing her finger toward the massive growth before she turned and strode back to her own pack and sank down to the floor.

Pharaun sighed and rolled his eyes, knowing he had pushed the high priestess too far. He would suffer more later for his little jibes. He looked over at Faeryl to gauge her reaction to the confrontation. The ambassador from Ched Nasad merely shook her head at him, scorn plain on her mien.

"I would think you, of all people, would be more than a little disgruntled that she's planning to strip your mother's mercantile company bare," he said quietly to her.

Faeryl shrugged and said, "It's no concern of mine. My House merely works for her—for House Baenre and for House Melarn. They own Black Claw together, so if she wants to steal from her partners, who am I to stop her? As long as I get home . . ."

Pharaun was surprised to actually see a wistful look on the ambassador's face.

The Master of Sorcere grunted at Faeryl's response and turned once more to inspect the material that blocked their way. He was both fascinated at seeing it in person for the first time and desperate to seek a possible way around it. He knew that the Araumycos filled countless miles of caverns in this part of the Underdark, but travelers had sometimes been able to find ways around or through it.

Valas was already climbing up the surface of the growth, pressed tightly against it, working his way toward the upper reaches. Pharaun could see that the passage they had followed opened into what must be a larger cavern, for the ceiling, like the passage itself, rose abruptly. He could see that the scout was making his way toward a narrow gap between the growth and the side of the cavern, perhaps hoping that there was a way to squeeze through, though to where, Pharaun had no idea.

Pharaun considered the diminutive mercenary from Bregan D'aerthe to be a bit uncouth, but nonetheless, he was glad the wiry guide was along for the trip.

"How long do we have before that gives out?" Faeryl asked, staring back the way they all had come, back toward the inky blackness.

Pharaun was surprised that she spoke to him. She was emboldened, the wizard supposed, from their earlier conversation. Not bothering to look at the ambassador, Pharaun continued his inspection, producing a tiny flame at the tip of his finger with which he began scorching the fungus. Where the fire touched the growth, it blackened and withered, but it did not burn a hole through to anywhere.

"Not long," he said.

He sensed rather than saw her discomfort at his offhand comment. The wizard smiled despite himself as he worked, bemused at the irony of Faeryl's situation. It had not been that long ago that she had been desperate to make this journey, to return to her home city.

Desperate enough to try sneaking out of Menzoberranzan and crossing Triel Baenre, the most powerful matron mother in the city, in the process. Faeryl had failed, of course. She had been captured at the gates, and she had wound up as Jeggred's imprisoned plaything to boot. Pharaun could only imagine what the draegloth might have been doing to her in the name of sport, but somehow the Zauvirr had earned a reprieve from Triel and had been assigned to participate in this little excursion to Ched Nasad.

In the end, Faeryl had achieved what she wanted, but the wizard wondered if she was still glad of it, despite her previous remarks. Even if she did get home, she was faced with the prospect of informing her mother, the matron mother of House Zauvirr, that Quenthel was coming to take everything. Absolutely everything. Regardless of the feasibility of such a move and the contingent's ability to actually pull it off unmolested by House Melarn, Faeryl and her mother would be the ones caught in the middle. He did not envy her position.

Plus, every time Jeggred so much as turned his gaze in her direction, she flinched and moved away. The fiend seemed to enjoy this, taking every opportunity to enhance the ambassador's discomfort through a suggestive smile, a lick of his lips, or a studied examination of his razor-sharp claws. It was clear to Pharaun that Faeryl was close to fully losing her composure. If that happened, he supposed they might have to actually let the draegloth have her and be done with it.

Then, of course, there was the matter of the supplies. Faeryl, like the rest of the members of the small excursion, had been forced to carry her own belongings for the better part of a tenday, something no high-born dark elf was accustomed to. Sedan chairs borne by slaves and porters was more her style, as it was Quenthel's. Leaving those thralls behind to stave off pursuit had been regrettable but necessary, and even with Jeggred's ability to carry a substantial portion of the load, the rest of them still had sizable burdens. He could hardly blame Faeryl if she was wondering whether this journey was nothing more than a huge mistake.

From Quenthel's demeanor it seemed she already knew that, or perhaps didn't care if Lolth's silence extended as far as Ched Nasad at

24

least and that their journey of exploration had become more akin to a raid. That was fine with Pharaun, but still he suspected there would be more to take from Ched Nasad than a store of magical trinkets.

Glancing at his pack once more and feeling the tension in his own shoulders, Pharaun wished for maybe the tenth time that day that he could summon a magical disk to bear their supplies. So many of the drow noble Houses made steady use of such a handy spell that the matron mothers generally insisted their House wizards learn it while attending Sorcere, the arcane branch of the Academy. Pharaun had never bothered to familiarize himself with it, though, since he had his haversack with its magically roomy interior. Even loaded up with all of his grimoires, scrolls, and more mundane supplies, it weighed a fraction of what a normal pack would. Besides, back at the Academy, if he had ever had cause to transport something with the magical disk, there was always a ready supply of students on hand who could have performed the task for him. Still . . .

Pharaun dismissed the notion, reminding himself for the tenth time that his magic was an all-too-precious commodity. With the goddess Lolth still strangely silent, none of her priestesses could gain the favor of her divine magic, leaving both Quenthel and Faeryl severely hampered and limited in power. The wilds of the Underdark were no place to be while vulnerable. Besides, there was no small amount of satisfaction in watching Quenthel, the High Priestess of Arach-Tinilith, the clerical branch of the Academy, labor with her burden.

Quenthel sniffed, startling Pharaun out of his reverie. The high priestess gestured toward where the scout was still climbing. Only his legs were still visible. The rest of him disappeared into the crevice formed between the wall of the cavern and the fungus.

She turned to Ryld and said, "Your friend is looking for a way through. Stop daydreaming and help him." Turning then to Pharaun, she added, "You, too."

Deciding that he had tormented her enough for the moment, especially with Jeggred so near, Pharaun smiled and bowed low, flourishing his *piwafwi*, then continued to examine the Araumycos.

As Ryld joined him, the wizard muttered, "It's times like these when I find her most charming, eh?"

"You shouldn't taunt her," Ryld murmured back, sliding along in front of the fungus and reaching for his short sword. "All you're going to do is cause us anguish later."

He took an experimental swipe and sliced a section of the growth away from the main body. It fell to the floor at his feet, and he bent to pick it up, but it was already beginning to blacken and decay.

"Oh, I think you mean 'me,' my stout friend," the wizard replied, removing a small vial of acid from a hidden pocket in his *piwafwi* and pouring the contents on the surface of the fungus. "I'll be inundated with enough anguish for the lot of us before we ever reach Ched Nasad, I fear."

Where the liquid coated the growth, the fungus began to sizzle and blacken.

Ryld paused and cast a glance over at his friend. The warrior looked taken aback. Despite their many years of friendship, Pharaun knew that even Ryld still occasionally found the wizard's behavior uncouth.

It's the price I pay for my winning personality and clever wit, Pharaun told himself wryly.

He watched as a reasonably sized hole was eaten through the fungus. There was only more fungus beyond it.

"We could try to hack or burn our way through this stuff forever," Ryld grumbled, moving farther along the face of the blockage to a point directly beneath where Valas had ascended. "There's no telling how deep or how thick it is."

"True, but it's fascinating, nonetheless. Thus far, I have discovered that it can be damaged by acid, fire, and physical cuts. Regardless, the pieces I remove simply dissolve into a dark, decayed mass. Remarkable! I wonder if—"

"I certainly hope you don't mean to tell me that you're exhausting all of your potent wizardly forces on this thing," Ryld asked, glancing back at the still-darkened curtain of magic behind them. "We may need your tricks far more desperately in a moment."

"Don't be dull-witted, my blade-wielding companion," Pharaun answered, tucking a piece of rosy stone back into a pocket.

"With my talents, I have more than enough to go around for everyone, even our charming pursuers."

Ryld grunted, and at that point a large hunk of fungus hit the floor of the cavern at Ryld's feet, already in the process of blackening. Ryld took a single step back, out of the line of fire, as several more pieces plopped down where he had been standing.

"It would appear that Valas is cutting his way through to somewhere," Pharaun observed, peering up to where the scout had, until recently, been visible. "I wonder if he's just experimenting or if he has actually discovered a means of egress."

The wizard craned his neck, trying to get a clearer view.

"There's a way through up here," Valas said, reappearing in full. "Come on."

"Well, that answers that question. Time to go," Pharaun said, turning to the rest of the group. He directed Quenthel and Faeryl upward, pointing to where the scout was visible. "We only have a few more moments before my wall of force wears off."

The other drow and the draegloth began floating upward, able to ascend through the magic of their House insignias. One by one, they disappeared through some unseen hole until only Pharaun was left. He began to magically rise up himself, realizing for the first time just how glad he was that they were not turning back to fight more of the tanarukks.

Aliisza smiled as she watched the last of her tanarukk charges tremble and lie still. The black tentacles that had destroyed them still curled and flailed, looking for anything new to latch onto. The alufiend was careful to stay out of reach of the grasping black appendages, though she knew that she could have removed them magically, if necessary. In fact, she could have intervened and dismissed the wizard's spell, rescuing her charges, but she had decided against it, and it wasn't because she feared to waste the spell. She was more curious than anything.

Aliisza knew that the dark elves and their demon would be more than capable, as drow tended to be. She moved back along the passage through which she and her squad of tanarukks had followed the drow, knowing that at least two of them had seen her. Yet they continued to turn away, as though they were running. Aliisza doubted the drow were there for any reason related to Kaanyr Vhok.

The alu wasted no time returning to the point at which she had set out with only the single squad, rejoining the larger force of which they had been a part, the force she commanded.

"They have moved into higher halls," she announced to the milling tanarukks, directing them along a new route. "We will cut them off at Blacktooth Rock. Do not tarry. They move fast."

With barely more than a grumble, the horde of humanoids set off, and it didn't take them more than a few minutes to reach the great intersection known to the Scourged Legion as Blacktooth Rock. It was a large, multi-leveled chamber where many different passages connected, and Aliisza wasn't even sure what the dwarves who'd cut the chamber once used it for. Much of it had been filled with the fungus colony the stoutfolk called Araumycos. There were still enough open passages there, however, that patrols of the Scourged Legion passed through frequently, and she knew that unless they utilized some magic to change their course, the passage the drow had taken to escape would ultimately lead them there as well.

The alu-fiend was still considering what she would do upon confronting the drow when her small battalion of tanarukks intercepted a second contingent of the humanoids, one she had sent to cut off escape along another route.

"What are you doing here?" she asked the sergeant, though she was actually glad for the reinforcements. "I assigned you to the Columned Chamber to watch for anything coming from the north."

"Yes," the sergeant answered. He was a hulking specimen who stood a good head taller than any of his fellows, his speech thick due to his prominent tusks. "But we got word that a large force of gray dwarves was spotted moving through the south part of Ammarindar, and a second patrol, one that had been stationed farther to the north and east, has completely disappeared."

"By the Abyss," Aliisza whispered. "What is going on?"

She considered for a moment, then issued orders for a small squad of tanarukks to return to Vhok's palace to report the news, while she and the remainder of the force continued to pursue the drow.

They know something about all this, she told herself as they set out, *and I'm going to find out what it is.*

Pharaun no longer jumped whenever Ryld silently returned after skulking along the group's back trail, so he showed no reaction when the warrior suddenly materialized in the group's midst. Splitter was still sheathed across the master of Melee-Magthere's back, so Pharaun knew that they were in no immediate danger. Nonetheless, he paid careful attention as his old friend began to convey a report to Quenthel in the silent hand language of the drow.

Our pursuers are on our trail again, the burly warrior signaled. *Several squads, all closing the gap.*

The snake heads hissed, echoing their mistress's irritation at this news before Quenthel quieted them with a whispered word.

How long before we are overtaken? she responded.

In the darkness, Pharaun saw Ryld shrug. *Perhaps ten minutes, no more.*

Quenthel replied, *We must rest, at least for a few moments longer. Besides, Valas has not yet returned. Figure out which way he went.*

She gestured at the intersection. Ryld nodded and moved to examine the walls near the three-way tunnel. If Valas had left some sign of the direction he'd taken, Ryld would find it, and they could continue.

Pharaun sighed, regretting ever having suggested they come this way to reach Ched Nasad. Passing through the domain of Kaanyr Vhok had been a risky choice, but one that Quenthel had finally insisted on, preferring speed over safety. So, the group moved through the Ammarindar, the ancient holdings of an even more ancient dwarven nation, long since wiped out.

Pharaun knew that Kaanyr Vhok had laid claim to the area since the fall of Hellgate Keep, which stood somewhere overhead in the World Above. Vhok, a marquis cambion demon, was an intensely unpleasant host, as Pharaun recalled. Most caravans generally avoided his little patch of the Underdark, so the passages they traversed had been little traveled, which Pharaun had hoped would help maintain the group's secrecy.

Even moving as surreptitiously as possible, the team was unable to avoid attracting the attention of Vhok's minions, and several of the cambion's patrols were once again relentlessly pursuing them. Pharaun had hoped that sneaking through the Araumycos would have thrown the tanarukks off, but he realized that they—or rather, the she-fiend, he supposed—knew exactly where the expedition was headed, even if they themselves did not. He had no doubt that even more were moving to outflank them, cut them off before they could move out of the region and beyond Vhok's reach. The question was, could they stay ahead of the patrols this time?

The Menzoberranyr couldn't afford to have to deal with the demon lord. With the news they carried, avoiding drawing attention to themselves from any of the great races of the Underdark was paramount. And yet, Pharaun had the sinking feeling that was going to be no easy matter. No part of the journey to Ched Nasad was going to be easy, he was certain. There was risk in every move, just like on the *sava* board.

In its own way, Quenthel's decision to relieve the group of extra baggage—and baggage bearers—had been fortuitous. They could set a faster pace without all the extras the high priestesses had initially insisted they bring along. The mage glanced at Quenthel, knowing she struggled between the notion of setting a faster pace and being sick to death of carrying a load that made her shoulders slump when she thought no one was watching. Pharaun suspected they could have gotten by with even less, and Quenthel might yet lighten her load, discarding more unnecessary provisions, before they reached the City of Webs. If they found themselves in another running fight with Vhok's hordes, it might be sooner rather than later.

Almost as if he knew time was growing short, Valas appeared, followed by Ryld and Jeggred. The drow scout trotted into the intersection and hunkered down against one wall of the passage, absently fingering one of the many outlandish trinkets that adorned his vest.

As Pharaun and Quenthel moved closer, Valas began flashing hand signals.

Our route takes us into a large chamber ahead.

Valas gestured along the passage from which he had just returned.

What's there? Quenthel signaled impatiently.

The scout shrugged then signed, *More of the fungus, but it doesn't block our path this time. We're almost beyond Vhok's reach.*

Then let's go, Quenthel replied. *I'm sick of this place.*

Valas nodded, and the group set off again. The passages through which the scout led them were once again wide and smooth, cut from the rock of the Underdark by skilled dwarf hands. They seemed to be making headway in the direction they wanted to go, as Faeryl commented more than once that things were starting to look familiar to her. With any luck, they would be out of Kaanyr Vhok's domain and into the outskirts of Ched Nasad's patrolled regions in short order. Quenthel seemed content this time to let Valas and Ryld interpret the ancient Dethek runes inscribed on the thoroughfares of the long-abandoned dwarven city and go where they suggested, for which Pharaun was intensely grateful. The sooner they reached the comforts of Ched Nasad, the better he'd feel, at least physically.

The mage had been contemplating making a suggestion to Quenthel, proposing to her that they enter the city discreetly. He wouldn't put it past the high priestess to want to stroll in with banners unfurled and demand to see the most powerful representatives of the noble Houses, just so she could tell them all that she was taking what was hers, Ched Nasad be damned. He had to think of a way to convince her to swallow her pride and do the smart thing, instead. It would be so much better for all of them if they didn't attract a lot of attention to themselves, at least not in the city streets.

Besides, Pharaun thought, *why do I want to be the guests of a bunch more matron mothers? An inn, especially a particularly splendid inn, would be much more satisfying.*

The trick, he realized, was in how to go about convincing Quenthel. Trying to make it look like her idea seemed the best choice, but working out a good, subtle way to plant the seed was tricky where the high priestess was concerned. She'd already shown that she was difficult to maneuver.

Push a little too hard, and she'd slap you down just because you were a male. Don't push hard enough, and she'd be too busy being in a foul temper to see what you were dangling in front of her face. Pharaun could think of a number of arguments he could use just to convince her, rather than trying to trick her into doing it his way, but again, with Quenthel, he knew he could argue until he was out of breath, and she might still refuse.

Pharaun suddenly realized that the passageway had begun to ascend, and fairly steeply, too. He glanced up and saw the others laboring to reach the top of the rise. As they crested the ridge, they drew to a halt, and Faeryl said something softly as she pointed into the distance. The wizard wondered what they had spotted. He quickened his own step, and when he caught up with them he paused. The panorama of a large, softly lit chamber greeted him. At least he assumed it was a large chamber. Judging from the curvature of the walls, it was quite grand, but more than half of it was filled with the great fungus. He shook his head, more impressed with the Araumycos than ever. The entirety of the growth was a single living organism, as best as any wizard or sage could determine. That this was a different part of the same entity they'd encountered nearly an hour ago was astonishing, but knowing that what he had seen, at least to this point, was still only a tiny part of the whole thing made his head swim.

The chamber itself was natural, with a mammoth black stalactite that looked remarkably like a huge fang just beginning to bite into the fungus, being the most prominent feature. Evidence of dwarven stoneworking was also in abundance. The drow had entered at a point fairly high along the exposed wall of the cavern, the passage emptying onto a large, balconied ledge that overlooked the floor. A large ramp, wide enough to accommodate several wagons side by side, descended from this ledge on the left side, entering into a series of switchbacks that crisscrossed down the side of the cavern below the ledge until it reached the floor. There, a smooth, paved road led to intersections scattered along the floor where other roads shot off to more switchbacks, eventually rising to a number of tunnels. In many cases, the pathways simply disappeared beneath the massive, pasty-gray fungus.

To Pharaun's eye, the whole place could have been a tiny city, similar to a portion of Menzoberranzan, except for two notable differences. First, the architecture was obviously and repulsively dwarven, all thick and blocky and dull to the eye. Second was the dim but pervasive light, which seemed to glow from almost everywhere and gave the whole chamber, indeed the entire stone surface, a pale, sickly gray glow. In Menzoberranzan, the city's velvety was blackness was broken by rich, luxurious hues of violet, green, and amber scattered across the cavern floor and ceiling. Here, everything was visible, glowing from some soft magical light that illuminated everywhere, but nothing had any color.

The dark elf wizard missed his home, longed to sit atop the balconies of the Academy and look out over the city. He yearned for even the simple pleasure of observing Narbondel, its red glow tracking the hours of the day and night. In the wilds, Pharaun had discovered that without the familiarity of the great clock in the City of Spiders he was losing all track of time, even though he had other, magical, means of following its passage. For a brief moment, Pharaun wondered if he would ever see Menzoberranzan again, and he felt a touch of— of what? Sadness? Was that what sadness felt like? It was odd, and the mage determined to shake it off.

What you need is a nice, hot, oiled bath, Mizzrym, followed by a deepstroke performed by a master masseur, and you'll have a spring in your step in no time.

With that encouraging thought, the wizard straightened up and turned his attention to his companions.

Valas had moved down along the ramp and had reached the first switchback. From Pharaun's vantage point, the diminutive scout looked truly tiny, giving the master of Sorcere a better sense of the scale of the chamber. Quenthel, Faeryl, Jeggred, and Ryld, meanwhile, were descending through the air to the next section of the path and were about halfway down, dropping in a loose cluster. Pharaun chuckled, wondering how the Mistress of the Academy was faring, still laboring with her baggage.

Well, Pharaun thought, that oil bath is waiting for you.

He took two steps toward the edge of the balcony to follow the high priestess and the others, when he felt rather than heard a disturbance behind him.

Chapter

THREE

Khorrl Xornbane could not help but tense slightly as the door to the private booth where he sat waiting slid partially open. His hand dropped instinctively to grip the doubleaxe at his side. Even when Zammzt slipped through the narrow opening on soft footsteps and settled onto the cushioned bench on the opposite side of the table, the duergar did not yet relax. He peered warily through the still-open partition into the hallway beyond, looking to see who might be lurking in a shadow, watching them meet. There were only three other individuals there, and none of them seemed to be paying Zammzt any attention at all. Two drow dressed as merchants, led by a third dark elf who was obviously a host of the Glowing Goblet, made their way to another booth and disappeared inside. Khorrl frowned as the host delayed a moment longer. The servant cocked his head slightly to one side, apparently listening to something that was said from inside the meeting cubicle, spoken too softly for the duergar to overhear.

He's just taking a drink order, the duergar thought. No need to get antsy.

Despite his self-admonition, Khorrl knew he would not rest easy for at least another minute or two. It would not be the first time some fool had allowed himself to be followed during a meeting with the duergar mercenary, and he never again wanted to be in such a position, caught unaware and forced to fight his way out of a corner. Not only had he barely escaped, but it had sullied his reputation to boot. That part had angered him most of all.

Finally, when he was certain no one was studying either of them on the sly, Khorrl relaxed, though he had to consciously release his grip on the doubleaxe to do so. He looked across the table at Zammzt, noting the lack of a House insignia anywhere on the plain-looking drow's clothing. For his part, Zammzt was reclining casually on the cushioned bench, the tiniest hint of a smile on his face. Though Khorrl didn't consider himself a great judge of attractiveness, especially in other species, it was plain enough to him that Zammzt's face was far from noteworthy. The drow was simply too ordinary looking. If he didn't already serve a noble House, he would have never amounted to much more than a common artisan, a step up from a slave but little more. Khorrl supposed the fact that he was such a shrewd negotiator was the dark elf's single biggest saving grace.

"I assure you, I was not followed," Zammzt said, interrupting the duergar's musings. "I would have known it, if someone tried, and there's no reason at all for anyone to do so."

"Why do you think I was concerned about that?" Khorrl asked, settling back himself. "I haven't accused you of anything yet."

"The sour look on your face and the furtive glances you keep casting out the door make it plain enough," the dark elf replied, "though I don't question your concern. You will no doubt be glad to know that I observed your arrival from a secure position, and I will tell you that no one followed you, either."

Khorrl stiffened slightly again, trying to decide if he should be insulted or impressed. Few creatures had managed to study him unnoticed, certainly not in recent years. For him not to notice Zammzt's observations was surprising, if what the drow claimed was true. The duergar narrowed his eyes, wondering if the dark elf was merely lying to impress him. He doubted it, but still . . .

"Then you must feel secure enough to speak freely, hmm?" Khorrl asked, baiting his boothmate to see what his reaction would be.

Zammzt's smile deepened the tiniest bit as he waved a hand in dismissal and turned his gaze on the table in front of him.

"Of course," he said. "Though I would think you'd prefer to wait until the host has brought us drinks first."

"I've already turned him down," Khorrl replied, giving his own wave of dismissal. "I don't care to partake while I'm doing business."

"As I'm well aware, Master Xornbane, from your reputation. I, however, have already requested that a refreshment be delivered to the booth. I believe I hear it coming now."

Khorrl turned his gaze for the merest of moments to the crack in the door, even as he opened his mouth to point out that he'd heard nothing. He started to turn back to Zammzt, but then did a double-take, for sure enough, the host from the other booth had appeared at the far end of the hall with a tray of drinks. Khorrl snapped his mouth shut again as he watched the servant first deliver a pair of beverages to the other booth, then proceed toward him and his companion. Apparently, in addition to his surprising ability to shadow someone, Zammzt also sported exceptional hearing. After delivering the drink and inquiring if the duergar had changed his mind and wanted something, the host departed. Zammzt reached over and pushed the partition shut the rest of the way.

"I think it's safe to discuss our business," the dark elf said, his red eyes glittering in satisfaction as he took a sip from his frosty mug. After a long pull, he sighed in delight and said, "Everything is in place. You should be receiving delivery of the first payment in the next day."

Khorrl eyed the drow for a long moment before finally nodding.

"And the amount is satisfactory?" the duergar mercenary asked. "None of my people goes into the city until I know that we'll be paid what I said."

"Absolutely. My mistress has instructed me to inform you that your fee is more than satisfactory. For the services you will be providing, she considers it a small price to pay."

"*Hmph,*" Khorrl grunted noncommittally. "That remains to be seen, doesn't it? If she leaves me hanging in the middle of the fight, it won't have been nearly enough, and you know it."

Zammzt smiled that knowing smile again and nodded in acquiescence.

"I can only assure you that she and her allies intend to see this through to the very end. Once they set foot down this path, there is no turning back for them, either. You should be well aware of that."

"Perhaps, but if things go sour for us," Khorrl said, running his hand across his bald gray head, "I will come looking for her personally."

"Please, please. There's no need for idle threats here. The initial payment is coming. Just be sure you have the first group ready to go when it arrives."

Khorrl nodded, more firmly this time. He had never reneged on a contract before, and he wasn't about to now. His clan was getting paid an exorbitant sum to fight, and his employer considered it money well spent precisely because of that reputation. Clan Xornbane might be merely a mercenary band in the greater scheme of the duergar hierarchy, but he had always made sure they honored their commitments. That wasn't going to change as long as he was the head of the clan.

"They will be there," he said finally.

"Excellent," Zammzt replied. "My mistress is counting on it. Despite your assistance, toppling the rival Houses will not be easy. That is why she and her allies are paying you such a generous retainer."

Khorrl frowned again, thinking of what work lay ahead. The drow was right; overthrowing one drow noble House, even when their clergy was hamstrung, was no small feat. He and his males were expected to help bring down several. The clan would suffer losses in this, no question about it, but they had been eager to accept this particular contract, anyway. The rich reward of helping the dark elves destroy themselves paled only slightly in comparison to the payment itself. Those among Clan Xornbane who survived would receive larger shares for this work than for their last four contracts combined. It was well worth the loss of troops, especially among the lesser races of the front ranks.

By the Abyss, Khorrl thought. *I might even consider retirement when we're through here.*

"We will do what we're paid to do. You know our reputation," the duergar said, affectionately running his hand along the handle of his doubleaxe. "Though I would feel a lot more confident if I knew for sure that your priestesses won't suddenly find themselves kissed by the spider queen in the middle of the fight. It would be our downfall, and yours too, most likely."

Zammzt spread his hands in a placating gesture.

"That is a risk, to be sure," he said, almost—*almost*—sounding apologetic. "But the opportunity for my mistress and her co-conspirators is worth it. Rest assured, you will not be forgotten in this. She looks forward to the moment when she can thank you from her new position as one of the highest-ranking matron mothers in the city."

Khorrl nodded one last time and prepared to depart.

"Very well, then," he said. "We will be waiting for the first payment. The schedule is set."

He rose, pulling his doubleaxe up beside him. Before he slid the partition open, he turned to look back at the dark elf, who seemed content to stay a while and finish his drink. Khorrl caught the drow's gaze and held it.

"We're committed now," the gray dwarf said. "There's no turning back. Blood will flow in Ched Nasad. Mark my words."

Spinning, Pharaun summoned his magical rapier from the ring into one hand, and clasped his *piwafwi* closed with the other, before he was completely turned around. As he pivoted into a defensive stance, releasing the rapier to dance in the air before him, he reached into the pockets of his *piwafwi,* selecting by memory and feel the components he needed to weave a certain incantation.

Perhaps a dozen steps from Pharaun, a shimmering blue doorway, similar to the extradimensional portal he was fond of using himself, was just closing, winking out of existence. The lovely creature he had spotted briefly during the rather one-sided battle with the tanarukks stood just in front of it, her smile accenting her arched eyebrows as she regarded him, arms folded casually beneath her prominent breasts. In particular, she seemed to find his floating, weaving rapier of interest.

"I'm sorry, did I startle you?" she purred, and Pharaun found her voice to be delightfully throaty.

"Oh, it's quite all right," the mage replied, eyeing the she-fiend from head to toe. She was dressed in tight, black, form-fitting leather, and while thigh-high boots and a corset seemed far from practical as travel-wear to the drow, he had to appreciate the effectiveness of the ensemble.

It compliments her wings so well, he decided.

"I wondered when you'd show up again," Pharaun said, noting with his second sweeping gaze the numerous daggers protruding from her belt and the tops of her boots. An enchanted ring he wore enabled him to determine that one of those daggers was obviously magical, as well as the long sword strapped to her right thigh. A ring adorning her left finger also caught his attention, for it radiated a strong protective dweomer.

"So you've been expecting me. How delightful!" she said, sauntering languidly over to a section of the balcony and sitting, leaning back and resting on her hands as she brought one long leg up to prop it on the railing. She appeared to ignore the fact that the rapier danced along as she relocated, keeping itself between her and the mage. "It ruins my grand entrance a bit, I suppose, but then again, I doubt you're terribly impressed with parlor tricks like mine."

"On the contrary," Pharaun replied, moving to take a seat a few paces away but maintaining the position of the rapier between the two of them. "I am always delighted to make the acquaintance of a fellow practitioner. You can't imagine how dull and dreary it can be, traveling with unimaginative companions who can't appreciate the difference between a divination and an evocation."

He swept his arm out over the side in the general direction of the other drow, who were far below him and well out of earshot.

Despite his casual manner, the mage was on edge and quite wary. He was sure the alu-fiend was sizing him up just as critically as he was her, and he considered everything carefully before opening his mouth. He certainly didn't want to reveal something that could get him into trouble with her later. Nonetheless, he was fairly sure she already knew where the rest of his companions were, and pointing out their positions lower in the cavern was not giving away too big a secret.

"Don't be too sure," she said, absently toying with the lacing that ran up the side of her corset, "I can imagine your predicament quite well. You forget the crowd I normally run with. They can't appreciate much beyond the next chance they'll get to eat or rut, much less the intricacies involved in spinning a good spell. What's a girl to do?"

When she finished, she gave Pharaun what he assumed must be one of her best pouts.

"Yes, I can see your point," the wizard said, chuckling. "It can't be much of a choice . . . rutting with the males, or seeking out a little more refined entertainment. I can't blame you for slipping away from them for a while."

"Oh, I never stray too far away from them," the demon said, looking at the wizard levelly. "One or the other of us might get into trouble."

Pharaun nodded slightly, acknowledging the hint. Still, he couldn't help but grin, delighted as he was to be able to engage in such clever innuendo. It was another thing he missed since taking his leave of Menzoberranzan. It wasn't just that most drow displayed a total absence of humor, his companions seemed even more staid than usual, though given the circumstances that wasn't totally unexpected. Still, they were a tight-lipped lot.

Quenthel was clinging too fiercely to the mantle of leadership to spend time mentally sparring with the wizard, Faeryl said very little at all, Valas was hardly in the same vicinity, and Jeggred's discussions had a marked singularity of topic to them. Pharaun had long since grown tired of hearing of the draegloth's desires to rend his foes in one messy way or another. Ryld had always been more willing to converse with him than most, but even the warrior had been pointedly taciturn for most of the journey. With the exception of a few brief discussions regarding Quenthel's heavy-handed methods, they had simply stopped the banter that had always marked the friendship between them.

It wasn't as though Ryld wouldn't talk to him, Pharaun admitted to himself, but things definitely weren't the same as before.

Before I left him to his death during the insurrection, the mage concluded, inwardly sighing.

Ryld had accepted the wizard's apologies afterward, claimed he understood the necessity of it, but in reality the pair's friendship had been damaged. It wasn't that Pharaun felt any real sense of guilt over the decision. He simply missed the benefits of the friendship.

"I said, you seem to be burdened with heavy thoughts."

Pharaun started, realizing that the she-fiend had been speaking to him during his ruminations. As he refocused his attention on her, he noticed that the rapier had sagged low from inattention and he snapped it back onto guard. Furious with himself for relaxing his vigilance, he summoned the weapon back to him and let it disappear back into the ring.

No reason to keep it out, he thought ruefully. *If she'd wanted to get past it and at me, she already had the perfect chance.*

The wizard bowed his head slightly, wordlessly apologizing for his lapse in manners. The alu-fiend only smiled.

"You certainly don't want to hear about my troubles," he said at last, his tone bright. "You obviously dropped in on this social visit for other reasons."

"Again, don't be so sure," the fiend replied, standing and stretching indolently. "It requires some fairly extraordinary circumstances to bring a band of dark elves through Ammarindar—"

"Oh, nothing of any real consequence," Pharaun interjected.

"—especially a mistress of the Academy and her retinue," she continued, ignoring the wizard's interruption. "Very extraordinary circumstances, indeed."

She was looking at Pharaun, perhaps gauging his reaction.

In fact, his reaction was the slightest straightening of his back and shoulders, but it was only the merest hint of his true surprise.

She knew.

A dozen thoughts floated through the mage's head in the next instant, considerations of who might have betrayed them, who back in Menzoberranzan had sent them off on this journey for the mere purpose of disposing of them in the clutches of Kaanyr Vhok and his minions, but the notions were dismissed again just as quickly. The risk of exposing the plight of the priestesses of Lolth was far too great to risk by such a method. The she-fiend had discovered their identity in some other way. Her broadening smile and sparkling green eyes told him that he had confirmed her suspicions.

"Oh, don't get too lathered up about it," she said, laughing. "Your secret's safe with us—at least, for the time being," she added, the smile gone. "But it brings me to my reason for being here. The Sceptered One, Kaanyr Vhok, Master of the Scourged Legions, lord of the portion of the Underdark through which you currently trespass, would delight in having an audience with you. I'm here to extend that invitation."

Almost as if on cue, there was a shout, dimly echoing, from far below. Without thinking, Pharaun turned and gazed over the edge of the precipice to the cavern floor below. There, Quenthel and the others had been in the process of crossing to a lower tunnel, one without switchbacks. Valas was rushing back from the mouth of the egress, apparently to join them. Behind him, a flood of tanarukks emerged from the passage and from others flanking it.

Observing the scene had taken but an instant, but it had been enough for the she-fiend to expend some sort of magical energy, which Pharaun could see radiating around her. He was on his guard, expecting an attack, but she did not move. Her green eyes, however, smoldered. Whether it was with lust or anger, he wasn't sure.

"I think you should accompany me back to the palace," the demon said, her voice husky. "You will like it there. Very much."

She began to saunter toward him as she spoke, and he could sense the energy flow over him. She was hoping to magically coerce him, somehow, the mage supposed. He backed up a step and put on his best apologetic smile.

"That, I'm afraid, is very much out of the question, at least for the moment. My companions need me."

The she-fiend's smile faded, and she pursed her lips in irritation.

"They are surrounded, you know," she said, pausing in her advance. "This is, at least for the moment, still an amicable offer. Go to them, convince them to return with me to Kaanyr's palace, and I promise you that the meeting will be cordial. My forces below have been instructed merely to hold their positions and prevent you and your friends from departing until I have a chance to make the offer to you. Will you do that?"

Pharaun smiled. "How well do you know Kaanyr Vhok?" he asked, his tone suggestive.

Her smile deepened, and her eyes glittered with what was definitely lust.

"Quite well," she answered, "but then again, he's terribly busy, so not as well as I would like. Come back to his palace with me."

Pharaun's own smile widened, and he asked. "What's your name?"

The she-fiend giggled once in amusement and said, "I almost forgot to tell you! I'm Aliisza. Now, will you come with me?"

"It's a delight to meet you, Aliisza, I'm Pharaun, and I'd love to accompany you, but for the moment, duty calls. Am I to assume that we will meet with resistance down there? Or has our discussion set your mind at ease to such an extent that we might pass out of Ammarindar unhindered today?"

Aliisza grinned and said, "I had my orders, dear. You were not to pass beyond the borders without a fight, but I tell you what . . . I'll give you a sporting chance, just because I like you." Her voice had turned husky again. "Just this once, I'll stay out of it. A few hundred tanarukks shouldn't cause you undue trouble, should they?"

Pharaun cocked his head to one side, as if considering that, then said, "Well, they will be a substantially greater difficulty than if we could move on unmolested, but as you say, it's a sporting chance. Until the next time we meet, then."

In answer, Aliisza nodded and smiled.

The mage leaned backward and dropped over the side of the precipice.

At Valas's distant shout, Quenthel looked up from where she had been staring absently at Jeggred's back, following the draegloth through the massive chamber. She spied the scout hurrying back from where he'd ventured ahead, and the high priestess spotted the hordes of tanarukks behind him, emerging from the sculpted tunnel wall. She swore under her breath, and the five snakes on her whip writhed in mimicry of her displeasure.

"We are cut off again, Mistress!" K'Sothra hissed. "Perhaps there is another way?"

"No, let us destroy them; taste their flesh and be done with them," Zinda argued, her own long black body straining forward eagerly.

"That's enough," Quenthel snapped, starting forward again to join with Valas.

The vipers quieted somewhat, but they still strained to pay attention to their mistress's surroundings, trying to sense any other possible dangers.

The tanarukks did not follow the scout but instead fanned out into a defensive formation. It seemed they were content to wait until the drow came to them.

So much the better, Quenthel thought grimly. They can line themselves up so that the wizard can decimate them most efficiently.

"What are they about?" Faeryl asked, trotting beside Quenthel. "Why aren't they chasing the male?"

She gestured toward Valas, who was only perhaps fifty paces from them.

"Why should they?" Quenthel countered, letting her long strides quickly close the gap between herself and Valas. "They somehow know we must go that way. It seems they're content to wait until we come to them."

Faeryl sniffed at this but said nothing more.

"We should wade through them and slice them, let their blood stain our feet as we tread upon their corpses," Jeggred suggested, his own long strides easily matching Quenthel's quicker ones.

The Mistress of Tier Breche looked over at the draegloth and saw him lick his feral lips in anticipation.

"Nonsense," she said crisply. "There's no need to get messy when they seem willing to oblige us by standing over there and letting Pharaun dispatch them with a well-placed spell or two. Right, wizard?"

When there was no answer, Quenthel spun to face him—only to discover that he was not behind her. Only Ryld kept pace with the two females and the draegloth.

"Where in the Abyss is that damnable mage?" Quenthel growled at Ryld, who raised an eyebrow in surprise and turned to look back.

"He was right behind me," the warrior replied, letting his gaze sweep back and upward, toward the tunnel through which they had originally entered. "I don't know—there!"

The weapons master pointed high up the wall, and Quenthel had to stop in order to turn around sufficiently to see where Ryld was pointing. When she spotted Pharaun, she muttered an invective under her breath. He wasn't alone. There was someone, a woman, in conversation with him.

"Who is that with him? What is he doing?" the high priestess asked no one in particular.

Ryld shrugged and said, "I have no idea, Mistress. I never heard him stop."

"Well, get him down here, now! I need him," Quenthel ordered.

Ryld made as if to protest, then shrugged, turned back, and broke into a rapid jog back along the thoroughfare. When she turned back, Valas had reached their position.

"So?" she asked the scout.

Valas took one deep, calming breath and explained, "They've cut off our route again, and they've made sure this time that we won't go around their flank."

The scout pointed to several other exits from the large chamber.

Quenthel could see already that more of the tanarukks were there, each group similar in size to the one directly in front of them. They were gathering on the ledges and ramps, just on their side of the tunnel openings. It wasn't hard to see that they were intentionally halting the drow's progress, trying to force them to turn back.

"Obviously, they aren't here merely to attack us," she said, thinking aloud, "so they must want something else."

"Perhaps I can explain," Pharaun said, materializing out of a shimmering blue doorway that hung in the open air only a few feet away. The portal snapped out of existence as the wizard primped himself a bit, straightening his *piwafwi* and adjusting his pack. "We've been invited to join Kaanyr Vhok, the master of those fellows, for a discussion."

"What are you talking about? Who was that woman you were speaking with back there?" Quenthel demanded, seething at how Pharaun seemed so full of himself all the time.

The fact that he could still freely use his magic, while she could not, continually galled her. Though he might never say anything, she knew he loved flaunting the fact of it in front of her every chance he could. To add insult to injury, he seemed taken with showing unbridled politeness toward her. She narrowed her eyes suspiciously. He wanted something, she was sure.

"We thought you were in trouble. I sent Ryld back to look into it," Quenthel said. She jabbed a single finger outward, pointing at the distant figure of the weapons master. "Now I'll have to send Jeggred to catch up with him while you stay here and explain to me what this is all about."

Before the high priestess could direct the draegloth to do her bidding, though, Pharaun cut in. "Oh, that's not necessary. Allow me but a moment." The wizard turned and faced Ryld, pointed his finger, and began to whisper. "Ryld, my dear friend, I appreciate your concern for me, but I am quite fine and standing here among our esteemed companions. You can return from your quest to rescue me."

In the distance, Quenthel saw the warrior start and straighten. He turned around as Pharaun spoke. Ryld seemed to shake his head in consternation, and Quenthel thought she heard him sigh, though of course it was only a whisper. By the time the mage was finished, Ryld was already trudging back in their direction.

"Very clever, mage," Quenthel said, clenching her teeth. "Now why don't you be as useful in other ways and tell me what you were doing up there."

"Of course. That was Aliisza, a charming and somewhat gregarious representative of Master Vhok's. She was lurking in the shadows back when we ran into them—" he gestured into the distance at the tanarukks—"in the previous tunnel. They answer to her, and she answers to Vhok."

"Well, how interesting," Quenthel said, folding her arms. "And just what did you two have to talk about for so long? You weren't, perhaps, coming to some sort of an agreement with her, were you?"

Pharaun looked genuinely pained and said, "High Priestess, I only listened politely while she extended her offer. I could not, of course, give her any sort of proper answer without first conversing with you. I suspected what your answer would be before I even mentioned the invitation, but I would be remiss in my duties if I didn't at least deliver the message."

"Indeed," Quenthel said. She knew good and well that the flamboyant wizard before her wouldn't have given a second thought to betraying her and the rest of them if it presented him with some worthwhile benefit. "Interesting that she chose you to be her messenger boy."

Pharaun grimaced, but only slightly.

"We share a common, uh . . . appreciation for the arcane arts," he said at last. "We spent a few moments in idle conversation about the difficulties of traveling with those who don't share that appreciation."

Quenthel snorted. "I'm sure you were interested in more than her wizardly skills."

The mage's grin didn't change, but his eyes hardened the slightest bit. Good, she thought. Remind him that you see right through him.

"Very well," she said. "We're certainly not going to go back with the brutes to see Vhok, so the question is, how do we get through them and on our way?"

"There's no way to get around them," Valas said, "unless the ambassador knows this area and has a notion of another route we can take," he finished, looking at Faeryl.

The Zauvirr priestess shook her head.

"We're still too far away from the proper outskirts of Ched Nasad for me to recognize any features with certainty," she said.

"Then we must slay them," Jeggred announced. "Let me engage them and cut a path for you, Mistress."

"No, Jeggred, there's no need, however much fun you might think it would be. Pharaun, here, is going to get us through this. Aren't you?"

The mage grinned bemusedly and said, "I might have an incantation or two that will allow us to make our way through to the tunnel. Aliisza has assured me that, in good sporting fashion, she will stay out of it. Slaying these creatures should be minimal trouble."

"I'm not concerned with that. Just clear a path for us," Quenthel commanded.

"Very well," he said as he began to move forward, weaving the beginnings of a spell as he did so.

Aliisza wasn't sure how Kaanyr would receive her latest news, but it didn't slow her steps. Tarrying to deliver it served no purpose. He would find out eventually, and she might as well pass it to him and get on to other, more interesting things. Besides, she wasn't really troubled by the prospect of the cambion's anger. He might fly off the handle from time to time, but he knew better than to direct it at her. Whether or not he flew into a rage this time, she had an idea that might just soothe his ruffled feathers and give her a bit of fun, besides.

Passing through the great doorway and into the throne room, Aliisza expected to find Vhok sitting on his throne, but he was not. He paced in front of it, which meant that he had serious things on his mind, serious in a bad way. The alu-fiend had a pretty good idea what those things were.

"Any more information on what that duergar horde is doing?" she asked as she approached him.

Vhok looked up from his contemplation, seemed to stare right through her for a moment, and at last said, "All I've been able to determine at the moment is that they don't seem to be headed in this direction, which is good."

"Good? Why?" Aliisza asked. She moved to sit on the top step of the dais. "I thought you liked the idea of a little sport for the Legions. You told me the other night that things were getting a bit staid around—"

"Because something big is definitely going on," Kaanyr interrupted, "and because they were responsible for wiping out the patrol to the northeast."

Aliisza had been about to stretch out, hoping to distract Kaanyr from all of this serious discussion for a few moments of romance, but she sat straight.

"That wasn't just a roving band of duergar," Vhok continued, "they were professional mercenaries. The Xornbane clan, if the evidence is correct. They don't go anywhere without major coin changing hands and big battles in the works."

Aliisza pursed her lips in thought.

"So if they aren't moving against us," she said, "then where?"

"Though I already have an idea, I was hoping you could tell me," Kaanyr said, looking down at the alu-fiend. "Where are my guests?"

Aliisza avoided meeting Vhok's gaze.

"I wasn't able to convince them to join us," she said carefully, "and after they defeated my little patrol as easily as they did, I thought it wise not to pursue the matter so directly."

"Defeated? Wiped out is more like it."

Kaanyr's tone was measured, and Aliisza could tell he was displeased.

So he already knew, did he? Is he spying on me, now?

She was glad she'd been up front with him on the subject. It had been tempting to fudge the truth a bit, to tell him that the tanarukks had not followed her instructions, but in the end, something had convinced her that she was going to have to start being a little more careful with Vhok.

"They are formidable," she answered at last. "The wizard with them is . . . interesting. He's the one I spoke with, and it was definitely he who plowed through the Legions. Drow are formidable to begin with, and it was a tactical error on my part to engage them in such a large chamber. They were able to easily evade the Scourged simply by getting up off the floor and out of range. Pharaun laid waste to the troops without much of a thought."

"I'm sure you did the best you could," Kaanyr said, waving her explanation away. Aliisza scowled at the insult but said nothing. "It's probably just as well. It seems that the gray dwarves are bound and determined to reach Ched Nasad, which is where our little visitors are headed, as well, I think. We weren't going to dissuade them from that without bringing the entire might of the Scourged Legions, as well as some of your sisters, to bear."

"I did find out a couple more things," Aliisza said, ready to spring her idea on Vhok. "They are all high-ranking nobles from Menzoberranzan, not just the priestess. The wizard is powerful enough to be a member, if not a master, of Sorcere, and some of the things he admitted to convinced me that most of the others are of similar rank."

"Well, that's all very interesting, but I probably would have inferred that from the fact that the Mistress of the Academy was out with such a small group to begin with. It still doesn't tell me what they're doing. It may help to answer the questions of why the grays are on the move."

"Well, I have an idea about that," Aliisza said, reaching the moment of truth. She wondered if Kaanyr would agree with her plan or choose to use someone else. "Whatever it is they're planning to do when they reach Ched Nasad, they all seem very concerned, very grim. Whatever it is, it's serious, and I bet they aren't the only drow in the city who are in the know about it. So why don't I sneak into Ched Nasad and snoop around a little?"

Kaanyr looked at Aliisza, pursing his lips. She wasn't sure if he was thinking about her idea or just studying her to see if she was up to something. Of course she intended to do just what she said, so he had no reason not to trust her on it, but if she had a little fun on the side, well then, what would be the harm in that? She needed a vacation from Ammarindar, from Vhok. Maybe a little time apart would do him some good, too, she thought.

"All right," he said at last, and the alu-fiend grinned broadly before she caught herself. "Go and see what you can find out. In fact, I want you to drop in on Aunrae. If there's something going on, the matron mothers will be in the know. I'd like to keep my relationship with her on good terms, at least for the moment, so be polite. And keep me updated. I don't want to have to come find you to see what you've learned."

Aliisza was nodding energetically as she stood up and headed out the door.

"I will," she promised, already contemplating the sort of disguise she'd like to use.

As Khorrl felt the wagon finally roll to a stop, he almost groaned aloud. His legs were cramping where he'd wedged himself into the hiding spot beneath the pile of supplies. He could barely stand to be there much longer, and he prayed to Laduguer that the trip was actually over. He couldn't imagine having to crouch there for even another few minutes.

The tarp over the top of the wagon was thrown back, and dim light shone down on the goods stacked beneath it. Of course, to anyone not properly prepared, that's all they would have seen—a wagonload of supplies for the city. Khorrl waited as he listened, not daring to move, in case it was merely another checkpoint. He didn't even want to breathe, for fear of being heard by whomever—or whatever— might be inspecting the wagon.

"It's all right," he heard a drow voice say, and he recognized it as belonging to Zammzt. The dark elf was near enough that there was no mistaking who he was talking to. "You can show yourselves, now. We're inside the storehouse."

With a thankful groan, Khorrl rose up, feeling his knees complaining. Around him, fourteen other duergar did the same, winking back into visibility one by one. They looked at each other, as if to confirm that everyone was all right, and began to peer around at their surroundings. Khorrl himself hopped awkwardly down from the wagon, grabbing his axe as he did so. Nearby, more wagons were being uncovered, and more of his fighters appeared, clambering out from between crates, barrels, and bales of foodstuffs. He knew that there were over twenty wagons, so he had about three hundred troops. More would arrive, in waves, over the course of the next several hours.

As Zammzt had promised, they were set up inside a large, open room, obviously a storehouse of some sort, though there were no goods there other than what was on the wagons. Ostensibly, the contents of the wagons were for the benefit of the Houses, but in reality, it was his army's supplies. They were going to be camping there for a few days, resting and preparing while the other duergar units arrived, all of them waiting until it was time to do their job. Khorrl hoped the storehouses would be left undisturbed, as promised.

A handful of drow moved about, uncovering wagons in order to free their hidden occupants or unloading the supplies and stacking them out of the way. Khorrl could see Zammzt looking a couple of wagons over, giving some young drow male a few instructions. When the dark elf was finished, he turned back to the duergar clan leader.

"I hope you find everything in order here, Captain Xornbane," Zammzt said, smiling. "I know it's not quite like roughing it in the wilds of the Underdark, but it should accommodate you well enough."

"It's fine, as long as no one comes snooping around here before we're ready to begin. The last thing we need is the city catching wind of us before your mistress is ready to fly her true colors."

Khorrl paced about as he spoke, trying to get the feeling back in his legs as much as surveying his temporary home.

"I seriously doubt that's going to be a problem," Zammzt said, smiling. Khorrl wanted to tell him to stop it. The grin reminded the duergar of a pack lizard's visage. "I've got loyal drow troops on guard duty around the storehouse, and you're sequestered here in the far back chamber. No one will bother you."

"If you say so," Khorrl answered doubtfully. He had seen more battles take a turn for the worse through the most simple, straightforward aspect of the plan going awry. "Just remember, all that beautiful treasure you gave me is already long gone, shipped off to safer parts. If you're thinking of turning the tables, you won't be seeing it again. It'll be an expensive betrayal."

Zammzt looked genuinely hurt, but only for a moment.

"I'm not sure you realize the risks my mistress takes, simply harboring an army here," said the drow. "If you're discovered, she too suffers the consequences. It really isn't in her best interests to turn on you, you know."

"Hmm," Khorrl answered. "We'll see."

"So, I presume you brought everything you need," the drow said, changing the subject, "but if there's anything else you want while you wait here, now is the time to ask. Though, for what we're paying you . . ."

Khorrl barked a deep laugh despite himself. The idea that he would bring his troops into such an uncertain situation without arranging for every provision, every possible contingency, was funny.

"No, we're fine. Now, when are we going to find out just exactly who we're supposed to be killing?"

"Soon, my gray friend," Zammzt said, that toothy smile blossoming again. "Very soon."

In the end, the battle with the tanarukks wasn't much of a fight at all. Pharaun had devastated rank upon rank of the slavering humanoids from a distance, even going so far as to decimate the reserve forces lurking in the back. He honestly didn't even find it sporting, especially when he was able to hover overhead, out of their reach, and attack them at his leisure.

The Menzoberranyr were well beyond the halls of Ammarindar, and after a night's rest they were closing in on Ched Nasad.

"We should be running into patrols by now," Faeryl grumbled as they hiked along. "We're within a quarter mile of the city. Something's wrong."

"I think we knew that before we left Menzoberranzan," Quenthel snapped.

The group found itself on the main thoroughfare that led into the city from the north, wondering when they would actually reach the surrounding outskirts of the city proper, the area protected by patrols. Pharaun couldn't blame Faeryl for being apprehensive. Even after several tendays of concern for her home city, he imagined that she might have held out some hope that she would find everything in order upon finally arriving. Still, he doubted that some disaster had befallen the city. Though they hadn't yet encountered any patrols, they were no longer alone on the road to the city.

Traffic flowing to and from Ched Nasad was a trickle of its normal self, at least according to the ambassador. Pharaun didn't doubt it. The avenue they followed was broad, wide enough for numerous caravans to pass in either direction, but there were no such convoys out and about that day. Most of those who shared the road with the Menzoberranyr were other drow, though the occasional gray dwarf, kobold, or goblin passed them as well. Those lesser beings gave the drow a wide berth. Any pedestrians who were headed toward the city were scattered just as far apart as those leaving, and Pharaun and his companions neither passed nor were passed by anyone.

The mage made a tactful attempt to bring up the suggestion he had been contemplating. "Quenthel, if something has happened here, similar to what we've been experiencing back home, it might be prudent to consider a less obvious entrance into the city."

"What do you mean?" the high priestess queried, looking sharply at Pharaun.

"Only that should we boldly approach and announce our stature and intentions, we might not receive the warm welcome we should under more ordinary circumstances."

"Why shouldn't they be glad to see us? Even relieved?"

It sounded as though Quenthel was growing indignant, and Pharaun struggled to find a way to explain his point in a way that wouldn't sound insulting.

Faeryl saved him the effort.

"Because they might think we're here to spy on them," she said.

Pharaun had to suppress a mild chuckle. It was, after all, the exact reason Triel had claimed when she imprisoned the envoy back in Menzoberranzan. It was a reasonable argument.

"Not if we insist upon meeting with the matron mothers of the highest Houses—" Quenthel began.

"With all due respect, Mistress," Faeryl interjected, "do you think you would react well to a high-ranking noble arriving in Menzoberranzan and insisting upon seeing you? During this time of crisis?"

Quenthel scowled and said nothing. Pharaun was relieved that the high priestess was at least willing to contemplate the idea.

"Even if they didn't think we were spies, they certainly would consider our visit to be highly unusual and would strive to keep an eye on us," the mage said. "We might be given the most luxurious accommodations and want for nothing, but we would also be absolutely unable to find out anything. Once we determine the state of things here, if it's really your intention to lay claim to the goods stored in the Black Claw Mercantile storehouses and take them back to Menzoberranzan, why draw undue attention to yourself? Were you planning to ask the matron mothers for them, first?"

Quenthel scowled at Pharaun as if the very idea of asking permission to take what was rightfully hers was preposterous. It was exactly the reaction he wanted.

"Faeryl," the wizard persisted, "even though the goods are rightfully the property of House Baenre and House Melarn, do you foresee Matron Mother Melarn—indeed, any of the other Houses—letting them out of the city?"

Faeryl smirked.

"Absolutely not," she answered. "I'm not certain how happy my own mother will be to hear about your plan." She smiled wanly and added, "I agree with the mage. The less you tell, the better your chances are of succeeding."

"Your arguments may have merit," Quenthel said. "So what else do you suggest? How do we enter unnoticed?"

"As traders, Mistress," Faeryl suggested, "members of the Black Claw Mercantile company. Triel said herself that we were here to check on House Baenre's financial interests, as well as to discover how widespread the problem is, so it's the truth, from a certain point of view."

"We don't look very much like traders," Valas said, trotting a little in front of the rest of them. "Perhaps Pharaun should use a spell of illusion to mask our looks."

"No," Faeryl replied. "Ched Nasad's guards are equipped to watch for that. They employ detection spells and devices to notice if you're trying sneak past them invisibly or under the guise of illusion. It's not necessary, anyway. You'd be surprised at what kind of bodyguards a wealthy trader would hire to protect her. I am a member of a trading house. If I tell the city guards that you're escorting me, and they get a good look at my house insignia, we shouldn't have any trouble, but you must remove your own insignia. They're likely to be recognized."

"Would you hire the likes of him?" Quenthel asked, pointing to Jeggred.

Faeryl frowned and said, "He could be a problem."

"Leave that to me," Pharaun said. "I have a couple of tricks up my sleeve that should aid us nicely. I can use them to get the draegloth past the patrols and into the city without them noticing him. As long as he cooperates, anyway."

Quenthel looked at Jeggred and asked, "Can you stay quiet and not try to tear the throat out of anyone?"

Jeggred regarded the high priestess askance but nodded.

"I am capable of subtlety when it is necessary, Mistress," he rumbled.

Sure you are, Pharaun thought.

"Very well," Quenthel said after a moment's deliberation. "We will enter the city incognito. Remove your insignia and try to look . . . common."

Everyone except Faeryl doffed their House brooches and began to stow as many of their finer accoutrements as possible.

"Pharaun," Quenthel said, nodding at Jeggred, "do what you must."

"First, I'm going to reduce you slightly in size, so that you aren't so, um . . . obvious," the wizard said, looking up at the eight-foot-tall creature. "You don't mind, do you?"

Jeggred grunted and glowered at the mage, but at a subtle gesture from Quenthel, he nodded acquiescence.

"Good," Pharaun continued. "Then, I'll cloak you with a spell designed to misdirect those divinations the patrols are likely to be using, and if you will don your *piwafwi,* pull the hood up, and stay in the back, we should get past them just fine."

"Yes, that should do nicely," Faeryl agreed.

"All right, then, here we go," Pharaun said, pulling a pinch of powdered iron from one of his many pockets and gesturing.

The draegloth began to shrink until he was no taller than any of the drow.

"Good," the wizard said, beginning the second spell.

When he was finished, he stepped back and said, "Now, draw that *piwafwi* around you to hide as much of you as possible."

"Yes, and lean on Ryld as though you're injured," Quenthel commanded. "Keep your head down like you're tired."

"Yes, good idea," Pharaun agreed, genuinely impressed. "We're all just road-weary merchants, ready for a hot bath and comfortable bed."

"Not a moment too soon," Valas said, his voice low. "I see a patrol up ahead."

Pharaun peered ahead into the distance and saw a large contingent of drow, some on foot, others riding lizards, moving down the road in their direction. They were fanned out across the width of the road, so there would be no way to avoid them.

"Just remain calm, and allow me to speak to them," Faeryl whispered.

The group began walking toward the patrol, with Ryld in the back, pretending to support a limping Jeggred. Pharaun could only guess at how much the warrior hated the scheme.

No matter, he thought. We should have little difficulty getting past these sentries. We're just drow, trying to reach a drow city. Why would we be any trouble to them?

As the groups drew close to one another, the patrol loosened weapons and slowed down, obviously preparing for trouble. One, the leader, Pharaun presumed, stepped forward a few more paces and held his hand outstretched before him, palm forward.

"Hold," he said, gesturing for the group to slow down. "State your name and business here."

Faeryl moved forward, past Valas, to come to a stop a few paces from the leader.

"I am Faeryl Zauvirr of House Zauvirr, Executive Negotiator for the Black Claw Mercantile." She removed her insignia and held it out for the patrol leader to get a good look and take it, if he wanted. "These are my caravan guards."

The sergeant or whatever he was stepped forward and took the insignia, then passed it back to an underling while he scrutinized Faeryl and the others, in turn.

"Caravan? What caravan? No goods have entered or left the city in six tendays, at least."

Faeryl nodded and explained, "Yes, I know. We are just recently from Menzoberranzan, but we lost what few goods we had in an attack along the way." She tossed her head back toward Ryld and Jeggred as a way of indicating her wounded companions, but with the suggestion that they weren't really important. The drow soldier in front of her peered over her shoulder for a brief moment, then nodded and returned his attention to her. "We wish to give our report and enjoy some civilization for a few days," she concluded, letting weariness creep into her voice.

Good, Pharaun thought. Tell them just enough of the truth to sound reasonable, without admitting anything.

"Attacked by what?" the leader asked.

The second-in-command handed the insignia back to him with a curt nod. Apparently it had passed muster, for the patrolman handed it back to Faeryl.

"What business is it of yours?" asked Quenthel sourly. "Do you always make it a practice of interrogating caravans this way?"

"Tanarukks," Pharaun said, stepping forward and placing his hand on Quenthel's arm. "She hates tanarukks. She's been in a bad mood ever since. A good deepstroke will do her wonders."

The Master of Sorcere could feel her bristle, but at least she didn't pull away from him. Beside her, the snakes of her whip stirred, but they didn't flail about as Pharaun feared they would.

The patrol leader glared at Quenthel for a moment but finally nodded and said, "We make it a practice when the city is—" he stopped himself from revealing more, then turned back to Faeryl— "You may pass, but good luck finding any 'civilization' to enjoy."

With that last bitter comment, he turned and motioned the rest of the patrol to part, creating a gap so that the entourage could pass through.

Faeryl nodded her thanks and motioned for the rest of them to follow her, then they were past the patrol and alone on the thoroughfare once again. Pharaun could see that the envoy was troubled by the patrol leader's words. He had to admit it was not a good sign.

"Let go of me!" Quenthel hissed, jerking her arm free, and the wizard blinked in surprise, having forgotten that he still grasped her and was steering her along.

"My apologies, Mistress," Pharaun said, bowing slightly. "In light of the situation, I thought it prudent to try to smooth things over the best way possible. In a way, though, it was good. You drew attention away from the draegloth."

"Fine," she answered, still scowling. "We got through them, that's the important thing. Now, let's see just how bad it is inside the city."

It wasn't long before the group had reached the gates of the City of Shimmering Webs. Continuing their masquerade as bruised and battered merchants, they passed through the guards there and found themselves inside.

It was chaos.

"You're late," Drisinil Melarn snapped as Ssipriina Zauvirr strode into the audience chamber of House Melarn.

The matron mother of House Zauvirr forced herself to suppress the hot retort that she ached to unleash, contenting herself instead with pursed lips.

"I am sincerely apologetic," Ssipriina lied, bowing low to the other matron mother, knowing she mocked the other drow simply through the use of such formal comments and antics. "It could not be helped. I had urgent business matters to attend to, issues that keep your coffers full, Matron Mother."

Ssipriina liked the dangerous glitter she was creating in Drisinil's hot eyes. It would be hard for the head of House Melarn to chastise her minion for working so diligently to keep her wealthy, and Ssipriina knew that. That's what made these subtle jibes all the more fun.

"Still, I sped here with as much haste as dignity would permit," Ssipriina added, "for I have good news. They have entered the city."

"You're sure?" the matron mother asked. "Do you have any indication that they've changed their plans?"

"Yes, I am sure of it," Ssipriina replied. "My male made contact with Faeryl only a few hours ago, and she informed him that they were headed toward the Fracture Gate in the lowest quarters of the city. Apparently, Mistress Baenre is still bent on stealing your goods. My spies saw them enter the city just a few minutes ago."

Drisinil sat in thought for a few moments, leaving Ssipriina standing expectantly. Finally, the matron mother stirred.

"They don't suspect that we know, do they?"

"I don't believe so. I have instructed Faeryl to be as agreeable as she can to whatever Quenthel is planning, and I have my spies set to keep track of them, wherever they go. They won't know a thing until it's too late."

"And you want to let them go through with it?"

"Well, not exactly, Matron Mother. I am suggesting that we let them get to the storehouse and get inside. We'll be there to catch them in the act. We'll have the proof, then, and we can present it to the other matron mothers."

"Hmm, yes, I like that," Drisinil Melarn said, shifting her considerable weight atop her throne. Her face held a look of determination. "I very much want to see Quenthel Baenre's face when she realizes she's not getting a single scrap of my wealth. I want her to realize she's just crossed the wrong House."

Truer words were never spoken, Ssipriina thought.

"Yes, of course. I will make plans for us to be there before they arrive at the storehouse. I trust that you wish for me to utilize House Melarn guards?"

"Absolutely," Drisinil said. "She needs to see just who she is trifling with. I want a strong presence there, Ssipriina, and when this crisis is over and the council lifts the ban on exportations, I'll make sure you're rewarded for your patience and diligence."

"Of course," Ssipriina said, bowing. "I will see to this matter personally."

✾   ✾   ✾

Ched Nasad was a bustling city filled with drow, duergar, and even the occasional illithid during normal times, but Valas found it suffocating. The scout was certain three times as many creatures occupied the place than was usual. It was brimming with desperate, starving masses who pushed and shoved their way along the thoroughfares, raising a deafening rumble and a pungent odor.

The gate through which the Menzoberranyr had entered was near the bottom of the City of Shimmering Webs, a metropolis filling a huge, **V**-shaped trench in the Underdark. The entirety of the city was crisscrossed with massive calcified webs set aglow with magic, a hundred or more layers of pathways that ran every direction and supported the population. Thousands of rounded, amorphous structures clung to these huge webs like egg-sacs or cocooned prey, thrusting up or dangling below and housing the citizens, guests, slaves, and their businesses. Right now, it looked like a writhing colony of ants swarmed over the webs, for as far as Valas could see overhead, the streets literally vibrated with the masses of humanoids taking refuge there.

The scout would normally have been in the lead of the entourage, but it was nearly impossible to move, so crowded were the streets. Instead, Quenthel had ordered Jeggred to run point, and the towering fiend was pushing his way slowly through the throngs. Valas stayed close behind the draegloth, and the rest of the group pressed in close behind the scout, fearful of getting cut off in the madness and winding up lost. Valas noted that time and again sullen-looking faces glowered at Jeggred while he growled and rumbled at everyone to stand aside. They all did, intimidated by the formidable creature.

There were few drow low in the city, but just about every other race was present. Many of the slave races, as well as representatives of the other major Underdark nations, clamored with one another, shouting, pushing, bartering, or just milling about. The Menzoberranyr stood out, and it was plain that they were being sized up by the populace. Sooner or later, there was going to be a problem.

More than once, Valas felt the brush of a hand or finger as someone in the milling crowd deftly attempted to pilfer a trinket from one of his pockets. He had already snatched two hands away from the charms pinned to the front of his shirt, leaving each with a nasty gash across the palm from one of his kukris.

Valas turned and glanced over his shoulder. Faeryl and Quenthel were both right behind him, the Mistress of Arach-Tinilith threatening bystanders with her horrid whip. Behind the two priestesses, Pharaun held his *piwafwi* closed and kept his head bowed, protecting himself from the press of the crowd. Ryld brought up the rear, using his bulk to shield the wizard in front of him.

This is ridiculous, the scout thought, shaking his head. We've got to get out of this part of town.

He started to lean over and tell Quenthel when a disturbance in front of Jeggred interrupted him. Valas turned back in time to see the draegloth pounce on an ogre armed with a greatsword that was blocking the path. A second ogre stood beside him, hefting a spiked club and glaring.

Jeggred leaped forward like a coiled spring, raking one of his razor-sharp claws across the front of the first ogre. The attack was so sudden, the creature didn't even have time to react. It stared down at its stomach as blood sprayed. Several screams erupted from the crowd as some struggled to get out of the way and others pushed and shoved to get a better view—or a chance to scavenge the bodies. The first ogre opened its mouth to scream, sinking down to one knee and holding its hands across its midsection, as Jeggred slashed again, ripping the humanoid's throat out. The ogre gurgled and flailed, wide-eyed with fear.

The second ogre snarled and swung its club at Jeggred, slamming the spiked weapon into the draegloth's shoulder. The fiend spun with the blow, his mane of white hair flowing behind him. The twist avoided the worst of the damage and brought Jeggred back to face his enemy from a crouched position.

At that moment, Valas was knocked sideways by a lunging goblin, teeth bared and daggers drawn. Before the scout could kick the wretch away from him, Quenthel lashed out with her whip. Several pairs of fangs sank into the goblin's flesh, and it fell to the ground, writhing and frothing at the mouth. Valas lurched back to his feet before more of the throng could surge over him. He put his back to Quenthel and openly brandished his kukris, holding back several shouting, cursing gray dwarves.

The entourage had formed a defensive circle, Valas realized. Ryld had Splitter out, and the wizard's magical rapier danced in the air before him, while Pharaun himself held a small wand of some sort, eyeing the increasingly angry crowd. Even Faeryl held her hammer in her hands, swinging it back and forth experimentally. Only Jeggred wasn't a part of the defensive formation, having moved a few feet off, finishing his bloody work with the two ogres. Out of the corner of his eye, Valas could see the fiend biting his foe, ripping chunks of the ogre's face off.

"We've got to get higher!" Valas yelled at Quenthel over his shoulder. When the high priestess didn't seem to hear him, he repeated himself. "Mistress Quenthel, we need to get to a higher section of the city. This is not working!"

Next to him, Pharaun jerked as a crossbow bolt snapped against his *piwafwi*. Someone was taking potshots from the crowd.

"What do you suggest?" Quenthel called back, extending her whip and flailing at an unfortunate kobold that had squeezed to the front of the gathering and was shoved forward from behind.

"Follow me!" Faeryl cried, and she began to lift from the ground, rising up into the air. "We must get to the mercantile district, and this is the fastest way."

"No," Valas groaned, eyes widening. "I can't—! I have no way to stay with you!"

But it was too late. The other drow had began to follow the ambassador's example and were lifting from the ground. Valas backed into the center of what had once been their circle, warily eyeing the crowd around him.

"Ryld!" he shouted. "Wait!"

Valas saw the warrior look down at him, but before the other drow could take action, Valas was grabbed from behind. He tried to spin around and slash out with his kukri, but the grip on him was powerful, and he couldn't get a clean swing in. A split-second later, he was glad, for Jeggred was the one who had a hold of him. Coated in blood that matted the fiend's fur, the draegloth held tightly to the scout as he left the ground. A couple of bold gray dwarves stormed forward, intent on getting in a parting swipe with their war axes at Valas's feet, but Jeggred still had a large, clawed hand free and slashed out at them, forcing the pair of duergar to leap back to safety.

Several more crossbow bolts whizzed by, and one sank into the draegloth's flank next to Valas, but Jeggred only grunted and spun away, levitating upward to where the other drow had gone. Valas looked back down where they had been standing only moments before. Even as the webbed street receded, the scout saw the mob swarm over the dead ogres, ripping items of value from the bodies.

Savages, he thought.

Above, Faeryl had stopped on a smaller side street several levels higher than where the drow had been previously, in a quiet space between rows of vendors. In the main thoroughfare, the crowds were less dense than below, but only slightly. Valas knew they were still relatively low in the city, for the glimmering glow of spectral light that emanated from the mesh of stone webs still dazzled his sight when he looked up, twinkling far into the distance overhead. He knew that the higher they got, the better the neighborhoods would be. Near the top of the cavern, where the trench-shaped chamber was at its widest, the nobles had constructed their sprawling Houses sufficiently beyond the stench and noise of the common folk far below. The Menzoberranyr had quite a ways to go before they would be in that vicinity.

"Is it always that . . . revolting down there?" Quenthel asked as the group settled to the stone avenue, huddling together and keeping their voices low. "Why do the matron mothers tolerate that rabble?"

Jeggred released Valas, who straightened and turned to look at the draegloth, wondering how much of the blood on the fiend was his enemies' and how much was his own. Much of Jeggred's fur was matted with the hot, sticky fluid, but other than the crossbow bolt in his hip, the beast didn't seem to bear any wounds. The scout examined his own clothing and noted sullenly that he was sticky with ogre blood, too.

"The lesser races are not permitted to wander so freely in the higher sections of the city without special permission," Faeryl explained. "It'll get better once we get a little higher."

"I doubt it," the high priestess said, sniffing. "I doubt the matron mothers would suffer such an embarrassment lightly. Likely they're dealing with more urgent problems, and I think we all know what those urgent problems are."

Over Quenthel's shoulder, Valas could see a trio of female drow who had stopped and were staring at Jeggred as the fiend yanked the crossbow bolt free with a grunt of pain. One of the dark elves whispered something to her companions, and the three of them scurried away.

Pharaun was making a point of dusting his *piwafwi* clean and straightening the garment so that he was looking stylish and well groomed again.

"You are most likely correct," the Master of Sorcere said, nodding in acquiescence. "Still, it would not hurt for us to find a place to stay for the night, gathering our wits and perhaps some more information, too. I'm sure that between the six of us, we can find out a little more about why the city is in this condition."

"Finding a place to stay may prove difficult," Ryld commented. "I wonder if there's a vacant room to be had in all of Ched Nasad."

Valas frowned, imagining the looks they would receive as they inquired after accommodations.

"If we can," the scout said, "your bodyguard will attract substantial attention. Even now, we are drawing looks. We should not stay out in the open for much longer."

Quenthel dug in her pack of supplies and produced a wand. Moving closer to Jeggred, she aimed the magical device at the draegloth's bleeding puncture wound and uttered a few words. The bleeding stopped, and the hole began to close.

"Be more careful," the high priestess admonished her nephew as she stored the wand once more. "Healing magic is limited."

"Even as overcrowded as the city is," Faeryl said, "the higher levels will not be that bad. I know of a place where we may be able to get rooms."

"Perhaps we need to rethink this," Quenthel countered. "It seems obvious to me that there are troubles here. I think it would be wiser to pay House Zauvirr and House Melarn a visit. We would be assured of accommodations there."

"No," Pharaun said, and Quenthel's eyes widened in surprise. The mage continued quickly, before the high priestess could lash out at him. "You may be right, but even so, you don't want to lose the opportunity to move about freely, do you? If we have any hope of staking a claim to the stock of goods and coin for your House, we must be able to avoid the matron mothers' notice."

"Well," Quenthel said, seeming to waver, "I'm uncomfortable with the idea of living like commoners in an inn, but your argument still makes sense."

Valas watched as the high priestess bit her lip, deep in thought.

Pharaun continued, trying to press home his advantage, "You know they will tell us nothing if there is a problem. They will keep that information to themselves at all costs. This way, we can explore a little bit, try to discover possible clues to Lolth's disappearance. It will allow us the chance to determine what has brought Ched Nasad to this condition." He leaned in close to avoid being overheard, as another pair of drow—males who had been strolling past this time—stopped and stared for a moment. "If nothing else, we can learn from this city's mistakes."

Ryld turned and gave the pair of males a level look, and they quickly averted their eyes and continued on their way.

"Whatever we do, we'd better do it now," the weapons master said over his shoulder. "Valas is right . . . we're attracting too much attention."

"Then shall I show us the way to the inn I know of?" Faeryl asked. "It's called the House Unnamed, and it's just—"

"You will do no such thing," Quenthel interrupted. "You seem far too eager to help us, and at the expense of your own House."

Faeryl gaped at the Baenre high priestess.

"Mistress Quenthel, I am merely—"

"Enough," Quenthel cut the ambassador off. "Until I decide to let the matron mothers know I'm here, you will not be warning them ahead of time. Jeggred, it will be your responsibility to make sure she doesn't try to sneak off."

The draegloth grinned, first at Quenthel, then at the ambassador.

"With pleasure, Mistress," he said.

Faeryl grimaced at the fiend's attentions, and Valas wondered just what had happened between the two of them prior to the group's departure. She'd behaved in that manner during the entire trip. He made a mental note to ask Ryld when they had a moment alone.

"Now," Quenthel said, turning to the other three of them, "which of you knows this city best?"

"I have visited Ched Nasad a number of times, Mistress Quenthel," Valas answered, and the other two males nodded in agreement, giving the scout center stage.

"Good. Find us an inn, someplace other than this 'House Unnamed.' Make it a good one, mind you. I won't put up with the squalor you might be used to."

Valas raised an eyebrow but said nothing. He found it interesting that the high priestess had changed her mind, agreeing to Pharaun's plan without actually admitting to it. He wondered if they would have words about it later, but for the moment, he was happy enough to do as she had instructed.

"The quickest way to get where we want to go is going to be by floating there," the scout said. "As long as Jeggred is willing to bear me, that is."

Quenthel looked first at the draegloth, then at Faeryl, and said, "You're not going to give me reason to have Jeggred or Pharaun kill you by trying to run away, are you?"

Faeryl glowered but shook her head.

"Good, then lead on, Valas. I am weary and would like to enjoy the Reverie on a proper couch for a change."

Jeggred lifted the scout up in one arm, and soon they were all rising easily toward the higher parts of the city. Faeryl had been right. As the group reached higher and higher elevations, the crowds abated somewhat. It was still busier than Valas had ever remembered, but at the higher levels, it was at least tolerable. He led them toward an upscale business section of the city, a zone where many of the lesser Houses, those with only enough power to make fortunes in trade as opposed to actually being powerful enough to run the city, maintained commercial offices.

It was this section, Valas knew, that many of the wealthy merchants from other regions of the Underdark frequented while visiting the city. The inns were extravagant enough that they would support the creature comforts expected by the trading community's elite, and they wouldn't do more than bat an eye even at someone as unusual as Jeggred. Valas hoped that there the Menzoberranyr would find a room that would satisfy Quenthel's need for pampering and not draw undue attention to themselves. If they could find a room at all.

Pharaun insisted that he be the one to negotiate with the innkeepers. The first two establishments nearly laughed in the wizard's face, and the third one made biting comments concerning the "Wrath of Lolth" before suggesting that a payment of submission for ritual cleansing would buy them the opportunity to share one room together. The fourth place had nothing either, but the proprietor there, a half-orc blind in one eye, suggested a place that was near the edge of the city, two sections higher. He claimed that his cousin ran the place and catered to mercenaries who hired on with caravans—or at least, they used to, when caravans still ran. Valas wondered which side of the family the relation was on.

It took a bit of searching before the group finally found the Flame and Serpent, a sprawling hive of stacked cocoon-shapes nestled together where one lonely strand of calcified webbing was anchored to the wall of the cavern. It held promise, if only by virtue of its out-of-the-way location and its appearance.

Quenthel balked upon first seeing the inn, but Pharaun suggested that they at least inquire inside before dismissing any possibility, and the high priestess once again let the male convince her.

She really must be weary, Valas mused. She's letting him run the show today. Well, one good night's Reverie, and that'll all change.

For a pleasant surprise, the inside of the Flame and Serpent was substantially more inviting than the outside had been. While Pharaun approached the innkeeper, a fat orc with silver caps on his tusks and two ogre bouncers to back him up, Valas looked around. There were certainly plenty of folk sitting in the tap room, and though Jeggred drew more than one lingering stare as he crouched beneath a ceiling that wasn't quite the right height for him, most of the patrons ignored them. Valas recognized why. They really were mercenaries, independents in the business for gold and little else, and as long as no one interfered with them or their livelihoods, they would keep to themselves. They were Valas's kind of folk.

Quenthel's expression was one of distaste, but Pharaun returned with a gleam in his eye and the good news that they had actually managed to get the Flame and Serpent's last two rooms. When the wizard mentioned the price, Quenthel rolled her eyes, but Valas realized they had probably still gotten a bargain.

"Only two?" Quenthel said doubtfully. "Then the males will have to share one, while Faeryl and I take the other. Jeggred, you, of course, will remain with me."

Faeryl's face looked stricken at the prospect of sharing her quarters with the draegloth, but she said nothing.

The rooms were not in the same area of the inn. The larger of the two, the one Quenthel claimed for her own, was a round chamber with a separate bathing room. It was near the front of the structure, with several small windows that looked out over the city. From their vantage, the females could see the magnificent glowing web streets stretching off into the distance both above and below. The smaller chamber was at the rear of the Flame and Serpent, an elongated room with two beds and a divan for a third person. The lone window opened to the wall of the cavern, where rivulets of water ran down, leaking through from the World Above and trickling down to the bottom of the **V**-shaped city, where it fed beds of fungi.

It's not much of a view, Valas decided, but it might prove useful for leaving the inn unobserved.

"I want to rest for a while, so you three," Quenthel said, looking at the males, "stay out of trouble. We will convene at the end of the day and discuss what to do next over our meal. Until then, leave me alone!"

With that she stalked off to her chambers, dragging Faeryl and Jeggred along with her.

Valas agreed to rest on the couch, and as the three of them unpacked a bit, Pharaun stood and stretched, cracking his back.

"I don't know about you two," the wizard said after a bit, "but I'm too excited to flop around here. I fancy a drink somewhere and maybe a chance to hear more of the buzz around town. Are you two interested in accompanying me?"

Valas looked at Ryld, who gave the scout a nod.

"Sure," they both said in unison, and the three of them set out together.

Three drow males moving through the streets of Ched Nasad proved to be much more anonymous than five drow and a draegloth, though Pharaun supposed that a large part of it was due to the fact that he, Ryld, and Valas were sauntering along back web streets in a higher section of the city. As they strolled, listening to the din of business all around them, the mage couldn't help but be thrilled at the exploration of the city. Unlike Menzoberranzan, Ched Nasad was a cosmopolitan collection of sights, sounds, and smells that permeated the entire city. He could certainly detect subtle differences as the trio moved through various sections of town, but regardless of where they found themselves, the wizard absorbed it all, noting that the air vibrated with a kind of clamor, the feel of wheeling and dealing, that was only present in the baser areas of Menzoberranzan.

It was certainly more lively than Tier Breche, where Pharaun spent far too much time cloistered in the towers of the Academy, hidden away in Sorcere. Back home, he had made a habit of only getting out into the main city when he needed supplies or the occasional drink and bit of fun. It had been that way for many years, at least while his sister Greyanna longed to kill him. With her no longer posing a problem, he made a note to himself to partake of the more colorful neighborhoods of home more often.

As they strolled, Valas and Ryld seemed to be looking everywhere at once, but Pharaun knew that their attentiveness to the cacophony around them was due to a different reason than his own. Certainly, he was wary of a pickpocket or thug, but for the weapons master and the scout, it was what they had trained themselves to do for years upon years. They had honed their skills of wariness and observation to keen levels, and their entire beings reverberated with it. Pharaun doubted seriously that anyone in the city would get the drop on him while his two companions were in tow. It was a comforting thought, if only because it allowed him to truly relax and enjoy the splendor of the City of Shimmering Webs.

The mage certainly understood why Ched Nasad had been dubbed such. The tangle of streets crisscrossed in purples, ambers, greens, and yellows for hundreds of feet in every direction, and it was a marvelous sight. Everywhere the three of them walked vendors hawked mushrooms, or jewelry, or potions. Pharaun noticed that the goods seemed of an inferior sort, though, and few people were buying—everyone had a hint of something in his eyes. Fear, he decided. Everyone looked afraid.

Once filthy looking drow male had small cages, each one holding a small four-armed humanoid with multifaceted eyes, mandibles, and a spidery abdomen. They were no more than a foot tall. Peering closer, Pharaun could see that the creatures had web-spinning capabilities. They shrank back as he studied them.

"You wish to buy one, Master?" the male asked hopefully, jumping up from where he had been sitting cross-legged.

"Infant chitines," Valas said. "The adults are hunted for sport, and whenever a nest is found the babies are brought back here and sold as pets."

"Interesting," Pharaun replied and briefly contemplated purchasing one, though from the look of things, the drow male was having little luck drawing any interest in his wares. "I'd consider getting one—as a present for Quenthel, you know—but these seem over priced."

The male's hopeful stare faded to disappointment, and he sat down on the edge of the street again.

Ryld snorted, and Valas shook his head.

"They're not too expensive," the scout said as they walked on. "The market's probably just flooded with them right now."

"Why is that?" Pharaun asked.

"Because chitines and choldriths worship the goddess, too," Valas answered quietly.

"Choldriths?"

"Chitine priestesses. Same racial stock, larger and dark-skinned. No hair, human eyes. I suspect that they may be suffering the same calamity that has befallen our own clerics."

Pharaun's curiosity was piqued.

"Really," he said, musing. "It might prove useful if we could track down some of these choldriths and find out if they are suffering the same fate. It's obvious that Ched Nasad endures the goddess's silence, too, and once we get proof, Quenthel may be at a loss for what to do next. This would give us the means to explore further, find out if Lolth's reticence is universal or just limited to our own race."

"It's a nice idea in theory, mage," Ryld said, shooing a goblin vendor away who was trying to convince him to buy a bowl of slugs, "but you'd be hard-pressed to track any down, and struggle even more to elicit information from them. The drow hunt them for sport, so the chitines and choldriths have learned to flee or fight to the death."

"Hmm," Pharaun responded, spying a little shop selling something he wanted. "Perhaps, but my particular talents could come in handy in such an endeavor."

The mage's companions followed him to a cramped kiosk selling spirits, which was hanging at the corner of two fairly large web streets. To reach it, customers had to slide down a steep ramp of webbing to the front of the vending stand, then ascend a ladder of webbing to return to the street. Pharaun studied the small crowd of people gathered around, each in turn descending the slide and purchasing a flask or mushroom cap of beverage.

"You'd think they could have put steps in on both sides," the Master of Sorcere sniffed disdainfully.

"Oh, by the Dark Mother," Ryld said, shaking his head. "I'll get us something."

With that, the warrior moved through the crowd, very few of whom were actually buying, instead begging coin or a sip from the paying customers. Ryld ignored them and descended upon the vendor, while Pharaun and Valas stood out of the way of traffic and took the opportunity to absorb the sights again.

When Ryld returned, he had a bit of a strange look on his face.

"What is it?" Valas asked.

"That gray dwarf charged me ten times what this swill is worth and seemed to take a certain delight in it."

"Well, a bit of gouging is to be expected, when caravan traffic has dried up," Pharaun said.

"Yes, but when a goblin asked for the same thing right after me, I heard the proprietor sell it to him for half what he charged me."

"Maybe the little thrall is a regular," Valas offered.

"Possibly," Pharaun said, opening the flask that Ryld had procured and inhaling a waft. He jerked his head back and scrunched up his face a bit. "I suspect it has more to do with relishing the opportunity to earn a little payback against the drow." He took a sip of the brandy and passed the flask to Valas. "After all, who regulates the commerce in the city? Who gets first choice of all the best vending locations? Who runs the caravan system? Who acquires the best trade goods?"

"In other words, who sticks it to the other races with regularity?" Ryld finished.

"Exactly. The gray dwarves, the trogs, the kuo-toans, and everyone else in this city know that the ruling class has fallen on hard times, and despite the fact that they've been allowed to trade in a city of dark elves, they won't waste a chance to earn a spot of revenge. And Ryld," Pharaun added, gesturing to the flask that Valas was handing to the warrior, "you would have been had at one-tenth the price."

Ryld shrugged, took a sip, and said, "You're drinking it, aren't you?"

The three companions continued on, sharing the flask and discussing the prospects of acquiring some sort of tangible confirmation that Lolth was absent from Ched Nasad. Pharaun continued to be deeply intrigued by the idea of investigating other races known to worship the goddess, and even as he contributed to the conversation, he mulled the concept over. It would require some research. Given time and Quenthel's willingness, he had a good idea where he might go to perform the study.

The mage's musings were interrupted when the trio ascended a webbed staircase, turned a corner, and found themselves on a colonnade overlooking an open plaza. From the congestion in the mall, Pharaun thought it obvious that refugees had taken to using the place as a sort of campground. Still, there was enough room to move along the raised walkway around the perimeter without brushing shoulder to shoulder with the riffraff, and the three dark elves glided along, ignoring the pleas and demands for coin from the unwashed around them.

A shout from below drew the drow's attention, and when Pharaun peered toward the center of the plaza, he spotted the source of the disturbance. A priestess was standing in a fairly open area, three or four hobgoblins gathered around her. She seemed to be mumbling something, but from a distance Pharaun couldn't make out what it was. The female drow raised her arm back and tried to lash out at one of the hobgoblins with a scourge, but the creature easily stepped aside, and the priestess stumbled forward from the exertion. She was quite drunk, Pharaun realized.

"Filthy animals," the priestess barked, staggering back upright. "Stay away from me!"

Pharaun noticed her unkempt state. Her *piwafwi* was soiled and sloughed half off her shoulders, her lustrous white hair was disheveled, and she held a bottle of something the wizard presumed to be liquor in her other hand.

The hobgoblins merely laughed at the drow before them, casually circling, which caused the priestess to turn, trying to keep an eye on them all. The effort made her stumble again, and she nearly went down in a heap.

"I don't think I've ever seen such a thing," Valas breathed. "The gall those subcreatures have is truly bewildering."

"Let's put a stop to this," Ryld said, taking a step forward.

Suddenly, Pharaun was aware of magic around him, an effect that seemed to be centered on him and his two companions. He reached out and put a hand on the warrior's arm.

"Wait," he said. "Let's see what happens."

When Ryld looked at the wizard quizzically, he continued, "Drawing attention to ourselves is not the best way to investigate. Besides," the mage added, "We might see once and for all if our theory is correct. This might be the proof we need."

The wizard flashed in sign language, *I think someone is watching us, observing us magically.*

Both Ryld and Valas raised eyebrows in concern, but before they could turn and look around, Pharaun cautioned, *Don't draw attention to the fact that we know. Just pretend we're watching the spectacle.*

Pharaun briefly considered dispelling the magic, but he discounted the idea because he knew it would only give their spy notification that they were aware of his or her presence. Instead, he pretended to turn his attention back to the brewing fight below while in actuality scanning the plaza for signs of someone looking at him rather than at the hobgoblins. There were a great many magical auras radiating from many different individuals, but no one, as far as the wizard could observe, seemed to be staring in his direction.

The hobgoblins seemed content for the moment to keep their distance, though they were increasingly pressed from behind by a gathering crowd. For her part, the priestess seemed to have lost interest in her detractors and was standing relatively still, her eyes closed, swaying slightly. She was mumbling something, but Pharaun again could not make it out.

Well, spy or no spy, he thought, I want to know what she's saying.

He reached into one of his many pockets and produced a tiny brass horn, with which he cast a spell. When the magic was complete, the wizard could hear the priestess's mutterings as though he were standing right in front of her.

"—beseech thee, our Mistress Lolth, return to me. Give me your blessings. Do not abandon me when I am your loyal an—*aieee!*"

One of the hobgoblins had chosen that moment to prod the drow with a sharpened stick, and she shrieked as she jumped, losing her grip on the bottle of spirits. It fell to the calcified pavement and shattered, spilling only the trickle that remained.

"Damn you, thrall!" she screamed at the hobgoblin that had molested her, attempting to stalk forward, her hand outstretched as though she were going to throttle him.

A second hobgoblin casually reached out with his own short spear and tripped the priestess, who went sprawling.

She rose to her hands and knees and began shouting, "My goddess, come to me, aid me! Do not abandon me, your loyal servant, who will obey—"

"Your goddess is dead," the first hobgoblin snarled, kicking the drow.

She grunted from the impact and toppled to the side, clutching for her scourge.

"No!" she shrieked. "Lolth would not abandon us! She is mighty, and her faithful are mighty!"

The four hobgoblins advanced together, and the drow priestess tried to kick at them, but the creature in the lead easily sidestepped the attack and jabbed down at her with his spear. Pharaun saw the point draw blood from the dark elf priestess's thigh.

Ryld snarled and flashed, *This is not right. We should do something.*

Valas nodded in agreement and produced his two kukris, one curved dagger in each hand.

The mage laid a hand on each drow's shoulder to slow them.

You only put our mission in danger, he signed. *As you can see, no other drow move to help her.*

He gestured down into the crowd, where several other dark elves were in attendance, observing dispassionately.

She has lost her faith and deserves no less, Pharaun admonished his companions.

It is not the priestess I am worried about, Ryld replied, a sullen look on his face, *but to allow those vermin to believe they can so blatantly confront a superior being spells trouble for us all. They should be put in their place.*

Perhaps, Pharaun responded, *but we need anonymity if we are to finish our task. Confronting those beasts does nothing to further our own goals.*

The wizard is right, Valas motioned, sagging back from the edge of the colonnade. *If the matron mothers hear that three outsiders interfered in what may very well be one of their own plots, we will no longer be able to walk this city unhindered and unobserved.*

If they're not already watching us, Ryld flashed. *Are we still being observed?* When Pharaun nodded yes, the warrior continued, *We've got the proof we sought, anyway. Let's return to the inn. I no longer have the stomach for this city.*

Pharaun nodded, though he did not share his friend's sentiment. Together, they turned and strolled back the way they had come, ignoring the screams of the priestess as the hobgoblins opened her a hundred times with quick, controlled thrusts of their short spears. After a few steps, the magical scrying vanished, and Pharaun cast his gaze around once more, hoping to find the source. He did not, and the three of them departed the plaza.

Behind them, the crowd that had gathered around the confrontation stirred and grew rowdy. Several other drow in the throng found themselves pushed and prodded as they tried to extricate themselves from the roiling multitudes. The other races were growing bold after witnessing the murder of a dark elf. Shouts rose up, curses to drow and their missing goddess. Finally, the handful of dark elves scrambled free, either rising up above the aggressors around them, or pushing through to more open streets. The mood was turning ugly in Ched Nasad.

SIX

Aliisza, disguised as a lovely drow female, perched on the roof of a quaint shop that stood along the side of a street leading to the plaza, and she watched the comings and goings of the citizens, slaves, and visitors of Ched Nasad. The store offered fashionable, decorative silk wraps and other clothing, but the fiend crouching on its rounded, co-coonlike roof was not interested in making a purchase. Instead, she watched intently as Pharaun and the other two drow males turned away from the slaughter of one of their own race and strolled calmly in the other direction. She observed them as they disappeared down one of the calcified webs that served as a street in the unusual city. When they were almost out of sight, she hopped down from her van-tage point and strode off after them.

Aliisza was not terribly surprised that the three dark elves she was shadowing had not aided the drunken priestess. She had seen far too much nonchalance in the city since she had arrived for it to strike her as odd. Still, she got the distinct impression that the entire group from Menzoberranzan was making a great effort to avoid drawing attention to itself. She intended to find out why, but first things first.

The alu could not help but smile as she made her way along the streets, following the wizard and his companions while pretending to shop for trinkets in the bazaars and markets. She studied the myriad lines of calcified webs that stretched across from one side of the massive cavern to the other, glowing faintly with magical, flickering light as far as the eye could see. She half expected to see some great, lumbering spider making its way across the vast webbing.

They sure do love their spider motifs, she thought wryly. Everything they do revolves around the great Lolth, Queen of the Spiders. You'd think they would learn to diversify a little bit, try to become a little more well-rounded.

She grinned at her own little joke. Drow were such odd creatures, she decided. On the one hand so deceitful and chaotic, always turning on one another, but on the other hand trying to live their lives by some code or structure, based on the tenets of faith set down by a demon who was as unpredictable as could possibly be.

At least they universally agree on one thing, the alu concluded, they all think they're superior to every other species in the Underdark, and on the surface, too.

Aliisza watched as a gaggle of kobold slaves, pushed along by their hobgoblin slavemasters, scurried from one web street down a sloped ramp to the next web street below. All in all, she had seen more species of creature in Ched Nasad than she could imagine being gathered anywhere else. The "lesser races" outnumbered the drow by two to one, she figured, and included surface dwarves, orcs, quaggoths, bugbears, and others, almost all of them slaves. The one possible exception to this was the gray dwarves, who traded honestly enough with the drow that they were tolerated in the city as merchants. In addition, Aliisza had seen an aboleth with its host of caretakers, illithids, grell, and what she suspected must be a deep dragon, for though it too was disguised as a dark elf, she detected the unmistakable scent as it strolled by.

The one notable exception to the eclectic collection of visitors were the beholders, for which Aliisza was not in the least sorry.

There's a race that's even more fond of itself than the dark elves, if that's even possible, the alu thought.

Eye tyrants were nothing but trouble as far as Aliisza was concerned, but fortunately they were in a perpetual state of war with the drow, so none were ever seen in the vicinity. If she had caught even a glimpse of one inside the great **V**-shaped cavern, she would have turned and headed the opposite direction as quickly as was fiendishly possible.

The alu blinked, realizing that with all her daydreaming, she was letting her quarry slip away. Glancing around, she spotted the trio of drow heading along a segment of web street toward a wall, into an out-of-the-way part of the city. She realized that they were in the mercantile district, and she recognized quickly enough that Pharaun and the others were headed for an inn set along the end of the dead-end thoroughfare.

Good, she thought. Now I can keep an eye on them and still enjoy the sights and sounds for a few days. Maybe I can even get the wizard alone for a little while. . . .

🕷 🕷 🕷

Faeryl Zauvirr brooded on the plush bed while Quenthel stalked back and forth in the room they shared at the Flame and Serpent. The high priestess didn't like to be kept waiting during the best of times, and she certainly didn't like being kept waiting in the middle of a strange city, tendays away from her homeland, and by three males, no less.

That damnable Mizzrym and his infuriating smile, Quenthel thought. I should have Jeggred rend him the moment he returns.

But she knew she couldn't eliminate the wizard or even allow him to be injured. As much as she loathed the situation, Quenthel knew she was dependent on Pharaun as a resource.

But when we return to Menzoberranzan . . .

The unfinished thought hovered in her mind, not so much because she didn't know what was to be done with the irritating mage but because she didn't know when, or if, she would see her home again.

It had been so long since she'd last felt the presence of Lolth, had last bathed in the goddess's glory and favor, that she wondered if she even properly remembered what it felt like.

Will it ever return? Is she gone?

Stop it! Quenthel silently scolded herself. *If you are being tested, fool, then right now, your score is not high. Not high at all. Even if she did send you back for a purpose.*

Jeggred opened the door and entered, stooping as he did so to avoid the low jamb overhead.

"They are back," he growled, sliding the door shut behind him.

"Where in the Hells were they?" Quenthel asked, still pacing.

"They went for a walk," the draegloth answered, shrugging.

Quenthel looked over at the creature, who was leering at Faeryl. The ambassador looked miserable under the fiend's scrutiny, and Quenthel wanted to laugh, remembering some of the things Triel had told her about the Zauvirr's torture at the hands of Jeggred. Even so, this was not the time.

Quenthel snapped, "Are those worthless males coming, or must I send you to fetch them?"

"They will be here shortly," Jeggred replied, turning away from Faeryl to crouch in a corner. "The mage told me he had something he needed to look over before they joined us." Even down on his haunches, the draegloth was as tall as the high priestess. His white mane of hair cascaded out behind him as he examined the claw of one hand, picking some fleck of something from its surface with the hand of one of his smaller arms. "They have been drinking," he finished, not looking up.

Quenthel swore, drawing a look from Faeryl, but the high priestess didn't care.

Out carousing, like foolish boys! she seethed. *When we return, they shall be put to work in the rothé fields.*

There was a knock at the door, and Quenthel stopped pacing at last, planting her hands on her hips as Jeggred rose to answer it. When he swung the portal open, Pharaun, Valas, and Ryld filed in. Quenthel was surprised to see the grim looks on the faces of the three males.

Before anyone had a chance to speak, Pharaun flashed, *Someone was watching us today, with magic. No one say a word until I ward the room.*

With that, he produced a small mirror and a tiny brass horn and used them to cast a spell of some sort, though Quenthel could not see any visible difference. Not that she expected to, but the idea of the wizard performing spells of his own accord, like everything he did, made her uneasy.

"The city is about to boil over," Pharaun said when he was finished casting. He took a seat on the couch and avoided looking directly at Quenthel.

He knows he's about to catch it, the high priestess thought.

"What do you mean? Who's been watching you? And what were you doing out there, anyway? Didn't I instruct you to get some rest and meet back here before the evening meal?"

"Actually, you did not, Mistress," Pharaun answered as the other two found places to lean against the far wall. "You said that *you* were going to rest, and you specifically told us to leave you alone. Under such circumstances, I didn't see the wisdom in disturbing you with trivialities like a refreshing walk."

Quenthel sighed. Once again the wizard was twisting her words around, using them to his advantage.

"As for who was watching us, I can't say. It might have been nothing, just a curious mage checking out some unusual-looking characters as a matter of course and moving on. Then again, it could have been someone specifically worried about us. I didn't see who was scrying. When I returned, I pulled out my grimoires and studied a spell that would detect scrying, though not stop it from happening. If I give a signal, everyone must be silent."

Quenthel nodded once, curtly, knowing that the wizard was taking wise precautions.

"Very well," she said. "What did you discover while you were strolling through the city that makes you believe it is about to 'boil over'?"

"It's true," Valas said quietly from his corner. "The lesser races are growing restless. We witnessed an attack today."

"So what?" the high priestess responded. "They squabble among themselves all the time back home."

"Yes, but this was a gang of them, assaulting a priestess," Ryld said. He was glowering, though at whom, Quenthel was not sure. "They were bold enough to kill her in front of everyone in an open plaza."

"They would dare?" It was Faeryl, sitting on the edge of the bed, her red eyes glittering with anger. "And you did nothing?"

"Truth be told, she was quite inebriated," Pharaun said, reclining on the couch. "Still, she provided us with the proof we needed. Ched Nasad's clergy suffers the same, ah . . . challenges that you do, Mistress."

Quenthel had folded her arms beneath her breasts and moved to stand in front of the wizard.

"You did nothing to aid her?" she asked, turning her gaze toward the other two males, watching as they looked away, some notion of guilt on their faces.

Pharaun shrugged and said, "To have interfered would have only drawn attention to the fact that we were in the city, Mistress. If we are to continue to investigate, we must maintain our inconspicuousness. Besides," he added, leaning forward again, "she was pleading for Lolth to return to her, right there in the open courtyard. She had clearly lost her resolution and was not, in my most humble opinion, fit to serve the goddess."

"In your—!" Faeryl seethed. "The opinion of a mere male is counted upon for very little in most issues. In the matters of the sisterhood, it matters not at all!"

She stood, taking a step toward the wizard. With a gesture from Quenthel, Jeggred was instantly between them. The ambassador shrank back from her one-time tormentor.

"Faeryl, my dear, in this you are usually correct," Quenthel said in her most soothing voice. It was one she rarely used, but in this instance she believed it was warranted. For his part, Pharaun gaped at her, which made her smile. "But, my dear, think on it," the high priestess continued. "The wizard is actually correct, though he may have stumbled upon this conclusion accidentally, addled with brandy though his mind seems to be. I understand your fears, but you must not let them eat away at your logic. If a priestess loses her faith in such a public spectacle, does she do her sisterhood any service?"

Faeryl shook her head as she backed away from Jeggred, returning to her spot on the bed.

"No, of course not," she mumbled at last. "She shames us all with her cowardice."

"Precisely," Quenthel said, nodding sagely, "and as foolish as it was for them to be out and about in the first place, these three silly boys would have only caused more harm to our progress if they had made a spectacle of themselves as well."

"Forgive my impudence, Mistress Quenthel," Faeryl said, her tone dreary. "I have returned home to find my city on the brink of implosion, where thralls dare to assault priestesses in open markets. As you love Menzoberranzan, your city and homeland, so I love Ched Nasad and do not wish to see her come to this end. I forgot myself in a moment of emotion."

Quenthel dismissed the apology with a wave of her hand.

"Understandable, in this time of crisis," she said, "but you must learn to control that emotion if we are to move forward."

"Do I take it, then, that you believe there is still more to be uncovered?" Pharaun asked.

"Perhaps," the high priestess answered, pacing once more. "I am willing to hear what the rest of you think, before I make my decision."

It was Valas who spoke first.

"I think it's unsafe to remain in the city for long, Mistress," the diminutive scout said. "We have discovered what we came here to learn, and I think it would be wise to return to Menzoberranzan before riots fill the streets and we get caught up in another slave revolt, or worse."

"I agree with Valas," Ryld added. "It is clear to me that the clerics here have handled the vanishing of Lolth less well than you and yours back home. There is little they can do for us."

Quenthel looked to Pharaun, knowing he would have something completely different and unorthodox in mind.

Pharaun shifted a bit, eyeing the other two males before saying, "I think we might do better to investigate further. Valas opened my eyes to another possible avenue of study, one that I would like to take advantage of. There are other races who venerate the Dark Mother besides drow, and it would behoove us to discover whether or not they, too, suffer her loss."

Quenthel nodded and said, "An interesting idea, but not one of much practicality. We are not loved by many others, and I doubt that those who worship Lolth would too freely impart such secretive information to us. Notice how we haven't been too forthcoming ourselves, even to the dark elves of our sister city. However, as there is still business I consider unfinished here, we will not be going just yet."

"Yes, precisely," Pharaun replied. "While you're busy with all that, I plan to at least look into my theory. I think I might know of a way to confirm it by tomorrow."

"I have other work for you tomorrow," Quenthel said, giving the wizard a cold gaze. "Faeryl, Jeggred, and I shall pay a visit to the storehouses of Black Claw Mercantile and take what rightfully belongs to House Baenre while the three of you find a means to transport it back. I intend to get out of the city with those goods as quickly as possible. The caravans are long overdue in Menzoberranzan, and we are here to make sure due payment is made."

Pharaun scowled briefly, and Quenthel was expecting an argument, but the wizard merely stood, nodding again.

Pharaun was surprised when Quenthel asked him to remain behind for a moment after dismissing the rest of the group, along with specific instructions to Jeggred to keep an eye on Faeryl, instructions that made the ambassador actually tremble. The wizard stood silently as Quenthel closed the door, then he cocked an eyebrow at her when she asked him if his detection spells were still in place.

"Yes, as a matter of fact, they are," the mage responded. "The divination should remain in place for a full day."

"Good," the high priestess said, nodding in satisfaction. "You're pretty talented with divining information, are you not?"

Pharaun could not help but grin but sat on the couch as he spread his hands ingenuously, wondering why she, of all drow, would pay him a compliment.

"I manage to get by," he said.

"I want you to do something for me," Quenthel said, biting her lip.

Pharaun tipped his head to one side, surprised, for it was not at all like her, especially in recent tendays, to pay him a compliment, much less ask a favor of him.

We are indeed a long way from Menzoberranzan, he thought wryly.

It would give the wizard leverage if he could perform a genuine task for her, but of course the first notion that popped into his head was the prospect of being played. Shrugging, he motioned for her to speak further.

After a lengthy pause, the high priestess said, "I want you to determine the identity of someone."

" 'Someone?' " Pharaun asked. "Surely you have more for me to work with?"

"Yes . . ." Quenthel answered, biting her lip again, "someone who was trying to kill me."

Pharaun sat upright on the couch, looking directly at the female in front of him.

"Kill you?"

He was surprised, not because it was so inconceivable that Quenthel was the target of an attack—merely being the Mistress of Arach-Tinilith brought with it a host of enemies—but because she had decided to trust him enough with this confidence and the task. If that was indeed what she really wanted. Maybe she was just trying to occupy his time, keep him from something else. A hundred possibilities swirled in his head.

"Someone back in Menzoberranzan sent several demons after me," Quenthel said. "Sent them right into the Academy. Fortunately, my prowess was sufficient to fend off the attacks, but I would like to put a stop to them before we return. It is a waste of both the lives of my charges and the magic I have been forced to consume in the effort."

Pharaun nodded, thinking. Someone powerful enough to bend demons to his will had to come from Sorcere, he reasoned. Certainly, plenty of mages in the school of magic had the wherewithal, but how many of them were so interested in eliminating Quenthel Baenre?

"I will look into it," the Master of Sorcere said. "If I can determine who sent the fiends in your direction, you will be the first to know it."

"Good," Quenthel said. "You will tell no one of this, not even the other members of our expedition."

"Of course not, Mistress," Pharaun replied. "This issue is between the two of us, and the two of us only."

"Very well," the high priestess said, indicating that the meeting was at an end. "Ferret out my enemy, and when we return to Menzoberranzan in triumph, I will make certain you are duly honored for your part. Your future at Tier Breche will be as bright as Narbondel."

Pharaun bowed low as a gesture of thanks.

If by that you mean I will glow with the flame of a thousand of your killing spells, he thought, *then we shall see.*

"I look forward to the accolades, Mistress Quenthel," the mage said aloud, and with that he pulled the door open for her and followed her out to attend to the evening meal with the others.

Gromph sat at his bone desk, mulling over his inability to peer into the Demonweb where Lolth resided. None of his usual scrying spells had been successful, and he was growing irritated. He was considering ways to get around this dilemma when the message arrived. It was a mere whisper, but Gromph nonetheless recognized Pharaun Mizzrym's magically transmitted voice.

Reached Ched Nasad. City in chaos; matron mothers ruling in name only. Investigating new possibility, more information next communication. Quenthel to visit Black Claw tomorrow.

Gromph's mouth tightened at the mention of his sister.

Hopefully, she will not come back, he thought.

The archmage knew of the spell the other wizard was using to communicate, and he was aware that he could whisper an answer to his counterpart. Unfortunately, he had not prepared for this. Thinking quickly, he whispered a few instructions.

"Focus attention on gathering information to aid our own situation. Keep me apprised of all new possibilities. Report on success at Black Claw with next—

"—contact," Gromph finished, but he knew that the spell had winked out before he'd managed to utter the last word. He shook his head, disgruntled, but he knew the Mizzrym was clever enough to figure out what he meant, regardless. Whether he would follow those instructions or not was an entirely different matter.

The Baenre wizard sat back in his chair, contemplating for a moment, pondering what condition the expedition team was likely to be in. He especially wondered how his sister fared and if the strain of his own attacks, coupled with the journey, had taken their toll. He certainly hoped so.

He suspected that she and Pharaun were clashing on a regular basis. The wizard was too independent, too full of himself to know when to placate the high priestess, and she had been too long inside the Academy, too used to getting her own way, unwilling to listen to advice, no matter how reasonable.

That's my sister, the archmage thought, frowning.

It often seemed to Gromph as if both of his sisters made poor decisions for no other purpose than to spite others. Even if Quenthel did survive her journey, Gromph thought she might very well be ripe for the slaughter when she returned. If she returned. If Quenthel were to lead the expedition into disaster in Ched Nasad, it would certainly be to Gromph's advantage. He could be rid of both her and the Mizzrym fop in one very charming blow. Yet, the fate of Menzoberranzan might very well rest on their shoulders. Was sending them off together the wisest choice?

Still uncertain what his next step would be regarding his own investigations of Lolth's domain, but with a whole new set of issues to deal with, Gromph arose from behind his bone desk and hurried to find his sister.

Triel scowled slightly when she saw Gromph enter the audience chamber. It was not a time for public petitioning, and though her brother was hardly some common supplicant, she had hoped to avoid any visitations for a while. The matron mother straightened herself in the overly large throne as her brother approached. The archmage bowed low and stepped close, further irritating the matron mother. She liked everyone to keep a little distance.

Gromph kept his voice low, leaning in so as to nearly whisper, "Triel, I have news."

Triel doubted the guards outside, flanking the doors, were going to hear a normal conversation, but her brother had not become Archmage of Menzoberranzan through carelessness. She inclined her head to listen.

"Do tell," she said.

"Quenthel and the others have reached Ched Nasad," the archmage said. "Pharaun Mizzrym reports that the city is in an uproar. Apparently, Menzoberranzan is not the only city afflicted with Lolth's disfavor."

"We don't know that it is disfavor!" Triel snapped. "There may be another explanation."

Gromph inclined his head slightly in apology.

"Afflicted with her absence," he corrected himself. "But the matron mothers there have done a poor job of keeping the situation quiet."

"How bad is it?"

"I gathered that trouble could be brewing . . . major trouble."

Triel sighed. As much of a relief as it was to find out Menzoberranzan was not being singled out for some sort of punishment, the news didn't get them any closer to discovering why the Dark Mother had chosen to disappear. Triel was at a loss as to the next step.

"Did he say what they were planning to do?" she asked her brother.

"Quenthel seems intent on following through with your instructions to bring back goods from Black Claw," Gromph replied.

The idea of more magical supplies lifted Triel's spirits slightly, but only slightly.

"Then I suppose they'll be returning within a few tendays," she said. "We are really no closer to an answer than we were when they left. It is only a matter of time before Menzoberranzan is in the same difficulties as her sister city."

"Unfortunately, you may be more correct than you understand."

"What other dire news do you have to report?"

If this was the way her mornings were going to start out, Triel considered remaining in Reverie until the midday meal a preferable alternative to actually rising and dealing with the issues at hand.

"I have received reports that our patrols are encountering a lot more activity around the perimeter of the city."

"What kind of activity?"

"Exactly what you might expect," Gromph said. "Though nothing has actually happened, no skirmishes breaking out, our patrols have spotted what looks to be scouting parties surveying our situation. Duergar, deep gnomes, and even kuo-toans have been spotted in greater-than-normal numbers."

"They know. They can tell that things aren't right."

"Perhaps. Or, they could simply be passing by . . . traveling to somewhere else, and we've simply grown more sensitive to their presence."

"I doubt it," she replied. "This can't last. We're going to have to confront the situation soon. I will bring this up at the next council meeting."

"Of course," Gromph said and made a move to withdraw.

Triel motioned that her brother was dismissed and told herself that it was time to get on with her day, but she continued to brood atop her throne for some time after that.

Quenthel was thankful she had Jeggred along for the trip from the Flame and Serpent to the storehouse district. The mood of the city had grown worse since even the previous day, and the drow received more than a few menacing looks and jostles as they moved through the streets. Fortunately, the trio didn't have to travel far to get to where they needed to go, and much of the journey was made by way of levitation. Faeryl was in a sullen mood, despite the fact that she seemed more than eager to aid the Menzoberranyr. Perhaps she was still displeased with Quenthel's lack of trust, or maybe she simply couldn't abide Jeggred's presence. The high priestess couldn't blame her. The draegloth took such delight in tormenting Faeryl, Quenthel almost felt sorry for the younger drow. Almost.

Quenthel had sent the males to procure transportation for the return trip to Menzoberranzan. She wasn't about to haul her own provisions on her back again, whether they managed to locate a stockpile of goods or not, and if they did they would need sufficient pack lizards and guards to ensure the materials arrived safely.

Valas had warned the high priestess that anyone worth his salt was going to command an exorbitant price, if he could be convinced to work at all, but Quenthel didn't care and told the scout so.

Why is it, Quenthel thought as they approached Black Claw's storehouses from a back street, where there were fewer folk milling about, that with males you always have to explain things to them in exacting detail? Why can't they just do as they're told and be done with it?

Pharaun was the worst, she decided. Quenthel had no doubt that the wizard was off doing his own little tasks, completely ignoring her instructions to him to help Valas and Ryld. He had an infuriating habit of ignoring her wishes, and she would have to do something about that—when they got back to Menzoberranzan, of course. She needed his talents too much until then.

"Now, remember," Quenthel warned Faeryl as they neared the office side of the storehouse. "Tell them only what I instructed you. If I'm not happy with this little encounter, Jeggred will make sure it's not a problem in the future."

The draegloth was strolling along behind the two priestesses, and Faeryl stole a quick glance over her shoulder at him. Quenthel noticed her faint shudder and smiled to herself. It turned out to be quite useful that Triel had set Jeggred upon the girl back in Menzoberranzan. It had made her so . . . compliant.

"Yes, Mistress Quenthel," Faeryl replied. "I understand."

The three of them were at the door to the storehouse, where a contingent of six House Zauvirr guards barred the entrance. Faeryl approached boldly, even as the males goggled at the sight of the towering draegloth behind her.

"We must inspect the stores," Faeryl said in what Quenthel thought was a surprisingly commanding voice. "Stand aside and let us enter."

The male who appeared to be the leader managed to pull his gaze away from Jeggred long enough to look at her quizzically.

"I don't know you," he said. "What is your business?"

Faeryl stepped closer, standing a little taller so that he was forced to peer up at her scowling face. She grasped the House insignia that was pinned to her *piwafwi* and thrust it into his view.

"You know this, don't you?" she snapped, shaking the insignia. "You're here to keep out the riffraff, stupid boy, not bother a personal envoy of Matron Mothers Zauvirr and Melarn."

Quenthel noted with satisfaction that the lad gulped, visibly shaken as he moved with haste to the side, allowing Faeryl access to the door. The ambassador stepped inside, with the high priestess and Jeggred right behind her. As Quenthel strolled past, she smiled sweetly at one of the males, who still gaped at the draegloth, his eyes wide.

Inside the storehouse, which appeared to have been spun from webbing and hardened to stone, Faeryl led the way through an office area, through a large door, and into a cavernous chamber that had been subdivided into storage areas by low walls. Her footsteps echoing in the vast storeroom, Faeryl walked across the stone floor, hurrying past row after row of shelves and bins. Quenthel followed her, figuring the ambassador knew the way to the most valuable hoards of magic.

Quenthel supposed there was a secure section of the store-house, and she began to worry. Any magic of value would likely be warded.

I should have brought that fop Mizzrym along, after all, she chided herself.

"Mistress!" Yngoth hissed, rising up from the whip. "We are in danger!"

Quenthel spun around, looking for signs of a threat, but she could see nothing.

"What danger?" she demanded. "Where?"

"A force is here . . . drow," Zinda answered, and all five of the snakes were agitating against her hip.

"Drow and others," Zinda added.

Someone's hiding, the high priestess realized. What have you done, insolent child?

A heartbeat later, a small host of drow appeared from behind a low wall, soldiers with swords and hand crossbows at the ready, and a handful of House wizards, too. They were all from House Zauvirr. Quenthel recognized two of the dark elves as matron mothers. It was obvious simply by their demeanor and bearing. One bore the insignia of House Zauvirr, and she was smiling coldly. The other, a rather plump drow, was most definitely not smiling and in fact looked quite distressed.

"By the Dark Mother," one of the males standing near Faeryl breathed, raising his crossbow and sighting down it at the fiend.

"He's dangerous," Faeryl called out, but several of the House wizards were already in action, casting spells even as the draegloth sprang forward, his teeth bared and his claws out, ready to shred anyone and everyone to ribbons. Faeryl took an involuntary step back, shuddering. Jeggred remained still, crouching as though he would spring again, snarling in fury, but unmoving otherwise.

"That will hold him," one of the wizards claimed.

Quenthel gasped in surprise, looking back and forth between Jeggred and Faeryl.

"Yes, Quenthel," Faeryl called out. "He has been rendered helpless. He cannot extract you from this."

Quenthel returned her glare to Faeryl as the soldiers fanned out, moving to surround her but staying well back. Many of the males aimed crossbows at her, and the wizards and priestesses all seemed ready to invoke various spells, should the Mistress of the Academy decide to bolt or attack. The snakes of Quenthel's whip writhed in agitation, snapping at anyone who stepped too close.

"You insolent little whelp of a drow," Quenthel snarled, shaking in fury as she looked at Faeryl, who only smiled sweetly in return. "All that time being so agreeable, and it was a lie. I knew you were being too accommodating. I should have let Jeggred have his way with you back in the wilds. I will see you flayed for this."

"That might prove difficult, *Mistress* Quenthel," Faeryl said, putting as much sarcasm as possible into her tone when she came to the honorific. "If you give this situation just a moment's thought, you will see, I'm sure, that you are overmatched. It really would be better if you surrendered this foolish standoff."

Quenthel blinked, weighing the ambassador's words. Finally, reluctantly, she realized that she was overmatched and nodded.

"Excellent, Mistress," Faeryl said. "Now, I think it would be a wise idea for you to lay down your arms and all of those wonderful trinkets I know you carry about yourself."

Quenthel's glare deepened, but she carefully set the whip down at her feet.

"Come on, Quenthel," Faeryl admonished. "I've been traveling with you for several tendays now. I know about the ring and the rod and all the other things. Don't make this more difficult."

Sighing, Quenthel began to remove the various items, and when Faeryl seemed satisfied that the high priestess could no longer be a significant threat, she ordered her to step away from the pile of goods.

As others swooped in and gathered up Quenthel's possessions, Faeryl stepped closer to Quenthel, smiling again.

"I am sorry it had to be this way, Quenthel," she said, "but I'm sure you understand."

Quenthel, who had regained some of her composure, smiled right back.

"Oh, I quite understand, Ambassador. My sister will be highly disappointed when she learns what you have done, but I wouldn't worry too much about that. It's a shame though . . . if there's one thing Triel will miss more than her sister, it would have to be her beloved son."

Faeryl didn't let her smile falter, but Quenthel thought the ambassador might have swallowed just a little nervously at the thought of the Matron Mother of House Baenre hearing the news that her draegloth had been destroyed.

Faeryl shrugged and said, "That's a worry for another time, Mistress. Now, if you will be so kind as to walk with me, I'll introduce Matron Mother Drisinil Melarn and my own mother, Mistress Ssipriina Zauvirr. They are most interested in hearing more about how you planned to steal our provisions and take them back to Menzoberranzan with you."

"Those goods belong in Menzoberranzan. They are ours by right," Quenthel said, angry all over again.

In the back of her mind, a part of her told herself that she really did need to learn to control her anger better, but she didn't want to listen.

Faeryl laughed cynically. "You didn't actually think I was going to let you steal from my House, did you?" she said. "From my city? You are mad!" Taking a calming breath, the ambassador continued, ice dripping from her voice, "Look around you, Mistress Baenre. This is what's left of your precious stores of goods."

For the first time, Quenthel realized that the rows and rows of shelves and bins were mostly empty. There was nothing in there to take. She had been thoroughly tricked, from the beginning of the journey, perhaps, played for the fool that she was. The betrayal was not unexpected, and Quenthel knew that had the roles been reversed, House Baenre would have carried the situation to the same conclusion. What galled her was that whatever foolish Baenre whelp had been responsible for the logistics of the deal had never bothered to put enough troops loyal to the House in place to ensure that nothing like this ever happened. Quenthel suspected that whatever loyal forces had been here had been summarily rounded up and executed when the crisis grew. The fact that no one was there now was a testament to that.

"What have you done with it?" Quenthel demanded, half interested in the answer and half stalling for time so she could assess the situation better.

Though there were a number of drow troops there, there was still a chance she could escape—though it would require leaving Jeggred behind.

Faeryl laughed, "Oh, don't worry. Black Claw made a tidy profit recently. The stock has been put to a far better use than what you intended, Mistress."

The mockery in the girl's tone was unmistakable.

"That's enough, Faeryl," Ssipriina Zauvirr said, taking a couple of steps forward. "There's no need to ruin the surprise we have in store for our guests."

As Faeryl lowered her head slightly in deference to her mother, she made her face stony smooth, but Quenthel knew that behind that facade, the Zauvirr daughter was delighted to have thwarted her.

Matron Mother Melarn also stepped forward—or rather, two heavily armed drow stepped forward, escorting her between them. She still frowned deeply, but she said nothing.

Ssipriina Zauvirr strolled halfway toward Quenthel and stopped.

"When my son managed to get into private contact with Faeryl and she was able to tell us what you were planning, we of course wasted no time in preparing for your arrival. I have to say, I am more than a little surprised that you actually expected to slip a storehouse full of goods out of the city, out from under our noses, without us noticing, but that's really of no consequence. As my daughter indicated, House Zauvirr has put the profits to a far better use."

Quenthel blinked in confusion.

"House Zauvirr?" she asked. "You are merely the caretakers. This company belongs to Houses Melarn and Baenre." The high priestess turned to the other matron mother and said, "Are you permitting this? Are you content to let these deceitful, low-class *merchants* make the decisions for your investments? You are far more trusting than I."

Drisinil Melarn didn't say a word, though she grimaced slightly when Quenthel spoke to her. Ssipriina Zauvirr laughed, a quick, bitter sound.

"Oh, she is far from content, Quenthel Baenre, but she has little choice in the matter."

Quenthel realized just why Matron Mother Melarn seemed so unhappy. The two drow flanking her were not escorts but guards.

"You would dare?" Quenthel asked. "You have laid hands on the matron mother of a high House of your own city and hope to get away with it? How can you expect to survive, when . . . when—"

The high priestess clamped her mouth shut, unwilling to finish the thought.

When Lolth will not grant you spells.

"Oh, not to worry," Ssipriina said, smiling even more deeply than before. "With the funds I've made selling off your valuables, I have ensured that House Zauvirr will never again kneel before the likes of you two."

Her eyes glittered red as she finished, and Quenthel saw pure hatred burning in them.

"Captain Xornbane, if you please?" Ssipriina called.

All around the drow gathering, appearing from nowhere, a horde of gray dwarves stood in a large circle, brandishing wicked-looking axes and heavy crossbows. Clearly, they had been standing there for a few moments but had simply been invisible. The duergar looked confident, ready for anything.

Quenthel felt the pit of her stomach leap into her throat, but before she could take any action she felt an invisible force seize her and hold her motionless. She couldn't move a muscle and saw that Drisinil Melarn was in a similar condition.

"Shall we kill them now?" one of the duergar asked, stepping forward.

Chapter

SEVEN

It's fortunate that Valas has been here before and knows the lay of the land, Ryld thought as he pushed his way through the throngs behind his companion.

The streets were more crowded than the previous day, if that was possible, and the warrior was sure that they would have made even slower progress if they'd been negotiating the web streets without a clue as to where to go for the right kind of information or the right kind of folk.

Ryld and Valas had set off shortly after the morning meal, the scout leading the larger drow into the lower quarters of the City of Shimmering Webs. At Quenthel's instructions, they were trying to find someone, anyone, who had supplies, equipment, and bodies available to serve them on the return trip to Menzoberranzan. Ryld still doubted the likelihood of the priestess acquiring anything worthwhile in the Black Claw storehouses, but he wasn't one to quibble with the Mistress of Arach-Tinilith. He had seen the folly of that with

Pharaun. Or rather, he had seen the difficulties. Pharaun seemed to be getting away with his insidious little remarks more and more frequently, and the warrior realized, too, that the mage had begun following his own agenda more consistently.

Ryld pushed past a cluster of illithids—illithids! Five of them standing on a street corner, and no one paying them any mind—and he followed the scout into a particularly squalid-looking taproom.

Ryld couldn't get Pharaun off his mind. The mage seemed to be able to talk anyone around to his way of thinking, and when that didn't work, he'd figure out a way to do what he wanted anyway and explain it all away later.

The warrior wondered how often his old friend had done the very same thing to him in order to get what he wanted.

Valas shouldered his way through the crowded bar, heading for the back of the place. It always seemed to be at the rear tables where information was brokered, and in this tavern it was no exception. Ryld took up a position to watch his companion's back while Valas sat down across from a surly looking drow whose *piwafwi* was tattered and stained. The drow was definitely no noble, though Ryld would never hold that against him. Growing up on the streets of Menzoberranzan, the weapons master knew as well as anyone what it was like to be born a commoner.

A *sava* board rested on the table, and a game was in progress. Ryld could see that whoever had been across from this drow had played himself into a bad position and left before the inevitable conclusion. He found himself wanting to sit down and push a piece or two about, trying to stave off the endgame, but he forced himself to turn away, watching the crowded room for signs of trouble.

"We're looking for pack lizards," Valas began, setting a few gold coins on the table as he reached out and made a play on the *sava* board, "some supplies, and a few sellswords who can guard all of the above."

The drow snaked a hand out from under his shredded *piwafwi* and scooped up the gold before Valas had even completed his move, one that was not really of much help to his position, Ryld noted.

Better to let the fellow continue winning, the weapons master surmised.

"You and just about everyone else in the city," the drow chuckled, flashing a crooked smile that revealed several missing teeth. "Those kinds of things require more gold than the two of you are bound to have," he added, giving Valas and Ryld an appraising look.

"Don't worry about the coin," the scout replied while Ryld returned his attention to the room. "Just point us in the right direction."

"Well, then," the informant said, "I know a gray dwarf who might still have a few lizards available—for the right price, mind you—that would serve you well enough. How about buying a round of drinks while I get someone who can take you to him?"

Ryld pursed his lips in consternation. He had hoped this would be a quick affair, but of course it was not to be.

The drow slid out from the table, clapped Ryld on the shoulder, and said, "My, you're a healthy one, aren't you?" before pushing through the crowd.

Ryld stole a glance down at Valas, who seemed to be studying the *sava* board. The scout made no move to lure a serving boy over.

"Are you going to order those drinks, or should I do it?" the weapons master asked his companion.

"Don't worry about it," Valas answered, looking up. "When the wretch returns, I'll tell him I couldn't get anyone's attention in so crowded a place."

Ryld nodded and turned back to wait.

It didn't take long for the filthy drow to return, and he had not one, but four big half-ogres in tow. Ryld's eyes narrowed at the sight of them clearing a path through the crowd none too gently.

"We may have trouble," he muttered at Valas, who craned his neck to peer past the warrior.

"Let me out," Valas insisted, pushing Ryld forward enough to slip out from behind the table.

The scout stood next to the warrior, and Ryld noticed that Valas had his kukris in his hands, though he kept them down at his sides where they weren't easily seen.

"These are the fellows I was telling you about," the drow informant said to the biggest of the half-ogres. "They're the ones that's got lots of coin."

Ryld groaned inwardly as the half-ogre, who stood a good head taller than the drow, grinned ominously.

"We were just about to go fetch a round of drinks, as you suggested," Valas said, making as if to step past the half-ogre, who was blocking their way. "I guess we'll need a couple extra. Ryld, why don't you come help me carry them all? Then we can talk business with you boys."

"I've got a better idea," the half-ogre said, his voice deep and rumbling. "Why don't you sit down and tell us just how much gold you actually have? Then we'll decide if you can leave or not."

"I don't think that's such a good idea," Valas said, his voice steely cold. "We'll just take our business elsewhere."

"I suppose a half-ogre would be stupid enough," Ryld said to the scout, "to think that just because Lolth has gone quiet, we've forgotten how to fight."

The half-ogre smiled and said, "That's a pretty good joke, dark elf."

Then the creature lunged.

In the end, it was the most straightforward approach, Pharaun decided, that would grant him entry into one of the wizardly institutes. He knew all too well from his working knowledge of Sorcere's defenses that most forms of arcane stealth would likely be detected, however careful he might be. It was the nature of mages to be distrustful of other mages, and he had discovered that with a handful of different academies, schools, and research organizations to choose from in Ched Nasad, the local spellcasters were even more wary of one another.

Apparently, competition between the associations for luring new talent inside their halls was fierce, and the prestige garnered from successful recruiting paramount. True to drow nature, the societies weren't above using any method, however violent and underhanded, to shift the balance of power. What better way to get inside, Pharaun reasoned, than to pose as a prospective new member? All that it required was doffing his House insignia and asking at the front gates for the opportunity to speak with someone who could give him a tour, expound upon the amenities and responsibilities, and so on. He could easily pass himself off as a wayward wizard in need of a home without revealing his true level of expertise or the means by which he had acquired it.

The first place Pharaun visited was the imposing halls of the Disciples of Phelthong, run by the Archmage of Ched Nasad himself, Ildibane Nasadra. Pharaun figured that being the largest and best endowed of the various schools, it would have what he sought. However, he was careful to explain to the minor official who was sent to escort him that his interest, his area of specialty, lay in the study of creatures. It would be paramount for the facility to have a vast menagerie on hand if he was to feel truly at home. When he discovered that the Disciples did not maintain such a zoo, he politely declined to take a tour.

The second place Pharaun chose to investigate was known as the Arcanist Conservatory. It was neither the most impressive nor the least, but he picked it on a hunch. The drow who met with him after he'd explained himself to the sentries at the front of the edifice was an enchanter by the name of Kraszmyl Claddath of House Claddath, a short, surprisingly stocky fellow with slightly yellowing hair and bad teeth. Pharaun feigned skills of a middling nature as he introduced himself, and Kraszmyl seemed genuinely delighted to escort his guest through the premises.

"Tell me, Master Claddath, does the conservatory maintain a collection of live specimens on site?"

"Well, if you mean the best menagerie of creatures from both the World Above and the Underdark, properly housed and cared for, then yes."

"Oh, how delightful!" Pharaun didn't have to fake his excitement. "This sounds like the right place for me."

"Tell me, Master Pharaun, what is your particular expertise with this area of study?"

"Well, my last assignment was for a merchant who wanted me to study various breeding effects on rothé herds," the mage lied, "but I have a special interest in a new field. I am most curious to learn more about chitines and choldriths."

"Really?" Kraszmyl seemed nonplussed at the idea as he led Pharaun deeper into the confines of the conservatory. "Why in the world would you find such base creatures of interest?"

"Oh, they are tremendously fascinating!" Pharaun gushed. "While we find them to be nothing more than simple hunting sport, they actually have a unique culture and religious focus that in several ways mirrors our own."

"Oh, I see," Master Claddath said woodenly. "I hope you're not one of those odd cretins who actually thinks we should cease our hunting."

Pharaun laughed. "Certainly not," he said, "but imagine the possibilities if I could make them more of a challenge?"

"Yes, I could see the value in that. Well, here we are," the guide said, ushering Pharaun into a wing of the facilities that contained countless cages, cells, and holding pens.

Pharaun had never seen such a collection of species before, and he was more than impressed.

"It is spectacular!" he said.

"Yes, it is, Master Pharaun, but I have concluded by your reaction that you have seen nothing of the sort before. Now, why don't you tell me the real reason for your visit to our little conservatory today?"

Pharaun carefully reached into a pocket of his *piwafwi*, extracted a fragment of glass, and turned to look at the other wizard, who was shielded by a number of protections. He held a wand in his hand that he pointed at the visiting wizard, and Pharaun knew that the drow had already used it. Some sort of enchantment magic, he guessed.

Trying to charm me into explaining myself.

"Is this the way you greet all of your prospective new members?" Pharaun asked, smiling.

Kraszmyl looked mildly surprised, then tucked the wand away.

"No, just those wizards who show up out of nowhere, claiming to want to join our ranks."

The other wizard produced a second wand and aimed it at Pharaun.

"Especially those foolish enough to claim—"

Kraszmyl Claddath's words hung in the air, unfinished, as he transformed into glass. Of course, his *piwafwi,* the wand, and several other trinkets that adorned his body remained intact, but the flesh itself was pure, clear crystal.

Sighing in satisfaction, Pharaun pocketed the fragment of glass.

"If you hadn't been so busy expounding on my foolishness, you might have heard the words to my spell," he said to the inert figure, moving closer.

Being made of glass, the short, stocky drow was heavy. Pharaun persevered though, moving the transformed dark elf into exactly the right position.

"Now, let's see if we can find what we're looking for."

The Master of Sorcere felt the urge to hurry, for he doubted the menagerie would remain unattended for long. It would require many first-year students to clean and feed all the imprisoned specimens.

Moving through the aisles of cages, he looked around, trying to find what he needed. Even in his haste, he was truly impressed with the collection before him. He caught sight of some rather large cages in the back, but he had no time to satisfy his curiosity.

A pity, he thought, rounding a corner and continuing his search. *I would like to spend a few tendays here.*

Finally, after several rows, he came across the object of his desire. Sitting sullenly, her four arms sealed in some sort of resin casts, a lone choldrith glared up at him with decidedly humanoid silvery-white eyes. He squatted down to examine her.

She had charcoal-gray skin and was completely hairless. A set of diminutive mandibles, so small that Pharaun doubted they were functional, flanked her more humanoid mouth. Her ears jutted up beyond the top of her head, similar to a drow's but even more pronounced. Pharaun thought they looked vaguely like horns. From what little he already knew and had managed to learn about the species, he understood the necessity for the casts, to keep the creature from casting spells and freeing herself.

"I have a proposition for you," he said in the common language of the Underdark. The choldrith stared back him, saying nothing. "I imagine you can understand me well enough, but just in case . . ."—he fumbled in his pockets for a few items—"it's a good thing I came prepared, eh?"

He produced a tiny clay ziggurat and a pinch of soot. Quickly, Pharaun wove a pair of spells, one to speak her language and the other to understand it, then tried again.

"If you will answer my questions, I will free you," he said.

Her eyes widened with hope, then narrowed with suspicion.

"You lie," she said in a strange, clicking speech, like the sound of a spider. "All drow lie to us."

"Perhaps that is true most of the time, but in this, I do not. I have nothing to gain by keeping you here and everything to gain by getting some answers."

When she only stared at Pharaun again, he asked, "What have you got to lose? You're trapped in a cage in a drow city, and your arms are encased in resin to keep you from calling on the Dark Mother. Except that doesn't matter, because she, too, has forsaken you, hasn't she?"

The choldrith's eyes widened again, and Pharaun knew it was true.

"You know about the goddess?" the creature asked.

"Yes, and I'm trying to find out where she's gone."

The wizard wasn't sure, but he thought he might have detected what would pass for a smile on the face of the wretched being.

"Then she does not love the dark elves more," she said, apparently to herself. "She has not abandoned the spider people in favor of you."

"No, her absence has been spread generously about to all her worshipers, it would appear," Pharaun answered. "What I'm trying to find out now is why?"

"The Dark Mother weaves her own webs. The Dark Mother seals herself away, but she will return."

"What? How? What tells you this?"

"I will tell you no more, killer of spider people. Free me or not, I have answered your question."

"So you have," Pharaun acknowledged, "and I will let you out of the cage. How you find your way home is up to you."

The wizard unlocked the cage door and stepped back. The choldrith edged warily toward the opening, eyeing Pharaun, obviously expecting a trick. He gestured toward the exit, palm open and up, and took another step back. The creature darted out of the cage and was halfway down the hall before the wizard caught himself laughing. He wondered how she would get the resin from her hands, but it was no longer his concern.

"Now that I know, it's time to go," he said aloud to himself. "But first, I can't resist a little peek . . ." and he turned to stroll toward the larger cages he had seen earlier.

Many of the larger cells were empty. It was the ones that were occupied that made Pharaun gasp. A creature unlike any he had ever seen before floated in one of the magically sealed chambers, something horrible and fascinating all at the same time. Its body was gray and soft, like the brain matter of creatures Pharaun had dissected in his younger days, with multiple tentacles hanging down from beneath it. A beak of some sort protruded from the front of the creature, but the wizard could not see any discernable eyes. It hovered in the prison, its tentacles hanging limply. Pharaun gazed at it a moment, then moved on.

The next creature he encountered was very familiar to the mage. The eye tyrant was a small specimen, no more than two feet in diameter. An adolescent, he surmised. The creature's eyes were all milky-white and scarred, effectively blinded and disabled. Still, watching the creature, Pharaun felt a little sense of dread.

From the other side of the great chamber, there was a shout, followed closely by a great crash and the sound of tinkling glass. The wizard smiled. That would be Master Claddath, warning me that people are coming. Thank you for the tour, Kraszmyl.

The mage wondered what kind of magical alarms he was triggering as he created one of his blue extradimensional doorways and stepped through to the outside of the Arcanist Conservatory.

No matter, he thought, allowing the magical passage to wink out as he floated between two levels of web streets, near a wall of the great cavern. They'll simply think my presence there was an attack from a rival institution. If anyone thinks to ask the sentries, I shall be famous.

With that, Pharaun drifted down to the street below and started on his way back to the Serpent and Flame.

He would have accounted the stroll back to the inn pleasant, had the streets not been so busy. All along the way, he caught snatches of conversation that centered mainly on the growing discontent of the citizens, the imminence of an attack from beyond the gates by all manner of fiendish armies, and the conviction that Lolth had abandoned the city to its fate. More than once, he witnessed the beginnings of a confrontation, but each time he saw trouble was beginning to brew, he wisely took a different route, frequently levitating either up or down to a different level to avoid the brawl.

"Pharaun," a voice called to him as he was making his way through a lane filled with cheese shops, wishing the odors were a bit less . . . well, stale.

Surprised and perhaps a bit unnerved at being flagged, he stuck his hands in his *piwafwi,* contemplating what sort of spell he might use to extract himself from trouble.

The wizard turned to find himself gazing at a beautiful drow female, her silvery white hair in lustrous curls down to her shoulders. She arched one high eyebrow at him and smiled, and he felt as though he knew her. Her dress was a bit unusual, and it lacked any sort of identifying insignia. Most telling of all, though, were the several auras of magic that she radiated, and he knew that she was not revealing everything.

"I beg pardon . . . do I know you?" Pharaun asked.

In response, she merely winked and crooked her finger for him to follow. Wondering what dangerous game he might be embroiled in but fancying a bit of fun, the wizard turned and sauntered after her. The female led him along a few streets, mostly back ways, and up a number of sections, until they found themselves in a residential area. The drow ducked into a small abode and turned and looked at him expectantly.

Pharaun hesitated at the doorway, looking around the street for any signs that would clue him in.

"Come on," his companion said, sticking her head back out. "Come inside."

"Why would I want to do that?" the wizard asked. "You've very obviously cloaked yourself in some obscuring magic, so your efforts to deceive me are only partially successful. I think my well being and I will remain out here, thank you all the same."

She simply smiled, and before his eyes the cloaking aura faded as her hair grew from light to dark, and her ebony skin transformed to the color of purest alabaster. The clothing she had attired herself in was transformed as well, into a black leather corset.

Pharaun smiled back.

"Hello, Aliisza," he said.

"Now, come inside so we can talk," the alu-fiend said, motioning for the mage to follow her and disappearing inside.

The interior of the home was small, if tidy, but it had the look of being lived in for a long time. The entirety of the place glowed with a soft violet hue, enough to illuminate the time-worn couch and table in the front room.

"I daresay this is not your place," Pharaun asked as he watched Aliisza slink across the floor and settle provocatively on the couch.

"No, I'm just borrowing it for a while," the demon said, reclining and propping a leg up. "I won't be here that long. Unfortunately, a home, unlike everything else in this city, is a bad investment at the moment. I doubt I could find a buyer, even if it did belong to me."

Pharaun grinned wryly as he settled into a chair across the room from the winged woman.

"So you've noticed the unstable marketplace, have you?" he replied. "A shame, that, but then it's not your worry, since it's not your place. Where are the owners at the moment?"

The alu-fiend smiled again, but her green eyes sparkled dangerously as she answered, "Oh, I don't think they'll be coming back. We've got the place all to ourselves, you know."

She turned over onto her stomach, propping herself up on her elbows and letting her feet wave lazily in the air above the backs of her thighs.

"Well, then, that holds promise," Pharaun said, his smile widening as he leaned forward. "But a clever girl like you must have things to do, places to go, Kaanyr Vhoks to see."

Aliisza made a face. "Come now, wizard. You're not going to

plead honor or some such nonsense to me, are you? Kaanyr is a long ways away."

"It's not so much the Sceptered One I worry about, you lovely creature. It's me. My mother always told me not to get involved with bad girls, especially if they had wings. I'm just a wandering wizard, far from home. You might take advantage of me."

The alu-fiend giggled.

"Contrary to what your mother might have told you, we 'bad girls' aren't always looking to take you home to the Abyss with us. Sometimes, we just like the look of a fellow."

Pharaun looked down at his hands as he said, "Sure. And you just want to have some fun, right? I'd love to stay and keep you company, but I really do need to—"

"Pharaun, I already know what's going on," Aliisza said, her tone serious. "Your Spider Queen has vanished without a trace, leaving no scraps of magic for the ladies, and you came all the way from Menzoberranzan to find out why. I really couldn't care less. Well, that's not entirely true. I can't wait to see Kaanyr's face when I tell him, but it can wait. I just thought that before I head back to him and you went on your merry way back to your home, we might enjoy a little conversation."

She sat up, swinging her legs over the side of the couch to face him.

"Besides," she added, reaching up and beginning to loosen the laces of her corset, "you and I didn't get to finish sharing magic tricks."

"No one's expecting me for a bit," Pharaun chuckled. "I suppose I could stay for a little while."

Ryld knew Splitter would be next to useless in such tight quarters, so he had already reached down and grasped his short sword. He slid the blade smoothly and easily from its sheath in one smooth motion, remembering the feel of it in his hand, the balance, even as he brought it up to defend against the onrushing half-ogre. He parried the blow from the creature's upraised mace, then made a neat slice across the beast's midsection.

The half-ogre jerked just the tiniest bit in surprise, and Valas was on the creature from nowhere, drawing one of his kukris across its hamstring. There was a burst of light and a crackle from the strangely curved blade as it struck home, and the beast howled and toppled as it clutched its gut and leg in pain.

Out of the corner of his eye, Ryld spotted sudden movement, and he ducked just in time to avoid a hurled mug. The cup passed over his shoulder and hit the wall near the table, shattering in a spray of pottery. Ryld didn't waste the moment evaluating the source of the attack. He slashed at another of the half-ogres, drawing a thin opening across its upper arm that welled with blood as the creature staggered back, then the warrior was spinning away and parrying a large cudgel that a third foe, off to his right, swung at him.

The confrontation was drawing the attention of other patrons in the taproom, and Ryld could hear more than a few of them cheering the half-ogres, cursing him and Valas, and perhaps eyeing a chance to get in on the action themselves.

This is about to get really ugly, the warrior thought, warily waving the blade between himself and the half-ogre that blocked his way out.

A crossbow bolt struck him in the ribs, but his *piwafwi* and breastplate prevented the missile from penetrating. Still, the force of the shot staggered him the slightest bit, and the cudgel crashed down on his left shoulder with a loud crunch. His entire arm went numb, and he nearly lost his footing when something hooked his leg from behind and tried to topple him.

This is madness, the warrior thought as he scrambled back against the wall, shoving the table between himself and the rest of the patrons. Valas was nowhere to be seen.

"Get him!" someone snarled from the crowd.

"Kill the dark elves!" another cried.

Yet no one seemed eager to approach him.

Ryld kept his short sword leveled at the threats in front of him as he scanned the room for his companion, wondering if the scout had abandoned him in favor of escape. It would hardly have been the first time Ryld found himself in such a position.

When a pair of quaggoths—huge, white-furred humanoids sometimes known as deepbears—lunged at the warrior, Ryld was forced to return his attention to the difficulties at hand. Slashing with his short sword, he parried the spear the first creature tried to thrust through his chest, then sidestepped the second one's attack, which came very near to gashing his throat. A second crossbow bolt thunked against the wall near him, shattering against the stone.

At the same moment, Valas flashed into view again, having been hiding somehow in the middle of the crowd. The scout plunged both kukris into the back of the first quaggoth. Ryld blinked in surprise but took advantage of the opportunity to spin and slash low, cutting the second deepbear across both knees. Both creatures collapsed in sprays of blood as Valas joined Ryld against the wall.

"That was impressive," Ryld said as he and the scout kept the shouting, cursing throng at bay with their weapons.

"When those two came for you, I saw a chance and took it."

"How do you want to get out of here?" Ryld asked, surveying the room for any signs of escape. "Just fight our way through?"

"I don't know about you, but I've already got a means of escape," Valas replied. "See you on the outside."

With that, the scout backed into a shimmering blue doorway that had suddenly appeared at his back. Ryld had no time to gape as the door vanished from sight, leaving him alone against the horde of angry tavern patrons. A hobgoblin was closing warily from the right, while an orc and a strange lizard creature closed from the center and left, respectively.

Typical, he thought. Everyone but me must be able to blink in and out with those damnable doorways.

Ryld lunged in and cut high at the orc before spinning to deflect a blow from the lizard creature's short blade. The warrior kicked out at the hobgoblin and slashed again at the orc, this time catching his foe right across the cheek. Blood spattered, and Ryld began to work his way through the crowd, knowing he couldn't remain against the wall and hope to survive.

As he got in among the crowd and his opponents swirled around him, Ryld had an idea. Dropping to one knee, he made a couple of defensive thrusts as he reached down with his other hand and slapped the floor, calling up magical darkness. Nearly the entire taproom was engulfed in the inky blackness, and the battle cries of the crowd changed to the noise of confusion and panic. The darkness didn't bother Ryld. He was used to fighting blind, feeling and hearing his foes as easily as he'd watched them before.

The reaction of the pressing throng was exactly what Ryld had hoped for. Not eager to attack a foe they couldn't see and unwilling to get hit themselves, the crowd edged away from the warrior, giving him ample room. Reaching up, he slid Splitter off his back. With Valas gone, he no longer had to worry about controlling or shortening his swing. With the greatsword, he would be able to cut his way out much more quickly.

Not waiting for the unruly patrons to regain their wits, Ryld began slashing and cutting with bold stokes, clearing a path toward the door. The screams emanating from around the weapons master were unnerving to the rest of the brawlers. Quickly enough, Ryld emerged from the darkness, finding himself near the exit of the establishment. A couple more onlookers stood by the doorway, but when they saw the burly warrior appear with his greatsword leveled at them, they quickly scattered. Bruised and bleeding from several small cuts, Ryld darted through the exit and out onto the street.

Valas was leaning against a wall on the opposite side of the street, watching for him.

When Ryld saw the scout, he pursed his lips in displeasure, but before he could voice his anger, Valas nodded and said, "A lot easier to cut your way out of there without worrying about hitting me, wasn't it?"

Ryld opened his mouth to retort, realized that Valas was right, and snapped it shut again.

Finally, after the two of them began making their way down the thoroughfare, the warrior said, "The next place we try, we're taking a table near the front door."

It was only after Ryld realized that they weren't having to push their way through the crowds on the street, who parted for them warily, did he realize that he was still carrying Splitter in his hand, the blade dripping with blood.

"Yes, Captain Xornbane, by all means, dispatch them," Faeryl's mother said as the gray dwarves closed in on both Drisinil and Quenthel.

The two drow and the draegloth, unable to flee, stared about themselves. While Jeggred merely seethed with rage, straining to break free of the magical hold over him, Quenthel and Drisinil looked wild, desperate. The duergar who had spoken motioned, and several of the other gray dwarves moved in, axes lifted.

"Wait!" Faeryl exclaimed, then leaned in close to whisper with Ssipriina privately for a moment. "Mother, let's not kill the two Menzoberranyr yet. I'd like to keep them for a while."

"I think that would be an extraordinarily bad idea," one of the males near her mother said, also leaning in.

Faeryl glared at the impertinent male, whom she seemed to recall was not of the family but had worked diligently as an aid for a number of years. Zammzt, she thought his name was. She wrinkled her nose slightly, for he was far from pretty.

"Do you always butt into conversations you were not meant to hear?" the ambassador asked.

Zammzt merely bowed in acquiescence and said, "Forgive me, but I am only looking after the House's best interests. If this plan of subversion and surprise is to succeed in overthrowing House Melarn, then no one who knows the truth can be allowed to live. If the drow or the fiend are able to relay to anyone—anyone at all—what transpired here today, you will lose your backing from the other Houses. No one will support your rise to the council, Matron Mother. It's an unnecessary risk."

Matron Mother Zauvirr studied her daughter carefully for a moment then said, "He does have a point."

"Mother, believe me," Faeryl replied, "they will never get the chance to talk to anyone. I will make sure of it."

Ssipriina finally nodded and said, "All right, you've earned the chance to extract a little revenge, I suppose, but you must make certain that they do not talk to anyone, especially not Halisstra. Do you understand?"

Zammzt clicked his tongue in consternation, but he apparently knew better than to argue further. He had made his case and had lost. He moved off to engage in conversation with some of the House wizards.

Faeryl, elated, said, "Of course, Mother. I understand all too well. If our plan is to succeed, everyone must think these two were plotting together."

"Precisely. Now, I must go and prepare. We still have a lot of work to do."

With that, Ssipriina Zauvirr departed, Zammzt falling in beside her, his head leaning in close to discuss issues privately.

The ambassador moved back over to Quenthel once more.

"You see, *Mistress* Baenre," she said, trying to emphasize the honorific to the point of sounding absurd, "we didn't really steal the Black Claw merchandise. You did. Or at least, that's how it will appear when we report finding members of two powerful Houses meeting in secret, having already smuggled desperately needed supplies out of Ched Nasad and preparing to steal even more.

"I'm sure they'll wonder why Matron Mother Melarn would have wanted to turn her back on her own city in favor of Menzoberranzan, but unfortunately, they won't be able to ask her, since she resisted us and had to be killed."

Faeryl signaled to the commanding duergar and watched with a warm feeling as three of the gray dwarves stepped close. At her nod, they raised their axes high and swung. Behind her, Faeryl heard Quenthel's muffled cry of protest, but she didn't bother turning around.

There was no more than a grunt from Drisinil as three axes slammed into her flesh, but the blades bit deeply and the fat drow's eyes widened in pain and terror, though she couldn't react in any other way. The three duergar yanked their axes free and prepared to strike again, but Faeryl motioned for them to hold. She wanted to watch as Drisinil died slowly.

"You'll never look down your nose at me again, you fat rothé."

Drisinil's red eyes blinked and widened, seeming to plead with Faeryl in some way, but the younger drow only smiled as she stood casually, hands on hips, and watched the matron mother's lifeblood drip into a puddle on the floor around her motionless body. Drisinil shuddered, and her eyes began to glaze over. Her breathing was rapid for a moment or two, then stopped. Her lifeless eyes stared at nothing.

Faeryl turned back to Quenthel, who had been able to see the murder. The high priestess seemed to look both terrified and furious, all at the same time. The ambassador stepped in close to the Baenre noble and smiled.

"Of course, they'll be told that you were caught while trying to flee the scene, though you and I will know better, at least for a time. You and Jeggred are going to receive a stay of execution, just as I did back in Menzoberranzan. Aren't you pleased? Instead of dying right away, you'll get some of House Zauvirr's hospitality, just as I was graciously entertained by your sister."

Faeryl spat the words at her captive, the smile gone from her face. All of the hatred, the fear, surged to the forefront of her thoughts.

"And as for you, you wretched, foul-smelling beast," Faeryl

said, turning to Jeggred, "I will ensure that you learn what true pain is."

The draegloth's eyes bored into her balefully, but she forced herself to stare resolutely back at him for three long breaths before finally turning away.

"Gruherth," Faeryl called, looking for one of her brothers in the throng of drow still milling about, "I want those two moved—secretly, mind you—to the dungeons in House Melarn."

Gruherth appeared and said, "We'll need a safe way to transport them."

"I'll take care of that," another wizard said, stepping closer to the fiend.

Pulling a few items from his pockets, the mage cast a spell, and a large white bubble formed around the draegloth. At the instruction of the wizard, four guards lifted the sphere—with surprising ease, Faeryl noted—and began to carry it into another part of the storehouse.

Very quickly, the same spell was applied to Quenthel, and four other drow boys bore her milky white sphere away, too.

Faeryl turned and looked for the duergar leader.

"Captain . . . Xornbane, is it?"

The gray dwarf who had given the order to kill Drisinil nodded.

"As I understand it, the next step in our plan is to get your company inside House Melarn unnoticed."

"That's right," the duergar repeated, folding his arms across his chest impatiently.

"Have all the arrangements been made to deal with this?"

"They have," he said, then he turned and trudged off after Faeryl's mother, leaving the ambassador to fume at his rudeness.

Gruherth reappeared.

"We're ready to begin moving everything through to the interior of House Melarn," he said to his sister. "Mother wants you there at the front so that we can throw off suspicion in case there are Melarn troops in sight once we begin crossing through the portal."

Faeryl grimaced but nodded. She had forgotten how much at her mother's beck and call she had been when she was last in the city. Still, she decided, it was better than being at Quenthel's beck and call.

Much better.

Aliisza wriggled her toes in delight as she stretched out on the bed next to the wizard. It had been quite a while since she had felt this good, and it wasn't merely the physical pleasures that delighted her. This Pharaun was quite the wit, she had decided, boisterous and clever for a drow.

"How come you're so unlike the rest of your race?" the alu asked him, rolling over beside him and walking her alabaster fingers up his slender, graceful black arm, enjoying the contrast in color. "Every other dark elf I've ever met and talked to has been so staid and boring. You, on the other hand, make me laugh."

Pharaun, with his head propped on his hands as he lay stretched out on his back, smiled.

"Just unlucky, I suppose."

Aliisza furrowed her brow in confusion and asked, "What?"

"Can you imagine how it must be for me, being around 'staid and boring' drow all the time?" he asked, sitting up and folding his legs beneath him. "No one ever appreciates my witticisms. I offer up clever remarks, and I either get funny looks, if I'm speaking with other males, or scowls, if I'm in the presence of the ladies. It's damned depressing. So I say it's just bad luck. I was born a drow, but I was given a much sharper intellect than most of my species."

Aliisza giggled and rested her chin on both hands, gazing at the dark elf's red eyes.

"Oh, come on," she said. "It can't be that bad. At least you get to talk to other drow. Look at me. I spend the entire day herding tanarukks around."

"Oh, yes, the tanarukks. A few grunts and an obscene gesture, and they've recited their clan history, right?"

Aliisza laughed outright.

"They're not so bad as all that, but they certainly aren't ones for clever humor. Not even Kaanyr likes to devote this much time to just . . . talking—" She paused, seeing the wizard's smile turn into a frown. "What now?"

"Why did you have to go and mention his name? I was doing just fine until you brought up your other lover. That's no kind of pillow talk, you know."

"Sorry. I won't do it again," Aliisza promised. "But tell me . . . how is it you manage to spar with this high priestess of yours? I thought the females of your species didn't put up with too much of that nonsense."

Pharaun groaned and fell back against the pillow.

"She goes from bad to worse," he moaned to no one in particular. "Why do you keep bringing up these most unpleasant subjects? You're torturing me! Was I that unsatisfying?"

Aliisza punched him on the arm, laughing.

"Just answer the question."

Pharaun eyed her for a moment. He seemed suddenly wary.

"Why are you so curious?"

Aliisza shook her head.

"No real reason. Just curiosity, I suppose."

Pharaun rolled away from her to the side of the bed and asked, "Why are you here? In Ched Nasad, I mean."

Aliisza pouted just a little. She really hadn't meant to put him on edge, and now she had to think of a way to calm the wizard down again. She decided the truth, or just enough of it, was the best medicine.

"Because Kaanyr Vhok wants me to find out what's going on."

"You told me you already knew. In fact, you explained to me what's going on. What else are you looking for?"

"Nothing," the alu replied, reaching a hand out to stroke the back of the drow's arm with her fingers. "I have all the information I'm supposed to get. Well, except for visiting one of the matron mothers to see if she wants Kaanyr's assistance. They have some old pact or something. I'm still here because you're here."

Pharaun eyed her a moment longer, then chuckled and shook his head.

"I knew this was a bad idea," he said at last. "The matron mothers of this city are the one big thing I'd like most to avoid, and here you are, preparing to drop in on one. Somehow, that just doesn't bode well for me."

"Oh, stop it," Aliisza said, arching one of her eyebrows at the mage. "I'm not about to tell any matron mother about you. I wouldn't want word getting back to—back to you-know-who"—she smiled again "—though I don't see how you can avoid the matron mothers, given the company you're traveling with."

"What, Quenthel? No, that's not a problem. She knows House Melarn won't be too agreeable to her plan to take the Black Claw goods back to Menzoberranzan, so—" The wizard stopped in midsentence. "I shouldn't be telling you this. I am a sex-addled idiot."

He stared at Aliisza intently, his red eyes glittering.

The alu-fiend stared back, but she couldn't help but smile.

"What are you doing, considering whether to try to kill me to keep your secret safe?" she asked. Arching one eyebrow she shimmied back away from the wizard, leaning back on her elbows provocatively. "I have a better idea," she said, feeling her voice grow husky with desire. "Teach me another magic trick instead."

Pharaun, feeling a combination of exhilaration and dread, left Aliisza in the little house. Exhilarated from the satisfying afternoon he'd spent with the alu, he was dreading all the things he'd let slip. Though he'd repeatedly told himself to be wary, he'd stumbled several times thus far. Being with the fiend had reduced his normally sharp instinct for caution to some half-remembered sense of danger that he knew he ought to be cognizant of but wasn't. It was just an accepted practice that a drow never opened himself up to a fiend, that he should keep his dealings strictly business, and yet here he was, sharing her bed and spilling his best-kept secrets. Still, if he had to pick a risky diversion, Aliisza was quite the prize.

Whatever his apprehensions, Pharaun found that his steps were light as he made his way back to the Serpent and Flame. He had useful information to share with the rest of the Menzoberranyr, and he also had a couple of divinations he wanted to attempt that he hoped would clarify a bit just exactly what was going on in the Abyss. Plus, he might still have time to fulfill that request of Quenthel's. All in all, it was turning out to be a truly memorable day.

Despite his own elation, Pharaun could still feel the tension of the city buzzing in the air, and he was careful to avoid the worst of the crowds. After the experience of the previous day, he didn't think it wise to get caught up in a chest-thumping competition with a congregation of disgruntled citizens. He made certain to spend most of his time floating from section to section, avoiding completely the calcified webbing ladders that connected different levels.

The mage stopped along the way at a dingy-looking shop called Gauralt's Spices, a place that purported to offer hard-to-find components for spellcasting. Valas had mentioned it to him that morning before they set out on their separate errands, and Pharaun found it exactly where the scout had said it would be. Of course, getting what he needed might prove to be another matter, but Gauralt, a drow male who ran the place, was able to supply him with the four strips of ivory and the particular incense he needed, and he was on his way again in no time.

Back at the inn, none of the rest of the mage's companions had returned. He supposed that Ryld and Valas might spend most of the day attempting to round up the needed supplies and mounts for the return journey, but he was somewhat surprised that Quenthel, Faeryl, and Jeggred had not come back from the storehouse. He couldn't imagine what would require them to spend that much time there, but then it was just as well.

If she was here, he told himself, she'd simply find something to snipe about, anyway.

He began to make a mental checklist of the spells he wanted to cast. First, he would use his new components to try to track down who was trying to kill Quenthel.

And probably offer to help, he added, grinning.

He also planned to try again to take a peek into the Demonweb Pits.

It was a spell he had tried more than once back in Menzoberranzan, with no luck whatsoever, but he hoped it would yield more satisfying results away from the City of Spiders. The Master of Sorcere had no basis for this supposition, but he thought it was still worth an attempt.

Pharaun retrieved the four strips of ivory he'd acquired, along with the incense, and sat down to perform the spell. Casting it would leave him weary and low on spells, but if the knowledge he gained from it was useful, he would count the cost worthwhile.

The mage arranged the four strips of ivory into a rectangle upon the carpeting, lit the incense, and closed his eyes. It was not a spell he cast often, and it required a careful application of chanting and specific questions. He couldn't stumble at any point, for he didn't know when the next opportunity to try it would arise.

With the incense burning and the spell begun, Pharaun asked his question, beseeching the elemental forces of magic and the planes of existence to grant him a meaningful answer.

"Reveal to me the enemy of Quenthel Baenre of House Baenre in Menzoberranzan, the enemy who seeks to destroy her, who calls forth demons to slay her in the very temple where she reigns."

The burning incense flared, and smoke filled the room. After a moment, a message formed in Pharaun's mind, words uttered by the wind, or perhaps the Weave itself. However it was delivered, the message that Pharaun received was clear.

The one who seeks the high priestess's death shares her blood and her ambition. Quenthel's enemy sprang from the same womb but is not of the womb.

Pharaun blinked, his red eyes taking in the darkened room as the last remnants of the incense burned out and turned to ash.

Sprang from the same womb but not of the womb. A sibling, but not a female. A male? A brother? Gromph! It had to be. . . .

Pharaun was surprised, not so much that the Archmage of Menzoberranzan would wish his sister dead but by the fact that he hadn't see it before then. Gromph had much to gain by eliminating the only real rival for Triel's ear. The archmage could not have designs on the throne of House Baenre itself, but he could be the puppet master, pulling the strings behind the scenes. Quenthel disagreed with everything her brother said, and vice versa, so she was an obvious and powerful impediment to any ambitions he might have.

Adding to that was the fact that Gromph had the knowledge of the Academy's defenses and had the capability to summon forth the fiends used in the attacks. It was a talent few others possessed, at least few others with the interest to do so. There were other powerful wizards within the halls of Sorcere, and Pharaun supposed that some of them would like to see someone replace Quenthel as the Mistress of the Academy, but Gromph was the one who stood to gain the most.

Though he knew the answer, Pharaun wasn't sure what to do with it.

On the one hand, he considered, I'm here with Quenthel. Does telling her aid me more? Or do I simply seal my fate upon returning to Sorcere? If I tell Gromph that Quenthel is trying to find out who's after her, even do him a favor by misleading her—or eliminating her, a small part of his mind suggested—does my standing at Sorcere improve, or will he be unable to protect me from Triel's wrath?

Of course, Pharaun knew that most of his decisions hinged on the eventuality of returning to Menzoberranzan, and he was planning to argue with Quenthel against that course of action. There were still too many variables, too many possible outcomes, before he would know which side of the siblings' conflict to join. He could stall Quenthel for a while. She wouldn't know what might be involved in his quest for her information. For all she knew, he could be working through a spell that actually took days to complete or negotiating with an elemental of some sort, making a bargain to exchange some commodity for a casting of a spell he himself did not know. There were a number of lies he could tell her to keep her waiting.

For the time being, then, he decided he would stay mute on his findings and see which way the rothé herd roamed. When the time was right, he would play it to his advantage. Either outcome, and he would improve his station within the Academy.

Pharaun rested a few moments longer on the floor, recovering from the exertions of the spell then began packing up his paraphernalia, stowing the strips of ivory away in a pocket of his *piwafwi*.

Next, Pharaun removed a small mirror from his haversack. He briefly wondered if using the same spell he had just employed to find Quenthel's enemy would work better in these circumstances, but he couldn't cast it again without resting for a few hours then studying his spellbooks. Firming his resolve, the wizard began chanting the words needed to activate the magical scrying.

The Master of Sorcere knew the spell was dangerous. Attempting to look in on a deity without permission could have disastrous ramifications. Still, he was intent on trying, if only to discern more of what was going on in the wake of the goddess's absence. Drawing on the memories he had of his strange visit to the Demonweb Pits those decades past, he finished the spell and peered into the mirror, which was reflecting a cloudy image of elsewhere rather than his own dark-skinned face.

Pharaun gazed into the magical window for several minutes, waiting and hoping that he might recognize something in its murky depths. There was nothing. He willed the spectral eye that he knew was on the other end of his spell to glide forward, remotely peering this way and that, trying to catch a glimpse of something, anything solid in the formless fog.

The mage felt a tingle, a warning in the back of his mind. He mentally scrambled to release the spell, to sever the connection with the eye at the far side of oblivion, and he almost succeeded, but not quite. A backlash of energy slammed into him, hurtled outward through the mirror like a punch, while at the same time Pharaun sensed a wall of force sliding down, cutting him off from his magical eye.

As his senses returned, Pharaun realized he was sprawled on his back, blinking as his eyes tried to focus on the ceiling. He groaned and sat up, seeing that he had been hurtled backward from the mirror more than ten feet. He rose onto wobbly legs and staggered back over to the mirror. It was cracked, its glass surface spider-webbed into hundreds of fissures. He stared at the ruined mirror for a moment, wondering if the pattern was representative of something or merely a coincidence.

Well, that answers that question, Pharaun thought. A mere mortal cannot penetrate the veil that has settled over the sixty-sixth layer of the Abyss, but perhaps a higher being can.

The Master of Sorcere shook his head and sighed as he gingerly gathered the fragmented remains of the mirror.

Why do I go through this trouble? he thought as he tried to figure out where he should discard the ruined thing. Everything I do for everyone, and all I get is grief in return. I'll bet other folk don't go through this much trouble to track down their deities, he thought wryly. I'm sure they just look them up anytime—

The wizard froze in the middle of the room, the beginnings of an idea forming. He almost smacked himself in the head.

Of course! he thought. I've been going about this all wrong. Why didn't I think of this before? We're asking the wrong . . .

Tossing the mirror down in a tinkle of glass, Pharaun began to pace, mulling his idea over more carefully. A plan was beginning to form, one that was getting him excited. The hardest part, he realized, would be figuring out how to convince Quenthel.

It was not long after that that Ryld and Valas returned from their own excursions.

The wizard took one look at the pair of them and quickly surmised that their endeavors had not only ended unsatisfactorily but violently. Both drow were glum as well as bloodied and bruised. Valas walked with a slight limp, and Ryld seemed unable to lift his left arm above his waist. Almost as one, they dropped their gear on the floor and dropped down onto their Reverie couches.

"I gather that things did not go well today," Pharaun commented. "No chance to haul Quenthel's supplies out of here?"

"Three places," Valas muttered. "We tried three places and got into two scuffles for our troubles."

"There just isn't a pack lizard to be had, it seems," Ryld added, rubbing his eyes with his good hand. "If there is, no one is ready to sell it to outsiders."

"I don't find that hard to believe," Pharaun replied, "considering that no caravans have entered or left the city in such a long while. Everyone is holding tight to what they have, riding the crisis out."

Pharaun busied himself straightening his own things while the other two males sat still.

"I'll wager with you for who has to tell her," Ryld said to Valas. "Rock, knife, and parchment?"

The scout shook his head.

"Let's just make the wizard tell her," he said, pointing to Pharaun. "He seems to delight so in tormenting her, anyway, so what's one more bit of bad news out of his mouth?"

Ryld nodded, and Pharaun found himself smiling.

"Well, we all have a reprieve, at least for the moment," the mage said. "She and the other two haven't returned from the storehouse."

"Really?" Valas asked, sitting up. "I would have thought they'd return before us for sure."

Pharaun shrugged and said, "As would I, but none of them are here."

"That's fine by me," Ryld said, leaning back against the wall and closing his eyes. "The less I have to see of that damned draegloth, the better off I am."

Pharaun pursed his lips, realizing that what he was going to suggest next might not set well with either the weapons master or the scout.

"I found out something today, too," he said quietly.

Ryld opened one eye and looked at the wizard.

"Oh?"

Valas leaned forward on the edge of the bed.

"Have you determined what has happened to the Dark Mother?"

Pharaun chuckled and said, "Not exactly, but I did learn that her disappearance has not been limited to our own race. Other species feel her loss, as well."

"I don't know whether to consider that good news or not," the scout said, sitting back again.

"Nor do I," Pharaun agreed, "but I have also learned that something is sealing us out from the Demonweb Pits. I have attempted to scry there in hopes of learning something of the goddess's condition—

indeed, if she yet exists—and I could not penetrate inside. A barrier protects it and keeps me, and others, outside."

"A barrier? You're speaking now of things I have no experience with," Ryld said. "What kind of barrier?"

"A potent one. I was nearly blasted into powder for my troubles," Pharaun said, a wry smile on his face. "I have tried it before, even spoke with Archmage Gromph before we left Menzoberranzan. He has experienced similar problems."

"It sounds as though whatever the Spider Queen is doing, she does not wish to be disturbed," Valas said.

"If it's her who's doing it," Ryld countered. "Perhaps another god has erected the barrier to prevent us from seeing her."

"Exactly!" Pharaun said eagerly. "Surely someone knows—or can find out—what we cannot discover."

"I thought that's what our mission was . . . to discover Lolth's fate," Valas said. "That's why we've come here."

"Yes, you are correct," Pharaun said, nodding, "though this business with storehouses of magic items seems to have become a higher priority. In the interest of bringing us back to the more fascinating part of our little expedition, I have an idea. I want to enlist help from the outside."

"Help? From whom?" Ryld was sitting up, too.

The wizard began to pace again as he explained his plan to his companions.

"A mere mortal, even someone with my acumen, can't penetrate the veil that has settled over the Demonweb Pits. Something is obviously intent on keeping us out. We need to enlist someone else's help in finding out what's going on there. Someone not of our own ilk."

Both of the other drow were watching the wizard intently, doubt plain on their faces.

"You can't mean . . ." Ryld said.

"Another god."

The weapons master seemed aghast. Valas said nothing but might have been contemplating the possibilities of such an act—and the ramifications.

"Perhaps a higher being," Pharaun continued, "especially one in close proximity to the Demonweb Pits—from one of the other layers of the Abyss—could, or possibly even already has, discovered more than we can possibly hope to on our own. Maybe we can convince one of them to tell us what has transpired or is transpiring inside.

"Not directly, of course," Pharaun added hastily, "but through an intermediary . . . a follower."

"You play a dangerous and foolish game, Pharaun Mizzrym," Ryld said, shaking his head. "The Dark Mother may find such a course blasphemous, a betrayal to the faith."

"Or she may congratulate me on being so innovative, so willing to examine and explore, whatever the risk. The other choice is to admit defeat, return to Menzoberranzan, and sit on our hands as our way of life ends."

"Quenthel will not be happy with this plan," Valas cautioned. "She will most likely consider it a personal affront to her."

"Yes, well, Quenthel is too focused on lining House Baenre's coffers to appreciate the larger picture before us. I'm beginning to wonder how wise a choice she was to lead this expedition. Don't stare at me like that, Ryld. . . . You've questioned more than a few of her decisions since we departed."

"Never openly. Not to her face."

"She's not here now, is she? My friend, I play with fire, I know that, but if I don't act where my heart lies then I've failed our race far worse than she. I'm content to steer things from behind the scenes, letting her believe she controls our tempo, our course, but such a method requires patience, more than a little frustration, at times, and the possibility of being thwarted or exposed. It would stand a much greater chance of success if the three of us worked together to maneuver her. I could use your help."

Valas had his chin in his hand, thinking. Ryld shook his head, lines of worry creasing his brow.

"You fight against millennia of tradition and habit, Pharaun," the weapons master said. "I can't say that I welcome the idea of returning to Menzoberranzan no better off than when we left, but usurping the high priestess's authority might very well see our heads on the parapets of House Baenre."

"The wizard has already been at it for a couple of tendays. . . ." Valas said.

"Perhaps, but until now, it was simply him against her; he hadn't brought us into it."

Pharaun clicked his tongue in exasperation.

"Do you honestly think that she won't hold us all responsible, regardless of the relative levels of involvement?" the Master of Sorcere asked. "She will blame you simply because you are a male, Master Argith."

Slowly, Ryld nodded.

"I suppose you're right," he said. "It still doesn't make me feel any better."

"I'm not suggesting we bind her with cord and throw her in a box, Weapons Master. All I'm asking is that you support me when I make a suggestion, that you back me, however subtly, when she and I disagree. Help me convince her that moving forward, rather than back to Menzoberranzan, is the wiser course of action."

"You make sense," Ryld replied, "but right now, your idea is just that. We must find someone willing to serve as the conduit. Do you know of any such creature?"

"I do," Valas said quietly.

Pharaun crouched down in front of the scout and asked, "You do? Who?"

"There's a priest I know, a follower of Vhaeraun."

"Vhaeraun," Ryld said in a clipped tone. "I doubt we'll receive any aid from him."

"Perhaps, but Tzirik is actually an old associate of mine," Valas replied.

At Ryld's surprised look, the scout added, "When you wander the wilds of the Underdark as much as I have, you have to be decidedly more pragmatic than in the cozy confines of Menzoberranzan. Tzirik Jaelre owes me a favor. If we can get to him, I think he might help us."

Valas turned to Pharaun and added, "Assuming, of course, that you have a notion of what he should do once we get there."

Pharaun replied, "I will when we find this priest. In the meantime, you keep this Tzirik Jaelre to yourself until I have words with Quenthel. At the right moment, mention that you know him, and we'll show her the wisdom of seeing this through to the end."

"I only hope the end comes later, rather than sooner," Ryld said grimly.

Chapter

NINE

Halisstra couldn't breathe. The blood pounded in her ears, making it difficult to hear what Matron Mother Zauvirr was saying. She didn't want to listen, anyway.

"I wish it wasn't true, Halisstra, I really do, but there's no getting around it. We caught her in the act, and when we confronted her, she wouldn't surrender. Your mother tried to flee, and the soldiers just did their jobs. By the time I got to her, I couldn't help her."

Halisstra shook her head, trying to rid her thoughts of the hated words. Her mother, dead. It wasn't true. It couldn't be!

"No!" Halisstra cried out, pushing Danifae away. Her battle captive, all flimsy silks, was reaching out to her, trying to comfort her. "You're lying!"

She struggled to spin free, to get out of the room, but she found all avenues of escape cut off. Matron Mother Zauvirr's troops seemed to be standing idly by, as though they were merely guests in someone else's home, but they were strategically placed about the room to guard the doors. She looked around for some of her own family's soldiers, but there were none to be found. Matron Mother Zauvirr had planned well, delivering her devastating news from a position of strength.

Wilting, Halisstra sank down to the floor, unsure what to do. Only Danifae settled down next to her, making soothing noises and trying to reach out to calm her. She didn't want to be calmed. She wanted to slap the other drow, smack her across the room, but she knew better. If she had any hope at all of surviving this horrid situation, she would need the battle captive's aid. She had to think.

It wasn't so much that her mother was dead. Of course that didn't bother her. In other circumstances, she would have delighted in it, but there weren't any other circumstances. Her mother had been caught in an act of open treason against the city, or so Ssipriina claimed, and Halisstra had no way to refute it, despite the fact that it was a ludicrous notion. Her mother would never risk herself so openly, especially not aiding foreigners, regardless of how good the relationship was between their Houses. Not to mention the fact that smuggling the goods from Black Claw Mercantile out of the city would ruin House Melarn. There was nothing to gain from it and so much to lose.

Of course, when Ssipriina arrived in House Melarn's audience chamber, sat right down in Drisinil's throne and made her revelation, the unspoken implication was there. Drisinil was not acting alone. When the rest of the council learned of it, they would likely find Halisstra just as guilty of the crimes as her mother. They would imprison or execute everyone in the family, dissolve House Melarn, and divvy up its assets. Unless she found a way to counter it.

She had no doubt that Ssipriina was behind it all, was somehow benefiting from the destruction of House Melarn, but in order to make it work, she would have to eliminate Halisstra, too. Halisstra had to move fast, but she knew that the other drow wasn't about to let the First Daughter of House Melarn out of her sight. Her only chance to get help was to send Danifae, and that would only happen if Ssipriina Zauvirr believed the battle captive was more interested in saving her own skin than in supporting her mistress.

Halisstra glanced over at Danifae, taking a deep breath to calm herself, then began to flash signs at her servant, working secretively so that only her companion could see.

You have to turn on me, she signaled. *Convince them that you'd just as soon see me dead. Then get help. Go to House Maerret.*

When Danifae gave an almost imperceptible nod, Halisstra reached out and slapped her. Hard. The blow sent the battle captive falling backward, skidding across the floor. Danifae's eyes widened as her hand flew up to her cheek, but before she could open her mouth to spoil the effect, Halisstra screamed at her.

"How dare you suggest such a thing! I would never consider it!"

Danifae's red eyes narrowed, and whether the venomous look was genuine or part of the ploy, Halisstra wasn't sure.

"Then rot in a cell until they put your head on a pike, Mistress." She stood, deliberately brushing her backside, straightening the flimsy silks that did little to conceal her curvaceous body. "If you won't, then I'll do it and save myself."

Danifae turned to Ssipriina and said, "Mistress Zauvirr, I humbly beg you to help me procure my release from *her.*" She sneered this last as she jerked a thumb down at Halisstra, who was still sitting on the floor. "I'm sure we can come to some sort of arrangement that you would find gratifying enough to release me from my servitude."

Ssipriina alternated between looking at the battle captive before her and the noble daughter on the floor, blinking in surprise at the outburst. She opened her mouth as if to say something, then snapped it shut again.

Danifae, taking advantage of the silence, continued, "I'm just now starting to recall conversations with Mistress Halisstra that I think might implicate her. Given a few moments alone in her chambers, I could recall even more evidence that proves her foreknowledge in these disgraceful, treasonous acts."

She looked down at Halisstra, a knowing smirk on her face.

Despite the fact that she knew her servant was playing the part—at least she hoped that's all it was—Halisstra shuddered at the look on Danifae's face. Not having to try very hard to look scared, Drisinil's daughter took another deep breath.

"Matron Mother," Halisstra said, "I assure you I had absolutely no previous awareness of any possible plots of my mother's. My battle captive is obviously lying to you, trying to save her own worthless hide in exchange for damning me with false accusations. You cannot possibly accept the word of a battle captive. She would tell you anything to see me come to a bad end."

Ssipriina looked down at Halisstra for another moment and laughed.

"Of course she would, silly girl, and how fortunate for me." The matron mother turned to Danifae, smiled, and said, "Perhaps we can come to some sort of an agreement. Go and see what you can uncover."

Danifae smiled and bowed deeply to Matron Mother Zauvirr, then turned to depart. As she spun on one heel, she looked down at Halisstra, sneering.

As Halisstra let her gaze follow the backside of her servant, she heard Ssipriina take a deep breath.

"Now, what to do with you . . ." the matron mother said in a most unpleasant tone.

Faeryl Zauvirr loomed over her prisoner, smiling in delight. The beads of dampness that glistened on Quenthel Baenre's forehead ran in rivulets into her eyes, making her blink and squint. Her mouth was frozen in a grimace of pain and misery, though it was difficult for her to effect any other expression, with the rothéhide-bound dowel wedged so deeply into her mouth. The bit was held tightly in place with braided cord tied tightly behind her neck. Her long white hair was matted limply around her head and spread across the top of the table upon which she lay.

Faeryl stepped back from the table where Quenthel was stretched tightly, her wrists and ankles locked into manacles at either end of the long, narrow rack. The high priestess's naked body was taut, like the string of an instrument, and coated in a sheen of sweat that glimmered in the light of the braziers, but still Faeryl was not satisfied.

"Perhaps we should try the needles again," the ambassador mused aloud. "They fit so easily beneath the toenails, and it is such fun."

Quenthel grunted and shook her head, her red eyes wide.

"No? Then maybe there's something in here that I can use to amuse myself," Faeryl said, turning to one of the braziers and sorting the tools resting in it. "Some of these are glowing nicely, now. I've heard that these blunt ones are especially good for the eyes."

The grunts increased in rhythm and went up an octave.

Facryl put her face back down in front of Quenthel's again, but she was no longer smiling.

"We've only scratched the surface, *Mistress* Baenre," she spat, once again stringing the honorific out. The sarcastic tone was becoming second nature to her. "We've got endless hours to enjoy this, and I want to make sure you experience every last little 'pleasantry' Jeggred inflicted on me."

Quenthel closed her eyes as a muted groan passed the bit shoved in her mouth.

Faeryl supposed the high priestess might be trembling, or perhaps it was simply the quivering of muscles, strained from being stretched so long. She chuckled and turned to examine the other prisoner.

Jeggred had been bound tightly to a stout column, lengths of chain encircling him from ankles to chin. The bonds were so tight, the draegloth could move only his head, which he tossed from side to side as he strained to break free. He snarled as Faeryl looked at him.

"Oh, I know," she cooed, stepping closer. "You want to gut me, don't you? You want to spill my blood and dance in it."

"You will die a slow, painful death," the fiend rumbled. "I will see to it personally."

Faeryl waved her hand in front of her nose.

"Stop talking, you vile beast. Your breath is most foul."

Jeggred only growled.

Faeryl fixed him with her gaze and said, "Do you remember the things you did to me?" She almost shuddered but forced herself to remain still. "I am going to repay you for it . . . every bit of it. I'll send your carcass back to Triel when I'm through."

Jeggred smiled.

"You can't begin to understand the methods of meting out pain. My attentions were but a part of those methods, and there is nothing you can conceive of that I will notice at all."

"Oh, really?" Faeryl replied, her lips pursed. "We'll see. My advisors have told me what things you feel and don't feel. 'He resists the burn of acid and fire, and he will not suffer from cold and lightning,' they said. But we'll find something. Yes, we will. Maybe sound, hmm? There is something you don't like, and when I discover what it is, you'll enjoy it for endless hours. I promise you."

There was a soft step upon the stone floor near the doorway. Faeryl turned in irritation to see what the intrusion was all about. It was Zammzt.

"What do you want?" Faeryl demanded.

She knew the aide was there at her mother's behest and that she was undoubtedly being summoned to attend to the matron mother. It didn't make her very happy, and though she could not take her annoyance out on her own mother, she could easily do so on the ugly male. The dark elf bent his knee and dipped his head slightly.

"I beg pardon, Mistress Zauvirr, but your mother requires your immediate presence in the audience chamber."

"Of course she does," Faeryl snarled. "If she has the slightest notion that I am not indisposed, she finds something for me to do."

When Zammzt hesitated for the slightest of moments, Faeryl gave him a cold stare.

"Well," she asked, "what are you waiting for? Go tell her I'm on my way!"

Zammzt scurried out of the torture room and disappeared around the corner, his *piwafwi* flying behind him. Faeryl returned her attention to Quenthel.

"I'll come back and visit with you some more in a bit," she said, "and when I do, I really want to give those needles another try. Maybe the fingernails this time, hmm?"

The bound form on the rack emitted a whimper.

"Oh, good, I'm pleased that you like the idea, too."

❀   ❀   ❀

Danifae Yauntyrr didn't really expect Matron Mother Zauvirr to grant her free run of the entire House, and her suspicions were correct. As she departed the audience chamber with a final sneer back in Halisstra's direction, she was also careful to note Ssipriina's slight nod at two of the guards standing near the door. As she stepped through the portal, the guards silently and unobtrusively fell in behind her. The battle captive pursed her lips in the slightest hint of frustration, but she wouldn't have expected anything else. It really didn't matter. She'd just have to put on a bit more of a show.

Ignoring the two House Zauvirr soldiers who followed her, Danifae made her way back to Halisstra's private chambers, where she also took Reverie so that she could attend to the noble drow's every need. She guessed that the guards would not be so invasive as to follow her in, and again, her intuition was right. She strode through the door and shut it behind her. Once she was alone, she began to pace, mulling possibilities over in her mind.

Halisstra had just provided her servant with a perfect opportunity to free herself from the other drow's subjugation. Danifae almost laughed at her mistress's gullibility, thinking that Danifae would run to try to save her. After ten years as Halisstra's battle captive, Danifae wanted nothing more than to be rid of the wretched drow and her domination. She wanted nothing more than to return to Eryndlyn. The problem was, with Halisstra's binding in effect, Danifae wasn't sure she could actually get free, even with Ssipriina Zauvirr's help. In fact, she suspected that once she actually did turn on Halisstra and provide the "proof" of Drisinil's daughter's guilt to the matron mother, Ssipriina would simply let her perish along with Halisstra.

Danifae knew she had to ensure her own freedom first and not depend on another for it. But how?

She hated the effect of the binding, for it was insidious in its effectiveness. Though Danifae didn't truly believe it, she sometimes wished that the compulsion of the binding fully controlled her mind, rather than merely restricting her ability to distance herself from Halisstra. She told herself that it would have been better to serve the Melarn daughter as a mindless zombie rather than of her own accord, attending willingly to avoid the consequences of straying too far from her mistress. It locked her to Halisstra as surely as a length of chain around their ankles.

In the early years, Danifae wanted desperately to throttle her mistress, but Halisstra's death would bring about her own, and Danifae would experience her own demise in a slow, excruciatingly painful manner. That was the nature of the binding. It sustained her somehow, kept her alive as long as Halisstra willed it. Distance was not a factor, but the moment Danifae disregarded Halisstra's wishes and went her own way, she had no doubt that the other drow would simply let her wither away like a mushroom with its roots hacked off. Displease the dark elf, and with a thought, Danifae would succumb. By the Dark Mother, she hated it.

The binding's magic was alien to Danifae. She didn't understand what was required to sever it or if it even could be severed by any hand other than Halisstra's. The risk of discovery was too great to allow her the chance to inquire, and besides, Halisstra rarely let her servant out of her sight. With Halisstra under arrest, Danifae had the perfect opportunity to follow through, to finally find out what could be done, and there was no time. Halisstra was going to die unless Danifae convinced Ssipriina Zauvirr to find a solution to her problem, and she doubted that the matron mother would lift a finger to help her, even with her promises of damning testimony against the daughter of Drisinil Melarn. That only left Danifae with the option of actually saving Halisstra.

Damn her! the battle captive silently screamed as she sat on her mistress's Reverie couch, pounding a pillow for good measure. She wanted to rip the stuffing out, but long years of the fear of punishment had trained her to resist letting her emotions get the better of her, and she stayed her hand. Taking a deep breath to calm herself, she considered the situation.

The next problem, she realized, was that even if she somehow managed to extricate Halisstra—and by extension, herself—from this mess, life as they both knew it might very well be over. They might survive the coup, but even then, where would they go? Without Lolth's blessings to aid them, it was an especially bleak outlook.

Making up her mind, Danifae decided the next thing to do was to figure out who in House Melarn was still Halisstra's ally. The first thing she considered were the House guards. They had disappeared, and she had a pretty good idea why. Ssipriina had likely already gotten to them and given them the standard offer: change allegiance to House Zauvirr, or find themselves unemployed or dead. She doubted there were any who would still rally to Halisstra, but she had to at least look.

Danifae opened the door to the hallway and was slightly surprised to find the two guards who had followed her no longer present. She supposed that they assumed she wouldn't try anything as long as the House was locked down and had decided to go find something more interesting to do.

Just makes it easier for me, she thought, smiling as she slipped out.

She hurried on her way.

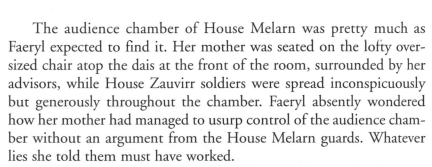

The audience chamber of House Melarn was pretty much as Faeryl expected to find it. Her mother was seated on the lofty over-sized chair atop the dais at the front of the room, surrounded by her advisors, while House Zauvirr soldiers were spread inconspicuously but generously throughout the chamber. Faeryl absently wondered how her mother had managed to usurp control of the audience chamber without an argument from the House Melarn guards. Whatever lies she told them must have worked.

"There you are," Ssipriina said impatiently. "Come here. I want to go over your story once more before the others get here."

Faeryl sighed but dutifully approached the throne.

"Mother, I have the details memorized. I think I can—"

"You will go over them with me and continue doing it until *I* am convinced, you ungrateful brat! You will not stop until then."

Her mother looked entirely too comfortable in the throne, which was certainly grander than anything they had in their own manor. That was the difference between a merchant House and a truly noble House.

Faeryl longed to return to the dungeons, where she could rule over her charges in peace. She hated having to attend to her mother's demands. Where Quenthel was concerned, even if it was a little pond, at least she was the big fish. It was always that way. At the storehouse, when she'd orchestrated the transport of the prisoners, she had been in charge, however briefly. Under the scrutiny of her mother, she was the petulant child once more.

Faeryl dreamed of holding the reins of power someday, but being the fourth daughter in her House, and having been sent to Menzoberranzan to represent House Zauvirr and House Melarn, to boot, she recognized the limitations to her chance to rise to the top. Even were she to someday sit upon the throne Ssipriina Zauvirr was hoping to claim through her orchestration of the day's events, Faeryl would still answer to others.

"Now," Ssipriina said, ticking off points one by one on her hand, "you were forced to come with Quenthel and the others. You notified me at the earliest opportunity what House Baenre was planning. We set up an ambush to catch them, and only then did we discover that Drisinil was in on it. Do you understand?"

"Yes, Mother," Faeryl responded sullenly.

"Good. When the matron mothers get here, stay out of sight until I call for you. Do you understand?"

"Yes, Mother."

"And stop that. It's childish and petulant."

Faeryl frowned, but she clamped her mouth shut.

"That's better," Ssipriina said. "Now I think we need to get those males summoned here as quickly as possible. Zammzt, I think that's a job for you."

When a knock sounded at the door to their room, Pharaun expected to see Quenthel standing there. It was late, and the Master of Sorcere was beginning to wonder if something untoward had befallen the high priestess and her two companions. As he opened the portal, though, the wizard was instead surprised to discover a strange and rather plain-looking drow in the livery of a noble House.

"I beg forgiveness for disturbing you," the male said, "but I am seeking the wizard Pharaun Mizzrym and the warriors Ryld Argith and Valas Hune."

Pharaun kept his body planted firmly between the visitor and the interior of the room, shielding the other dark elf's view of it. Behind him, he could hear Valas and Ryld unsheathing weapons.

"Who are you?" the wizard asked, considering which spells remaining in his repertoire would suffice to defend himself against an attack.

"My name is Zammzt. I come at the behest of Matron Mother Ssipriina Zauvirr of House Zauvirr, Matron Mother Melarn of House Melarn, and Quenthel Baenre of House Baenre. Are you one of the three?"

"Perhaps," Pharaun answered, gauging the fellow's potential as a threat. The drow was, at the very least, radiating a number of magical auras. "It would depend on why you're looking for them."

"Mistress Quenthel is a guest of Mistress Drisinil Melarn of House Melarn. I am here to extend an invitation to you to join them for a banquet in your honor."

"Oh, how delightful," Pharaun said. "I assume that you can escort us there, as well?"

"Indeed, Master, uh . . ."

The mage rolled his eyes and said, "Pharaun. I'm the wizard."

"Certainly, Master Mizzrym. I have been instructed to escort you to House Melarn."

"I see. Well, then can you give me a moment to clean up? I'd hate to attend a dinner in my honor looking like this," the wizard said, gesturing at his *piwafwi*.

"Certainly, Master Mizzrym. I am at your convenience. The dinner will not start without you."

"Excellent," Pharaun replied. "Give me just a moment, and we'll be right out. You can wait for us down in the common room."

With that, he shut the door and turned to his companions.

"Either she got caught or she decided she was not getting treated well enough by the inn staff," Valas said, frowning.

"Either way, it is no good for us," Ryld added. "And I was just beginning to enjoy not being under any matron mothers' thumbs."

"Well, then . . . which is it, good masters?" Pharaun asked them both. "Out the window or to a dinner party?"

Ryld and Valas looked at one another.

Finally, Valas sighed, "Dinner."

"Very good," Pharaun said, "but before we go, I want to spend a few moments in contemplation of my grimoires. I have a feeling I might be in need of some arcane fortitude before the night is over."

"Yes, I think that's wise," Valas agreed. "Ryld and I could stand a bit of healing magic, if there's any to be had."

"Why don't you two go search the priestesses' room and see what you can turn up?" Pharaun suggested. "I know Quenthel had that wand, but she's likely to have kept it with her. There might be a potion or two, though."

The scout nodded, and he and Ryld slipped out of the room.

Pharaun opened up his haversack and pulled out his spellbooks, which were conveniently on top. That was the thing he truly loved about his magical carry-all. Whatever he needed always seemed to be on top. He sat down to peruse the pages.

The wizard could not recoup all of the incantations he had cast during the course of the day, as he would need to spend several hours resting before his body had recovered sufficiently for that, but he had wisely decided to hold off on committing the full compliment of spells to memory that morning, so he had an opportunity to choose four or five that would best suit the occasion.

Now, Pharaun wondered, what sorts of magical wizardry would be particularly useful for a dinner party?

He settled on his choices and began to study.

Nearly an hour later, the Master of Sorcere looked up at the sound of the two other males reentering the room.

"Ah, perfect timing," he said. "I think I'm ready to go. Did you have any luck?"

Ryld answered, "It took a bit of rummaging, but we managed to confiscate two potions from Quenthel's belongings. That's one more thing we agreed that you get to tell her when we see her next."

Pharaun chuckled, "Well, I must say, the draughts did you a world of good. You're certainly much more presentable than you were a mere hour ago. Are we ready, then?"

"I believe so," Valas replied. "We did a quick surveillance of the inn, and it appears that our escort is alone. Nothing suspicious about him so far."

"Then I suggest we leave at once," the Master of Sorcere said. "I'm starved, and I fancy a taste of something better to drink than the swill we purchased last evening."

Ryld and Valas exchanged looks, and the three of them found their way to the common room. The drow who called himself Zammzt was there, waiting patiently, but the look on his face told Pharaun that he was beginning to get a little nervous.

Probably wondering if we gave him the slip, the wizard thought. Worried about what he'd tell the matron mother when he had to report back that we wouldn't cooperate.

The stroll to the House would have been pleasant, Pharaun decided, if the streets weren't plagued by the occasional angry mob. Twice, the four of them had to make a quick dash down a side street or float to another level to avoid being engulfed in a tide of trouble-makers. At one point, Pharaun thought he'd have to blast a way through the throng with a bolt of lightning or a ball of fire, but it never came to that. In order to keep up with them, Valas was forced to transport himself by way of an extradimensional doorway. This from an item Pharaun had, until then, been unaware the scout carried.

"You know," he said as they moved into the highest levels of the city, where the most lavish of the nobles' manors were located, "I quite seriously doubt we should remain for the full evening."

"What, you think the city is growing too dangerous?" Valas asked wryly. "If we had given it any thought, we might have considered packing our supplies and bringing them with us."

Pharaun slowed a step, thinking, but then he proceeded, saying, "You're right, but if the situation warrants it, I can return for the goods myself later."

The four drow arrived at last at House Melarn, an impressive bulge in the upper reaches of the city. The whole of the thing was stacked above the level of the street and also hung below it, and it covered an area two or three blocks wide and just as deep. To Pharaun, it looked like a massive cyst of some sort, which, he supposed, had been the intent of the architects who'd fashioned it.

The food and spirits had better be worth it, the wizard thought, sighing as he followed the others inside. Right now, it just looks like a prison.

Aliisza loathed the form she'd chosen for herself, finding it ugly and without civility. Oh, certainly any orc who spotted her would have thought her beautiful, but the alu-fiend considered the race repulsive as a whole. Still, it had its advantages.

At the moment, that advantage was that Pharaun would not recognize her. Following the wizard and his two drow companions through the web streets of Ched Nasad, being led by a fourth drow—whom she found to be rather unattractive—Aliisza didn't want her lover of earlier in the day to spot her. As well, she found it easier to avoid notice as one of the baser creatures rather than as one of the dark elves. The drow citizens might have outnumbered the rest of the other races combined, but they appeared to be fearful of being alone in public, and though Aliisza certainly didn't fear for her own well-being, she thought it best to draw as little attention to herself as possible.

Besides, she found that she could overhear more interesting conversations if she was not in dark elf form. The other beings tended to stall or whisper whenever they saw any drow about, but they were not so mindful of their words when it was just an orc, beautiful for her race or not. Aliisza could certainly understand why.

There was talk of rebellion or of invasion everywhere she went. Half the inhabitants seemed to think the crisis in the City of Shimmering Webs was an opportunity to end the drow reign once and for all, while the other half believed that someone else was already in the process of doing just that and that everyone already living there would pay the price for it. One thing was constant, whatever other opinions were revealed: Everyone blamed the dark elves for their problems.

It was the drow, she heard, who had angered Lolth. She had turned away from the city, leaving it to fend for itself. Others said that Lolth had grown weak and ineffectual from the complacency of her worshipers, and this had allowed other deities to overwhelm her when she wasn't expecting or prepared for it. The most intriguing rumor of all, of course, was the tale that seemed most recent. Spreading like wildfire, it claimed that the matron mothers had discovered a traitor in their midst, one of their own who had collaborated with a high priestess from beyond the city to bring Ched Nasad low.

There were a dozen variations on that story. The traitors consorted with demons, the traitors were actually demons in disguise, the traitors were stealing from the city, the traitors were preparing to attack the city. . . .

Aliisza had little doubt about the veracity of the story, for she suspected that the high priestess must be Quenthel. Somehow, the Menzoberranyr had been apprehended in the middle of her little scheme, the one Pharaun regretted mentioning. She was curious about Pharaun's role in the rumor, or the portion of the story that included a matron mother. The alu-fiend wondered if Pharaun had been swept up in the events or if spending the afternoon with her—she shivered with delight at the memory of it—had allowed him to stay clear.

Even if he hadn't gotten entangled in the matron mothers' schemes thus far, he was bound to eventually. She knew this with a certainty born of having seen the political machinations of her own kind drag even the most unwilling creatures into its webbing. Pharaun would have a part to play in the unfolding events, as much for his inquisitive, forceful nature as for his relationship with the priestess he so casually followed.

Regardless of what the wizard wanted, he was in the company of a stranger, someone obviously of a noble House by the insignia on his *piwafwi,* and he didn't seem to be under duress or coerced. Perhaps he didn't know what was going on. Aliisza would have to puzzle on that some more. One thing was certain, however: The effect the rumor was having on the populace was not good.

Aliisza knew she shouldn't care if Pharaun had been apprehended. Theirs had been a relationship of mutual satisfaction, no more, no less. He was a pleasant diversion from Kaanyr Vhok, and she knew she would return to the cambion, had always intended to do so. Pharaun knew this as well, and the fact that he wasn't bothered by the informal nature of their "chance meeting" in the streets was what had made him so delicious.

But the alu-fiend did care, at least enough to consider whether or not she should figure out if he needed her help. She supposed she simply wasn't quite ready to give him up.

She also knew that that wasn't the only reason she hadn't yet returned to Ammarindar to report to Kaanyr Vhok all she'd discovered thus far. Perhaps it was the multitude of sights and sounds in the city that attracted her still. Perhaps it was the exquisite feeling she got whenever creatures of the race she chose for her disguise—whether it be dark elf, orc, or yet some other species—admired her form. It had been too long since she'd experienced that. She also wanted to see events unfold in the city. She sensed the tension in the air, and she wanted to witness the violence, the chaos, should something come to pass. Ched Nasad was more than ripe for such a thing. The place was literally buzzing with energy, with anticipation.

The four drow she followed moved casually, yet they always seemed to be adjusting their course to avoid the largest crowds, and they never tarried near side web streets or alleyways. It was clear to Aliisza that they were moving warily. More than once, they magically bypassed the worst of the crowds, levitating or using the magical doorways that both she and Pharaun employed from time to time. They led her into the higher sections of the city, and soon it became apparent to Aliisza that she would have to either stop or change shape in order to continue unhindered. There were going to be few orcs that high in the cavern, and she would draw attention to herself in her present guise.

Changing back to the drow form she'd used earlier, she followed the four dark elves farther, until they arrived at a large noble House, which they entered.

Aliisza found a quiet spot atop a building on the opposite side of the street and settled down to wait.

Khorrl Xornbane knew that his fidgeting was a bad sign, but he couldn't help it. He and his clan had been hiding and waiting for so long he could hardly stand it any longer. Hiding several thousand duergar was never easy, but trying to do it in the middle of a city full of drow was taking its toll on his nerves. He was thankful that the waiting was almost over.

Until then, the fighting had been relatively easy and pain-free. Ambushing the matron mother and her retinue in the storehouse had been almost too simple. She obviously trusted the other matron mother far too much, and it had cost her. He wondered if anyone had discovered the bodies of her soldiers and advisors. They would, soon, he knew. The smell would lead someone to them.

Khorrl and his duergar were inside the manor itself, out of sight in an unused wing of the place, in a barracks where no soldiers were currently quartered. It was driving Khorrl mad. His sentries had not reported anyone even coming near the halls where he and his boys waited, but if anyone found them, the plan was ruined.

"Captain." An all-too-familiar voice came from the shadows at the edges of the storehouse.

Khorrl felt his heart begin to race with anticipation. Zammzt stepped from the shadows, a wry smile on his face.

"So?" the duergar asked.

"We've gotten the word," Zammzt replied. "It's time for you to go to work."

Khorrl rubbed his hands together in delight. At last. He began going over the plan in his head once more as he issued orders, and Zammzt faded back into the shadow from which he'd emerged.

The real fighting was about to begin.

Faeryl was fast growing bored with all of it. She wished the matron mothers would simply see things as her mother had laid them out so carefully, declare House Melarn treasonous and dissolved, and permit House Zauvirr to rise to a position of prominence so that Ssipriina could sit on the Council. But of course, there was the prerequisite squabbling that had to take place, first. Faeryl supposed she would care a whole lot more if she stood to gain more, but her mother would still be ordering her around—and getting ordered around in turn, even if it was by someone other than Drisinil Melarn.

There's always someone using you as their footstool, Faeryl thought, no matter how high you reach. Even Triel Baenre was forced to nod her head in subservience to the whims of Lolth, and it's possible that the Dark Mother herself has been forced to—

"Faeryl, stop wasting our time with your idle fancies, and pay attention," Ssipriina Zauvirr said, snapping Faeryl out of her thoughts.

"Sorry, Mother," the younger drow answered, chagrined.

She focused her attention on the conversation at hand, for at least the matron mothers were no longer talking as one.

"I *said*," Inidil Mylyl declared, emphasizing the word to make sure everyone in the room understood that she was put out at having to repeat herself, "that hearing the tale in its entirety once more would go a long way toward clarifying just exactly how this managed to happen right under our noses. Perhaps Faeryl can indulge us for a few moments more to explain this."

Faeryl groaned inwardly. She had already explained herself three times to the first matron mothers to arrive. They had not been happy with several parts of her story, so she was going to have to tell the whole thing once more for those matron mothers who had chosen, for whatever reason, to arrive late. Of course, they were the most powerful drow in Ched Nasad, used to keeping others waiting and daring anyone to question them on it. She felt queasy as she crossed to the center of the room.

"Yes, of course, Matron Mother Mylyl," she said as politely as she could.

Compared to the collection of nobility in the room, House Zauvirr was still inconsequential and could be held accountable for everything Faeryl had done and said up to that point. Embarrassing one's own mother in front of her superiors was no way to climb to a higher position within a House, and the ambassador knew that both her tone and her explanation had to be handled just right.

"For the sake of understanding," she continued, "let me start by saying that House Zauvirr represents House Melarn in certain business interests, and I represent House Zauvirr's efforts on behalf of House Melarn in Menzoberranzan. I serve—or did serve, rather—as the ambassador to Triel Baenre herself. When the difficulties arose, they were, as you now know, experienced in Menzoberranzan as well. Concerned about this and the lack of caravan traffic between the two cities, I petitioned Matron Mother Baenre to allow me to return here in the hopes of finding out what was wrong.

"Triel refused, and in fact, effectively placed me under house arrest, for what concerns I never found out. She eventually imprisoned me when I tried to leave on my own. While I did not wish to damage the relationship between our Houses and House Baenre, my loyalty and concern lay solely with my own family and those families we serve here in Ched Nasad. I was ordered put to death for treason, but thankfully, the execution never occurred.

"Triel changed her mind at some point, choosing instead to forgive me whatever sins I supposedly committed. She assigned me to journey with her sister, Quenthel Baenre, and several others here to Ched Nasad to reestablish trading and to determine if more information was available concerning the, uh . . ."

"Child, we all know that Lolth has vanished. You don't have to tread around the subject." It was Matron Mother Aunrae Nasadra, the uncrowned queen of Ched Nasad, leader of the most powerful House in the city. Faeryl swallowed as Aunrae added, "Get to the point."

The ambassador nodded and continued. "Menzoberranzan had suffered an uprising, a slave revolt supported by outside forces. Containing it consumed a substantial amount of the sisterhood's divine resources. Matron Mother Triel sent the group of us here to find out if Lolth's disappearance was limited to Menzoberranzan or felt across all tribes of drow, but she also wanted Quenthel to procure any divine magic she could lay her hands on here. Quenthel and Triel had apparently rationalized that since House Baenre held part ownership in Black Claw Mercantile, anything the storehouses stocked was her city's by right. Once I was able to covertly relay this to my mother via my brother and his magical contacts, we worked together to set a trap and catch the Menzoberranyr in the act. It was only when we all arrived at the storehouse that we discovered Matron Mother Melarn was actually aiding the visitors. My mother confronted both of them together, and Matron Mother Melarn tried to escape."

When she finished, Faeryl realized she was out of breath from rushing through the rest of her explanation. Matron Mother Aunrae had that effect on everyone.

"Drisinil was killed, cut down trying to flee," Ssipriina added, drawing attention back to herself. "I would have done whatever I could to spare her if I could have reached her in time, but it was too late, and my own magic is too weakened to stave off the passing."

"So you conspired to allow them to sneak into the city, going so far as to mislead a city patrol?"

The matron mother who asked this question was Jyslin Aleanrahel. Her features were sharp, almost fierce, and her reputation as a malicious, greedy drow who found fault in every action was legendary. Faeryl had never liked her, but she was hardly in a position to show that sentiment.

"They have no doubt been sent to spy on us," Jyslin continued, "and their supposed story of reestablishing contact here was simply a falsehood meant to keep you off-balance. I daresay the males still loose in the city are sending sensitive information back to their superiors even now, especially if this wizard is as capable as you alleged before. I might have expected you to be a more clever girl and keep them out of the city, but I suppose that's too much to ask."

"This is foolish," Umrae D'Dgttu, matron mother of the second most powerful House in the city said. "We've heard the story, some of us several times now. It is clear to me that House Zauvirr acted with the best intentions of Ched Nasad in mind. I move that we dissolve House Melarn forthwith."

Umrae was one of Ssipriina's secret allies, Faeryl knew. This was it. They were beginning the process, giving her mother what she wanted. Dissolution of House Melarn was the first step in granting Ssipriina a seat on the Council.

"I concur," said Ulviirala Rilynt, another of the four her mother had bribed. "The treason of House Melarn seems clear enough to me."

Faeryl stole a glance at Ssipriina and saw that she was trying hard not to smile too broadly.

"I'm more concerned with the veracity of their story," Lirdnolu Maerret said. "So far, all we've had to go on is this fanciful tale Ssipriina and her daughter have woven, with no neutral observer able to substantiate it. House Zauvirr stands to gain quite a lot by seeing Drisinil and her ilk dead. I for one am unwilling to so quickly assume they're telling the truth simply for the good of the city."

"Quite true," Jyslin Aleanrahel agreed. "Let's hear Drisinil's daughter speak."

Faeryl opened her mouth to protest then snapped it shut again. The matron mothers knew well the propensity drow had for scheming, and this was the challenge Ssipriina had cautioned her would come. There were some who would want the whole truth and would look to try to trap House Zauvirr in a lie, or if they were allies of House Melarn, try to pin whatever blame they could on Ssipriina. Her mother had cautioned Faeryl for patience during this time. When their new enemies were exposed, or if the decision didn't favor Zauvirr, their secret mercenary army would step forward.

Halisstra Melarn was brought from the dungeons below to answer for her mother's crimes. She was almost forcibly led into the chamber, flanked by two large female guards. She had been stripped of her fine clothing and was dressed in only a thin shift. She cast her eyes about the room, searching faces, perhaps hoping to find some sympathy or support among those present.

It was rumored that Halisstra had a soft streak, that she never seemed to show the type of tenacious ambition her mother wanted to see in her daughters. She was more interested, those rumors suggested, in slumming with her battle captive, Danifae, using the other drow's good looks to attract males to carouse with. There were even some who whispered that Matron Mother Melarn would have cast her out of the family, given the right circumstances. Faeryl knew that the slumming part was true, and that gave her an idea.

She spread her hands helplessly, as if acknowledging that she had failed in some way. "I beg your forgiveness for whatever flaws you see in our plan, Matron Mothers," Faeryl said quietly. "I am as disappointed as you that a House of our own beloved city would conspire with foreigners at our expense. I now recall additional damning evidence that might put this debate to rest."

"What?" Ssipriina said, leaning forward, obviously loath to see her daughter possibly ruin her own carefully laid web of lies.

Faeryl studiously ignored her mother.

"What do you mean?" Jyslin said, her eyes narrowing.

Faeryl was sure she had the advantage. Though she had not mentioned it before—since it was a lie she had only conceived of on the spur of the moment—there was no way Jyslin could challenge her for leaving it out of her story the first time. Faeryl could pretend she'd simply forgotten it until then.

"It's just that, right after passing through the gates of the city, I had the good fortune to spy Mistress Halisstra and her consort, Danifae Yauntyrr. I was surprised to see them in such a sordid section of the city, but I considered it a stroke of good fortune, nonetheless. I made a specific effort to move into their line of sight so that they would see it was me and notice I was with strangers. I thought for certain they had spotted me, and I even flashed a quick message to Danifae, but she either didn't recognize me or didn't want anyone to know they'd been there. She turned Halisstra away, and the two of them melted into the crowd. At the time, I didn't think anything of it, but now I realize that she must have been there to signal Quenthel and the others."

Halisstra's eyes grew wide at hearing Faeryl's accusations. She sputtered to find the words to defend herself.

"I . . . we never . . . Matron Mothers, I assure you that we never saw the ambassador and her companions in the lower sections of the city. I am innocent of the charges leveled against me."

Faeryl smiled to herself. Halisstra had specifically avoided denying that she had been there. It had been a gamble, supposing that the two of them might have been in the vicinity in the last couple of days, but it had paid off. The unwanted attention was being focused on Halisstra.

"Perhaps I am mistaken," Faeryl quickly interjected. She smiled at Halisstra, who was staring daggers at her in return. "It was crowded there, with all of the refugees and the base-born males in their revelry, so it's easy to understand how I only thought Danifae had caught the eye of someone in my party. The two of you were obviously seeking someone else."

Faeryl wanted to grin at her own cleverness. By pulling back, admitting she had made a mistake, she doubly damned Halisstra. The seed of doubt had been planted in everyone's mind, and the less she tried to force them to accept her theory, the more likely they all would be to believe it; such was drow nature. For those who chose to believe Halisstra's innocence, that left only one other reason for her to be in such an improper part of the city. Either way, it shed an unpleasant light on the daughter of a traitor.

Ssipriina turned to Jyslin Aleanrahel and said, "Matron Mother, I am only a trader, unused to the machinations of the higher nobility. If I had foreseen how greatly this would have displeased you, I would have conceived of a better way to deal with the crisis at hand. As it was, I still hope you will consider that I was keeping only the best interests of Ched Nasad in mind, acting in all ways on its behalf."

There was a general murmur from the matron mothers as they put their heads together, no doubt discussing the additional implications of guilt Faeryl's little tale had just heaped upon House Melarn. At the very least, the suggestion that Halisstra had been carousing with the commoners of the city meant that her disgraceful behavior was of the worst sort and she was unfit to rule a noble House. That half of it happened to be true only made the whole incident sweeter to Faeryl, who was simply glad she was no longer the drow everyone else was looking down their noses at.

"Enough!" Aunrae Nasadra shouted, rapping her rune-covered staff upon the floor. Even in such an impromptu meeting, the eldest and most powerful matron mother commanded absolute respect, and the room fell silent. "This nonsense is the reason we face the bleak loss of our goddess's favor. How can we expect Lolth to grant us her attention when we waste so much time and energy on such ridiculous discussions as who's stepped in the most rothé muck?" The matriarch walked among the others, peering at them all. "Whether or not House Melarn's progeny chooses to whore around with low-born males in the seamiest underbelly of Ched Nasad is of no concern to me."

Faeryl stole a glance at Halisstra, whose face was down in humiliation.

Matron Mother Nasadra paid neither of them any heed.

"The streets are not safe for most drow," she said. "We all know the extra precautions we had to take even to come here. Our city is on the verge of disaster, mothers, and yet we must stand here and discuss the fate of a noble House, one high enough to have a seat on the Council.

"Ssipriina has suggested that we dissolve House Melarn and offer up Halisstra and these remaining outsiders as sacrifices to appease the masses as much as the Dark Mother. While we know nothing about why our beloved Lolth is angry with us, that she *is* angry with us, we are certain. Will this help? Will it bring her blessings back to us?

"If we make an example of the traitors and let the whole city see us do it will it quiet the citizens for a time? Perhaps, but more importantly, will it satisfy all of you? Will you return to your Houses satisfied that a House has fallen and that the hierarchy has shuffled sufficiently? There are things more fragile than the peace of our city, but they are few in number. This backstabbing, while inherent in our nature, is misplaced during this time of difficulties."

"What if this Baenre priestess's companions know something?" Halisstra asked. "What if they have an inkling of what troubles the Dark Mother? If you simply kill me, then you get what you want—one less House to stand in your way—but if you kill them, whether as spies or as sacrifices, you might lose valuable information."

"Shut your mouth, child!" Ssipriina hissed. "You've shamed us enough for one lifetime. Do not think that you can escape justice merely by pretending to be loyal now. It's too late for that."

Halisstra would not be deterred. She proceeded, ignoring the dark stares the matron mothers gave her.

"What if this wizard has discovered something?" she asked. "Faeryl has already told us he is clever and was not above antagonizing Quenthel. I would not put it past him to know more than he's letting on. Why kill him, when he might be so inclined to parlay with us? Could he be willing to reveal his own secrets? Perhaps even for a price? There are those among you who do not wish to hear what he has to say. He might expose the lies you have told concerning my mother and me."

Aunrae smiled and said, "Tell me, child, do you think Lolth would grant such a vision to a male? Do you think she would allow a *boy*, however clever, to unlock the secrets of her silence?"

"These are desperate times, Matron Mother, you said so yourself. I would not close any possible avenue of redemption, however thickly cloaked in folly it may seem. Of course, I have few avenues of redemption for my life left. I have my own desperate times. Whether you wish to question him or not, I merely ask that you bring him as a witness into these proceedings. His words could prove my own innocence."

Faeryl frowned, not liking where this was leading. She was beginning to think it had been a mistake to put the full plan into motion until Pharaun and the others had also been brought into custody, or better yet, killed. Maybe she could get to him before the rest of them had a chance to speak with him, take care of it herself, one way or another. Perhaps then her mother would stop treating her like a child.

Aunrae nodded, her mouth pursed as though considering the younger drow's words.

"You argue for your life, Halisstra Melarn, but still your pleas have some merit. We will wait to pass sentence on you until we've had a chance to hear all sides. As for the 'clever boy,' when he comes to us, when we have him in our possession, we will extract whatever information he has, fully and without paying any price. Somehow, I do not think Quenthel Baenre had established the proper leashes on her wizard. I do not intend to make the same mistake."

"Matron Mother Nasadra," Zammzt called from the back of the room, where he had just entered. "They are here."

Pharaun, Ryld, and Valas had been led inside and shown to a waiting room, an all-too-familiar sight to each of them and one that did nothing to set their minds at ease. They were left alone, or rather with only sentries posted at each of the exits to keep them company. Pharaun occupied his time strolling through the chamber, admiring the frescos and statuary that were in abundance there, primarily exhibiting the motif of spiders, webbing, and the glory of the dark elves. There were a goodly number of musical instruments as well, some he didn't even recognize. The Master of Sorcere supposed a good many of the works related to the history of House Melarn, but to Pharaun it was all just so much pomp and circumstance. Ryld and Valas, meanwhile, had their heads together in consultation, most likely discussing tactics for extricating themselves in the event that things went bad.

When the double doors at the far end of the room were thrown open, Pharaun turned to see not one but several ostentatious drow females—matriarchs all, he was sure—waiting in the large audience chamber beyond. They were attended by a retinue of House wizards, soldiers, and younger females, all of them in House livery and many of them, Pharaun noted, radiating magical protections and other spells.

"Good evening, and welcome to House Melarn," one some-what tall and slender drow said imperiously, waiting on the throne as the three males moved into the room. "I am Matron Mother Ssipriina Zauvirr."

Pharaun bowed slightly as he moved to a place in front of the throne, far enough back so as not to seem threatening. Ryld and Valas moved to join him as the other matron mothers gathered around the throne, and the assortment of wizards, priestesses, and soldiers flanked everyone else.

Pharaun knew the woman was Faeryl's mother, of course, but he couldn't guess what she was doing on the throne of House Melarn.

The mage looked around the chamber, trying to find Faeryl. She was there, though off in a corner of the room, as if she were trying to avoid notice.

If I didn't know better, Pharaun thought wryly, I would have to assume they're expecting some sort of trouble.

Neither Valas nor Ryld said anything, but the wizard could feel them on either side of him, tense and ready to spring.

"We are honored and delighted to be guests in your House, Matron Mother Zauvirr," Pharaun said. "To what do we owe this auspicious occasion?"

And where in the Abyss are Quenthel and Jeggred? he silently added.

Ssipriina Zauvirr sniffed and replied, "On the contrary, Pharaun Mizzrym, I should be the one thanking you and asking you why you have graced the City of Shimmering Webs with your august presence. The reputation that preceded you, telling of a confident, self-possessed mage of no small skill, was only half the story, it seems."

Pharaun smiled in the most disarming way he could muster as he shifted his weight to one foot, letting the other turn out slightly.

"Everyone has her own opinions, as always, Matron Mother. That is not to say that anyone is in error, only that affectations and realities do not always mesh, and for good reason."

"Of course," another matron mother said, moving forward from Ssipriina's left, "and our opinion is that you and your companions, while affecting the appearance of simple travelers or even emissaries from our sister city of Menzoberranzan, are in reality spies, here to steal from us and expose whatever weaknesses you thought you might be able to find to the world at large."

So much for affectations, thought Pharaun, shifting his weight uneasily.

He felt, rather than saw Ryld, to his left, and Valas, to his right, both stiffen at the undisguised accusation.

"Easy," he muttered under his breath. "Save the foolish heroics for the 'all-else-fails' part of the program."

Smoothing his face as best he could, the mage spread his hands in gracious acquiescence and said, "I'm sorry, Mistress . . ."

"Matron Mother Jyslin Aleanrahel, of House Aleanrahel."

Pharaun swallowed then said, "Matron Mother Aleanrahel. While I'm sure our efforts at avoiding attention must seem terribly surreptitious, I can assure you that we meant nothing antagonistic. We only wished to—"

"To avoid being confronted like this?" Jyslin interjected. "How well did that serve you?"

Pharaun sighed and said, "Not well at all, it appears, but my companions and I still aren't completely sure we understand your concerns. I must profess, I am confused as to why we're meeting here, if none of you is Matron Mother Melarn."

Several of the matron mothers gave each other knowing glances. Pharaun was thoroughly confused. He continued to scan the room and saw something else quite odd: a drow, obviously nobly born but stripped to her underclothes and held prisoner between two stout guards, and it wasn't Quenthel.

"Oh, we have no concerns," Jyslin Aleanrahel replied. "Not anymore. Until you arrived, we were concerned that we would not be able to detain you, that you might try to slip out of the city. We were concerned that you would report your discoveries to your superiors back in the City of Spiders. We were more concerned that you would try something foolish, like concluding your high priestess's ill-conceived plan of theft and spying. You've cooperated nicely, though, so we feel we have the situation well in hand."

Ryld made an almost inaudible strangled noise, and the mage felt the warrior shift his weight. In response, several of the soldiers, who had unassumingly fanned out to more completely surround the trio, tensed as though expecting Ryld to lunge at them.

Pharaun frowned.

"I wasn't aware that our high priestess was planning anything of the sort," he said. "If something is amiss, we must all work to see that it is rectified. Just tell us where she is, and I'm sure we can resolve whatever—"

"Quenthel Baenre was caught committing treasonous acts against Ched Nasad," yet a third matron mother said, stepping out from behind the throne. Pharaun sensed that this one, with a graceful age about her face, might just be the most formidable drow he'd ever met. "There was no doubt about her guilt. She died trying to flee the scene of her crimes."

Pharaun blinked, reeling. Dead? Quenthel Baenre was dead? He wasn't sure whether to laugh or be worried. Behind him, he heard both of his companions' gasps of surprise.

"She was caught conspiring with House Melarn to illegally enter the city and steal valuable resources belonging to us," the older drow said, "and we believe she was also committing espionage on behalf of Menzoberranzan. We consider these to be crimes against the city, against all drow, and most especially against the Dark Mother herself."

Conspiracy? Pharaun thought. How ridiculous could they be?

He stared at the throne where Faeryl's mother sat, and he was beginning to understand who was behind it, and perhaps why.

No wonder Faeryl was so eager to help us, he thought. She was leading us by our noses the whole time.

"Furthermore," the matron mother continued, "you, by association with Quenthel, are accused of the same charges. You are under arrest, and you will be confined on the premises until such time as we can determine your guilt or innocence."

"Not today," Ryld said, taking a step forward and reaching for Splitter.

As one, a multitude of soldiers brandished hand crossbows, and at least half a dozen wizards and priestesses appeared to ready spells.

"Ryld, you fool, wait!" Pharaun growled, still trying to keep his voice low. "There are better ways . . ."

Valas reached a hand out and stopped the larger drow from finishing the act of unsheathing his greatsword.

"Not yet," the scout pleaded. "We've got no chance like this."

Ryld snarled, but he released the hilt of his weapon and stepped back again.

"Good," the third matron mother said. "You are not as foolhardy as Faeryl suggested. Though the bravado is misplaced here, I'm sure it's served you well in the past."

"Mistress . . . ?" Pharaun began.

"Aunrae Nasadra, of First House Nasadra," the drow finished for him.

Of course you are, the wizard thought.

"Mistress Nasadra," he said, "while I am shocked and saddened by the news of Quenthel's death, I implore you to hear me out. I have absolutely no knowledge of any conspiracy between her and anyone here in the city. There must have been a great misunderstanding."

"I doubt it," Aunrae replied, "but you may yet have a chance to prove it and spare your neck. Simply tell us the truth. Did you or did you not sneak into the city and meet in secret with Drisinil Melarn, matron mother of House Melarn, in order to steal goods out of Black Claw Mercantile's storehouses?"

Pharaun looked around at the myriad faces staring expectantly at him—and at the scores of weapons leveled at him and his two companions—and he did the only thing he could; he lied.

"Absolutely, Mistress Nasadra," he deadpanned, and everyone including Ryld and Valas gasped. Before the other two Menzoberranyr could refute his false admission, he continued, "Or rather, Quenthel must have. It all makes sense, now. You see, Mistress, she ordered my two companions and me to track down caravans that could help transport a large amount of goods, without telling us what they were for. Mistress Baenre told us males very little, you must realize.

"Right before we set out to follow her instructions, I overheard her speaking with Faeryl Zauvirr, the ambassador to Menzoberranzan who was accompanying us. I recall that she said something about meeting with her mother and one other, though of course at the time, I didn't know to whom she was referring. She asked Faeryl something to the effect of, 'and you're certain the meeting place is secure? We can't afford to be seen, you know.' "

"You pompous, smart-mouthed liar!" Faeryl screamed from across the room. "Kill them now and be done with it!"

Pharaun did all he could to avoid smiling. Around him, everyone began to talk at once, and though he heard more than a few snatches of conversation condemning him and his outlandish story, he knew that he had sown the seeds of doubt. Already, though, the troops who had surrounded them—troops wearing the insignia of House Zauvirr—began to advance uncertainly upon the three of them.

"All right, wizard," Ryld hissed, "we're out of time. What are we going to do?"

Pharaun opened his mouth to tell the warrior that he had absolutely no idea, when a sudden and violent shudder rocked the chamber, causing everyone to stumble and flail about, their center of balance disrupted. A split second later, a monumental thundercrash penetrated the walls, deep and loud, and reverberated through the entire room.

"By the Dark Mother," someone cried as everyone looked at everyone else in confusion and panic.

A servant ran into the chamber, a wild look of fear in his eyes.

"Mistresses! It's duergar! Hundreds of them, surrounding us . . . they're attacking!" Another sonic shock knocked the liveried boy to his knees, and he seemed to hug the floor in terror. "They burn the stones themselves, Mothers. The city is burning!"

Aliisza was more than a little surprised to see the horde of duergar seemingly appear out of thin air around the great manor Pharaun and his companions had entered. From the looks on their faces, though, she wasn't nearly as surprised as the drow who were guarding the place. The gray dwarves, whom she estimated numbered between two and three thousand, had formed a line along one side of the manor house before making themselves visible by firing off a volley of crossbows. They also lobbed several dozen small clay pots, which burst into orange balls of flame upon impacting the stonework wall that surrounded the manor.

The few drow who'd been lounging around near the palatial front gates scrambled for cover as the hail of bolts and incendiary bombs struck. The blast from the initial attack shook the entire web street, and Aliisza had to improve her grip to avoid slipping and falling from her roost on the roof of the building on the opposite side of the open plaza. When she could look again, she saw that few of the dark elves had survived the first attack.

An alarm was quickly sounded inside the courtyard of the cyst-like building, and more drow appeared from inside, a large contingent of them, in fact. Aliisza watched as they formed a line across the protective wall and returned fire with their hand crossbows. Several duergar dropped before the barrage, but the gray dwarves exhibited wise tactics, throwing up a shield wall with the front rank and firing a second volley from behind that protective barrier. In several places, the stone itself seemed to burn from the duergar fire bombs, and the fire was spreading.

In the plaza, citizens of Ched Nasad scrambled for cover, and in the distance, Aliisza could see a large column of troops marching, one web street over, in her direction. The duergar were about to have unwanted company . . . or so she thought.

That's when the second mass of gray dwarves appeared inside the courtyard, flanking the drow who had formed up to defend the front gates.

Oh, how clever, the alu-fiend thought. They look like they've done this a time or two.

Pharaun never hesitated.

"Scatter," he said sharply to the two drow with him.

He willed a spell into being. Ordinarily he would have needed at least a few seconds to speak the phrase and perform the gestures to bring the effect about, but he had enhanced this particular magic, and this conjuration simply happened as he thought it, with no gestures, words, or delays. A thick, roiling mist appeared, obscuring everything around the wizard. He knew that Ryld would know how to take care of himself, and he hoped that Valas would understand, too. He promptly dismissed them from his mind as he levitated upward.

Another concussive blast shook the House, though the wizard, hovering in the air, only heard it this time. He floated all the way to the ceiling, casting a spell of invisibility on himself. He knew it wouldn't completely obscure him from the more clever wizards and matron mothers, but it would at least prevent the common soldiery from spotting him. From below, he could hear the turmoil and confusion as a host of drow reacted to both the messenger's words and the rumbles in the foundation.

When he reached the ceiling, Pharaun reached inside his *piwafwi* and extracted a small pinch of diamond dust. He incanted once more, watching as the dust vanished in a sparkle of light. It would further conceal him, he hoped, this time from detection magic.

By then, someone had had the presence of mind to magically dissipate Pharaun's mist, and the floor below was clear once more. The Master of Sorcere surveyed the entire chamber, looking for signs of Ryld and Valas. The scout was nowhere to be found, which didn't surprise the wizard in the least, and Ryld had maneuvered himself off to one side of the room. The weapons master crouched behind some statuary, Splitter in hand, watching as the enemy ran here and there.

He won't stay hidden long, Pharaun reasoned, knowing the matron mothers still intended to mete out their own personal justice just as soon as they could restore some order.

Considering quickly, the wizard dug out a bit of fleece from one of his pockets. With it he manufactured another spell. This one he cast at Ryld, creating a little enhancement to the warrior's hiding place. When he was done, a new, illusory statue stood where Ryld was, further concealing him.

Pharaun turned his attention back to the center of the room, where several wizards were standing, some of them casting. Another was carefully turning, peering in every direction, and Pharaun could see that magic emanated from the drow.

They're looking for us, the Master of Sorcere realized.

Fumbling around in his pockets, Pharaun found what he was looking for: a tiny hammer and bell, both made of silver. Striking the hammer against the bell, the wizard produced another magical effect. This time, the results were flashy.

A horrid vibration beat through the floor beneath the wizards' feet, causing them to clap their hands over their ears and stumble about. Even the one who'd been scanning the room seemed startled, though he planted his feet and continued searching. As the vibration reached a crescendo, the stone of the floor itself could no longer stand the strain and began to fracture. A thousand spiderwebbing cracks shot through the floor, making footing unstable and knocking many of the wizards down. The floor continued to fracture until it was nothing but pulverized powder, half a foot deep. The downed wizards kicked up dust as they flailed about, trying to regain their footing. Several of them didn't move at all.

Excellent, Pharaun thought, but his elation was short-lived. Ryld had been discovered and was engaged in a fierce battle with several House Melarn soldiers and at least two priestesses. Though blood streamed from a gash across one arm, the warrior was otherwise holding his own, but Pharaun knew that it wouldn't last long if anyone was able to bring magic into play. Already, the mage could see a priestess unfurling a scroll. Before he could act, though, Valas stepped up behind her, seemingly from nowhere—How does he do that? Pharaun marveled—and plunged one of his two curved daggers into the small of her back. As the cleric dropped woodenly to the floor, the scout was turning away, and Pharaun lost sight of him again when the wizard turned his attention for a moment to the other side of the room.

There, several of the matron mothers had come together, protected by a significant portion of their entourage, and were huddled around something Pharaun couldn't see. He considered whether to strike at them while they were in such close proximity but dismissed the idea.

Don't want to draw any more attention to myself than necessary, he decided.

Pharaun felt the tingle of magic being cast at him, and he saw another wizard with his finger pointed in his direction. Somehow, they'd discovered his position. Pharaun realized he was glowing with a pale violet flame, despite his invisible state. Already, several other wizards were looking in his direction, and a handful of soldiers were arming crossbows.

Damnation! the mage thought.

He quickly pulled his *piwafwi* around himself and turned away as the first volley of bolts crashed into the ceiling around him. He felt a pair of the missiles strike his back, but the *piwafwi* did its job. There was no way he could eliminate the faerie fire around himself without also dismissing the invisibility, he knew, but if he simply let himself be a target, he would wind up a pincushion. Shaking his head in consternation, Pharaun quickly dropped from his position, pulling up just short of hitting the floor.

The contingent of wizards and soldiers had followed Pharaun's descent and were moving to close with him. Two soldiers brandishing long swords came at him from opposite sides, and though he was able to duck the first attack cleanly, the other one caught him flush across the arm, penetrating his *piwafwi*. Blood spurted from the gash as the mage cried out in pain. A heartbeat later, he and his two adversaries were engulfed in a torrent, as though they had danced their dance into the center of a waterfall—only it wasn't water. It burned like fire, and both of the sword wielders shrieked and thrashed as their skin blistered and reddened. Pharaun felt his own skin bubbling and boiling as he flung his *piwafwi* up to shield his face and threw himself clear, moving at an unnaturally rapid pace, thanks to the magic of his boots.

Rolling free of the downpour of acid, Pharaun summoned his rapier as he leaped to his feet, continuing his forward progress right at two more soldiers. He used the hovering, dancing rapier to hold the pair of drow at bay just enough so he could pass between them before they even knew he was coming. Once he was through, he headed in the direction of Ryld, while more crossbow bolts and a couple of streaking missiles of light and fire fizzled out as they reached his form.

Valas had hidden himself away again, but Ryld was hard at work, surrounded by no less than six opponents. With each swing of Splitter, the burly warrior parried several weapons at once. His chest was heaving, and he was covered in blood from a dozen small wounds. He didn't appear capable of going on the offensive with so many foes surrounding him.

As Pharaun closed with his companion, he had the magical rapier slash at the back of one of Ryld's adversaries. The blade jabbed into the drow soldier from behind, causing the poor fellow to arch his back in agony and crumple to the ground. Grimly, Pharaun ordered the rapier to return and protect him as he began to conjure another spell.

Backing himself into a defensive position near the same statues that Ryld had used to hide himself earlier, the Master of Sorcere extracted a second pinch of the powdered diamond. This time, though, the spell he wove created an invisible barrier between himself and the dozen or so soldiers and wizards who had been pursuing him. The location where Ryld had chosen to hide was more or less in a corner of the great audience chamber, and Pharaun took advantage of that by stretching his invisible wall at an angle, sealing himself and the Master of Melee-Magthere off from most of the rest of the chamber, with only the five drow who were still surrounding Ryld to contend with.

The Master of Sorcere turned his attention to aiding Ryld as the other soldiers painfully discovered his magical wall. He ignored the thumps they made as the first two or three slammed into the barrier, but he couldn't help but smile. Ryld had fatally wounded a second foe, a priestess who was writhing on the floor in a growing pool of blood. Pharaun drew out his own crossbow and loaded the weapon even as he brought his dancing rapier to bear on a drow male who was trying to get in behind Ryld.

The rapier slashed, grazing the guard's shoulder, and as the soldier turned to protect himself from this new threat, Pharaun fired his crossbow, striking true. The soldier grunted in surprise and pain as the bolt took him in the shoulder of his weapon arm. He dropped his long sword and staggered backward, eyeing the rapier as it flitted about in front of him. Pharaun reloaded the crossbow and was taking aim when Valas stepped from a shadow and finished the guard from behind. Eyes wide, the drow gasped and tried to say something, seemed confused that his words wouldn't form, then died, sliding to the floor as the scout freed his kukri from its victim.

"I assume that's you, wizard? What's the point of being invisible if you're going to glow all purple like that?"

"I'm glad to see you wound up on the right side of things," Pharaun said, then staggered as another rumble shook the building. "By the Dark Mother, what is going on out there?" he said, steadying himself from the aftershocks.

"Whatever it is, I don't know if it's better to be out there or in here," Valas replied, wiping his curved dagger clean on the dead drow's *piwafwi*. "We've got to get out of here."

Pharaun nodded, forgetting that the scout couldn't see him, then he said, "I agree" before turning to see how Ryld had fared.

The warrior was facing only a single opponent, stepping warily around the slick pools of blood as he feinted a few times. His ploys weren't terribly effective, and he was gasping for breath. His close-cropped white hair was matted red with blood.

Valas crept forward, ready to get in another attack from behind the moment an opportunity presented itself, so the mage turned his attention back to his magical wall, confident his two companions had the situation well in hand.

On the other side of the barrier, several of the drow wizards were levitating, testing to see if Pharaun had left any gaps along the ceiling. Another wizard was obviously casting, trying to find something that would dispel the effect. Soldiers stood at the ready, fingering their weapons and eyeing Pharaun and his two companions balefully. Pharaun knew by sense that the magical partition still held, but it would only be a matter of time before their enemies would find the right combination of magic to bring it down.

At that moment, Pharaun noted the smoke on the far side of the room. It was where the matron mothers had been, but they were no longer there.

Of course not, the mage thought sardonically. They're not going to come out until they know we're in custody again.

The smoke, however, was thick and black and seemed to be pouring into the room through a hole in the wall. He could see flames licking the stone, and he realized what was going on.

"We've definitely got to get out of here," the mage said to Valas.

"That's what I said," Valas replied, "but you seem to have sealed us in here."

Ryld had dispatched his final adversary and sank down to one knee, trying to regain his breath.

"Hello, Pharaun. It's good to 'see' you. You two aren't going to walk through walls again, are you?" Ryld asked, heaving himself to his feet again.

On the other side of the barrier, some of the House Melarn delegation had lost interest in them, turning and pointing back at the smoke or running toward it. Whatever was happening in the obscured side of the audience chamber, they were very agitated.

"Alas," Pharaun answered the warrior, "I have exhausted my quota of wall-walking for the day. I'll have to rely on more conventional means of egress, I'm afraid. Still, we shouldn't tarry. That smoke is from the same stuff we had to deal with during the insurrection back in Menzoberranzan."

"The fire bombs that burned the very stone?" Valas asked.

"Then that means . . ." Ryld added.

"Precisely. We may be contending with associates of Syrzan, or others, who are inciting the populace to riot and arming them with the same tools of destruction."

"I thought you said the alhoon was operating alone, an outcast from its own kind," Ryld said, turning in circles and analyzing every nook and cranny of the corner of the room.

"I did," Pharaun admitted. "In my conversation with the thing during our captivity, it claimed that very thing. Perhaps whoever supplied it or its minions with the alchemical incendiary jugs is serving multiple fronts."

"Regardless of who's doing it, we know how grave the situation is," Valas said. "We need to get out of the city."

"Again, I agree," Pharaun said. "I suggest we make a run for it once I lower the barrier."

"Into that mob?" Ryld countered. "We should try to find another way out."

"But that's the quickest way to the streets. We don't know our way around in here, and House Melarn could be an inferno before long."

"Look," Ryld argued, "you may be feeling fine, but I can't take another stand-up fight right now." He gestured at his own bloody form. "There's got to be other ways out of this House. Let's go find one." The warrior gestured toward a door in the corner and added, "Leave your barrier up and let's go."

Valas nodded and said, "Ryld is right. We can't fight through all of them. Let's try another route."

"Very well," Pharaun sighed, "but if the House falls down around our ears, I will personally blame both of you."

He gestured toward the door, inviting Valas to lead the way.

For the first few minutes, the halls of House Melarn were remarkably empty as Ryld, Pharaun, and Valas limped their way through them. Occasionally, the trio heard running footsteps in the twisting, winding passages that threaded their way through the massive structure, but they were able to avoid confrontations by either taking a detour or momentarily hiding. It appeared to the Master of Melee-Magthere that most of the inhabitants were focusing their attention outside, where the bulk of the fighting was taking place.

As they reached an intersection, Valas held up his hand for a halt, and the scout slunk off in one direction, investigating the route ahead. Ryld and Pharaun pressed themselves against the wall, trying to remain out of sight. The wizard was no longer invisible, nor was he glowing with that annoying, flickering purple hue. Ryld had taken care of that with a pass of his enchanted blade. The warrior could see that his companion's skin was blistered, and he imagined that Pharaun was in considerable pain. His own wounds troubled him only when he thought about them.

Don't you have some sort of magic that can help us locate an exit? Ryld flashed to the wizard as they waited.

Pharaun shook his head.

Such spells exist, but I don't know them, he silently replied. *Without knowing the way, we could be down here forever. This is a fool's errand, Ryld.*

Then perhaps we should just follow the soldiers. They can unwittingly lead us out of here.

Pharaun waved away the warrior's suggestion, though whether it was in exasperation or acceptance, Ryld wasn't sure.

The risk of discovery or disaster is greater if we do that.

Ryld shrugged but gave no other reply. Instead, he turned to watch for Valas's return.

Why do I bother arguing? the weapons master thought as his listened for telltale sounds. *He's already made up his mind.*

Valas returned at that moment, gesturing for them to follow him. Together, they crept forward into a new corridor, and Valas pointed to a doorway on the opposite side.

That's a kitchen, he signaled, *and beyond it is a pantry. On the other side, here*—the scout pointed to a door near the trio—*is a mess hall. I think we're in the barracks section.*

Well, that's not a good place to be, Pharaun gestured. *We want to avoid the guards, not come bunk with them.*

Valas gave Pharaun a baleful look and motioned for the other two to follow him. *I think there's a stairwell leading up just past this area,* he flashed as he led the way through the passage.

Ryld thought they might actually get lucky and get through the guards' quarters unnoticed, but as they neared the opposite end of the passageway that bisected the barracks and the mess, they heard the approach of a large contingent from ahead of them. As one, the three drow turned to scamper back in the other direction, but at that moment several House Zauvirr soldiers appeared at the other end. They were pinned between the two forces.

"Damn!" Pharaun growled as he reached inside his *piwafwi.* "Hold them off while I see what I can do."

Nodding, Ryld slipped Splitter free and approached the group coming from where Valas had indicated stairs.

If we can cut through them, the warrior reasoned, *at least we can continue the way we want to go.*

The soldiers, numbering four, gave a shout of warning and unsheathed their weapons.

"Come on, you son of a drider," one of them snarled, stepping in with a long sword and a short sword together, one in each hand.

The other three fanned out, looking for a chance to flank the burly intruder. Ryld kept his blade level and loose, waiting and watching, shifting from foot to foot in hopes of preventing any of his foes from getting past him and to his back, or reaching Pharaun. He worried that his hands, still covered with drying blood, would be too slick to wield his blade properly.

The first opponent stepped in, slashing with his short sword up high, then bringing his long sword through in a sweep across Ryld's midsection. The weapons master ducked below the first slice and parried the lower blow with Splitter.

Try that again, and I'll have you down to two short swords, Ryld thought, watching to see if the other drow would fall into a pattern.

To his left, another of the soldiers was trying to scoot along the wall, obviously hoping he could squeeze past Ryld, but the Master of Melee-Magthere was keeping them all in his line of sight. He made a quick slash to the side, causing the soldier to flinch back. Ryld bounced back to the middle of the corridor, still watching the drow with two blades. The other two drow, both on Ryld's right, were waiting and watching.

Fine with me, Ryld thought, keeping his main attention on the one in front of him.

The drow changed tactics this time, stepping in with the long sword leading, and proceeded through a flurry of blows with only that weapon, watching how Ryld blocked them. When Ryld swung through a parry and counterattacked, the other warrior was ready, deflecting the stroke with the short sword. Unfortunately, the engagement allowed the drow on Ryld's left to finally shoot past him.

"Pharaun!" Ryld called, "watch out!"

He stepped away from the center of the hallway, angling backward to keep his opponents in his sight, and the weapons master could hear cries of pain and terror behind him. He hoped it was the other group of drow, and not his two companions. The male with two swords pressed in again, and this time Ryld was ready for him. When the first swipe from the short sword passed high, Ryld knew that the long sword would follow low. This time when the stroke approached Ryld cut sharply with his own blade, neatly slicing the long sword in half. The broken end skittered away with a clatter.

"Damn you, motherless rothé!" the other drow snarled, but he gasped in the next instant as Ryld's momentum spun the weapons master fully around in a circle and into him again.

His cut was quick and true, and the opponent dropped to the floor with a groan. Ryld didn't waste time watching him fall. He was already sidestepping the attack from the soldier who'd gotten behind him and who was trying to cut at him from the back. He took a short spear in the side of his leg for his troubles and growled in pain as he back-stepped from the attack, limping. He couldn't let himself get turned away from anyone, yet they were moving to do just that by surrounding him.

Appearing as if from nowhere, Valas caught the soldier with the long sword from behind, sliding an arm around his neck and planting one of his kukris into the fellow's back. Seeing the attack, Ryld quickly turned and parried several thrusts from the short spears. The final two drow had hoped to get in close and attack Ryld while his attention was focused on the opposite side, but they'd lost their chance.

Ryld stepped fully into the middle of the hallway again, wanting as much room as possible to use Splitter. When the two House Zauvirr soldiers saw that the odds were down to two to one and would quickly be even with Valas beside him, they faltered and began to back up.

A staccato series of glowing bluish-white missiles shot past Ryld, slamming into the two drow as they tried to turn and flee. A few of the magical streaks of light fizzled out as they reached their targets, but far more of them struck true, causing the two soldiers to shudder and convulse as they went sprawling to the floor. Ryld glanced back to see Pharaun holding a slender length of some darkly stained wood cut from a tree on the surface world.

The wizard nodded in satisfaction and tucked the wand away.

"We mustn't tarry," he said, "Everyone in the entire House probably heard that."

Curious, Ryld took another glance back past Pharaun to where the other contingent of drow had been. They were all dead, clutched in the grip of the black, shiny tentacles the mage sometimes summoned. The tentacles continued to squeeze and contract around the bodies of those unfortunate soldiers or flailed about blindly if they had nothing to grip.

Turning back, Ryld followed the other two past the dead drow and into the stairwell.

🕷 🕷 🕷

Halisstra stumbled and lost her balance as the deep rumble shook House Melarn. To either side of her, the guards who were "escorting" her into the audience chamber stumbled as well, losing their grips on the drow noble's arms as they flailed about, trying to regain their collective balance. All around Halisstra, shouts rose as drow began to mill about uncertainly in the confusion caused by the vibration, whatever it was. Stunned as much by the proceedings that had been taking place in her mother's House—her House now, Halisstra realized—as by the shock wave that tore through the place, Halisstra merely stood in place, dressed in only her underclothes and with her arms securely manacled behind her back, staring at the chaos around her.

When the liveried servant from House Nasadra ran into the room, announcing the fighting outside, Halisstra blinked in astonishment.

Duergar? Attacking House Melarn? Why in the Abyss would they—

A second blast rocked House Melarn and knocked Halisstra off her feet. Or rather, it would have if someone hadn't caught her from behind.

"On your feet . . . I've got to get you out of here."

It was Danifae, dressed for battle and looking remarkably like just another guard in a House Zauvirr *piwafwi*.

Halisstra struggled to right herself with Danifae's help, then turned to look at her battle captive. The servant was not normally permitted to arm and armor herself, but she was currently wearing her old chain shirt and buckler and had her morning star at her side. Halisstra wondered how Danifae had managed to get to her accoutrements, which had been locked away in Halisstra's rooms, but she wasn't going to take the time to complain just then.

Halisstra heard a shout from behind them, and she turned, expecting to see her original guards realizing she was free. Instead, she discovered that a thick mist had filled the room, and she could see very little beyond a couple of paces away.

"Come on," Halisstra hissed, scrambling through the mist toward the back of the room, to a doorway leading deeper into the House where her own chambers were located. "Back to my rooms, and you can get these—"she held her arms out away from her back to indicate the manacles—"off me."

"Of course, Mistress," Danifae said, steering her superior by one arm through the thick, obscuring mist, along the wall and toward the door. "We'll thank someone later for hiding our escape with this fog."

"You mean, that's not something you and Lirdnolu Maerret planned to help extricate me from Ssipriina Zauvirr?"

Danifae laughed once, a bitter chuckle.

"Hardly," she said. "Despite my convincing performance before Matron Mother Zauvirr, you didn't really expect her to let me wander free did you? I had no way to reach House Maerret. No, that commotion back there was someone else's doing."

Once the two of them were out of the audience chamber and into the hall, Halisstra could see better, and she set off regally toward her own chambers, despite the fact that she was half-naked and bound. She hadn't managed more than three or four steps before a third rumble staggered her. She gasped as she lost her balance and stumbled against one wall of the hallway, but Danifae was there, catching hold of her mistress and steadying her as the tremor quieted.

"What the blazes is going on?" Halisstra demanded as they righted themselves and hurried on their way.

"I don't know for sure, but I can hazard a guess," her subordinate replied as they turned a corner. "There are riots welling up in the streets."

"Perhaps," Halisstra said, "but why would duergar target House Melarn?"

"That, I can't say," Danifae replied, "but my guess is it has more to do with Ssipriina Zauvirr's attempt to overthrow House Melarn than anything else. Regardless, it served my purposes well enough. Perhaps we can find out more in a little bit, after we get you out of those restraints."

"Yes," Halisstra answered, thinking. "Let's start with finding out where in the Nine Hells all of our House guards are."

"I can tell you that right now," Danifae offered as the duo turned another corner and entered Halisstra's chambers. "They accepted an offer they couldn't refuse: serve House Zauvirr or die."

Halisstra sighed.

"Is there anyone still loyal to me?" she asked, though she feared she already knew the answer.

"Possibly your brother, if he's still alive, but he's at the Dangling Tower and can't do us much good here," Danifae said, turning Halisstra around so that she could take a look at the locking mechanism on the restraints. "As for inside the House right now? I doubt anyone would be willing to aid you, except maybe those three males in the audience chamber, the ones from Menzoberranzan, and only if you win their trust." The battle captive shook her head. "I can't get these off right now. Better to break the chain and worry about them later."

"Fine . . . but what do you mean, 'win their trust?' How could I do that?"

Halisstra began to pace, pondering her options. Though she had managed to escape the matron mothers for the moment, she was still trapped—inside her own House, of all places—and doubted it would take long for Ssipriina's guards to close in on the two of them.

Danifae didn't answer right away. Halisstra turned to repeat her question and saw the other dark elf grab the noble's mace from where it stood in the corner by her bed. She was momentarily startled when Danifae returned to her side and pushed her to her knees, but she quickly understood the battle captive's intent, and positioned her hands near the floor where Danifae could strike the chain while it was against the stone.

"You could start by telling them that their high priestess is still alive," Danifae finally answered, drawing the mace back for a hard blow against the chain joining the manacles.

"What?" Halisstra gasped, turning to look at her servant. "Quenthel Baenre is alive?"

For a brief moment she wondered if her mother had also survived.

Danifae held her downstroke at the last moment when her mistress moved.

"Hold still!" she commanded, repositioning Halisstra for another try. "And yes, the Baenre priestess is alive. I saw both her and her demon companion in the dungeons earlier. While I was prowling around, trying to figure out what to do, I saw that male Mistress Zauvirr called Zammzt hurrying from that direction."

Danifae smacked her morning star hard against the chain, but the links didn't break.

"A few moments later," she continued, "Faeryl Zauvirr appeared, also coming from the lower levels. Curious, I decided to see what she was doing down there. She has them both bound to within an inch of their lives, and Quenthel Baenre is stretched tight on the rack at the moment."

Danifae lined up another blow with the mace.

"Then Ssipriina is lying! I can free the high priestess and get her to prove my innocence."

Halisstra felt elation for the first time since the catastrophic day had begun.

"Possibly," the battle captive answered dryly, taking another whack at the restraints, "but I doubt many of the matron mothers will choose to believe her. She may still be guilty of her crimes, even if you are innocent of yours. Enough of the matron mothers have an agenda that precludes you walking free from this. More likely—*ah ha!*"

The link Danifae had been pounding on finally crimped enough to separate the manacles.

Helping Halisstra to her feet, the battle captive continued, "More likely, they'll simply accuse you of trying to help her escape and offering that as a cover story."

Halisstra eyed the steel restraints still on her wrists, already finding them annoying, but they would have to wait. Free, at least for the moment, Halisstra's fear melted away. She was furious, and she couldn't decide who bore the majority of her anger.

"Well, I'm not just going to sit here while everyone else brings down House Melarn around my ears. Help me get ready, and let's go find that Baenre."

"As you wish," Danifae said, moving rapidly with the decision having been made.

With her servant's help, Halisstra quickly began to dress, first attiring herself in a set of plain but functional clothes, then donning her armor, a fine suit of chain mail bearing the coat of arms of House Melarn and several enchantments. Once that was on, Danifae handed Halisstra her mace and shield and scurried about the room to gather up other things Halisstra normally had with her when out in the city or beyond.

When Halisstra was dressed, Danifae grabbed her morning star, each of them wrapped themselves in a *piwafwi* marked with the insignia of House Zauvirr, and they were ready.

Outside Halisstra's rooms, the halls were quiet. No one had yet been sent to hunt for her, it appeared, for which the priestess was silently thankful. Once away from her private quarters, Halisstra began to breathe a little easier. No one would question two House guards moving through the halls.

That's when the two of them came around a bend in the hallway and spied three strange drow, two of them bruised and bleeding, creeping through the gloom. They were definitely not members of the household, but it took Halisstra another moment or two before she realized they were the three Menzoberranyr.

"Damn," one of them said, reaching inside his *piwafwi* as the other two brandished weapons and advanced warily.

Chapter

TWELVE

Matron Mother Zauvirr wasn't merely angry. Angry was for subordinates who knew to hold their tongues in the presence of their superiors despite their feelings. Angry was for those times when you had to slap a child because it didn't know any better. No, angry wasn't nearly strong enough a word to describe what Ssipriina was feeling. Someone was going to pay for this foolishness. Someone was going to *die*.

She stormed through the hallways of her own House Zauvirr, having slipped out of Drisinil's manor during the confusion and magically transported herself back home. There was something she wanted to get, something she needed, though she hadn't expected to, when the day started. She almost hoped that someone would cross her path as she marched along, that someone would make the mistake of accosting her, of interrupting her train of thought for some idiotic and perfectly pointless reason. She really hoped they would . . . it would be fun, in a distracting sort of way, to watch some hapless male bleed out as she ripped him up. She was furious enough to do it with her bare hands.

A guard would do nicely, she thought. Any foolish boy who even looks at me.

All of her planning, wasted. All of the careful manipulation, the bribes, the theft, the smuggling of valuables and troops, even the fortuitous arrival of the damnable Menzoberranyr and her clever scheme to fit them into the plan was for naught. Someone had blundered, and she would have his head.

I had them in the palm of my hand, Ssipriina thought. They were ready to anoint me. Even after that ridiculous story the wizard made up.

That obvious attempt to derail her plans wouldn't have stopped her. No one would have believed him, even after her foolish daughter reacted. Ssipriina thought Faeryl had sounded like the petulant child that she still was.

I should never have brought her in on this.

Ssipriina realized her mind was wandering. It was the fury, keeping her from thinking straight.

Faeryl I can deal with later. There's nothing to be done except to fight and win, but it would have been so much easier if the gray dwarves had remained out of sight. Who told them to move out?

As the matron mother arrived at her rooms, she decided that ferreting out the guilty party would also have to wait until later. Her full attention was needed elsewhere. She was about to spring something on the entire city. Something very special. Ssipriina grinned when she imagined it.

Faeryl stumbled and fell against the corridor wall when House Melarn first began to shake.

The servants were screaming, and from somewhere she heard, "Mistresses! It's duergar! Hundreds of them, surrounding us . . . they're attacking!"

A second shock wave rumbled through the House.

"They burn the stones themselves, Mothers. The city is burning!"

With a sinking feeling, Faeryl knew it for the truth. She had lived through this experience before, though it had been in the bowels of House Baenre, chained to a column. Even so, she remembered the rumbles from above, felt the vibrations in the ground. When she had been freed by Triel Baenre and invited to join the mission to Ched Nasad, she had gotten all the details of the insurrection in the streets of Menzoberranzan from others. Their descriptions of the jugs of fire, the fire that burned stone itself, were vivid. She could only imagine what it would feel like on a web street of Ched Nasad.

Faeryl groaned. Her mother's plan was falling apart. The duergar weren't supposed to appear unless the negotiations with the other matron mothers went badly. Despite that idiot Pharaun's asinine claim of her involvement in the conspiracy, the situation was far from out of hand.

Mother pulled the trigger too soon, the ambassador decided. She must have gotten cold feet and didn't bother to tell me. How typical.

Shaking her head, Faeryl scrambled up to her feet again as the room was enveloped in a thick, murky fog. She knew who was most likely behind it. As much as she wanted to slice Pharaun into a thousand tiny pieces, there was too much confusion.

Besides, the ambassador grudgingly admitted, he and his boys are not to be trifled with. I'll let mother's wizards take care of them. I've got to get rid of Quenthel and that loathsome beast.

Faeryl felt her way along the wall, stumbling as yet another blast rocked House Melarn. The mist cleared, and she could hear the sounds of combat on the far side of the room. She resisted the temptation to look, as much as she hoped to catch a glimpse of the wizard's demise. Instead, she managed to make her way to a door just as several dozen House soldiers came in, jostling her aside in their efforts to defend the audience chamber.

"Fools!" Faeryl hissed at them.

Almost shaking with rage, she departed the audience chamber and hurried toward the lower levels. She passed few other drow in the corridors, all of them looking confused. None of them seemed to know the origin of the disturbances, and at one point the ambassador overheard at least three priestesses discussing an earthquake as they passed her, going the opposite direction.

Faeryl didn't care to explain to them what was really happening. It was not her House. Turning a final corner, the ambassador hurried into the torture chamber where she had left Quenthel and Jeggred. They were not there. The room was not empty, however. One of the House torturemasters was methodically straightening tools that had been upset with the booming thumps from outside.

"Where are they?" Faeryl demanded, gesturing to the rack where Quenthel had been restrained.

The torturemaster turned and looked at her vacantly, not understanding.

Growling in exasperation, the ambassador repeated herself.

The other drow looked at her, then comprehension lit his features. "Oh, they're not here," he said.

Faeryl rolled her eyes and said, "I can see that, you foolish boy. Where *are* they?"

"That ugly drow, Zammzt, ordered them taken to a cell," the torturemaster replied. "I saw to it personally."

Another severe blast rocked the room, and tools were scattered everywhere. Faeryl managed to grab hold of the column where Jeggred had been chained for support, but the other drow was not so lucky. He went down in a pile—and even more unfortunately, one of the many braziers of hot coals tipped over onto him, showering him with burning cinders. Screaming, the drow scrambled away from the embers, but he was already a conflagration, his clothes ignited and smoking as he flailed helplessly about.

Faeryl bit her lip in irritation.

Now, why do you suppose he would have moved them, and to where? she thought, turning to leave.

She decided she'd have to ask someone to show her, and she departed.

Pharaun faltered for only a moment at the sight of the two drow priestesses before him. One, quite simply, was beautiful. The other, while lacking the graceful curves and fluid motion of the first, was obviously nobly born and not unpleasant to look at, either. Then, getting a closer look, the wizard recognized her. She was the drow who had been in chains in the audience chamber only moments before. In fact, he realized, she still wore the manacles she'd been shackled with, though the connecting chain between them had been severed. Neither of the females looked happy to see him, Ryld, or Valas.

"Damn," Pharaun muttered, returning to his senses.

He reached inside his *piwafwi,* fumbling quickly for the wand he'd used to dispatch the drow soldiers not too long before. In front of him, Ryld went on guard, raising Splitter into an aggressive position as he advanced warily. Valas slipped to the opposite side of the hallway, automatically fanning out with Ryld to come at the adversaries from either flank.

The lovely creature who'd first caught the mage's eye hissed in vexation and brought a morning star out in front of her. She had a buckler on her other arm held to the side where Valas was closing.

"It's them!" she snarled, taking up a position in front of the other drow as though to defend her.

Both dark elves seemed quite capable of taking care of themselves, and Pharaun noted the finely tooled chain mail each of them wore. The one to the rear actually sported the House Melarn insignia on hers, and the wizard guessed she must be one of the dead matron mother's daughters.

Pharaun had his wand out, but before he could invoke the trigger words to use the thing, Ryld stepped in and launched a short series of strikes at the dark elf in front of him, who managed with some difficulty to parry the attacks with both her weapon and her buckler. The Master of Sorcere knew that Ryld was not really pressing his attack yet. The weapons master was attempting to size up the skill of his competition with a few well-placed feints before closing in to finish the job efficiently.

Valas continued to creep in from her other side, and she backstepped more than once to prevent the scout from getting behind her. Pharaun aimed the wand and prepared to recite the activation phrase, when the other drow, the daughter of House Melarn, spoke up, causing him to falter.

"Hold, Danifae."

The drow in front retreated another couple steps, but she did not drop her guard.

"We have no quarrel with you," the still-unnamed Melarn said. "I know you don't have reason to trust us, but we're not the enemy. . . . They are."

She gestured upward, to the floors above.

Ryld took a threatening step forward then he too stopped and held his guard. Valas was watching both sides with glittering eyes, kukris at the ready.

"How convenient," Pharaun said, smiling coldly. "The imperiled daughter, implicated in her mother's treason and with no friends, making a peace offering. At least until we let down our guard, right? Then you turn us over to Matron Mother Zauvirr, claim you captured us, and hope she lets you off the hook."

"I could easily say the same about you, but I won't," the Melarn daughter replied. Without taking her eyes off Pharaun, she added, "Danifae, I said stand down!"

Pharaun raised an eyebrow at her tone of command. Danifae nodded in acquiescence, stepping farther back until she was side by side with her mistress.

"Well, you're right about that," Pharaun said. "We don't have any reason to believe you. If you're on the outs with Mistress Zauvirr, what are you doing down here, all decked out in your finest armor?"

"We're trying to save our own skins," the daughter said, a bit more testily than Pharaun thought necessary, considering she was trying to broker some sort of truce, albeit temporary. "I think we both might have been played by Ssipriina Zauvirr. If you come with us, help us, we might be able to get you information that will help prove it."

"Lower your weapons to the ground," Ryld said, "and we'll consider listening to you."

"I think not," the daughter countered. "At least, not until we have some assurances that you won't attack us the moment we do. I don't know for sure that you *weren't* in league with my mother."

Ryld snarled, raising Splitter and advancing again. Valas was doing likewise, still looking to maneuver around to the priestesses' left side.

"Ryld, Valas, wait," Pharaun called out quietly.

He had no doubt that the two warriors could dispatch the drow females with relatively little difficulty, as long as the wizard was backing them up with a careful selection of spells, but he was intrigued. Ryld cast a quick glance back over his shoulder at the wizard then shrugged and held his ground.

"I can assure you that we have never met your mother and had no dealings with her, ever. That wild tale in the audience chamber above was merely a contrivance to stall for time—ruffle everyone's feathers, so to speak. You seem to know who we are," Pharaun said, addressing the daughter of House Melarn, "but we are at a disadvantage. Who are you, and what is this information you are planning to use to buy our trust?"

In a flash of bluish light, Valas was stepping through a dimensional doorway, and as the one named Danifae turned to face the point where the scout had been standing only a split-second earlier, the Bregan D'aerthe scout was behind her, one hand gripping her wrist tightly where she held her morning star, the other hand holding a kukri at the line where her jawbone faded into her graceful neck. Though she was several inches taller than the scout, Valas was easily able to keep her overbalanced by shifting his hip under hers and levering her up off her feet.

Danifae's eyes bulged wide as she realized she'd been outmaneuvered, and she flailed about helplessly for a second or two until she grasped that the blade was at her neck, at which point she froze.

"Lay them down," Ryld said to both drow females, gesturing to their weapons with his greatsword. "To the floor, nice and quietly."

The Melarn daughter gasped in surprise at Valas's maneuver, narrowed her eyes, and took half a step toward her companion. When she realized she was outmatched, she sighed and settled her mace to the floor at her feet. Danifae sagged a bit in Valas's grasp and relinquished her weapon to the other female, who set that down as well.

"Excellent!" Pharaun said as Ryld kicked the two weapons safely away. "That wasn't so bad, now was it?"

"You could have trusted us," the daughter spat. "We gave you no reason not to."

Pharaun laughed out loud. Ryld stifled a chuckle of his own, and Valas, who released Danifae but kept his kukri carefully placed in the small of her back, was grinning behind her.

"You are a dark elf," the wizard said finally, regaining his composure. "That alone is enough for me not to trust you, but beyond that, if you think we're going to trust anyone in this cursed city, you're the biggest fool I've met in a while. Yet, I am not completely uninterested in negotiating, so you may still get a chance to redeem yourself. You can start by answering my questions. Who are you, and what is the nature of this information?"

The Melarn daughter grimaced but finally answered, "I am Halisstra Melarn, as you have surmised by now, I'm sure. This is Danifae, my personal servant. What I meant was, your friend the high priestess and her demon companion aren't dead."

Pharaun felt his eyes bulge at this revelation. He heard both Ryld and Valas breathe in sharply.

"Really," the mage said, trying to sound offhand as he regained his composure, "and how would you know that?"

"Because I've seen them," Danifae, still locked in Valas's grip, answered.

"Apparently," Halisstra said, "Ssipriina Zauvirr simply told everyone that the priestess was dead so that there would be no demands for her side of the story. They probably *should* have killed them, but I guess Faeryl had other plans for her."

At the mention of the ambassador, Pharaun tilted his head.

"You know Faeryl Zauvirr?" he asked.

"Yes," Halisstra replied, "I know her. We grew up together. Since our Houses have—or rather, *had*—a business relationship, her mother and mine spent quite a bit of time together. She might very well be with the Baenre priestess right now. I suspect she's torturing them both."

"Is that so?" Pharaun asked.

Ryld, who still had his greatsword trained on the two females, snorted, "Why does that not surprise me?"

"I wonder how the esteemed high priestess managed to get herself caught in the first place?" Pharaun pondered aloud.

"It was an ambush," Halisstra said. "When they were at a Black Claw Mercantile storehouse. Faeryl was in on it, I guess. Her mother met them there with a host of guards who subdued the high priestess and the demon that was with them. They claim they had to kill my mother, who was trying to escape, though now I wonder if she truly is dead."

"Well now," Pharaun said, even more intrigued than before, "some things are beginning to make more sense. Now I know why Faeryl was being so agreeable during the trip here. She wanted Quenthel to go to the storehouse. It was their plan to take Quenthel all along."

"Not just Quenthel, but all of you," said Halisstra. "I'm guessing she intended to capture all of you at once, but when you didn't appear at the storehouse with the others she had to amend her plan. She'd be quite pleased, I'm sure, if you were all dead."

"Yes," the mage said wryly, "we were informed of that very fact not an hour ago. Needless to say, we weren't too keen on the idea, ourselves."

"So where's Mistress Baenre?" Ryld demanded. "We're going to find her and leave. You can help us or join everyone else who's gotten in our way thus far."

Halisstra looked appraisingly at the warrior.

"What is it you expect to accomplish by finding her?" she asked.

"We're going to get her out of here, and we're going to go find—"

"Weapons Master Argith," Pharaun interrupted, pulling the warrior to the side where they could talk privately. "I'm not sure that's really the wisest course of action. We need to get out of here before the whole House falls down, don't you agree?"

"And leave the Mistress of the Academy here?" Ryld countered. "We should try to find her."

Pharaun looked questioningly at his companion and asked, "Why in the Underdark would we do that?"

Ryld's eyes flashed in anger.

"You may be eager to be rid of her, wizard," he said, "but I am not."

"Oh?" Pharaun replied, growing hot himself. "If I didn't know better, I would think you were sweet on the high priestess. Have you forgotten so soon her disdain for you?"

"Whatever your own ambitions are, I still serve the task I was given by Matron Mother Baenre and the rest of the High Council. Quenthel still plays a large part in that, and I have no desire to betray Menzoberranzan herself to suit my own personal vendettas."

Another shock wave tore through House Melarn, and Pharaun was forced to rise into the air to keep his balance.

"Can we argue about this later?" Valas interjected, still gripping Danifae as the two of them tried to maintain their balance. "I agree with Ryld, at least for the moment. We may yet need Quenthel, who is still our best connection to the Dark Mother, and the only one who can tell us if we're succeeding in reconnecting with Lolth. If we do find Tzirik, it may behoove us to have her there."

Pharaun sighed, chagrinned that he had raised his voice enough to be overheard.

"Very well," he said. "We will attempt to find her before we depart, but remember what I said. If the House falls down around our ears, I will personally blame both of you."

He smiled, hoping a little levity would ease the tensions. Ryld still scowled but nodded curtly once the decision was made.

Another rumbling shock wave rocked House Melarn and forced everyone to shift their feet in order to keep their balance. Halisstra looked around with no small level of concern in her eyes.

"If you want to find your high priestess, then let me take you to her," she said. "Danifae and I have no quarrel with you, as I admitted before, and everything I've told you thus far is the truth. We have no allies here, and neither do you. Joining together could be mutually beneficial."

"All right," Pharaun said. "We'll suppose for the moment that we're going to trust you to take us to her. It will make our chances of getting out of here in one piece markedly better, but just to make certain you don't consider trying anything, shall we say, troublesome, I think Danifae here will accompany us with her arms bound behind her. Valas and I will keep a good eye on her while you and Ryld keep to the front."

Danifae's eyes widened the slightest bit in protest at the suggestion, but Halisstra nodded after only a moment's consideration.

"Very well," she agreed. "We'll do it your way—for now. First, you must do something for me. You must answer a question, if you can. What is the state of things out on the streets? I have not had a chance to find out for myself since the shock waves began."

Pharaun shrugged helplessly.

"I fear I cannot tell you with any degree of accuracy," he said. "You were in the audience chamber when the attacks began and heard the warning cry. These duergar appear to be organized, though. My suspicion is that someone else, someone powerful, is behind them."

Halisstra looked sharply at the wizard and asked, "What gives you that impression?"

"The blasts we're feeling are due to incendiary alchemy. We encountered similar destruction back home recently. Whoever is supplying the duergar with them may be associated with the forces we dealt with in Menzoberranzan, and I will warn you now, the stone does indeed burn. We will be at risk as long as we remain inside your House."

Halisstra looked fearful, but she nodded in thanks.

"Then the sooner I can get you what you want, the sooner we can get outside and find out for sure. Danifae, I want you to comply with their instructions. Do you understand me?"

With a small sigh, the other drow female nodded.

"Yes, Mistress," she answered then moved over so that Valas could use a length of cord to bind her hands securely behind her back.

"Wonderful. It's nice to see how we're all getting along so well together," Pharaun said. "Now, Halisstra Melarn, why don't you lead the way?"

"Before I do, allow me to help you in a more immediate way. Let me heal your injuries."

Pharaun glanced over at Ryld, who subtly shook his head, frowning. Shrugging, the wizard decided to ignore his companion's concerns. His face hurt where the acid had burned him.

"All right," he answered, "you can tend to me. But if this is a trick, my two compatriots here will see to it that it never happens again."

"I understand," Halisstra said. "I'm just going to pull a wand out, so please don't get jumpy, all right?"

Pharaun nodded and waited as the daughter of Drisinil Melarn produced the wand and utilized it. The mage immediately felt the effects of the divine magic and breathed a sigh of relief.

"Thank you," he said.

Quickly enough, Halisstra similarly healed both Ryld and Valas.

"There . . . you see?" she said, tucking the wand away again. "We really are on your side."

"Indeed," Pharaun replied noncommittally. "We'll just develop the trust slowly, I think. If you please?" he said, gesturing down the hallway.

Halisstra eyed the wizard for a moment, as if assessing whether or not she was making a mistake, then turned and set off down the corridor. Ryld walked close by her side, Splitter hovering protectively close to her.

Aliisza was not certain exactly when the battle outside the noble House had gotten so out of hand, but it was clearly becoming a major engagement, drawing the attention of the entire city.

Sitting on the edge of a building that hung off the side of a web street several street levels above the raging combat, her feet dangling off into space, she watched anxiously as yet another wave of goblins and kobolds crashed into the ranks of duergar positioned around the spacious structure.

The alu wasn't sure why she felt worry over the outcome of the clash. Oh, she understood well enough that she actually felt concern for Pharaun's well-being. She just didn't understand why she did. She wouldn't have imagined that she would care at all for the drow, and indeed her feelings were nothing close to true affection. Still, she found him clever and amusing, and she had enjoyed her time with him earlier in the day.

I guess I'm just not through with him, she decided.

So she waited and watched, wondering if he was going to get out alive. She knew he might have managed to transport himself and his two companions someplace else by means of an extradimensional doorway or similar magic. That was the most likely possibility, actually, and she doubted he was still inside. For some reason, though, she felt compelled to stay and watch. Something in the back of her mind told her that the wizard was still there.

At least the battle is interesting, Aliisza mused.

The gray dwarves had soundly defeated the initial force of drow, pinning the dark elves between the two lines of attackers like steel caught between hammer and anvil. The dark elves were flattened and slaughtered in a matter of moments. Some lucky few had managed to get inside the front door of the manse, but the duergar were in the process of battering that down. Aliisza doubted the portal would hold much longer.

Beyond the walls of the estate, more drow marched to relieve the siege or perhaps to gain their fair share of the spoils. Arriving quickly, driving slave troops before them, the new force was larger than the duergar's, and the gray dwarves found their position reversed, defending the house rather than attacking it. Though the goblins and kobolds outnumbered the duergar by a substantial ratio, they were no match for the gray dwarves' battle tactics and incendiary pots. Three times, the drow had forced their army of lesser beings to assault the walls, and three times they had been repulsed, suffering heavy casualties.

Aliisza understood the tactic all too well, though. The duergar were forced to expend magic to defend themselves, and the drow were happy to sacrifice their shock troops in exchange for draining the gray dwarves' reserves of magic. They were only slaves, after all. A few more waves, and perhaps the duergar would begin to break.

The only problem, Aliisza realized, was that the duergar had utilized such a large quantity of the incendiary clay pots that most of the plaza was burning. The air was getting thick with smoke, and the drow were forced to stay back from the spreading conflagration. In several places, the palatial house was burning too, and Aliisza wondered how much damage the building could sustain before it began to break apart. Though she knew the stone-shaping forces used to build the city had made the web streets and their attached structures as strong as steel, the abode was still precariously perched. If enough of the stone burned, the whole house might break away.

That would be a sight to see.

Aliisza spotted a commotion down a side street, not far from the plaza where the bulk of the fighting had been taking place. There were a handful of drow there, but little else. The alu supposed they might have been a scouting or screening force.

The fiend decided to move in for a closer look. She stepped over the side of the roof and dropped down to another, two levels below, magically slowing her descent. She crouched low as a half-giant passed, not wanting to distract the creature.

The half-giant strode along the wide street, its war axe held loosely in its hand. The blade of the weapon was slick with blood, dripping a trail behind it as it moved. The air was thick with smoke.

A gang of dark elves, soldiers led by priestesses and wizards, poured into the street in the distance, organized and grim, seeking to stop the half-giant. Before they could take three steps in the direction of their quarry, a huge chunk of something crashed to the street between them. The weight of it shook the street, and the sound it made was like a thousand blades striking a thousand shields. It made the half-giant nearly fall, and it had to drop to one knee before it completely lost its balance.

Aliisza peered through the smoke to see what had landed atop the web street. It was nothing but a smoking pile of rock, but the fiend could tell that it had been a part of the street overhead. Actually, it looked like part of the street and a couple of buildings. The whole pile of rubble was ablaze, thick plumes of smoke pouring off it. She looked up, wondering where the chunk of the city had come from.

Even through the smoky haze, Aliisza could see a thoroughfare above them, crossing at an angle, connecting to the besieged House. A large chunk of the road was missing, as if a huge bite had been taken out of the immense spiderweb strand. Flames still licked the stone of the causeway where it had broken off, bringing a small part of the House with it. The rest of the immense structure still sat where it had, but Aliisza realized that more of it could go at any moment. The alu saw how dangerous it was to be down there, below the burning stone.

The half-giant must have sensed this too, for it turned to move back along the street, retracing its steps. That's when a second drow patrol came into view. It was a small group, no more than five or six, but their leader was a wizard, and he had a wand in his hand. The wizard gestured with the wand and a crackling bolt of electricity shot out of the end of it, catching the half-giant square in the chest. The creature howled in pain as its hair burned away. It nearly dropped its war axe, and even after the attack was over, Aliisza saw that the beast couldn't work its fingers right for a moment. The dark elves swarmed toward it, crossbows and swords out and ready.

The half-giant wasn't so easily felled. Aliisza watched, fascinated, as the towering humanoid fumbled in its hip pouch and pulled out a handful of clay jugs. From one knee, it threw them in the direction of the charging drow. Miraculously, its aim was very good, and almost all of the containers flew toward the dark elves, who shied away when they saw what was coming. The jugs shattered on the street and burst into flame, sending a wall of fire and smoke skyward in a blast that Aliisza could feel on her face.

By the Abyss, Aliisza breathed, unable to tear her gaze away from this wonderful display of destruction.

Drow leaped clear of the attack and scrambled to get away from the conflagration, which charred the street in seconds. A couple of the dark elves managed to escape to the half-giant's side of the fire. Realizing they were pinned between the half-giant and the blaze, they looked for some avenue of escape, eyeing the huge beast warily.

Lumbering to its feet again, the half-giant began striding purposefully toward them, gripping its war axe with both hands. Almost as one, the drow turned and fled to the side of the street, leaping over the edge and drifting downward into the smoky vastness below.

At almost the same moment, the street shifted, tilting sideways, and the half-giant stumbled toward the edge. Aliisza watched as the massive humanoid looked around wildly, trying to find out why its footing had grown precarious so suddenly. She saw, too, that the fire it had started with its incendiary pots had already burned through a significant portion of the calcified webbing that was the street, and it was coming apart. The other end had already been weakened by the impact from the rubble, and a whole section of thorough-fare shifted and groaned. The alu knew it wouldn't remain together for much longer.

Amazingly, the half-giant ran toward the fire, taking great, lumbering strides that shook the crumbling roadway and caused chunks of it to fall away from the fiery crack. As the entire path shuddered and snapped free, tipping downward, hinged where the pile of slag had dropped on it earlier, the creature leaped, crossing the distance, passing through the roiling flames. Aliisza's mouth dropped in amazement. The half-giant cleared the flames, reaching the other side, landing with a mammoth *thump* that made the projecting end of the street that was still intact quiver and bounce.

Behind the half-giant, the falling piece of street went tumbling down into the darkness below, eventually landing somewhere with a thunderous boom. Ahead of the towering humanoid, three drow stood staring at the hulking creature, mouths agape. Even from her vantage point, Aliisza could see that the half-giant smiled as it advanced. It raised its war axe and plodded forward. The wizard panicked and turned to flee, leaving only two soldiers to face the creature. Surprisingly, they turned as one to meet the advancing half-giant. One of the two took a tentative step forward, measuring where and how he would attack, when he was shoved hard from behind by his companion, who turned and retreated.

The first drow stumbled, off-balance, right into the path of the half-giant. Aliisza smirked. The fleeing dark elf was sacrificing his partner so that he could escape.

Raising its war axe, the half-giant prepared to cleave the sprawled male in half. Desperately, the dark elf raised his long sword and rammed it into the half-giant's stomach.

The creature roared, arching its back, and its downward swing went awry, biting through the drow's arm instead of his torso. The dark elf screamed as the half-giant fell forward, collapsing on him and driving the sword deeper into itself.

The soldier had dealt the killing blow, Aliisza realized, as the half-giant lay on top of him, unmoving. The boy cried out in pain. He was trapped, pinned beneath the half-giant's weight and with only one good arm to try to free himself.

"Ilphrim! Ilphrim, help me!" the drow cried out, but Ilphrim was long gone, and the fire burned closer.

Aliisza sighed. The battle had been particularly entertaining, but it appeared to be over, though the wounded drow pinned beneath the half-giant still squirmed occasionally. She considered his companion's treachery, pushing him into the path of the rampaging half-giant, to be very clever. She laughed quietly.

The trapped and dying drow moved his arm again, futilely trying to shift the weight of the half-giant off himself so he could wriggle free, but Aliisza knew he would never do it, not with only one arm.

In a sudden and very uncharacteristic act of compassion, the alu-fiend leaped off her perch and floated down to where the dark elf lay feebly squirming. The drow spotted her and tensed, eyeing her warily. She only smiled and nudged a discarded dagger a bit closer to him, so that it was within reach of his free hand. Stepping back, she waited and watched to see if he would do the right thing.

The drow contemplated her for a moment, then he seemed to nod in understanding. He took hold of the dagger and saluted Aliisza with it before he started cutting pieces off the half-giant's corpse. It was going to take a while, and it was already messy, but he might just cut his way free before the web street collapsed.

Smiling in satisfaction, Aliisza turned away and headed back up to her original vantage point, worrying anew over Pharaun's fate.

The five drow worked their way into the bowels of House Melarn for what seemed like hours, though Pharaun was fairly certain they'd only been at it for about fifteen minutes. On several occasions, the group was forced to stop while a member of the House guard crossed paths with them, and once, Halisstra actually posed as a member of House Zauvirr, issuing orders to a group of sentries to head to the surface to help in the defense of the House.

"The lower levels are not usually very heavily occupied," Halisstra said at one point. "I suspect most of Ssipriina's servants and troops are above, aiding in the defense of the House. It's not much farther, now."

The mage nodded as the five of them continued on their way. More than once, Pharaun caught himself gazing in infatuation at the gorgeous creature beside him. She seemed to be considerably unhappy at the state of things, especially the fact that she was helpless to defend herself with her arms bound as they were, but she kept her gaze cast demurely down, and the wizard only found this to be even more endearing.

The group took one last stairwell down and found themselves in a dismal cell block. The hall was undecorated, unlike the posh elegance of the levels above, and the stale stench of unwashed bodies, faint though it was, gave a certain hint of what was to be found there. Halisstra led the five of them to a doorway at the end of a short hall. It was stout and obviously designed to withstand considerable force.

The drow priestess stepped up to the portal and waved her House Melarn brooch before it. There was an audible click as the magic of the insignia operated the locks set into the door. Halisstra pushed the door aside and moved through into the chamber beyond, which appeared to be a guard room, currently empty. At the far side of the chamber, a hallway stretched off into darkness.

Pharaun, spotting movement in the corridor there, put a finger to his lips and motioned for quiet.

Someone is there. Be alert—and no noise, he signed, pointing to both Halisstra and Danifae.

The two drow females nodded, and Pharaun gestured for Halisstra to proceed. As she entered the hallway, the others followed her in. The majority of the cells were empty, their doors standing open and the chambers within dark and silent. However, about halfway down, Pharaun could detect the low voice of someone speaking. It emanated from one of the cells on his right, and he could just see the door being swung shut from inside.

Moving as quietly as they could, the five of them closed the gap to the doorway. The portal was not completely sealed, and Pharaun was able to peer inside the cell. Quenthel was there, naked and crouched against the far wall. A heavy steel collar was around her neck, with a thick chain running from it to a bolt set into the stone of the wall. The high priestess was gagged with some sort of thick bit that was wedged tightly in her mouth, and her arms were obviously incapacitated, stuck together in some sort of thick, viscous black blob in front of her. She had been very effectively immobilized, and Pharaun understood all too well, completely prohibited from casting, should she

still have a divine enchantment locked away after all this time without contact with Lolth.

To one side, against another wall of the cell, Jeggred stood
glowering. He too was chained to the wall, thick bands of adamantine encasing his neck, arms, and legs. Pharaun could see that the
restraints were magically strengthened, but even so, the draegloth
strained against them, refusing to admit even for a moment that he
was not going to break free. Again and again, Jeggred jerked on the
chains, causing them to rattle against the wall as he tried to lunge
at the object of his wrath.

Faeryl Zauvirr stood just a little way out of the draegloth's reach,
her back to Pharaun and Halisstra. She was standing over Quenthel
in the middle of a scathing taunt.

". . . know you would have loved to tell the matron mothers the
truth, but it's too late for that now. I only regret that we didn't have
more time spend together, Quenthel."

Her voice dripped with acid.

"Come a little closer, Faeryl," Jeggred said, his deep voice flat with
malice. "Let me caress you like before, in the underhalls of the Great
Mound. Don't you want to feel my kiss again?"

Faeryl shuddered but ignored the draegloth, instead pulling a
dagger from her belt.

Halisstra tapped Pharaun softly on the arm.

Let me lure her out here, the Melarn daughter signed.

Pharaun nodded and stepped back, out of sight. Ryld pulled Danifae against the wall next to the wizard, while Valas took up a position
on the opposite side of the door.

"Still, it's going to be fun watching you both die," the wizard
heard Faeryl say.

"I'm afraid we have other plans for her, Faeryl," Halisstra said,
pushing the door open.

The ambassador hissed in anger.

"What are you doing here?" she snarled. "You should be dead!"

Then, apparently realizing that Halisstra had discovered her secret,
Faeryl's tone changed.

"You don't really think I'm going to let you walk out of here alive, do you? To run and tell the others what you found? I don't think so."

Halisstra's tone was equally cold.

"On the contrary. You don't think I came down here alone, did you? Danifae!" the Melarn daughter called out, back over her shoulder. "It's true. Run, and tell them what we found."

"I think not," Faeryl said, appearing in the hallway as though she had leaped past the priestess. "You're not going to tell . . ."

The words died in Faeryl's mouth as she spotted Pharaun, Ryld, and Danifae leaning against the wall.

"You!" she spat. "Halisstra, you cast your lot with *them?* You're a bigger fool than I thought."

The look in Faeryl's eyes was decidedly nervous, and her fear only grew as she felt Valas step in behind her and take hold of her arm. The point of the scout's kukri settled against the hollow of her throat.

Pharaun reached out and held out his hand, waiting for Faeryl to relinquish her dagger to him. Eyeing any possible avenue of escape, she appeared ready to bolt but realized she had no chance against so many. She relinquished the dagger, flipping the handle around and laying the weapon in the wizard's palm.

"Perhaps I am a fool," Halisstra said, "but at least I have them as allies, which is more than I can say for you. Did you enjoy your little game of lies? I hope it was worth it. I think it will be the last thing you enjoy. Ever."

"Watch her," the mage said to Valas as he stepped into the cell, Halisstra close behind.

It was obvious from the relieved look in Quenthel's eyes that she was glad to see him. Pharaun only smiled as he uttered a magical phrase. The collar around Quenthel's neck clicked open.

"Help her," he directed to Halisstra.

Pharaun then moved over to Jeggred, whose red, feral eyes glittered in anticipation.

"Your arrival was timely, wizard," the draegloth said, spreading his arms wide. "Free me so that I may rend the traitor and watch the life fade from her eyes."

"You will do no such thing," Quenthel said. Halisstra had helped the high priestess remove the gag. "Do not touch her, Jeggred. Do you understand me?"

Jeggred looked at Quenthel for a moment, but then the demon inclined his head in acquiescence.

"As you wish and command, Mistress."

Pharaun had but one more spell with which to unlock the restraints that held Jeggred, and he quickly utilized it to free one of the draegloth's arms. For the other bindings, the mage decided to cast a different spell, one that would suppress the magic that strengthened the adamantine. He quickly wove the dispelling magic and watched as the aura surrounding the metal faded from his sight.

"Try to break it, now," he said to Jeggred.

The draegloth jerked experimentally on the chains holding him to the walls, then he really leaned into the effort, but the adamantine links still would not yield.

Pharaun frowned.

"Perhaps a bit of cold, to make them brittle," he mused aloud, producing a small, clear crystal from his *piwafwi*. "Gather the lengths together in a group," he directed the draegloth. Jeggred did so, holding them in his free hand like a set of reins on a pack lizard.

Pointing the crystal at the sections of chain, the Master of Sorcere focused a cone of magically summoned arctic air along their lengths. When the incantation was completed, he gestured for Jeggred to try again.

This time, when the fiend began to work the restraints over, the frosty metal shattered, freeing him. He still had the collar and manacles around his neck and limbs, but that could be dealt with later.

"My thanks, wizard," the draegloth said, then strode over to where Quenthel was in the process of freeing herself from the last of the black, sticky, resinlike substance that her hands had been encased in.

Quenthel stood in the center of the cell, naked but seemingly oblivious to it.

"Do you make a habit of remaining maddeningly out of reach until the last possible moment, Mizzrym?" she said, scowling slightly. "You cut your arrival a bit close, didn't you?"

Pharaun sighed inwardly, realizing that whatever gratitude had been present before had been replaced by the high priestess's usual haughty demeanor.

"My pardon, please, Mistress Baenre," he said in as gracious a tone as possible. "We dallied with some of the local maidens as long as we could before rushing here at the last moment. I didn't think you would mind terribly much."

Ryld chuckled at the wizard's snide remark, while both Halisstra and Danifae gave him sharp looks, reminding him that the two members of House Melarn were unaccustomed to his disrespectful relationship with Quenthel. The Mistress of the Academy merely scowled at him then turned away to face Faeryl, who cringed, still under Valas's guard.

"Strip her and give her clothes to me," Quenthel commanded, eliciting a high-pitched squeak of protest from the ambassador.

Valas held the prisoner steady as Ryld stepped up to help him, and Halisstra jumped forward almost eagerly and began to disrobe Faeryl, who struggled to avoid the ignominious fate.

"Just who are these two?" Quenthel snapped, eyeing Danifae.

The battle captive cocked her head to one side, eyeing the high priestess in return, as though gauging how much she should defer to this new leader.

"I am Danifae Yauntyrr, Mistress Baenre, formerly of Eryndlyn. I am Halisstra Melarn's personal attendant."

"A battle captive?" Quenthel smirked, and Danifae merely bowed her head.

Quickly enough, Faeryl stood naked in the midst of the group, still held between Valas and Ryld, while Quenthel donned the ambassador's clothing. As the high priestess was dressing, she jerked her head in the direction of the collar, still chained to the wall where she'd been restrained only moments before.

"Lock her up," Quenthel commanded.

"No!" Faeryl protested, trying desperately to jerk free of her two captors. As Valas, Halisstra, and Ryld all corralled her, the ambassador shrieked and began to fight against her captors. "No! You can't leave me down here. . . ."

"Shut up!" Quenthel said, slapping Faeryl. "You sniveling, wretched creature, did you really believe you could get away with your betrayal? Did you honestly think you could defy me, a Baenre, and the Mistress of Arach-Tinilith? By the Dark Mother, child, the depths of your foolishness surprise me! Lock her up," she repeated, gesturing once more at the thick adamantine collar.

"No!" Facryl protested again, struggling as she was hauled over to the wall.

The ambassador flailed and kicked, but the scout and warrior held her tightly as Halisstra fitted the collar around her neck. When the adamantine band clicked shut, the imprisoned drow sobbed once, and as soon as the two males relinquished their grip on her, she began frantically jerking on the restraint.

Quenthel started to turn away, then paused.

"You can redeem yourself, if you like," she said to Faeryl.

"How?" the frantic dark elf asked. "Anything! I will do whatever you want."

"Tell me where my things are," Quenthel replied. "Tell me where all of my possessions were stored when I was brought here."

Faeryl's face fell in despair.

"I don't know," she sobbed, dropping to her knees in supplication. "Please don't leave me here. I will find them for you."

"Don't bother with her," Halisstra said. "I know where your things are, Quenthel Baenre."

Quenthel turned and eyed the daughter of House Melarn.

"Why should I trust you?" she asked.

"That is for you to decide," Halisstra answered, "but consider this . . . I led your males down here to find you, I lured the traitor out into the hall before she could kill you, and I live here and can find my way around. While that would ordinarily be a strike against me, as I told the wizard, I have no quarrel with you, and I do not want to see you suffer the consequences for House Zauvirr's betrayal of my mother."

Quenthel's eyebrows raised as she listened to the other priestess's words, then she looked at Pharaun.

"She speaks the truth," the wizard admitted. "At least thus far. She has thrown herself in with us, though she has few alternatives. The other matron mothers, led by Ssipriina Zauvirr, are wresting control of her House away from her, after the death of her mother."

"Hmm," Quenthel mused. "Very well. We'll address your status later. If you know where my things are, lead on."

"Wait!" Faeryl cried out, lunging forward against the chain around her neck. "She will betray you, Mistress. All the noble Houses despise you for your plans to steal from the city. You can't trust her."

"On the contrary," Quenthel laughed derisively, shaking her head. "She is a Melarn, a member of the only House in Ched Nasad I *can* trust. Let's go."

The high priestess turned to depart the cell, and Pharaun was stepping into the hall behind her as Faeryl wailed once more, "You can't leave me here!"

The ambassador began a chant, and Pharaun recognized the pattern of the words as a divine incantation, though he wasn't sure what sort of spell the dark elf might still have retained in her memory.

Before she could complete the invocation, though, Jeggred was in front of Faeryl. The draegloth flicked a hand out, across her face, slicing his long claws across one cheek and catching her by surprise so that she lost her concentration and the words of the spell died in her mouth, the magic lost.

Faeryl cried out, backing away and clasping her bloody cheek. She began to tremble, remembering all the terrible things Jeggred had done to her. She cowered from the towering fiend, folding herself into the corner, as the draegloth glared down at her. He did not raise a hand to strike her further.

Quenthel stepped up beside the demon, wrapped her hands lovingly around his arm, and smiled at the imprisoned drow.

"You know, Faeryl," the Mistress of the Academy purred, "You're actually right."

Faeryl only blinked at Quenthel, terror in her eyes.

"You said before that I couldn't leave you here. Sadly, it's true. There's no telling what other spells you might still have tucked away in that clever little mind of yours. Jeggred, my pet, repay her for the things she did to us. Take your time . . . enjoy the moment."

Quenthel strolled out of the room, along with Ryld, but Pharaun remained, as did Halisstra and Danifae.

Faeryl's first scream rang in Pharaun's ears, echoing in the small cell. The draegloth had not yet touched the ambassador, but as the wizard watched, smiling, Jeggred moved closer. Her screams rose in pitch, and they were suddenly silenced as Jeggred casually reached out with one large clawed hand and grasped her by the neck, just beneath the collar she wore, cutting off her air. Madly, Faeryl began to flail at the fiend, but he easily lifted her up and extended his arm out fully, so that the naked drow's feet rose off the floor, kicking at the air. She pummeled feebly at the draegloth's arms, and just as she was fading, Jeggred released her, watching as she crumpled to the floor, gasping for air. Before she could fully regain her breath, he reached down and poked a single claw up under her chin.

Pharaun saw that the talon penetrated deep into the soft tissue, probably through the dark elf's tongue, pinning her mouth shut. Faeryl squealed in pain, but it was a muffled cry. She reached up to try to pull the fiend's hand away, but he slowly, relentlessly began to lift her, forcing her to scrabble to her feet, clinging to his arm with both her hands to support her weight and keep the talon from plunging deeper, penetrating the roof of her mouth. Higher and higher the draegloth lifted, until at last Faeryl was on her tiptoes, frantically trying to lift herself off this impaling spike by her arms alone, tears streaming down her face.

Jeggred merely held her there, watching her squirm, using his two smaller hands to caress the ambassador. He brought his other hand up and flicked a claw across her exposed throat, slicing through her vocal chords.

With blood streaming from the gash in her neck, her red eyes wild with terror, Faeryl tried to scream, but all that issued from her was a muffled, wet gurgle. Jeggred laughed and let her dangle, unable to cry out at all.

Danifae and Halisstra turned away, but whether satisfied or disturbed at the fiend's display of ruthlessness, Pharaun was not sure. He was the only one who remained in the cell, and he couldn't draw his eyes away from the scene before him.

Blood ran down Faeryl's neck and chest, and her struggles were growing more and more feeble. Finally, perhaps growing tired of this sport, Jeggred raked at her again, across the abdomen this time, slicing cleanly so that her entrails were freed. The fiend let her drop to the ground at last, and Faeryl crumpled at the draegloth's feet, though Pharaun could see that she was not yet dead.

The ambassador blinked in shock and occasionally thrashed weakly as Jeggred crouched down. When Pharaun realized the demon was preparing to feast, dining on Faeryl even as she lay there, still conscious but too weak to fight him, the wizard finally had to turn away. The wet sounds of the demon at his meal followed him out into the hallway.

Gromph Baenre did not relish the latest message he had to deliver, for several reasons. First and foremost, it was not good news, and however much he was removed from the source of the report, he was still the messenger. Ordinarily, he wouldn't mind for that reason alone, for there were few individuals in Menzoberranzan who could actually take out their displeasure on him, the most powerful mage in the city. Of those few, most held on to only a shell of their former power and were relying on him to conceive of a way to restore it. No, being the bearer of bad news this day would not be as risky as it might on other days, but then he didn't often have to deliver such unpleasant information to his sister.

That brought the Archmage of Menzoberranzan around to the other cause for his distress. Triel Baenre was at home, which meant that Gromph had to go visit her, rather than the other way around. He detested leaving Sorcere, detested having to go to the Great Mound even more, and certainly didn't like doing any of it under such circumstances. It was yet another reason for him to add to his list of reasons why he wanted the crisis resolved. He was tired of all the inconvenience it was causing him personally.

As he flew over the streets of Menzoberranzan on his way to the Great Mound, Gromph peered below in consternation. He had sent word to the appropriate individuals in charge that more troops were to be dispatched, but he had yet to see the results of his orders. The disquiet below was growing again, and if they weren't careful, the nobles of the city would find themselves right back in the middle of another uprising.

Well, Triel could put her foot down again, he supposed, insist that the other matron mothers respond promptly when the call came for more soldiers, but he doubted it would make them quicken their pace one whit. They were going to tend to their own Houses first, High Council be damned.

Approaching the edge of House Baenre, Gromph settled himself to the balcony outside his sister's audience chamber. The guards on duty there peered at him warily for a moment, but when they saw who it was, they stiffened in salute. Ignoring them, the archmage walked briskly past them into the council chambers themselves, hoping to find Triel there. She was not.

Clicking his tongue in exasperation, Gromph passed out of the large audience chamber and into the hallway beyond, which led to her personal quarters. Arriving at the door to her suite of rooms, the archmage was greeted by a pair of stoic females, robust specimens who were well armed and apparently trained equally as well in the art of combat as divine magic.

The pair of guards crossed their heavy maces before the door.

"She is not to be disturbed," one of them said, her stare flat, making it clear she would brook no argument, brother or not.

Gromph sighed, making another mental mark to the tally of reasons he hated doing this. No matter how many times he had to push his proverbial weight around to get to see Triel in her private rooms, the matron mother's personal guards never made it any easier on him the next time. He'd had enough of it.

"I'm not going to stand here and argue with you about this, today. You've got one minute to tell her it's me and let me through, or I will leave you as two piles of smoking ash on her doorstep. Do I make myself clear?"

The flat stares turned mildly baleful, but after some careful consideration, the one who spoke finally nodded curtly and slipped inside, shutting the door behind her and leaving her partner to stare icily at the archmage while he folded his arms and tapped his foot.

Just when Gromph was seriously considering whether or not to make good on his threat, the door opened and the guard appeared again, motioning him through. Arching his eyebrow as though to say, "what else did you expect?" he pushed past her impatiently and shoved the door shut behind him.

Triel was not in the front room, though that didn't really surprise the wizard. Usually, if she was going to bother to be presentable for guests, she would see them in the audience chamber. He figured his odds were about even as to whether he'd discover her in the bedroom or in the baths, most likely with a lover. He tried the bedroom first, with no luck.

Moving through into the bathroom, Gromph found his sister, alone except for a pair of attendants, eyes closed and soaking in an oddly scented oil bath. The odor permeated the room and made him cough.

Triel opened one eye and looked at the wizard, then closed it again, making no move to greet him.

"You really shouldn't threaten my guards like that," she said, a bit testily. "They're standing there to keep the likes of you out, you know."

"A thousand apologies, Matron Mother," Gromph answered. "I will be certain to avoid helping you in the future. Please do drop by sometime and I'll be sure to keep you waiting outside *my* offices."

This time, both of Triel's eyes opened, but instead of growing angry, she appeared worried.

"What is it?" she asked. "Your news must be particularly unpleasant for you to behave so boorishly."

Gromph had to chuckle, but it was a bitter laugh.

"You know me better than most, sister. I suppose I should give you more credit. You're correct, though, the news is bad, and it comes from several fronts. Our patrols are telling me that traffic is picking up on the outskirts of the city. Nothing definitive, but they're growing fearful that we're due for some sort of aggressive act from somewhere, and soon."

"What sort of traffic?" Triel asked, shifting in the bath so that an attendant could begin to scrub her back with a rough cloth.

"Hard to say. Enough species come and go as it is, but they have reported an inordinate number of troglodyte sightings the last few days."

Triel made a noise in her throat, and at first Gromph wondered if it was in response to the ministrations of the attendant, but he realized it was derisive when his sister said, "Troglodytes? They've never been able to muster any sizable threat against us. You came all the way over here and harassed my guards to tell me that? Please."

Gromph clicked his tongue in vexation and strode across the tiled floor to take a seat on a long bench along one wall.

"No, of course not, but don't be so quick to dismiss any potential threat. More than enough generals saw their last battle from underestimating the enemy. We're vulnerable to any attack right now, and you know it."

"Fine, I'll take it under advisement," Triel said. "So, what else do you have to tell me? I'd like to enjoy the rest of my bath, but if you insist on giving me more bad news, I don't think I shall be able to."

Gromph shook his head.

"Yes, there is more bad news," he said.

"Oh, wonderful."

"I'm hearing bad things from our expedition to Ched Nasad."

The matron mother rolled over and sat up, shooing away the attendant. She seemed unconcerned that her upper body was exposed to him, though Gromph ignored that fact.

"What kind of bad things?" she asked, her tone grave.

"The last communication I received reported that riots were beginning. I haven't heard anything since, and the next reports are overdue."

"How long?"

"Two days. I already relayed that information to you."

"Do you have a means of contacting him?" Triel asked.

"Yes, but not for a while, and not really for the kind of conversation I suspect you'd like for me to have with him. Even with what I *can* do, I'll have to make preparations to use the appropriate magic."

"Fine, do that. In the meantime, what are your thoughts?"

Gromph considered the question then said, "Do I believe they are alive? Let's give them some credit. They are an enterprising lot, and I have no doubt that they can take care of themselves. That's half the reason you sent them away, isn't it?"

Triel's eyes narrowed slightly as she stood and let the oil cascade from her body.

"I do want them to succeed," she said. "It aids us nothing for them to perish, regardless of whatever benefits we both receive for having a few specific ones out of the way."

She motioned for the attendant to bring her a towel and had it wrapped around herself.

Gromph's stare was carefully neutral.

"I want them to succeed, too," he said. "My issues aside, this crisis affects every aspect of my studies and pursuits. My point was, if they were ingenious enough to be considered a threat here, I think they can take care of themselves in Ched Nasad."

"Find them," the matron mother commanded, "and let me know when you do."

"Even if I have to threaten your guards again?"

"Even if you have to leave them as piles of ash on my doorstep."

Gromph nodded and turned away as Triel began to dress with help from the two attendants. The archmage stopped and turned back to face his sister.

"Oh, and one more thing."

Triel looked over at her brother and asked, "Yes?"

"Will you please remind the other matron mothers of the importance of timely response to threats inside the city? I asked for reinforcements for several specific sections three hours ago, and they were still not in place when I came to visit."

"Again?" Triel sighed. "Yes, of course I will speak to them again."

"You know," Gromph added, almost as an afterthought. "It would probably help if House Baenre spared some extra soldiers for the cause. A show of good faith and all that."

"Really? Do you think we can afford to spare them?"

"I know of two right outside this door who could be put to far better use," the archmage replied, giving his sister a last, meaningful stare.

❈   ❈   ❈

"Explain to me again what you think I have to gain by trusting you," Quenthel said, gnawing at a strip of dried rothé meat.

The seven of them were hiding in a mess hall in an unused wing of House Melarn. Only Jeggred was no longer hungry, having sated himself back in the dungeon.

It certainly took Faeryl a long time to die, Pharaun thought, shuddering, as he sat watching the draegloth lick himself clean. The wizard was having a hard time blocking out the image of the drow, still moving, still watching, even as the fiend had begun to feast.

Ryld and Valas stood guard near the door, both of them obviously anxious to be on their way. The rumbles from beyond the walls had ceased for the moment, and Pharaun wasn't sure whether that boded well or ill for them. If the fighting had been quashed that quickly, it was only a matter of time before Ssipriina began searching for them again. He was eager to be away, too.

As Quenthel continued to inhale the food, Halisstra pursed her lips and tried again to defend her usefulness to the Menzoberranyr.

"I can get you out of the House without notice," she said. "I know the best routes to take. If we encounter any of Ssipriina's guards along the way, I might be able to dismiss them without incident. Until you're safely out of the city, having the two of us accompany you is to your benefit."

Quenthel nodded as she ate.

"Perhaps," she said, pausing to sip from a waterskin. "Or perhaps you would simply like to lead us into ruin in your own way, maybe by lulling us into trusting you so that you can betray us to Ssipriina. For all I know, you still hold me responsible for the death of your mother, or are at the very least angry about my intentions."

Halisstra rolled her eyes where Quenthel could not see, and Pharaun had to quell a bemused smirk.

At least I'm not the only one who finds her unbelievably irrational at times, he thought.

"Yes, all of that could be true, certainly," Halisstra said, "but then

I wouldn't have had much to gain by helping to rescue you when Ssipriina already had you in her clutches, don't you think?"

"Hmm," Quenthel said doubtfully, another bite of food in her mouth. She finished chewing and looked over at Pharaun. "What's your opinion?"

The Master of Sorcere sat up straighter, surprised that she was seeking his counsel.

I suppose that when you're surrounded by the bigger enemy, he mused, the smaller enemy seems a friend.

"Well, thus far they've given us no reason to doubt them," he answered. "Except, of course, their heritage itself. Regardless of whether you're inclined to trust a dark elf you've never met—a dark elf of a House that you so recently intended to betray, at that—our options seem severely limited without their company. I don't suppose we'd be all that worse off, anyway, should they decide to turn on us at an inopportune time."

Quenthel made a face at the wizard.

"Are you thinking with the right part of your body?" she asked sarcastically, nodding in the direction of Danifae, who sat on a couch off to one side, listening to the discussion.

When she became a part of it, she lowered her eyes demurely and folded her hands into her lap.

Pharaun smirked.

"Oh, absolutely, Mistress Baenre," he said dryly. "Nothing would please me more than to have additional females along on this trip, all with a ready suggestion on how something should be handled or a friendly comment on ways I might improve my demeanor for the benefit of everyone around me."

Halisstra's eyebrows shot up in surprise, and the wizard remembered again that she was unaccustomed to his manner with Quenthel.

For that matter, he thought, noting the high priestess's scowl, Quenthel herself is unaccustomed to my manner.

Taking a slightly more conciliatory tone, Pharaun added, "With all due respect, regardless of which part of my body I'm currently using to contemplate this matter, it seems undeniable that we stand much to gain and little to lose by trusting them, at least for the moment. Ask me again in half an hour, and my answer might be markedly different."

Quenthel chewed her rothé thoughtfully, though whether she was mulling his point or whether she was considering whether or not to allow Jeggred to dismember him, Pharaun wasn't sure.

"In any event," he finished, "we can ensure ourselves some degree of protection by keeping them close, under our scrutiny. If they lead us into a trap, we might yet negotiate with Ssipriina Zauvirr . . . turn them over in exchange for our own freedom. Only if we don't tell the matron mother what happened to Faeryl, of course," he added with a grin.

Halisstra's flat stare told Pharaun that she found both his humor and his insurance plan distasteful, but Quenthel seemed convinced.

The Mistress of Arach-Tinilith nodded after tossing back the last bit of water in the skin.

"Very well," she said to Halisstra. "You will serve as our guide out of this accursed House, and if you serve us well, you will be rewarded with your lives. Do I make myself clear?"

Halisstra swallowed once, but she finally nodded.

"I think at least for the time being that your weapons and magical trinkets will stay safe and sound in our possession. If you behave yourselves, you may earn them back."

Both of the other drow nodded their acquiescence.

"Good, then let's be on our way," the high priestess announced, dusting off her hands after finishing the dried meat.

"Before we go," Pharaun said. "there is the matter of 'where' to discuss."

Quenthel looked at the mage.

"We are returning to Menzoberranzan," she said. "The expedition was a failure. Universally, Lolth speaks to no one, and the goods I had hoped to bring back with me to help us defend ourselves do not exist. We have nothing to show for the journey."

"Exactly," Pharaun countered. "We have nothing definitive to bring back with us—yet. I say we push ahead, continue to try to determine what is happening."

"But we have nothing to pursue," Quenthel argued. "We know little more about the Dark Mother's absence than we did before we left."

"That's not entirely true," Pharaun said. "As I mentioned before, the goddess's absence is not limited merely to our race. Regardless, I have an idea. While *we* may not be able to discern any more information directly, we could enlist the aid of someone who can."

"Who?"

"A priest of Vhaeraun."

Quenthel rose from the chair where she had been sitting, fury plain on her face.

"You speak blasphemous words, wizard. We will do no such thing."

Even Halisstra had recoiled at the suggestion, Pharaun noted.

He raised his hands in supplication and pleaded, "I know it's unconventional, but hear me out before you dismiss the idea."

Quenthel began to pace, and Pharaun knew she was at least intrigued, if not happy, with the notion. Her desire to claim the glory of discovery in this matter rivaled his own, he supposed.

"Just what is it you think a priest of Vhaeraun—" Quenthel formed the god's name with a grimace—"could do for us? And where would we find one who could—or even would—aid us?"

Pharaun leaned forward eagerly.

"We struggle to see inside the Demonweb Pits," he explained, "but perhaps another god would not suffer the same difficulty. In this instance, with the proper sacrifices and deferential behavior, we might just be able to ask for a little audience in order to find out."

"Few of his ilk would even consider helping us," Quenthel said, waving her hand in dismissal, "and we know of none to even ask."

As Quenthel turned her back on him during her pacing, Pharaun looked over at Valas and nodded in encouragement.

Tell her, he signed.

Taking a deep breath and nodding, Valas said, "I know one."

Quenthel turned to face the diminutive scout.

"What?"

"I know a priest of Vhaeraun," Valas replied. "An old acquaintance of mine, Tzirik Jaelre. I think he would be willing."

"Really," Quenthel said, eyeing Pharaun and Valas alike, as though suspecting that the two were collaborating. "What makes you think he would help us?"

The mage carefully studied the tabletop in front of him.

She is too clever for her own good, he thought, knowing that if he admitted his foreknowledge, Quenthel was as likely as not to dismiss the whole idea just to spite him.

"He owes me a favor," Valas replied. "At the very least, he owes me enough to hear us out, even if he refuses. I don't think he'll refuse."

"How convenient. Pharaun?"

The wizard looked up, pretending to be thinking about something else.

"Hmm? Oh, yes. Well, it is very convenient that Valas knows someone who fits the bill. I wish you'd said something earlier," he said to the scout, "but I guess we can't all conceive of these flashes of brilliance. If Valas vouches for his friend then I say, what do we have to lose?"

Quenthel opened her mouth, possibly to retort, by the look on her face, but she never got the words out. A shock wave far stronger than any they had felt previously coursed through the House, knocking them and most of the furniture over.

"By the Dark Mother!" Halisstra screamed, stumbling against a wall. "The whole House is coming down!"

FOURTEEN

Ssipriina Zauvirr and several guests stood atop an observation tower overlooking House Zauvirr. Leaning against the balustrade, she stared out over Ched Nasad. Her abode was not far from House Melarn, but in that direction, the matron mothers could see very little but thick smoke. Despite the obscuring clouds, the fighting around House Melarn still raged, and the sound of it reached the matron mothers even high on the tower.

"This has gotten out of control," Umrae D'Dgttu said grimly, standing beside Ssipriina. "Your agent said nothing of this stone-burning fire when we agreed to this plan."

"Yes," Ulviirala Rilynt chimed in, pacing back and forth behind them, her numerous bracelets, rings, and necklaces clanking with each step. "I dislike the idea of so much destruction, especially right now."

"Nonsense," Nedylene Zinard scolded, also leaning against the railing very casually but with her back to the unfolding scene of ruin.

She seemed more interested in her lacquered fingernails than in the activity around her. "We knew going into this that we might have to be aggressive. If we are to remake this city to our liking, now is the time to act, and we can let nothing stand in our way. Not the other Houses and not our own misgivings. Sometimes you have to break a few lizard eggs to make an omelet. Sometimes you have to kill a few slaves to win the day."

"Perhaps," Umrae D'Dgttu said, her whip-thin frame belying her puissance as the most powerful cleric among them, "but this is unnecessary. You should not have summoned us to install you as a new member of the Council until you eliminated *all* of the Menzoberranyr. Allowing that wizard to weave his lies did not help your cause."

ShriNeerune Hlaund snorted. "The wizard's lies were inconsequential. Ssipriina was a fool to send her mercenaries out so prematurely."

"I did not do that!" Ssipriina retorted. "Someone else gave them the signal before it was time. I still held out hope that we could resolve the dissolution of House Melarn bloodlessly. These fire pots were not my idea either. The gray dwarves procured them from somewhere else without my knowledge."

"So you're saying that you don't even have control over your own House?" ShriNeerune sneered. "And you expect us to continue to back you? I should have known better than to support a merchant House."

Ssipriina's fists clenched, and she dearly wanted to strike the dark elf belittling her, but she held them at her sides.

"I'd be careful, if I were you," she snapped, staring coldly at the offending drow. "I'm still the one those grays answer to, and right now, we're winning. You could find yourself on the other side of the battle very quickly."

"Enough," Umrae said, stepping between the two of them. "What's done is done. Now is the time to fight, not argue. Ssipriina, did you bring it?"

Ssipriina kept her stare steadily on ShriNeerune's face for a moment longer, her eyes narrow in anger, but then she turned away.

"Yes, of course," she answered. "I have it right here."

"Then let's do this," the thin matron mother said, motioning for the five of them to gather together. "It's time to claim our legacy."

Ssipriina nodded and produced a small bundle wrapped in black silk. Undoing the covering, she revealed a crystalline statue of a spider, as black as darkness itself, broken into several pieces. The head and the abdomen were separated, as were two sets of four legs, one for each side of the figurine. The five matron mothers gathered around as Ssipriina held the cloth in the palms of her hands, the collection of parts sitting atop it, stretching her arms out for them to see.

"It has been many years," Nedylene said, reaching out with her lacquered nails and lifting one set of legs to examine them. "The city will tremble before our might. Let us begin."

"Hold them steady, Ssipriina," Umrae warned.

She took hold of the abdomen of the statue. One by one, the other three matron mothers each took up a part. They looked from one to another, and finally, when Umrae nodded, they fitted the pieces together, making the figurine whole.

"Quickly, now!" Umrae hissed, and Ssipriina wasted no time re-wrapping the completed statue in the cloth.

Already, the matron mothers could see that the bundle was squirming, growing larger.

"Hurry!" ShriNeerune hissed. "Throw it!"

Ssipriina did. She reached back and hurled the bundle out into the void, as hard as she could, and as one the five matron mothers watched the wiggling cloth tumble away from House Zauvirr.

The cloth fell away, and the assembled drow gasped as one. The statue had transformed into a living thing, a spider as black as the crystal it was born from, and it was growing rapidly in size. In the blink of an eye, it was the size of a rothé, and as it disappeared past the side of the web street it was still growing.

Ssipriina watched, awed, as the creature shot forth a string of webbing at the street, attaching a line to anchor itself as it fell. Then it was gone, vanished from their vantage point.

The five dark elves waited breathlessly, hoping to catch another glimpse of the thing they had created. The strand of webbing had jerked taut and visibly vibrated as it dropped straight down. Obviously, the spider was still attached to it. For a moment, there was nothing to see, though all five matron mothers strained to do so, anyway.

When the first black leg stabbed into view, feeling for a foothold on the web street, Ssipriina felt her heart skip a beat. The appendage was longer than she was tall. Slowly, delicately, the spider lifted itself into view, and all five matron mothers took an involuntary step back from the balustrade, even though their creation was dozens of yards away from them. It was as large as the street was wide.

"By the Dark Mother," someone breathed. "It's magnificent!"

The giant spider righted itself atop the street, and Ssipriina could hear the screams of those below, screams of terror as the spider was spotted. It began to scurry in the other direction, toward the masses of soldiers still fighting several streets away.

"By the Abyss," Umrae groaned.

"What? What is it?" Nedylene asked, worry in her voice.

"There is no link," Umrae replied, her eyes closed in concentration. "I can't control it."

Halisstra could feel her sense of impending dread growing. While House Melarn had not collapsed all together, as she had so direly predicted back in her rooms, it had certainly shaken violently more than once, and to her senses, familiar with every hallway, chamber, and nuance of the dwelling, it seemed to lean very slightly to one side. As impossible to fathom as the idea was, Halisstra wondered if the place was still stable. She wanted desperately to get outside and see for herself just what was happening in the city. The drow couldn't imagine violence so potent as to be able to physically disturb House Melarn.

The dark elf priestess was leading the others toward her mother's chambers, where she was certain Quenthel's personal belongings had been taken after the Mistress of the Academy had been imprisoned. Though she would have some competition from

Aunrae Nasadra, Ssipriina Zauvirr would certainly claim much of House Melarn's bounty for herself, including the high priestess's personal items, to keep as trophies of her affront to the city of Menzoberranzan, if nothing else. It remained to be seen if everything Quenthel Baenre had in her possession upon arrival in the city was still there.

The more she thought about the actions of Ssipriina and the other matron mothers, the more incensed Halisstra grew. Beyond the consequences of turning on House Melarn, they were potentially offending the most powerful House in Menzoberranzan. Plus, the course of action they had taken seemed to Halisstra to be a symbolic thumbing of the nose at the very idea of even *trying* to discover what was going on with Lolth.

At least Quenthel and the others are trying to figure something out, she'd told herself more than once since her entanglement with them. Lolth might value devotion, but Halisstra didn't believe the goddess expected her servants to sit back and wait for her to come save them, even if they showed overzealous dedication or sacrificed a thousand gray dwarves.

Truthfully, Halisstra had found herself wondering just what Lolth wanted.

Halisstra passed through a large intersection and turned down a new pathway, one even more lavishly decorated, if that were possible, with plush carpeting, murals, and images of House Melarn triumphs. They were entering Drisinil's personal quarters, and Halisstra was fearful that a large contingent of House Zauvirr guards would be posted to protect the chambers, insurrection outside or not. The dark elf's concerns were well founded, for as she rounded a corner, she spotted a squadron of troops milling about, blocking access to the door beyond, which led into Drisinil's private residence.

"What are you doing down here?" Halisstra demanded, hoping to throw the soldiers off-balance with her commanding tone. "You are needed on the parapets at once!"

"I don't think so," the sergeant said, eyeing the motley group following the First Daughter as he raised his sword and pointed it at her. "We received word that the traitor had escaped, and now you appear right here, conveniently for us. I'm afraid we have orders to kill you and anyone aiding you."

The soldiers fanned out, brandishing their weapons as they advanced.

Halisstra's first instinct was to bring her mace up to defend herself, but her hand was empty, for Quenthel had not yet permitted her to rearm herself. Danifae, who was at Halisstra's side, was no longer bound, but she had no weapon, either. Danifae did, however, carry a small knapsack with some of their other belongings. Quenthel had agreed to let them stop at Halisstra's chambers and pack a few things before departing, for if the House continued to thrash about like it had, there was no telling when they might have to evacuate, and there would be no better chance later.

Out of the corner of her eye, Halisstra saw her attendant falter a step, too, but before the soldiers could close the gap, a blur of yellowish-white fur flashed between the two drow, slamming into the front rank of troops with a deep, unsettling snarl and a whirl of arms and claws. There was a sickening sound of rending flesh before Halisstra realized that the draegloth, Quenthel's personal bodyguard, was the source of the carnage.

Halisstra's gasp of surprise came only after three of the soldiers, including the sergeant, went down screaming before the onslaught of the creature, their bodies horribly mangled and their blood splattered everywhere. Several other soldiers began to surround the draegloth, trying to stay clear of the fiend's savage claws, but at the same time looking for ways to press the attack. Jeggred crouched, watching his multiple foes as they swarmed around him, lashing out with their swords but unwilling to get in close enough to do any good. A handful were already backing out of the fray, producing hand crossbows.

Another figure darted past Halisstra, and a third, and she settled back against the wall as Ryld and Valas entered the fight. The larger of the two, whom she had found striking when they first came face to face, was wielding his greatsword in a manner she found comforting.

The blade seemed light and easy in his hands as he carved half the face off of one soldier and spun to swipe through the midsection of a second enemy in the same motion. The diminutive one, on the other hand, seemed content to slink up behind one of the drow soldiers still trying to find an opening inside Jeggred's deadly reach. The guard never heard or felt Valas coming, and when the scout planted his kukri into the small of the soldier's back, a flash of energy accompanied the stroke. The soldier arched his back in agony and crumpled to the ground as Valas pulled his blade free and stepped aside, disappearing into the shadows again.

"Get out of the way, foolish girl, and let them do their work," Quenthel snapped at Halisstra from behind.

The daughter of House Melarn glanced back over her shoulder to where the high priestess was standing. She saw the wizard producing some odd ingredient or another, which she knew meant he was preparing to fling a spell. In front of him, a rapier seemed to dance of its own accord in the air, as though it was defending him from any foes who might try to get close to him. She pressed herself against the wall to allow him ample room then sidestepped her way back to where Quenthel waited. On the opposite side of the passage, Danifae was doing the same.

"No sense getting in the thick of things when they're more than capable of handling it themselves," Quenthel explained, scowling. "At least they're good for that, if nothing else."

Halisstra wanted desperately to ask the other drow how she tolerated such insubordination from the three of them, especially the wizard, Pharaun, but she thought it best to keep her mouth shut and stay in the high priestess's good graces. It might be a long while before Quenthel trusted her, and she didn't want to do anything to jeopardize that.

A hissing sound accompanied a long, thin sliver of ice that shot from Pharaun's fingertips and streaked straight at one of the soldiers, embedding itself in the back of the drow's shoulder like a deadly icicle. The soldier cried out in pain and stumbled backward, but too late. Jeggred, seeing his foe's attention diverted, darted in and slashed with his massive claws, ripping through the muscle wall of the guard's abdomen and smiling delightedly as entrails began to tumble out. The force of the blow was so strong that it spun the dark elf around. With a sickening *plop*, the soldier fell onto his back, gazing sightlessly toward Halisstra while the contents of his body leaked out around him.

"Hold!" a voice shouted from behind Quenthel. Halisstra turned, along with the high priestess, to see a whole new force of soldiers, who had approached from the direction Halisstra and the others had come.

"Wizard, do something!" Quenthel ordered, stepping back as the new soldiers slipped their weapons from sheaths and trotted forward.

Pharaun spun around, and seeing the new threat, he stabbed a hand inside his *piwafwi* and produced several small items. His dancing rapier swung around and darted forward, bobbing and weaving through the air in an attempt to hold the new squad, which was even larger in size than the first one, at bay. At the same time, Halisstra heard the wizard utter some word or phrase under his breath. Though she didn't understand his speech, the effect was immediate and impressive. A blinding streak of lightning shot forward from the wizard's fingertips and struck the closest soldier squarely in the chest. Immediately afterward, several fingers of the same bolt crackled again, fanning outward from its first victim to strike the rest of the dark elves.

Halisstra cried out in pain and flung her arm up to shield her eyes from the flaring light of the bolt, cowering against the wall and cursing the wizard for blinding her and making her vulnerable to the soldiers' attacks. Her vision swam for several moments with the afterimage as she groped along the wall, trying to listen for the sound of imminent attack, but nothing came. Ahead, she heard one last gasp as someone was wounded, and the sounds of battle faded.

When her vision finally cleared, she saw Danifae and Quenthel looking as dazed as she felt. Pharaun appeared proud of himself, and the entire host of House Zauvirr soldiers lay on the ground to either side of her.

"Damn you, Pharaun," Quenthel snarled, her hands on her hips as she glared at the wizard, who was a few inches shorter than the high priestess. "You warn me next time you intend to cast a spell like that!"

Pharaun bowed, and Halisstra wasn't sure if it was meant to be mocking or not, but he said, "My apologies. There wasn't time to warn anyone. They would have been upon us if I hadn't acted as swiftly as I did."

Quenthel sniffed, apparently not completely satisfied with his explanation, but she said nothing else. After a moment, Halisstra realized that the Mistress of the Academy was looking at her.

"Well?" Quenthel said. "Lead on. I don't want another horde of Ssipriina's lackeys finding us still standing around their comrades' corpses."

Halisstra nodded curtly and turned toward the door. She was careful not to stare overly long at any of the bodies of the soldiers Jeggred had dispatched. She reached the door and waved her brooch in front of it, allowing the magic to do its work and unlock the portal. The priestess stepped inside and beckoned the others to follow her.

The interior of her mother's chambers was gaudy and out of style for Halisstra's tastes, but she paid the decorations no mind. As the rest of the group filed inside, she gestured toward the rest of the room and the different doorways.

"Mistress Baenre's things are here somewhere," Halisstra said. "If we spread out, we can find them more quickly."

As if to punctuate the need for urgency, another rumbling vibration bounced through the House, and Halisstra thought she heard the fracturing of solid rock.

"Never mind that," Quenthel said brusquely. "They're in there."

She pointed through one of the doorways.

"That's the bedrooms," Halisstra said, slightly puzzled at how the high priestess would know they were in there. "Come on," she said, and the entire group followed her into the interior chamber.

The oversized bed sat to one side, a huge, round affair that could accommodate five or six drow and probably had on more than one occasion, Halisstra supposed. In addition to that, there were a number of couches, chests, dressers, and tables for furniture, and rich tapestries covered every square foot of the walls.

Quenthel trudged across the room to a point between two tall armoires, where a tapestry woven of black fabric glowed in phosphorescent hues of green, purple, and yellow with an image of a drow priestess. Halisstra knew it was supposed to be her grandmother, and she wondered why Drisinil had kept it. Halisstra certainly didn't intend to keep anything to remind her of her own mother.

"Here," Quenthel said. "Everything's behind here."

"Well don't touch it, yet," Pharaun admonished, striding up beside her.

He studied the tapestry for a moment then nodded to himself as though satisfied. He took hold of a corner of the weaving and yanked it off the wall. Behind it was only bare stone.

Quenthel's scowl deepened, but the wizard simply produced a wand from inside the folds of his *piwafwi,* waved it about, and uttered an arcane phrase. He pocketed the magical device and went back to studying the space as the others gathered around. Danifae stood near Halisstra, and the priestess felt her attendant press something against her hand. Looking down, Halisstra saw that the battle captive had procured a pair of daggers and was handing one to her, on the sly.

Oh, you clever girl, Halisstra thought. She quickly palmed the weapon and tucked it into the folds of her *piwafwi,* out of sight. Then she returned her attention to what the wizard was doing.

"Yes, of course," Pharaun said, as though he had recognized something that should have been obvious to him. "All right everyone, step back. I can disarm the protective wards and sigils that are here, but I cannot deal with the more mechanical trap that I suspect is also present."

"That's all right," Valas said. "If you can remove all of the magical protections, I might be able to manage the rest."

Pharaun nodded and began to gesture and mutter, finally pointing toward the space between the two tall armoires with a flourish. Halisstra supposed the wizard must have some ability to sense the presence of various spells, wards, and charms, for she could not see what he was working on and had never known of a secret portal anywhere in her mother's rooms. Pharaun gazed at the wall a moment longer after he was finished with his casting then nodded for the scout to give it a try.

Valas moved up closely to the wall and began to inspect it little by little, inch by inch. Halisstra wanted to get in close beside him, to see what he was looking at, but she dared not disturb his concentration. At that moment, yet another in the series of rumbles shook the room, and Halisstra nearly lost her footing.

"By the Abyss!" Valas yelled, waving his arms in an effort to avoid falling against the wall. "This is no good. I can't do this with all of the—"

The scout's words were cut off as the whole room suddenly lurched and began to tilt. Halisstra fell to the floor as the chamber was no longer level but instead tipped to one side, away from the wall they had been inspecting. She realized she was screaming as she rolled along the floor. The movement stopped, but all through the House she could hear the horrendous sound of fracturing rock, loud popping noises that sounded as if the whole world was snapping apart.

"We've no time! We've got to get out now!" Halisstra heard one of the males yell.

"Not without my possessions," Quenthel insisted, sitting up and trying to stand on the yawing floor. "Get that door open—*now!*"

Pharaun, who had actually begun to levitate to avoid falling down, nodded as the others left their feet—all except Valas, who seemed perfectly capable of maintaining his balance despite the tilt of the floor.

The wizard removed a soft glove from inside his piwafwi. He donned it and began casting again as the floor made several popping sounds and began to tilt even more. A massive, glowing fist appeared, twice as tall as Pharaun, floating in the air in front of the mage. Pharaun guided the magical conjuration with his own gloved hand, turning it so that the knuckles were aimed at the point on the wall.

"Get back!" Pharaun yelled. "I don't know what kind of backlash this will create."

There was more popping from the structure of the House—closer, the sounds deafening—and Halisstra found she had her hands over her ears. Her heart was pounding in her chest.

We're going to die in here, she thought. The whole house is falling apart, and we're going to be crushed.

The magical fist lurched forward and slammed into the wall between the armoires, smacking against the stone with a powerful crunch. The wall cracked in several places. Pharaun directed the fist to back up and go again.

Quenthel was beside Halisstra, grabbing her by the arm.

"When he gets that wall down," the Mistress of Arach-Tinilith said, "we will need to hurry. What's the fastest way out of here?"

Halisstra looked at the other drow helplessly.

"We're in the very heart of the House," she answered. "The most protected point. It'll take us forever to get out, no matter which way we go."

Quenthel scowled, but then she nodded and moved away.

The giant fist had slammed into the wall two or three more times, and the wall was about to collapse.

One more blow should do it, Halisstra thought as she felt the concussions of more cracking and breaking beyond the room. If it's not too late already, she added to herself.

Around Halisstra, the others were wide-eyed, trying to maintain their balance and eyeing the walls, ceiling, and floor warily.

The next slam of the fist finally did the section of wall in, and it collapsed in a pile of rubble. Behind it, a small chamber sat dark and dusty, filled with shelves containing a number of items Halisstra had never seen before. Quenthel pushed ahead of everyone else and strode—or rather hiked, for it was like walking up a hillside—into the chamber, snatching up a five-headed snake whip with a gleam in her eye.

"Yes!" was all she said as she held the weapon aloft, the five vipers hissing and writhing joyously.

Quickly, Quenthel gathered up several other items that obviously belonged to her then eyed the other things displayed on the shelves.

"No time," Pharaun insisted. "We leave now!" Turning to Halisstra, the wizard demanded, "Which way is out? Get us there, before the whole place falls!"

Halisstra shook her head miserably.

"We're as far away from the exits as we can be!" she shouted over the cacophony of popping, shattering stone. The room lurched again. "There's no close way out!"

"Then I'll make one," Pharaun shouted. "Which direction is closest to the outside?"

Part of the ceiling on the far side of the room collapsed, sending a shower of stone fragments and dust into Halisstra's face. She covered her nose and mouth with one hand as she flung her arm up to shield her eyes from the stinging shards of rock that pelted her. She couldn't think. She was going to die. There was no way out, no escape—and no Lolth.

Halisstra felt the wizard's hands grasp her arms.

"Tell me," he shouted, "which way is the closest way to the outside, regardless of walls?"

Halisstra shook her head, trying to focus despite the panic rising in her chest. She spied Danifae clinging to Quenthel as both of them held on to the edge of the broken wall leading into the secret room. Jeggred had his claws embedded in the rock of the floor and was clambering along it toward his mistress.

The closest outside wall . . . which way?

An image appeared in her head, a mental map, and she knew that her mother's chambers backed up nearly to an outside wall, which meant that the secret room Pharaun and Quenthel had discovered was very close to the outside.

Frantically, Halisstra pointed to the hidden room.

"That way!" she yelled.

Pharaun nodded. Scrambling on his hands and knees, the wizard headed in that direction, almost slipping and sliding back the other way as the room tilted again. Halisstra began to slide along the floor, herself and decided against trying to stop, instead bracing her feet against the far, lowest wall. She craned her neck around to watch the mage as he began yet another spell. He seemed to have an endless supply of them. He dug in his *piwafwi* and pulled out something too small for Halisstra to see, then he began to gesticulate wildly in the direction of the wall at the back of the secret closet. Before her eyes, a tunnel formed right into the rock itself, and after about fifteen feet, it broke through into space beyond.

"Come on!" Pharaun shouted to everyone as the whole House seemed to be one solid rumble.

The noise of the cracking stone was deafening, and Halisstra had barely been able to hear the wizard. The room tilted over even more sharply, and Halisstra realized that it was nearly sideways, with the new opening to the outside almost over her head. She began to float, lifting herself magically toward the impromptu exit, as the other members of the group did the same. As she reached the top and was about to pass through into the open air of the city beyond, she saw that Jeggred had a hold of Valas. The draegloth lifted effortlessly toward the hole, and it was at that moment that Halisstra remembered that Danifae could not levitate either.

The House Melarn daughter looked down desperately and saw her attendant, crouched in the low corner of the room, near the collapsed ceiling, scrambling to stay atop the shifting pile of rock as the room continued to tip over. Danifae's eyes were blazing with fury as she gazed angrily up toward where everyone else was escaping the collapsing dwelling. There was another excruciatingly loud snapping sound as more stone buckled and popped, and Danifae, still inside the destroyed remains of House Melarn, was falling away.

Khorrl Xornbane was bloody and exhausted. His clan, gathered all around him, looked that way too. He had no idea how long they'd been fighting, but it was too long. They needed rest and water. They couldn't keep this up for much longer. Unfortunately, the captain of Clan Xornbane feared that the day would grow much worse before it got better. He hoped he was wrong.

Khorrl had already passed the word that his troops were to abandon their positions defending House Melarn. They had been besieged there for so long and had used up so many of their firepots that he feared the place was growing unstable.

I'm not going to lose my boys that way, he told himself.

The remains of his forces were reforming on the opposite side of the plaza from the House, and for the moment they were being left alone. It was hard to be sure how long that peace would last, though, because none of them could see very far in the thick smoke of the burning stone.

What Khorrl and his duergar could see told the tale clearly enough, though. The plaza was covered with the bodies of goblins and kobolds. Littered in between them were slightly fewer drow, though the number of dead dark elves surprised him. More dead gray dwarves than Khorrl would have liked were scattered here and there, too. It had been a hellish day, and it was far from over, the captain feared.

"Sir," one of his aides said, running up to Khorrl, "we've completely abandoned the estate. The last of the troops have formed a line from that corner—" the young gray dwarf pointed through the smoke toward the edge of a dwelling behind them—"across to the flank of our main position, there." He swung his arm across to the far right side of the plaza.

"Good," Khorrl replied, visualizing the battlefield in his mind, since he could no longer clearly see it with his eyes.

"Also," the aide continued, "there's another force of drow coming toward us, from that direction."

He pointed off to the left, where the plaza was joined by a large web street. It was, regrettably, the weakest point of Clan Xornbane's defenses.

"Friend or foe? Did you get a look at their House insignias?"

The aide shrugged and said, "Not in this smoke."

Khorrl sighed. He would have to send scouts out to reconnoiter the new troops. He said as much to the aide, who saluted him and started to turn away.

"Wait," the captain said, and the aide stopped attentively. "Get some boys up there—" Khorrl pointed toward the street one level above where they were currently positioned—"I don't want another swarm of those damned dark elves dropping in on us like they did earlier."

"Yes, sir," the aide replied, and hurried off to execute his captain's commands.

Khorrl sighed again and turned to call for water. From behind him there was a loud popping sound, a sound he knew too well—splintering stone. He spun back around and peered through the gloom of smoke in the direction from which it had come. All up and down the lines that protected the clan's position, the word was spreading, and it reached Khorrl quickly enough. House Melarn was burning to oblivion, and it was about to go over.

Khorrl shook his head, knowing what was about to happen. He hoped his aide was right and hoped that all his boys had gotten out of there. He lamented the ones who couldn't, for whatever reason.

The popping started again, and grew louder and more steady. He could feel the vibrations in the stone beneath his feet. He almost wished he could see it, but in a way, he didn't. It was going to be a deathtrap for anyone still inside.

The snapping, splintering sound of stone reached a crescendo, and there was one final explosion, a tremor that shook the entire street enough that Khorrl had to brace himself with his axe. There was a jerk, and the rumbling ceased. Khorrl knew the whole building had gone over the side, tumbling into the void.

A few seconds later, there was a horrendous crash from below. House Melarn had struck something. A heartbeat later, he felt the vibrations of the impact. It was subtle, but for that sort of vibration to travel through a web street and into the walls of the huge cavern, and back along the other web streets, the initial impact must have been devastating.

It might take out several more streets, the duergar mused grimly.

"Sir!"

It was the aide again, rushing up to his captain, his look wide-eyed.

"What is it?" Khorrl demanded, wondering what would so shake up the lad.

"A spider! A huge one, as big as a house! It's coming this way!"

Khorrl groaned, realizing just how much worse things had gotten. He hated being right.

FIFTEEN

As he floated up and out of the collapsing building that had at one time been House Melarn, Pharaun Mizzrym heard a cry of anguish below him. Looking downward, he spied Halisstra, still emerging from the gaping opening that led into the ruin of her mother's chambers. She was staring back down into the building.

For the rest of his days, the wizard wouldn't be sure what convinced him to do it, but sensing that someone was still inside, he made up his mind in the blink of an eye to cast a spell. Yanking off his *piwafwi* and tossing it to Ryld, he uttered a quick arcane phrase and began transforming himself into a loathsome and wretched creature. He had seen the horrid thing several times before and in fact had hunted them for sport a few times in his younger days. As he dropped back down toward the crumbling building, which was beginning to break away from the last of its moorings and drop into the space below, he changed from the handsome drow elf with the winning smile to a winged woman with scaly hindquarters. Though the form was repulsive, it did have one advantage over the wizard's natural shape: It could fly. Pharaun hoped his harpy shape would be strong enough to lift whoever was still trapped inside.

Halisstra seemed about to drop back down into the cavernous room, which was tilted completely on its side, but Pharaun grasped hold of her *piwafwi* and shoved her to the side. She looked up at him, startled, and gave a quick shriek of surprise and horror, even as she stumbled back. She fumbled for something tucked inside her own *piwafwi,* and the mage got the impression she had no clue it was him. She was about to attack him.

"Get up with the others!" he hissed, motioning with one of his clawed hands. "I'll go back."

He saw the flash of a dagger, and Halisstra relaxed the slightest bit, seeming to understand who the harpy really was. He filed away for later the fact that she'd secreted a weapon on her person.

Halisstra nodded and pushed herself up from the edge of the hole even as Pharaun folded his wings to his side and stepped over the opening so that he could drop through. Inside, he saw Danifae flailing madly atop a pile of rocks that had once been the ceiling, as the mound of rubble shifted beneath her. At that point, House Melarn was truly falling, and the two of them with it. He noticed that the rubble shifted and ground itself together as the building plummeted downward, grinding itself into oblivion. It almost seemed to be draining out of a hole below her, like some great hourglass. She was struggling to keep from getting sucked down with the stone, but her leg was wedged between two large blocks, and she could not gain a sufficient grip anywhere else in order to pull her limb free.

Pharaun sank quickly down to where the battle captive struggled, unfurling his wings at the last moment to slow his descent and come to hover beside the drow female. Danifae responded, reaching out to try to grab hold of the creature before her. Whether she realized it was Pharaun or not, she didn't seem to care. Pharaun extended his taloned feet in her direction and worked his way to within her reach. She was sinking ever deeper into the debris pit. It was up to her knee, and when it shifted, she arched her head back and screamed more in frustration than in agony.

The instant Danifae had a solid grip on him, Pharaun began to thrash with his wings, exerting himself to rise up and out, hoping it would be enough to remove her from her predicament. He felt the resistance—not just of her weight, but also of her trapped leg—but he tugged and flapped, working to free her. Finally, with one last heave, he felt the resistance give, and he was barreling upward, Danifae clinging tightly to his legs. He soared toward the opening as the room continued to drop, and there was a massive roaring crash and a blinding cloud of dust as he shot out through the widening hole.

Once free of the room, Pharaun realized he really wasn't flying upward at all but was hovering in place as the entire structure of House Melarn fell away beneath them. He saw it smash into a web street that stretched across beneath it, and when it struck the thoroughfare a glancing blow, the rubble tumbled around so that it was spinning as it fell. If they'd been a moment longer in freeing themselves, the wizard realized with a shudder, he never would have been able to navigate his way out of the hole. The room would have spun and tumbled with him and Danifae trapped inside.

Both of them watched for a moment, awed, as the massive stone structure plummeted downward toward the bottom of the city. Finally, with a sickening boom, it struck somewhere far below, and the concussive impact reverberated all the way up to where they hovered.

Pharaun was beginning to feel the strain of trying to fly while holding so much weight. Struggling to see through the thick, choking dust that had been stirred up, he eyed what was left of the web street where House Melarn had been, portions of it still aflame, and saw that chunks of it, too, were giving out. Instead of heading straight up toward that spot, he veered to the side, away from the worst of the damage. Where the calcified webbing broadened into a plaza it was still solid and firm. As he labored in that direction, another major section of the street fell away, following House

Melarn to the bottom. What was left was just a ledge jutting out into space.

The mage pumped his wings, steering the two of them toward the firmer pavement, past the ledge, which extended perhaps ten feet from the plaza and was twice as wide. When he was over the plaza, he sank down quickly, flapping his wings to force himself to fall off to one side rather than directly on top of Danifae. The drow female dropped right where he'd set her down and sprawled there, drawing deep, ragged breaths. He settled down next to her, none too gently himself, and collapsed. Little points of light swam in his vision as he gasped for breath in the dust-choked air. His limbs were leaden, and he could do nothing but listen to Danifae's and his own panting.

"That was some rescue effort," Ryld said, floating down next to the wizard. "I don't know what sort of terror you're supposed to be, but please don't ever try to save me looking like that. I'm liable to kill you before I know it's you."

Pharaun opened one eye and looked at the warrior as he mentally ended the transformation spell and returned to his own form.

"Certainly not," he answered between gasps. "You, my friend, would just have to extract your worthless carcass from poor Danifae's predicament yourself, should you ever find it thusly trapped. You haven't the beauty to warrant rescuing."

The other members of the group were all settling upon the plaza now, and as Halisstra ascended next to her battle captive attendant, she seemed to crumple, covering her face in her hands. Pharaun supposed he could understand her anguish. After all, her home was sitting at the bottom of the chasm.

"I owe you a very large debt, wizard," Danifae said. "My thanks."

Pharaun, propped up on his elbows, inclined his head in acknowledgement, still wondering what had possessed him to try the stunt in the first place. He certainly would have felt no regret at seeing the female plunge to her death, but in the end, he supposed, it would have been an awful waste.

"I'm sure there are ways you and I can find for you to repay me," he deadpanned, his face smooth.

"Yes," Halisstra said, looking up. "We both owe you. I will make certain we find a suitable reward for you."

She attempted to offer a genuinely warm smile for Pharaun. The wizard nodded again, intrigued by the suggestiveness of the drow's offer. He eyed the battle captive again, wondering just how willing she was to serve as recompense for the fact that she was still breathing. The look in her eyes made it clear she was not pleased, but she didn't voice her displeasure as the Melarn daughter then leaned in to inspect her counterpart in what Pharaun thought was a decidedly affectionate manner. Danifae's leg looked badly cut and bruised but not too much the worse for wear.

Quenthel clicked her tongue in exasperation and said, "Now that everyone is back from the brink of death, I think it's time to leave this city. First, though, we must see if we can salvage our other supplies back at the inn."

The others nodded in agreement.

"Let's go quickly," Pharaun suggested, aware of the noise of fighting, invisible through the haze but definitely coming closer. "We don't want to remain here for any longer than we have to, I think."

Pharaun stood, dusting himself off and picking up and replacing his *piwafwi* from where Ryld had dropped it only moments before. He gazed out across the city, for the first time, really, and the scene took his breath away.

"We may already be too late," the wizard breathed, overawed by the devastation he could only partially see, as so much was obscured by a hazy glow, or cloaked with thick smoke. The section of Ched Nasad where House Melarn had been was alive with flames. Recalling that he and Danifae had just escaped perishing in the monumental occurrence, he glanced down to where Halisstra and the other dark elf sat huddled together. Halisstra looked stricken, staring off into the vastness of the city as her attendant huddled close to her and whispered soothing words.

"Yes," Quenthel concurred. "This will get worse, much worse. Everyone stay alert. Master Argith, give the two of them their weapons," she said, gesturing toward Halisstra and Danifae. "I think they've earned the right to bear them after getting us out of that deathtrap."

The weapons master pulled a black circle of cloth from a pocket of his *piwafwi,* unfolded it, and threw it down upon the stone paving of the plaza. It transformed into a perfectly round hole, large enough for him to reach into. He began rummaging around inside it.

"I think our return to the inn will have to wait for later," Valas said, pointing. "We're not in the clear yet."

When Pharaun turned his gaze toward where the scout indicated, he groaned. Scores of gray dwarves were advancing in a line toward them from out of the smoke, faces grim, crossbows and axes brandished. Their front rank had formed a shield wall, while the second row prepared to fire missile weapons. They were mere yards away.

"Look out!" Halisstra cried, pointing in the opposite direction with the mace Ryld had just handed to her.

A host of drow soldiers and priestesses appeared out of the thick smoke, surging forward to meet the duergar head on.

When the fiery, smoke-choked estate finally ripped loose from the web street and tumbled into the vast depths of the city below, Aliisza looked on with a mixture of fascination and disappointment. She was certain the wizard was lost to her, yet she marveled at the capacity for destruction the drow displayed. They were tearing apart their own city, with the capable help of several other species. She wondered what any of them hoped to gain from it, but she didn't really care. She was just sorry she couldn't enjoy any more flings with the mage.

With her consort dead, the alu prepared to make her way out of the city. She had no more cause to be there, and delaying her departure any longer would only place her at risk, however slight. She would rather not have to confront a host of drow or duergar, and she certainly didn't relish the thought of large amounts of stonework falling on her.

Before she could follow through on her intentions to leave, though, Aliisza spied movement a little way down from where the palatial abode had been but moments before. She wasn't sure, for the air in the vicinity was choked with smoke and dust, but she thought—

There. Something was definitely hovering in the air, a wretched creature the fiend knew well enough—a bird-woman known as a harpy—and it had company, a second form gripped in its talons. The pair of them hovered in mid-air, struggling to stay aloft, and the harpy veered up and to the side, bearing its cargo with it.

As Aliisza followed the pair's progress, she caught more movement out of the corner of her eye and realized the harpy and the drow clinging to it were being followed. It was the wizard's companions.

The alu found herself laughing, realizing that Pharaun must be the harpy in a transmuted state, no doubt one of his many spells. He really was an impressive mage, she thought. Somehow, some way, the entire group had managed to free themselves from the building just before it collapsed and vanished into the bottom of the cavern, and along the way, they had picked up two additional members.

Aliisza moved cautiously closer, wanting to get a better look without being seen, and when she did, her eyes narrowed. That wretch Pharaun had rescued some tart, a beautiful drow who, despite her current disheveled look, was obviously a lovely catch for the wizard. Even as she watched, the mage transformed back into his natural form, collapsing beside the female, giving her the eye even as he caught his breath.

Aliisza was furious, watching the mage ogle the drow. She would tear that trollop's eyes out herself! She would—!

Shaking with anger, she prepared to swoop in and make good on her silent threats, but the rest of the group settled around the pair. Clenching her fists in fury, Aliisza restrained herself, but she wanted to know what was going on. Quickly, she cast a spell and began to magically eavesdrop on their conversation.

—must see if we can salvage our other supplies back at the inn.

Then let's go quickly, she heard Pharaun say. *We don't want to remain here for any longer than we have to, I think.*

Grinning, Aliisza ended the spell and flew off, still careful to avoid drawing attention. She had an idea forming, and she was pleased with herself for thinking of it.

⟡ ⟡ ⟡

"Get off this street!" Ryld urged, pointing to a smaller thoroughfare that ran past a temple off to one side where they might avoid
the worst of the clash. "Hurry!" the warrior commanded, sprinting
toward the side street.

Pharaun heard the call of his friend and tried to turn and scramble
toward the side street that Ryld had indicated, but the wizard wasn't
quite fast enough to avoid the press of drow streaming past him. Instead, he was buffeted along for several feet in the opposite direction
before he finally managed to slip off to the side, taking refuge against
a set of large stone stairs leading up to some immense public building.
A moment later, Danifae staggered alongside him, dropping to her
knees and panting for breath.

"Where are the others?" the wizard asked her, admiring her curves
even as the battle raged around them.

"Don't know," she gasped. "Were . . . right behind me."

"We can't stay here," Pharaun told her.

He began to look around for a better vantage point upon which
to watch for his companions without being in the midst of the
fighting.

The battle was raging in the plaza where Pharaun and the
others had become separated. A duergar stepped up to the pair of
them, smiled maliciously, and raised a spiked warhammer to strike
at the mage. Danifae was too quick, though, jerking her morning
star around and into the gray dwarf's midsection. The stout creature gasped as the wind was knocked out of him, and Pharaun
took advantage of the delay to cast a spell. A wide but thin fan of
flame sprang from the wizard's fingertips and caught the humanoid squarely across the face. The duergar shrieked and staggered backward, flailing at his burning beard. Others in the crowd
shifted and moved to avoid coming into contact with the blazing
creature, and finally the duergar fell off-balance and collapsed, unmoving, to the paved street.

"Come on," Pharaun insisted, taking Danifae by the hand and

leading her, still limping from her ordeal back in the collapsing House, up the stairs to the top of the landing.

A pair of gray dwarves started to follow the two of them then stopped about halfway up, aiming loaded crossbows. Pharaun spun away and yanked his *piwafwi*'s hood around him, using the cloak to shield both himself and Danifae. Two bolts smacked into the center of his back, giving him a vicious sting.

He cried out from the pain, sinking down to one knee. Angrily freeing his magical rapier, Pharaun turned back to face the pair of duergar, mentally directing the dancing weapon toward them. The wizard managed to engage the first gray dwarf, but the second one scrambled past the enchanted weapon and clambered up the steps toward him.

A blur of fur and claws landed on the steps between the mage and his foe, and Jeggred sliced and gashed at the duergar, spraying gouts of blood in every direction. The humanoid staggered back from the draegloth's onslaught, his arms held up defensively as he was cut down. When the first gray dwarf saw the fate of his companion, he backed down the steps and fled into the swirling maelstrom of skirmishing below.

"Stay here," Jeggred said, bounding back down into the crowd. "I will get the others."

Pharaun considered whether to obey the draegloth or ignore the beast. He would be much happier, he decided, if he could get up on top of the building, but he knew that Danifae was unable to follow him, should he choose to levitate there. He decided to await the return of Quenthel's pet.

"Back in here," he said to Danifae, stepping into the deeper darkness of the entryway and pulling her in after him.

From there, they could watch the street below without being so exposed.

Danifae pressed against Pharaun, trying to remain out of sight, but the effect was very distracting. The mage found himself pressing right back, while at the same time wondering how he could be so easily diverted during such a time.

It's not like you've never enjoyed the feel of the flesh before, he chided himself.

Still, he was glad that she lingered there, though whether her contact with him was purely happenstance or calculated, he wasn't sure.

The two of them did not have to wait long. Jeggred reappeared after a couple of moments, with Quenthel right behind him. Jeggred cut a swath through the crowd with his oversized claws, while the drow protected the fiend's back. As the duo forced their way through the throngs, more than a few fell before the draegloth's fierce strikes. Finally, they reached the stairs and hurried up to the landing.

"We're here," Pharaun said, gesturing for Quenthel and Jeggred to join him. "We've got to get to the roof," he said, pointing over their heads. "We can see much better from up there, and stay out of the fray."

Jeggred nodded and grabbed Danifae. Together, they began to levitate upward, reaching a spot on the roof that overlooked the sea of clashing bodies below. Pharaun and Quenthel followed quickly. The four of them settled down atop the rounded surface and dropped low, wanting to avoid creating too large a profile against the backdrop of the city. Pharaun did a careful inspection of the city streets one level up, trying to ascertain whether or not they'd been noticed from there. It appeared that they had not.

"Do you see them?" Quenthel asked no one in particular, and Pharaun returned his attention to the scene below.

The battle still raged, but it was beginning to thin somewhat as the body count grew.

"Nothing," the Master of Sorcere replied, and Danifae also shook her head.

"The warrior went running that way," the battle captive said, pointing toward a side street on the opposite side of the square. "I think Halisstra followed him."

"Yes, I heard him," Pharaun replied. "I tried to get there, but the surge was too much. When the fighting dies down, we can try to reach them."

"What about Valas?" Quenthel said. "What happened to him?"

Pharaun replied, "I don't know, but he can disappear even when you're looking right at him, so I don't think he's in much danger. He'll show up when we need him most."

By this time, the duergar were beginning to overwhelm the force of dark elves, and when reinforcements for the gray dwarves arrived, what was left of the drow turned and fled. Pharaun watched, hoping the throng of duergar would give chase, but they seemed content to hold up and regroup.

That's when everything went wrong.

Five or six crossbow bolts snapped against the roof next to the wizard, and a couple of them actually struck him in the back. Only the enchantments of his *piwafwi* protected him, but he was getting damned tired of being hit. Danifae was not so lucky. One of the bolts speared her through the calf, and she growled in pain as Pharaun leaped up to shield her with his own body.

A burst of flame and light exploded only a few feet to the wizard's right. Fire swept over the surface of the roof where they crouched as a second and a third burst landed near the first. The wizard flinched, then turned to see where the new attack was coming from. What he saw made his heart sink. The attackers, whom Pharaun could see were more gray dwarves, were perched atop a web street one level above them and near the back line of the roof. They hurled more firepots in the drow's direction, and Jeggred roared in anger, hit by one of the incendiary pots.

"Damn it, Pharaun, you've led us into a crossfire!" Quenthel snarled at the mage. "We've got to get off this roof. Jeggred, shield me."

Quenthel turned to peer over the side, and Jeggred positioned himself to shield the three drow with his body as best he could. Part of his fur was smoking, but the draegloth didn't seem to notice.

"We can not stand here," he said.

"I know," Pharaun responded, examining the bolt wound in Danifae's leg more carefully.

It had struck the same leg that was already injured but didn't appear bad, having missed the bone and penetrated only the fleshy part of her calf. He snapped off what he could, and the battle captive gave a slight jerk.

Quenthel made a disgusted sound, pulling back from the edge.

"All of this commotion has attracted their attention below us," Quenthel said in a harsh tone. "We can't go that way."

"Then we'll go over the other side," the wizard replied.

He shoved what was left of the bolt through Danifae's leg and out. She hissed from the sudden pain, but bit her lip and stifled any more sounds. More crossbow bolts and firepots were smacking down against the stone around them.

"Is it poisoned?" Pharaun asked the high priestess.

In answer, one of the viper heads on Quenthel's whip rose up and hissed, "No."

More of the firepots slammed down nearby, adding to the roar of the fire, which was hot and spreading across the rock surface of the building.

"We'll be roasted rothé meat in a moment," the mage said. "Heal her so we can go!"

"Forget her," Quenthel replied. "Come on."

The Mistress of the Academy stood and moved toward the back of the building, still skulking behind the draegloth.

Pharaun looked back down at Danifae, shrugged, and began to stand. The female reached up and grabbed him by the *piwafwi,* a determined look on her face.

"Don't leave me here," she said. "I can walk. Just help me up."

Another pair of explosions erupted near her head, and she flinched forward as Pharaun took hold of her by the hand and hauled her to her feet.

"You won't regret it," she said, giving the wizard a brief but obvious look. "I'll be worth it."

Limping, blood flowing from the puncture, Danifae began to follow Quenthel and the draegloth.

"Jeggred!" she called. "Carry me!"

Pharaun realized his mouth was hanging open, and he snapped it shut. As he trotted after the battle captive, he saw Quenthel and the draegloth freeze, and he swept his gaze to where they were looking, at the back side of the building. Rising up from behind the roofline was an immense, chitinous leg of something all too familiar. The leg sought footing upon the rooftop, and two more appeared, followed by the head of a spider of massive size.

"Lolth preserve us," Quenthel breathed. "Where did that come from?"

The immense spider pulled itself into full view, scrambling ponderously over the back edge of the building, each step making the entire structure shake violently.

"Oh, no," Danifae said. "They didn't . . ."

"They, who?" Pharaun asked, involuntarily backing up a step.

Even Jeggred seemed anxious, watching the enormous arachnid, black and shiny, heave itself fully atop the building. Its mandibles clicked as it peered about, its multilensed eyes glistening in the firelight.

"And what did *they* do?" the wizard added.

"The matron mothers," Danifae replied. "They summoned a guardian spider. The fools."

Quenthel sucked in her breath.

"Indeed," the high priestess agreed. "We must flee."

Pharaun wanted to ask the two females what in the Abyss a guardian spider was, but at that moment, the arachnid spotted them, though they had remained quite still. It leaned forward eagerly, coming after them.

As one, they turned and fled over the side.

As she reached the alley, following Ryld Argith, Halisstra turned to see who had caught up with her in the chaos of the swarming, fighting drow and duergar. Of the others, there was no sign.

"Come on!" Ryld shouted from up ahead, motioning frenetically for Halisstra to keep up with him.

Several duergar had followed them into the alley that ran alongside the temple and were closing in on her. She turned back for a moment, thinking to make a stand and drive them away, but a crossbow bolt snapped against the stone wall near the priestess, shattering and showering her with splinters. She turned again and ran, the gray dwarves pounding along after her.

As Halisstra caught up to Ryld, he fired his own crossbow once, to slow down the pursuit, and they sprinted along the alley together, weaving through the turns of the pathway, trying to lose their foes. The two of them turned one last corner and skidded to a stop. The alleyway ended at a solid wall, though one side was low, protecting some sort of covered porch.

"Damn," Ryld muttered, slipping his greatsword free. He turned back to prepare to face the oncoming gray dwarves. "Get ready," he told her, and Halisstra planted herself beside the warrior, her heavy mace feeling good in her hand.

"Why don't we just float up there?" she asked, pointing to the roofline as the first two duergar appeared.

The first of the gray dwarves wielded a wicked-looking, double-bladed axe, while the second had a heavy hammer that was easily twice the size of Halisstra's own mace. She readjusted the grip on her shield as the hammer-wielding dwarf advanced, hate gleaming in his eyes.

Ryld risked a quick glance upward before he stepped gracefully to the side, avoiding the first cut of the double-bladed axe and making a quick, neat cut of his own that the gray dwarf barely managed to parry.

"Only if we have to," the warrior replied. "No sense making ourselves a target for their crossbows."

Halisstra could see that though the duergar's weapon was larger, the creature was forced to put a lot behind each swing, while Ryld was able to sidestep and redirect his own weapon far more easily. Then the priestess was too busy thwarting her own attacker's strikes to watch the weapons master.

The first blow came low, aimed at her knees, and she dipped the shield down enough so that the hammer grazed it, scraping across as she spun back and out of the way to avoid taking the full brunt of the strike. The dwarf followed this with an uppercut swing, which Halisstra was forced to block with her weapon, again redirecting the hammer rather than trying to completely stop the swing. She brought her mace back around and waited, thinking to let her enemy tire himself by repeatedly over-swinging.

That was all good in theory, Halisstra realized, but when three more duergar appeared, she knew that she and Ryld had been cornered. This time, when the dwarf over-swung and she deflected the blow with her shield, she also kicked out, catching the gray dwarf with her boot in the side of his knee. The humanoid grunted and staggered backward a couple of steps, but another dwarf was there, ready to step into the fray. Halisstra moved to position herself next to Ryld again, working so that each of them could protect the other's flank, preventing the gray dwarves from getting inside their position.

Out of the corner of her eye, she saw Ryld, still battling with the gray dwarves. One of the humanoids lay dead at his feet, while another had a bloody gash across his thigh. Behind them, two more had appeared, and these had crossbows, which they brought to bear, waiting for openings to shoot at the two drow.

One of the duergar nudged his companion and pointed to the priestess. Together, they swung their crossbows around to put her in their sights, and Halisstra took refuge behind her shield. She felt one bolt strike her shield, but the other embedded itself in her shoulder. She grunted in pain and staggered backward, unable to keep her shield raised high enough for solid protection.

Another gray dwarf circled to Halisstra's shield side, seeing that her defenses were down, and brought his axe high for a new strike. She did her best to spin and face the duergar without exposing Ryld's flank, and she managed to parry the blow with her mace, but the crushing force of it made her stumble to one knee.

"Ryld! Help me!" she cried out, and as though sensing she was in trouble, the warrior was in front of her, battling all four of the foes at once.

The priestess risked a glance over at the gray dwarves who were reloading their crossbows. They were also pointing at her and grinning. Or rather, they were pointing over her head, Halisstra realized.

The priestess's heart sank as she took a peek above. More of the gray dwarves had already taken the roof, and these had thrown nets across the opening while she and Ryld had been engaged in the battle. They were trapped inside the alley, unable to escape. The duergar on the roofs also had crossbows, and as one of them fired at her, Halisstra flinched. The crossbow bolt whisked across her face, grazing her cheek. She felt wetness.

"Ryld!" she cried out as she stumbled to her feet again. "They're above us, too. We're trapped."

The warrior never acknowledged Halisstra's cry, so busy was he fending off four duergar. Slowly, he was being forced back, bloody gashes across his body, having to retreat a little at a time to keep the gray dwarves from surrounding him.

Gritting her teeth, Halisstra tested the end of the crossbow bolt that protruded from her arm and almost wretched from the pain that doing so produced. Her shield arm useless, the priestess rose to her feet anyway, gripping her mace and moving next to the warrior once more. She tried to stay beside him, to guard his flank and enjoy a similar protection.

One of the four gray dwarves was dead, but Ryld was breathing heavily. A duergar slipped around to Halisstra's side, trying to get inside her defenses. She swung her mace hard and caught the duergar closing in on her on the shoulder, feeling the satisfying crunch of metal on bone. The gray dwarf growled in anguish as he dropped his axe and fell back out of Ryld's reach.

Two more stepped in to take the wounded one's place, and Halisstra had to press in too closely to Ryld to avoid being struck down. Her movement hampered the weapons master's ability to fight, and he took a cut across his forearm as a result.

"By the Dark Mother," Ryld snarled, whipping Splitter around to cleave the offending gray dwarf's head completely off.

The body flopped to the ground as the head rolled away, past another duergar, who watched it pass him with a look of horror on his face.

Another crossbow bolt clacked against the stone of the street near Halisstra, and two more struck her armor, bouncing off. Ryld jerked as a bolt flew close to him, but he never turned his attention away from his adversaries, never deviated from his fluid motion and quick, precise strikes. Still, he and Halisstra were being backed into a corner, the priestess saw, and they would make easy prey for the snipers on the roof.

The first firepot exploded right behind Halisstra, making her jump and nearly get her head taken off by an axe. She scrambled away from the flames as she warded off another blow from the axe-wielding enemy in front of her with her mace, feeling the vibration of the blow all the way up her arm. Two more of the flaming contraptions smacked against the end of the street, the clay pots shattering and spilling fire everywhere. She risked a glance up and saw another one hurtling toward her. Somehow, her wounded shoulder screaming in agony, she managed to bring her shield up with both hands and deflected the pot so that it skipped off and hit the pavement between her and her opponent.

The gray dwarves fighting with them began backing up, and Halisstra saw that the duergar on the roof were creating a fire screen to seal her and Ryld off, trap them between the flames and the wall. She knew that they intended to pin the two drow down, and pick them off at their leisure. There was nowhere for the dark elves to go. They were going to die.

SIXTEEN

The second time he got no reply from the distant wizard, Gromph slammed his fists down atop his bone desk in frustration. Two sendings, and nothing. What had happened to Pharaun? Why wouldn't he answer? The Archmage of Menzoberranzan rose up and began to pace.

Two different spies had already contacted him with reports of heavy fighting in Ched Nasad. The matron mothers were squabbling over something, it appeared, and like it or not, the team from Menzoberranzan appeared to be in the thick of it, but Gromph couldn't get any confirmation from the team itself. He considered whether or not he should try one last time.

Realizing he couldn't force the wizard to answer—Pharaun might be receiving the magical whispers and was simply unable to reply—Gromph decided against any further waste of magic. It was possible that Pharaun was unwilling to give himself away in the company of others who didn't know the full extent of what he was up to.

Or he's dead, Gromph thought.

It was a possibility, however unlikely that seemed. Pharaun Mizzrym had a knack for keeping himself out of the worst sorts of trouble, and coupled with Quenthel and the others, the archwizard had a difficult time imagining that they'd succumbed to whatever violence inundated the streets of the City of Shimmering Webs. Still, it wasn't impossible.

If the team was dead Gromph felt no remorse.

Gromph sighed and reached into one of the drawers of his desk, extracting a scroll tube. Pulling the bundle of rolled parchment free of the tube, he found the page he was looking for and tucked the others away again. Spreading his selected sheet out on the desktop, the archwizard took a deep breath and scanned through the spell once before preparing to cast it. He was just about to begin the incantation to try once more to reach the wizard when a thought struck him.

Just because he'd been communicating exclusively with Pharaun didn't mean he had to continue that way. Why not try some of the other members of the team? It was possible Pharaun was dead or incapacitated, but that didn't necessarily mean that all of them were. Quenthel was the most likely choice, but he didn't relish the thought of talking to her. Who would his next choice be? Ryld Argith.

Nodding to himself, Gromph read through the arcane words on the scroll, weaving the magic that would allow him to contact the warrior. He completed the phrases and felt the magic coalesce.

"Ryld, this is Gromph Baenre. No word from Pharaun. Give me an update on the situation. Whisper a reply at once."

Gromph sat back and waited for a response. It was deathly quiet in his secret chamber. If Ryld Argith answered, the archwizard would undoubtedly hear it. The silence seemed to stretch on, and Gromph was just about to throw up his hands in frustration and despair when the reply came. When he heard it, his blood actually ran cold.

I'm separated from Pharaun and the others, don't know where they are. Duergar are everywhere. The whole city is burning. We're cut off, no way—

Gromph slumped in his chair, sighing long and loudly, shaking his head in displeasure.

Triel is going to spit rocks when she hears this, he thought. How long can I hold off telling her? On the other hand, maybe Quenthel is dead.

The archmage caught himself smiling as he rose from his desk to go find his sister.

As Pharaun ended his descent at the steps of the building, he could see a sizable force of duergar, waiting and watching. Without hesitating, he took a couple steps forward then crouched and smacked his hand against the stone, summoning a sphere of darkness. Quickly, he retreated back up the steps just as Jeggred settled to the ground next to him, with Quenthel on his other side. A couple crossbow bolts whizzed by, but he ignored the missiles, motioning the other three to move into the protection of the porch where he and Danifae had taken refuge before. It was a small space, especially with the draegloth in attendance, but they all fit and when crouched down were at least partially shielded from the duergar on the street below. More importantly, they were out of sight of the spider.

Danifae sank to the stone floor, and the wizard could see that she was bleeding steadily from the wound in her leg. The battle captive opened her own pack and pulled out a strip of cloth. Wrapping the makeshift bandage around her leg, she held it there as Pharaun assisted her by tying it off. Quenthel looked on impassively.

Pharaun stole a glance at Quenthel and signed, where Danifae could not see, *If you heal her, we can move much faster.*

Quenthel shrugged and replied, *She is not a necessary part of this group. I will not waste the magic on her. There might not be any left later for you, if I did.*

Pharaun pursed his lips, wondering what it would take to convince Quenthel that the battle captive was an asset they could not do without. He turned his attention back to Danifae.

"Can you walk on it?" he asked her.

"Yes," she answered. "I can keep up."

"We will not wait for you, if you cannot," Quenthel said sharply, "and I will not permit Jeggred to be slowed down by carrying you. Do you understand?"

"Yes, Mistress," Danifae said.

Pharaun saw that her eyes narrowed a bit. He gestured with his palms down where Quenthel could not see, indicating for Danifae to be patient. He was not about to abandon her, even if he knew full well that she was playing upon his desires just to save her own hide.

At that moment, a single massive spider leg settled on the stone between the alcove and the shield of magical darkness that the mage had summoned, and a portion of the arachnid's body hove into view. It was the underside of the creature, Pharaun noted, holding his breath as he felt the tremor of it settling its weight on the web street. Beside him, the two females were wide-eyed, and Jeggred watched the scene warily, but none of them moved. As the spider glided down and away from their hiding place, the wizard sighed softly in relief. It had not noticed them.

Out beyond the protective blackness, Pharaun could hear the shouts of duergar—cries of terror—as the spider moved quickly away from the building where the mage and his companions were hiding. The vibrations of its steps grew ever softer as it departed.

Good, Pharaun thought. Chase them for a while.

"What in the Abyss is a guardian spider?" he asked aloud.

Danifae shrugged and said, "I don't know as much about them as Halisstra. You'll have to ask her if you want the details, but I can tell you that the matron mothers have, in the past, brought these creatures forth for various purposes. They must have conjured one today, maybe to turn the tide of the fighting."

Quenthel sighed and shook her head.

"Madness," she said quietly. "The matron mothers of this city pick the most foolish time to war with one another."

"I wouldn't limit the appellation of foolish solely to the matron mothers of *this* city," Pharaun muttered under his breath.

Quenthel glanced at him, but he simply smiled, and she turned her attention back to the unseen ruckus beyond the sphere of darkness, apparently not having clearly heard his remarks.

"Dispel the darkness," the high priestess ordered the wizard. "I want to see what's happening."

As I said, Pharaun thought, shaking his head.

Sighing, the mage gestured and the sphere of blackness vanished, revealing the street beyond. The spider was out of sight for the moment. In the street, nothing moved, though there were plenty of dead strewn about, duergar and drow alike.

"It seems to have wandered off," Quenthel observed, rising to her feet. "We should be going, too, before it comes back."

"Let's give it another couple of moments," Pharaun suggested, still unnerved at the appearance of the giant creature. "Just to make sure it's completely gone."

Quenthel scowled at the wizard then turned to the draegloth and said, "Go see."

Smiling, the fiend bounded out from their hiding place to peer in both directions.

At that moment the duergar chose to come out of hiding.

Scores of them poured out from around the corner and from the building across the street, as though they had been waiting for the drow to emerge from their hiding place.

"Get 'em!" one of the gray dwarves shouted.

The duergar formed up a semicircle, surrounding the dark elves' position, and Jeggred leaped back into the alcove as the first volley of crossbow bolts peppered the walls around them.

Cursing, Pharaun ducked low, using the elevation of the porch as a screen. He pointed his finger toward the street and spoke the arcane phrase that would trigger one of his spells. At once, a cloud of roiling smoke, shot through with white-hot embers, formed beneath him and began to flow away from the building and across the street. The duergar, many of whom had their crossbows loaded again and were aiming at the small group, eyed the fiery haze warily as it appeared and began to churn toward them. As it reached those in the front ranks and engulfed them, they began to scream and flail, scorched by the embers.

Gray dwarves fell back before the cloud as it burned their kin where they stood. The smoke was thick and black. It moved away from the building, and the screams of the duergar intensified as more and more of them succumbed to the scorching heat.

Pharaun crept out a little way to watch his handiwork. Jeggred stood beside him, unafraid of a stray missile, eyeing the cloud with delight.

"Can any of them survive?" the fiend asked.

"Not if you go dance among them," the Master of Sorcere replied. "The fire can't hurt you, right?"

"That is correct," the draegloth answered, and he bounded into the smoky fog.

The incendiary cloud had pushed across to the opposite side of the street. Bodies of duergar were scattered across its surface, charred and smoking. Several of them were openly burning. Jeggred emerged from within the roiling smoke, which Pharaun redirected to flow down the street, in the direction opposite they wished to go. It would continue of its own accord for some minutes before dissipating, ensuring that another horde of the enemy couldn't come up behind them. The draegloth was dripping with blood but had a very satisfied look on his face. He had an amputated arm in his hand and was chewing on it as he trotted back to where the three drow were crouched.

Pharaun studiously ignored the fiend's dining habits as Quenthel asked, "Are they all dead?"

"Either dead or running," the draegloth answered. "The street is clear."

"Then we should proceed. The spider could return at any moment, and we have no time to waste. Where did you say the others went?" the high priestess asked Pharaun.

The wizard pointed toward the alleyway where he had seen Ryld vanish moments before.

"The weapons master went in there," he said. "It's possible that one or both of the others joined him."

Before Pharaun could take more than a couple of steps, though, the street heaved and shook.

"Damnation!" he heard Quenthel cry out, and the mage risked a glance back.

The spider had spotted them and was skittering along the street, easily stepping over the roiling cloud of flame Pharaun had sent in that direction. The arachnid came toward them, and fast, its mandibles flexing eagerly.

Pharaun turned and fled from it.

*   *   *

"I'm telling you, I want that thing killed, now!" Ssipriina Zauvirr screamed. "If you don't do it, we are all in a midden heap of trouble!"

She loomed over Khorrl Xornbane as the two stood on the steps of an upscale fashion shop, abandoned in the fighting, situated in the interior of the gray dwarves' position on the plaza. The shop was well back from the lines of battle, but Khorrl could plainly see the spider in the distance as the matron mother pointed at it. The massive creature clambered over a building near where Clan Xornbane was locked in a pitched battle with a force of antagonistic drow.

"And *I'm* telling *you*, I'm not sending my boys to fight that thing!" Khorrl snarled back, losing patience with this haughty dark elf. "You hired me to win you a seat on your blessed council by defeating your adversaries, not to clean up your mistakes. You and your cronies brought it here, so you and your cronies can figure out how to stop it. It's not my fault you can't control it!"

"*My* mistakes? Let's talk about mistakes, Captain. Let's talk about you and your mercenary rabble taking to the streets prematurely, ruining my well-laid plans for ascension to the Council in one foolish moment. Mistakes, indeed! We wouldn't even be in this position if you had followed simple orders."

Khorrl wanted to slice the offensive drow in half right then. If she hadn't brought a retinue of bodyguards with her, he would have, but he was outnumbered, and he knew that even if he got in the killing blow he would be taken down shortly thereafter. Instead, he squeezed his grip on his axe and sucked in a deep breath, trying to still the trembling rage that coursed through his body.

"Prematurely?" he said through clenched teeth. "I received direct orders from your boy Zammzt. If he didn't have the word from you, go talk to him. Either way, *stop wasting my time!*" he finished with a roar. "I am not sacrificing my lads needlessly to kill your spider. In fact, we're done, here.

"Forghel!" he called out, looking for his aide. "Forghel, sound the retreat. We're pulling out."

Khorrl knew he played a dangerous game, turning his back on the dark elf, but he wanted to bait her, see if she would lose her temper.

"Liar!" Ssipriina screamed once more. "Don't you blame your foolish gaffes on my House. You will not abandon your—Don't you walk away from me!

"To the Abyss with you. *Kill him!*" she screamed.

Smiling to himself, Khorrl gave a shrill whistle, and instantly, a host of his boys banished their invisibility and magically appeared, surrounding him, axes and crossbows ready. The captain turned back to face the advancing retinue of drow, looking specifically for Ssipriina.

The dark elf's bodyguards had begun to chase him down, but when the additional duergar materialized, the drow soldiers faltered a moment. That was all the Clan Xornbane troops needed. Charging forward, Khorrl's boys took the fight to the drow.

Of course, Ssipriina Zauvirr was not foolish enough to remain too close to the fighting, but she gave the captain one last baleful glare as she turned and retreated back down the steps in the opposite direction.

Grabbing up a crossbow from one of his gray dwarves who was standing close to him, Khorrl sighted down the weapon, taking aim at the withdrawing matron mother. He fired, but the bolt clacked loudly off a stone column at the corner of the building as Ssipriina rounded it and disappeared. She would be back, though, the captain knew, and she would bring more of her damnable soldiers with her.

"Sir, look," Forghel said, running up beside Khorrl.

The captain turned and looked back the way his aide was pointing, and his heart sank. The immense spider was positioned in the middle of the street, rearing up on its back legs, while its front appendages

fluttered oddly in the air. A bluish line appeared in the air, as tall as
the spider itself, and widened into an odd-shaped field of blue light.
A second spider stepped through the magical opening, equally as large
as the first. It had somehow summoned a mate.

Ryld was growing tired. He didn't know how much longer he
could defend himself and Halisstra from the crowd of gray dwarves
that slowly, inexorably, pressed in at them from all sides. He knew he
was running out of room to retreat. Soon, he would find his back
against a wall, and there would be no more running.

Fire began to spill from above. The clay pots exploded all around
him, and he knew it was only a matter of time before one of them
found him.

Well, this is a fine way to go, the weapons master thought, ducking beneath a badly overswung hammer strike and cutting the duergar across his midsection. Backed into a corner in an alley, trapped
like a rat in a cage, and burned to death. Well, you wanted to get out
of Menzoberranzan and find a little excitement, fool. I guess this will
have to do.

Surprisingly, the gray dwarves backed away from him, maintaining their guard as they retreated, and Ryld let them go. He was
breathing heavily, his lungs feeling scorched from the acrid smoke
that was all around him. A dozen or more insignificant gashes covered
his arms and torso, burning like the stings of a viper.

If they don't want to fight, I'm not going to argue with them, he
thought gratefully.

He kept his sword level as a threat but risked a quick glance up to
the rooftops.

Sure enough, just as Halisstra had claimed, more of the foul dwarves
had stretched netting across the way, preventing the two of them from
escaping by that route. Ryld was certain he could pick them off with
his crossbow but not if he had to dodge ground troops and firepots
at the same time. He saw the duergar overhead hurl several more of

the horrid things down, but instead of aiming at him, they threw wide, so that the bursts of flame erupted between Ryld and his foes on the ground.

They're trying to seal us in, the weapons master realized. Trap us and kill us without risk to themselves.

He was judging the width of the flames, trying to determine if he could leap across them without burning himself too much, when he realized that Halisstra was speaking to him.

"Ryld," the priestess was saying. "Ryld, I can get us out of here."

The warrior glanced over at her, ignoring the taunts and jeers from above as the duergar took their time, savoring the moment before dispatching the dark elves.

"How?" he asked.

"I can cast a spell," Halisstra replied. "A magical doorway that will get us out of here, but you've got to buy me some time!"

"Ah, Pharaun's favorite trick," Ryld replied. He eyed the low wall that was behind the two of them, and he pointed to it.

"Get over that," he said. "We'll be better protected from above and can decide what to do."

Without waiting for her to follow, Ryld levitated upward until he was at a height just above the top of the wall, which had originally been slightly over his head. He quickly stepped across it to the other side and lowered himself once again. Halisstra, her shield arm hanging limply at her side, was only a heartbeat behind him. She tumbled into the corner with a grunt of pain as Ryld watched for pursuit.

When the duergar saw where the two drow were going, they began yelling in rage. From above, they began to fling more of the firepots down, trying to target the two dark elves, but Ryld pulled Halisstra inside the protection of the covering that hung partially out over the enclosed area. There was a door in the wall to his back, but it appeared stout. He tried it, and as he suspected, it was locked. Several of the firepots had landed inside the little courtyard, but the warrior and the priestess were far enough back away from them that they were in no danger.

"Won't they ever run out of those things?" Halisstra complained as Ryld saw a hand grasp the top of the wall.

Pulling out his crossbow, he waited until a head appeared then fired, catching the gray dwarf directly in the face. The humanoid shrieked and toppled backward.

"Eventually," he replied, reloading, "but let's not stick around to see how long."

"Where should we go? We want to be able to find the others again, right?"

"Yes. We need to get to—"

Ryld cut his words off short as several screams erupted from the other side of the wall. It was only then that he realized that firepots were raining down on that side rather than on theirs.

"What the—?" he said, and scooted forward to the edge of the overhang.

Cautiously, he peered up to the roofline. It appeared that the duergar who had been there were gone. Then, in an instant, he spotted a drow form rise up just long enough to fling another firepot down before ducking out of sight again. Ryld began to laugh.

"What is it?" Halisstra asked, moving up beside the Master of Melee-Magthere. "What do you see?"

"It's Valas," Ryld replied, pointing. "He's taken care of our snipers for us."

Ryld placed his fingers in his mouth and gave a shrill whistle. A similar whistle emanated from above a moment later.

"He knows we know he's up there," Ryld said. "Let's save your spell for later and go join him."

Halisstra nodded.

"Before we go," the weapons master said, crouching beside the priestess, "let me see your arm."

He examined the bolt for a just a moment. It was sunk deep enough in her shoulder that he would have to force it out the other side.

"This will have to wait until Quenthel can heal it. However . . ."

Before she could protest, Ryld snapped the protruding end off.

"Goddess!" Halisstra grunted as she jerked from the pain, squinting her eyes shut.

She reached her other hand up, but Ryld grabbed her arm and held it away.

"Don't," the warrior said. "You'll only make it bleed."

Grimacing, Halisstra shook her head.

"No," she said. "I can heal it. Just let me—"

She pulled her arm free and reached inside her *piwafwi,* producing a wand.

"Push it out," she said, taking the broken end of the bolt and biting down on it.

Ryld complied, bracing her shoulder with one hand and preparing to shove the head of the bolt through with the other. In one clean, quick motion, the shaft was out. Before she could jerk away from him, Ryld pulled it completely free.

Halisstra sobbed once, then she spat out the splintered shaft, waved the wand, and uttered a trigger phrase. The bleeding stopped instantly and the wound closed. The priestess sagged back and closed her eyes in relief.

"Let's go," Ryld said, reaching out to help her to her feet, "before those fires burn out and the grays are over this wall."

"Wait," Halisstra said, and produced a second wand from inside her *piwafwi.* "Let's make it a little harder for them to shoot at us."

Ryld arched his brow at her, puzzled. Quickly, she invoked the power of the wand twice, and the two dark elves were completely invisible.

Ryld reached out and found the priestess. He took her hand.

"So we don't get separated," he explained.

Together, the two drow rose upward, watching as duergar alternated between scattering from the firepots that Valas was hurling down on them with deadly accuracy and firing ineffectually at the scout with their crossbows. As they neared the top, Ryld pulled out Splitter and sliced through the netting, parting the material easily with the enchanted greatsword. He and Halisstra passed through the hole and settled to the rooftop near where Valas knelt, peering over the edge.

"We owe you one," Ryld said to the scout as he moved away from the edge to avoid any stray crossbow bolts.

The roof was covered with the bodies of a good half dozen gray dwarves.

Valas glanced over to where the warrior's voice had come from but didn't react otherwise.

"I saw you come down here and figured I'd try to catch up by coming the long way around," he said, rising up to throw the last of his firepots. "When I saw these cretins here, laughing and throwing these things down, I knew you were in trouble."

"Let's get out of here," Ryld suggested. "Do you know where the others are?"

"I think they got up on the roofs on the other side of the square," the scout replied, dusting off his hands and backing away from the edge. "We'll find them. The wizard will be all flash and glory when they run into something, so we can track them that way."

Ryld turned to follow the scout.

"Too true," he said.

The three dark elves made their way across the rooftops until they came to another side street a little farther ahead of where they'd originally been separated. Valas climbed down the side of a gaudily decorated shop that had plenty of hand- and footholds, while Ryld and Halisstra descended by their customary levitating method. By the time they were on the ground, the invisibility magic had expired.

"Lead on," Ryld said to Valas, gesturing, and the scout took the fore as the three of them prowled through the street, making their way back toward the main thoroughfare.

The ground began to vibrate.

"What in the Underdark?" Ryld muttered, steadying himself as the street bounced beneath his feet. "What is that?"

"I don't know, but it's big," Valas replied. He looked over at Halisstra. "Do you have any clue?" he asked her.

Halisstra shook her head, but she had a worried look on her face.

"Let's not stay and find out," she said.

Valas nodded and proceeded out into the main street. Peering in both directions, he had to reach a hand out to stabilize himself, for the quivering had grown stronger.

"Oh, no," Halisstra said, her voice stricken.

Ryld looked over at her and asked, "What? What is it?"

275

"Oh, by the Dark Mother," the priestess said, putting a hand to her mouth in terror. "They summoned one."

"Summoned *what?*" Ryld demanded.

"One of those," Valas said from the warrior's other side, and when Ryld turned to look, he saw the scout pointing.

The weapons master turned to peer in the direction his companion indicated and saw a spider the size of the entire square clambering into view. He sucked in his breath, feeling his knees go weak.

"Oh, no."

Pharaun knew that with his magically enhanced boots he could easily outrun the other drow, and that's precisely what he did. The wizard sprinted ahead, careful to maintain his balance on the quivering web street as the colossal spider pursued them. He had but a handful of spells left, and there was little if anything left in his repertoire that might affect the huge arachnid. A far better bet, he decided, was to misdirect the creature, perhaps conjure an obscuring mist that would allow him and the others to hide and sneak away while the spider was distracted—but he didn't dare stop to weave the spell.

"Pharaun!" someone shouted from ahead, and the wizard glanced over in time to see Ryld, Valas, and Halisstra standing in the mouth of a side street, gawking slack-jawed at the massive spider behind him.

He veered in their direction and darted into the shadow of the alley. Only then did he stop to catch his breath.

"I've never . . . seen anything . . . like it," the wizard panted. "Danifae called it a . . . guardian spider."

"Yes," Halisstra said softly, still staring at it. "The matron mothers must have called i—Oh, by the Dark Mother . . . it's summoning another one!"

Pharaun turned to see what Halisstra was talking about, looking past Jeggred and Quenthel as they came into view, running for all they were worth, with Danifae limping behind them. The spider had stopped pursuing them, and was rearing up on its hind legs, flailing about with its front limbs in the air. The wizard gasped when an enormous gate opened up in front of the spider, as large as the creature itself. Through the hazy murk of the bluish-white portal, the wizard watched, aghast, as a second massive spider clambered through and onto the street. The portal shut quickly behind it.

"Oh, no," Quenthel murmured. "How many times can they do that?"

"I don't know," Halisstra said from somewhere behind the wizard.

"Once is too many," Pharaun said. "We've got to get out of here."

He spun away from the massive arachnids, ready to sprint in the opposite direction.

"Wait!" Halisstra cried, pointing.

The mage glanced back once more.

Danifae was still limping badly and had not been able to keep up. As the second spider passed through the portal, it appeared on the opposite side of the battle captive. She was trapped between the two creatures, and was sprawled in the middle of the street as well.

"She's hurt!" Halisstra cried.

She took a tentative step forward to go to the aid of her attendant.

"Don't be a fool," Ryld said, grabbing the priestess by the arm as Jeggred and Quenthel joined them. "You'll only get yourself killed, too."

Halisstra jerked herself free and took another step out into the open.

"I don't care," she said. "I'm going to help her."

With that, the First Daughter of House Melarn dashed across the open area to where her servant was struggling to regain her feet.

The spiders sensed the movement, and both of them began to close in.

C h a p t e r

S E V E N T E E N

Pharaun cursed and took a step after Halisstra, thinking he might have to magically cloak the two of them in order to save them.

"Don't," Quenthel ordered. "Danifae was unlucky enough to be wounded. I will not exhaust either resources or time saving her. Let's go while the spiders are distracted."

"But—" Pharaun began, but when he saw the look in the high priestess's eyes, he shook his head and stepped back into the alley. He regretted the idea of losing them—or at least, losing the beautiful Danifae. "Very well," he said.

"I'm not leaving," Ryld said, and he turned to sprint out into the street, following Halisstra.

"No!" Quenthel shouted at the Master of Melee-Magthere, but it was too late. Ryld was already ten steps away, removing Splitter from its sheath on his back as he charged toward the closest of the two spiders. "Damn you all to the Abyss!" Quenthel raged.

Shrugging, Pharaun turned and followed the weapons master.

"Go after them!" Quenthel growled from behind the wizard.

Pharaun could only assume she was talking to him, though why she was ordering him to do something he had already made up his mind to accomplish, he couldn't fathom. Soon enough, though, the draegloth flashed past him, sprinting down the street in the direction he also traveled.

The mage pulled up a few yards from the closest spider, watching as Halisstra reached her servant and knelt down. Somehow, along the way, she had fumbled a wand free from her cloak, and she quickly utilized it, causing both drow to disappear. The spider, looming over the spot where the pair had just been visible, snapped down once, clacking its mandibles together in obvious frustration. The beast began moving its head back and forth, trying to find its prey. In the distance, the second spider had turned its attention to something else. Fortunately, it was not coming their way—at least for the moment.

Pharaun, of course, could still see the two females, for he was aware of the magic they radiated. It appeared to him that Halisstra was dragging Danifae to the side, out of harm's way, but the spider somehow sensed where the two females were, and it dipped its head again, missing a direct bite but coming close enough with its attack that it grazed Halisstra, knocking her down. Shivering in delight at having felt its prey, the spider raised up for another attack.

Ryld had almost reached the creature, and his long legs covered the remaining distance quickly. He leaped through the air, Splitter raised high overhead. As the warrior sailed past the hindmost leg of the giant spider, he swung the greatsword around with all his might, cutting cleanly through the appendage. Black blood spurted everywhere, and the spider reared up, kicking with its ruined leg and barely missing the weapons master.

At nearly the same time, Jeggred launched himself into the air toward another leg, grabbing a hold of the spider and climbing upward. Pharaun could see the draegloth's claws extended, and the fiend used them to great effect as he quickly ascended the creature's limb. Fearlessly, Jeggred slashed and clawed his way to the spider's body and began to climb the slick black abdomen, working his way higher and higher.

The effect of the two attacks was instantaneous. The spider jerked away from its intended meal and spun around, looking to bite whatever tormented it. Its one ruined leg twitched erratically, but otherwise the arachnid lost none of its stability. Ryld had rolled into a crouch after his sweeping sword strike, and he had Splitter up, ready to fend off the spider as it maneuvered to face him.

Pharaun shook his head and considered what he could do to aid in the fight. There was really only one choice. Most of his spells were gone, and the few remaining to him were not offensive in nature. He reached inside his *piwafwi* and produced a wand, a single segment of iron that was about as long as his forearm. Extending it outward, he uttered a trigger phrase and activated the magic in the wand. Instantly, a sizzling bolt of electrical energy leaped forward from the end of the wand, arcing through the air and crackling across the surface of the spider's head. The discharge caused the spider to recoil, chattering and quivering, from Ryld's position. As the last remnants of the bolt dissipated, Pharaun could see that the spider's leathery hide and multifaceted eyes were smoldering.

Pharaun started when he heard the twang of a bowstring strumming, and he glanced down to his right. Valas was there, kneeling, firing off a short bow. The wizard had seen the diminutive scout carrying the weapon all along, but up until then, Valas had apparently had little cause to use it. The Bregan D'aerthe scout lined up and released four shots in the time it took Pharaun to assess the situation, and his aim was true. The arrows embedded themselves in the nearest eye of the spider, one after another, puncturing the many-sided orb like a massive pin cushion. The spider thrashed about in response.

At the same time, Ryld was on his feet again, running with the spider, looking to get in another strike. This time, however, the warrior was not so lucky. As the jerking, pain-crazed creature spasmed along the street, one of its legs swept the warrior off his feet, sending the burly drow tumbling. Ryld landed hard, losing his greatsword in the process.

The massive arachnid was skittering straight toward Pharaun and Valas, and the wizard could see Jeggred on top of it, sitting astride the thing's huge neck, slashing madly with his claws and flinging gobbets of flesh and black blood everywhere as the fiend sawed into the spider's head. The spider reared and jerked, trying to shake Jeggred from its body, but the draegloth clung tenaciously to it, sinking his claws deeply into the beast's flesh to maintain his hold.

The wizard took an involuntary step backward as the onrushing spider closed the distance quickly, its rapid steps making the web street buck and bounce. Raising his wand, the mage fired off a second lightning bolt, letting it crackle over the spider's head, knowing Jeggred would be resistant to its destructive power.

The electrical discharge obviously hurt the massive beast—Pharaun could clearly see scorch marks on its shiny black skin—but it didn't slow a whit. It ambled drunkenly toward the mage and the scout even as Valas pumped a dozen arrows into it.

Goddess! thought Pharaun, backing up another step.

He wanted to turn and run, but he couldn't make himself stop watching the charging creature. Valas was back-stepping too, still firing arrows, but they were both in the spider's sight and it was clearly targeting them as the cause of its woes.

Just as the spider reached the pair of drow and snapped downward, Ryld leaped into view, swinging Splitter in a huge arc and smashing the blade savagely across the creature's face. The lightning bolt had obviously bought the weapons master enough time to retrieve his greatsword.

The arachnid jerked backward, more blood dripping freely from the fresh wound, but it was not to be so easily deterred. It snapped at Ryld once, twice, and the warrior fended the attacks off with his greatsword, laboring to keep the twitching mandibles away from him.

Pharaun scrambled backward again, happy enough to let the broad-shouldered weapons master bear the brunt of the combat. Pharaun raised his wand for a third lightning strike, hoping that would fell the beast, but before he could activate the wand the spider snapped down at Ryld a third time, and the warrior's luck ran out.

The spider's mandibles closed tightly around the Master of Melee-Magthere, who grunted in pain and nearly lost his grip on Splitter. The creature hoisted him into the air, squeezing its captured prey tightly, trying to crush the life out him. Ryld arched his back in agony and began desperately hacking at the mandibles with his sword.

Pharaun hesitated to expend his magical bolts with Ryld in the way, and Valas likewise seemed at a loss, sighting down a drawn-back arrow but faltering. There was no clear shot. Even so, Jeggred continued to hew into the spider's flesh. The draegloth's arms were completely coated with sticky black fluid.

Why won't the blasted thing die? Pharaun thought in dismay.

He was tempted to jolt the creature despite the presence of his companions then he remembered his other wand. Reacting quickly, the wizard managed to fish the second item from inside his *piwafwi* just as the spider stumbled into both him and Valas. The scout went sprawling, rolling into a tumble several yards away, while Pharaun managed to avoid the worst of the blow by leaping out of the way at the last moment, aided by his magical boots.

Landing to one side, the wizard flicked the wand at the spider and uttered the trigger word, sending a host of glowing projectiles streaming from its tip directly at the spider's eyes. The five missiles swerved unerringly around Ryld and struck the creature's eyes in rapid succession. The great spider flinched away, opening its mandibles to chatter in pain, dropping Ryld in the process.

The weapons master fell limply toward the ground but somehow still retained consciousness enough to halt his own descent, drifting the last couple of feet to the pavement. The spider, meanwhile, reared up, its face a bloody mess, Jeggred still slashing at the top of its head.

There's no way it can withstand much more, the wizard thought.

"Finish it," Quenthel said, pointing past the spider. "Kill it and be done with it."

Pharaun could see the second spider coming their way, so he quickly discharged a second round of screaming projectiles from the wand. When they struck home, the spider finally collapsed in the middle of the street, nearly landing atop the still-prone Ryld. The creature didn't move, though its legs and mandibles spasmed awkwardly.

"Withdraw!" Quenthel demanded. "The other one is coming."

Pharaun ran to help Valas get Ryld to his feet, and the trio scurried as fast as they could back into the alley. Jeggred leaped down from his perch atop the dead arachnid and joined them. They all reached the protection of the side street simultaneously, and Pharaun turned back to see what had become of the pair from House Melarn. Farther up the street, the wizard could see the magical emanations of Halisstra and Danifae. They were walking toward him as quickly as the limping drow could move.

"They're almost here," Pharaun said, gesturing back to where he knew only he could see the two. "Keep still," the Master of Sorcere warned. "It might sense vibrations."

The two groups waited, apprehensive. Halisstra and Danifae stopped moving, pressing against the wall of the closest building as the second spider came closer. Pharaun slipped back into the shadows.

As the beast passed, Pharaun prepared to cast the spell he'd considered earlier, one that would bring about a heavy mist, should they need it, but they did not. As the giant arachnid moved off, the vibrations grew calmer. Pharaun stole another glance and saw that the two females were drawing closer.

"You would openly defy me?" Quenthel snarled, slapping a still-woozy Ryld across the cheek.

Jeggred rose up to his full height and moved to stand beside the high priestess, backing her while she meted out her discipline.

Ryld staggered back from the blow, and a trickle of blood dripped from the corner of his mouth, but he didn't flinch from the high priestess's gaze.

"They aren't so expendable as you might think," he said weakly but with his chin in the air. "Give them a chance to prove themselves before you abandon them. It might be you she's rushing back to aid next time."

Jeggred growled and took a step forward, but Quenthel held up her hand in a signal for him to be still. The draegloth glowered at Ryld but obeyed his mistress.

"Your days of questioning my authority are nigh ended," Quenthel said, turning to face both Ryld and Pharaun together. "When we get out of this city, there will be some changes. I am tired of this."

As if to mimic the Mistress of the Academy's foul mood, the snakes of her whip began to shimmy back and forth, hissing in vexation.

"All I say is that you are too quick to dismiss them," Ryld insisted. "They are more valuable than you give them credit for."

"He's right," Pharaun said, "Halisstra has demonstrated some resourcefulness. Don't discount them simply because they are not from Menzoberranzan."

Quenthel scowled at the two of them in turn then drew in Valas with her gaze for good measure. Halisstra and Danifae reached their position, still invisible.

"I am sorry," Halisstra said upon arriving, "but I could not abandon her. She still has a certain value to me."

Quenthel snorted but waved her hand in dismissal, as though minimizing the entire episode.

"You are aware of the conditions under which you will be permitted to stay with us. Keep up, or fall behind. We will not suffer you to slow us down."

She just doesn't want to let on how much we defy her, Pharaun realized. She's pretending that remaining and waiting was her own act of generosity. The wizard smirked to himself.

Halisstra let Danifae down and produced a wand from her belongings. She waved it over the battle captive's leg and murmured a phrase that the wizard didn't quite catch, but then he saw that the puncture wound had healed. The dark elf moved to Ryld to administer a similar healing effort to him, but Quenthel intervened.

"Where did you get that?" the high priestess demanded.

Halisstra started, not expecting such a venomous reaction to her charity.

"It's mine," she began to explain. "I brought it—"

"Not anymore, it isn't. Give it to me," Quenthel insisted.

Halisstra stared at the high priestess but made no move to hand over her magical trinket.

"If you don't want Jeggred to shred you to several pieces right now, hand that wand to me."

Slowly, her eyes burning with anger, Halisstra passed the wand to Quenthel.

The Mistress of Arach-Tinilith examined the wand carefully, nodding in satisfaction. She turned and used it on Ryld herself. As the divine power of the wand flowed into the warrior, his worst injuries closed, though several small scratches and bruises remained. When she was satisfied with the weapons master's condition, she tucked the wand away in her own belongings.

"Now," Quenthel said, turning her attention back on Halisstra, "we will have no more of this wasteful use of curing magic taking place. I will be the one who decides when and if a member of this group receives divine aid, is that clear?"

Halisstra nodded.

"Do you have any more magic secreted away that I should know about? Believe me, I will know if you do."

Drisinil's daughter sighed and nodded. She produced an additional wand and handed it over.

"You cannot use that, though," Halisstra mumbled. "It's arcane in nature. I also . . . dabble in that sort of magic."

"I see. Well, if it becomes necessary, you might get it back when you've proven your worth. Until then, I keep them both."

The high priestess turned and strolled a few feet away, completely ignoring the drow female who stared daggers at her back.

"Halisstra," Pharaun said, trying to change the subject and hoping to show Quenthel that the priestess was useful at the same time, "both you and Danifae seemed to know where these giant spiders came from. What can you tell us?"

"They're guardian spiders," the dark elf answered, her voice thick with anger, "summoned only in times of great need. Those two were so small . . . the matron mothers who conjured them must have had a rather minor one stored away."

"You mean they get bigger than that?" Valas asked incredulously.

"Certainly," Halisstra replied, warming to the subject. "How do you think the webs of the city first appeared here? Upon arriving in the cavern, the first high priestesses, along with their wizard counterparts, summoned spiders of immense size to spin the webs upon which the city would rest. It was with Lolth's blessing that these sacred creatures came to us, and they were magically stored, transformed into crystalline statues. From time to time they are brought forth again to repair sections of the city or to defend the chamber. Normally, though, they're controlled through a mental link to do our bidding and to gate in more of their kind only when we command it. I don't know exactly how. That is a secret reserved for the matron mothers."

"Blessed Dark Mother," Ryld said. "Do you think the other one will bring more?"

"I don't know," the priestess replied. "I hope not."

"Look," Pharaun said, glancing ahead, where the spider could still be seen scuttling along the web street.

A force of gray dwarves were on a pathway above it, peering over the side at the spider below them. A number of them had begun throwing more of the damnable firepots at the creature. As the little incendiary devices struck the arachnid, they burst into flame, and the colossal spider reared up as it began to burn, looking to eliminate the source of the pain.

More of the clay pots were cast down, several of them striking the spider on the head and abdomen. Rising up on its hind legs, the spider attempted to reach the duergar, but they were too high overhead. The spider spun in place, turning its back on its attackers, and fired a thick stream of fluid in their direction.

"Webbing," Pharaun noted aloud, impressed.

The stream of webbing sailed accurately, attaching to the underside of the web street, hardening as it did so. The spider turned and began to scamper up the strand of sticky filament, pursuing the gray dwarves, who were desperately clambering to get out of the way.

"The fools," Ryld said. "They just managed to get its attention focused on them. Fortunate for us, though."

"Enough," Quenthel said. "We still need to get our belongings from the inn and leave this wretched city."

Pharaun turned to gaze at the high priestess, knowing full well that his expression was one of dumbfounded amazement.

"You can't be serious! Look around," he said, gesturing out toward other parts of the city, where the distant glows of more and more fires were visible through the ever-thickening smoke. "The whole city is in turmoil.

"Use your ears," he continued, gesturing in a different direction, where the screams of the fighting and dying echoed off the walls of the huge cavern. "We're running out of time. I'm sure the whole city is choosing sides and taking the battle to the streets, and yet you want to tempt fate by trying to go after more of your trinkets? I think—"

"Listen to me, *boy*," Quenthel spat, her face livid. "We just went through this with your warrior friend. You will do as I say, or you will be left here to die. If you've forgotten who I am, allow me to remind you that I am High Priestess Quenthel Baenre, Mistress of Arach-Tinilith, Mistress of the Academy, Mistress of Tier Breche, First Sister of House Baenre of Menzoberranzan, and I will no longer tolerate your snide remarks and your haughty insubordination. Do you understand?"

As if to back up her words, Jeggred stepped forward and with a menacing growl took hold of the collar of Pharaun's *piwafwi,* bunching it up in his clawed fist.

The wizard glanced over to Ryld, who still looked weakened from his fight with the spider. Nonetheless, he had his hand on the hilt of Splitter and was stepping forward, ready to come between the draegloth and the mage. But Pharaun could tell by the warrior's expression that he was trying to determine just how badly he really wanted to choose sides at this juncture.

Jeggred whipped his head around and snarled, "Don't even think about it, weapons master. I will tear out your stomach and feast upon it if you interfere."

Ryld's expression tightened as he took offense at the draegloth's threats, but Pharaun gave a quick, subtle shake of his head to warn the warrior off.

"*Mistress* Quenthel, since you are so passionate about recovering your valuables," Pharaun said, trying to make his voice sound jovial, "then let's make haste, before the opportunity is wasted."

Quenthel smiled, obviously pleased at having successfully asserted herself and regained the upper hand.

"I knew you would appreciate the importance of my decision," she replied, turning away.

"So, wizard, how do you propose we cross over to the Flame and Serpent?" she asked, appraising the devastation alongside Pharaun. "What magic do you still have up your sleeve that can get us there quickly and safely?"

"None, Mistress Baenre," Pharaun replied in all seriousness. "I have consumed over half of my magic for the day, and I'm not even certain how we'll get out of the city."

"That's not good enough, Mizzrym."

"I have a counter-suggestion," the mage said, pursing his lips. "Let me go get the goods while you and the rest of the group wait here and rest. It's out of the way, fairly easily defended, and I can find you again when I come back. I have a spell to get me to the inn and back quickly, I just can't take all of you with me."

Quenthel scowled, thinking, and Pharaun wondered if, as often as she frowned so severely, the high priestess even realized she was making such a face.

"Very well," Quenthel said at last, nodding. "Do not dawdle."

"Oh, I don't intend to. The less chance there is of large chunks of this doomed city falling atop me, the better off I'll feel."

Quenthel turned and explained the plan to the rest of the group. Everyone nodded in agreement, ready for a respite.

Ryld pulled Pharaun aside and asked, "You *are* coming back, aren't you?"

Pharaun cocked an eyebrow and replied, "Besides having a fondness for you, my brooding weapons master, I still truly desire to get to the bottom of this mystery. My chances are better with you all than without."

Ryld looked at him for a long time before nodding.

"Be careful," he said, turning to find a seat against a wall of the alley, his crossbow out.

"How do you intend to cross the city?" Halisstra asked.

Her face was drawn and tired. Still, her eyes glittered red, as with some new determination.

"I have a spell of flying that I can use to get there and back again fairly quickly," Pharaun answered. "Unfortunately, I would be much better off if I were not visible, but I have already played that particular trick today."

"Maybe I can help," the daughter of what once was House Melarn said. "Mistress Quenthel, that wand you just confiscated from me would serve us well, with your approval."

"What is it?" the high priestess asked, seemingly pleased by the deference shown her.

"A spell that will render him invisible, even should he attack a foe," Halisstra replied. "I assure you, it will not harm him."

Quenthel scowled and looked at Pharaun for some sort of confirmation. The wizard nodded. He still believed the two females newly added to the group were trustworthy, and they certainly wouldn't be in much of a position to turn on the rest of them now.

"Very well," Quenthel said.

She produced the wand and passed it back to the other female. Halisstra took it, offering her thanks to the high priestess. She targeted her wand at Pharaun.

"Wait," the wizard said.

He produced a feather from inside his *piwafwi*. Using the feather as part of the casting, he enchanted himself with the ability to fly.

Tucking the feather back into its customary pocket, he turned to the priestess and said, "All right, go ahead. It's always easier to cast when you can see your own hands."

She smiled faintly and nodded, then summoned the magical energy from the wand. In but a moment, Pharaun was totally invisible. Halisstra offered the wand back to Quenthel.

"No," the high priestess said, shaking her head. "You can keep it. I think you learned your lesson."

"Yes, Mistress," Halisstra said with a smile that did not reach her eyes. She tucked the wand away and went to sit down once more, beside Danifae.

"I'll be back shortly," Pharaun said.

He rose into the air before anyone could think to reply.

Danifae watched as the wizard disappeared, and she sensed when he departed the alley. Shaking her head, she sat back and watched the weapons master and the scout, both of whom paced, apparently eager to be away from there.

This is a strange lot I've wound up with, she decided. They are competent, and yet they bicker and argue unlike any group of dark elves I've ever seen.

The battle captive looked over at Quenthel, who was speaking quietly with the draegloth, Jeggred.

She's certainly an interesting one, Danifae decided.

It wasn't the first time she'd encountered a female like the high priestess—confident yet blustering at everything and everyone.

Still, Danifae thought, letting her eyes linger appreciatively over Quenthel's form, she's a fit leader.

Danifae turned her thoughts Halisstra. The First Daughter of House Melarn looked visibly shaken at the physical loss of her home, even though Ssipriina had already wrested possession of it from her. Danifae wondered how her mistress would hold up under that kind of duress. Certainly, there was no lamenting the destruction of House Melarn on her own part, but Danifae could imagine how it would feel if her own family had been wiped out in such a fashion. House Yauntyrr might well have been destroyed, for all she knew. It had been far too long since she'd last seen it. She didn't even know the fate of Eryndlyn itself in the current crisis, much less her own House.

"Let us come with you," Halisstra said to Quenthel. "Let us help you find the priest of Vhaeraun."

Danifae looked at her mistress sharply.

"What makes you think we're going to try to find the scout's friend?" Quenthel asked.

"I-I beg forgiveness, Mistress Baenre," Halisstra stammered. "I merely assumed—"

"Assumptions are best left to that miserable wretch, Pharaun," Quenthel warned.

Halisstra bowed her head.

"Of course, Mistress Baenre," she said. "Nonetheless, I would humbly ask that you permit me and my servant to accompany you. Our chances of survival are much greater if we stay together, and as you know, I have nothing left for me here."

The dark elf pursed her lips, obviously trying to control her emotions. Danifae thought it somewhat unbecoming, showing so much of her passion, but she would never say so, especially not in front of others.

Quenthel tapped her lips with her finger and nodded as though she understood the pain of Halisstra's plight, though Danifae seriously doubted the high priestess held any true compassion for Halisstra's situation.

"Yes, well, as long as you can continue to make yourself useful, and if you are willing to do what I say, then I see no reason why you cannot continue to travel with us."

Danifae cringed. No doubt this would take her farther away from Eryndlyn, not closer. She was going to have find a way to break the binding, and soon, and she thought perhaps the wizard had that capability. It would be easy enough for her to manipulate him into helping her, the way she caught him eyeing her all the time. Easy, indeed.

Halisstra bowed her head again in thanks and said, "If it is not too presumptuous, Mistress Baenre, may I ask what your intentions are?"

"Well, once we manage to get out of this city," Quenthel replied, emphasizing the words to show of what a daunting task that would be in and of itself, "I think we might actually pay a visit to this friend of the scout's. However infuriating the Mizzrym boy can be in so many other ways, he does occasionally have a good idea or two."

That's why you can't afford to alienate him or cause him bodily harm, Danifae surmised.

It wasn't difficult to see that Pharaun was really the most valuable member of the team. That raised the question of who was really the leader. Quenthel by default, but Pharaun by subtle necessity.

That will bear watching, Danifae thought with a smile.

Ssipriina surveyed the troops she'd assembled in the courtyard of her estate and grimaced. So few remained of what she'd started the day with. Would they be enough? She let her gaze roam over them . . . soldiers, priestesses, wizards. How many had she lost in the destruction of House Melarn? How many more in the hours since, battling the rival Houses, her own duergar mercenaries, succumbing to the guardian spiders?

The matron mother shook her head, thinking of that debacle. It was certainly a blunder, but she refused to label it ill-conceived. Animating the creature to fight for her House had been clever, an idea her allies had all endorsed. Certainly, none of them had been able to foresee that the mental link used to control the spiders was in some way tied to their connection to Lolth. Without the goddess, there was no link, but once Ssipriina and the others had figured that out, it was too late. They had all missed that, and she refused to accept sole blame for it.

Still, the damage could have been contained, if only that double-crossing fool Khorrl had done his duty. She had paid him a matron mother's ransom. He should have jumped at her every beck and call, but instead he turned his back on her, gathered his mercenaries, and was preparing to pull out of Ched Nasad all together. The loss of his support was a tough blow, but what galled her more was how foolish he'd made her look—foolish in the eyes of her peers.

The other matron mothers, upon hearing that the duergar were no longer in House Zauvirr's service, had washed their hands of the alliance, immediately withdrawing their support for Ssipriina's claims. They had their own Houses to consider and couldn't afford to weaken themselves further in a lost cause.

Lost cause! Yes, she had been made to look foolish, and she would not have that. Ssipriina Zauvirr would show them what a lost cause was.

Let the rest of them distance themselves from her. Let them rot at the bottom of the chasm. She was not going to let these setbacks foil her plans. Half the city might burn, but when the smoke cleared, House Zauvirr would sit at the top of the heap.

Khorrl Xornbane was going to pay as well, but would her remaining troops be enough? Between her own House and those from House Melarn who had switched allegiance, she had assembled a potent army, but so many had been lost.

That was Clan Xornbane's fault, too. They'd let the battle around House Melarn get out of control. It was their horrible firepots that made the stone burn, that allowed the House to fall. It was needless destruction, brought about after needless fighting.

Ssipriina had no doubt that the gray dwarf captain had spoken the truth. Zammzt could very well have been behind the premature exposure of her mercenaries, but why? Which matron mother was he in league with? Which of them had something to gain by watching her plans build up, then teeter to disaster? There were so many, but she would have to determine that later.

Ssipriina would miss Zammzt. She needed his efficiency, his battle acumen. She didn't have enough strategists to put in charge of the forces she'd assembled. The ugly male would have served in that capacity nicely. Faeryl would be a suitable replacement, but she'd not been seen since the chaos at the end of the gathering of matron mothers. Ssipriina suspected that her daughter had perished when the estate crumbled into the bottom of the cavern.

Foolish girl, the matron mother thought. Good riddance.

Sighing, Ssipriina shook herself out of her musings and swept her gaze one last time over her undersized army. They would have to be enough. She would lead them herself, and they would be enough.

"Gather yourselves," the matron mother said, moving to a protected place in the middle of the milling mass of drow. "It's time to claim what's ours."

Chapter

EIGHTEEN

Pharaun tried to stay near the perimeter of the city as he made his way toward the Flame and Serpent. For one thing, he didn't relish the thought of being crushed at any moment by falling debris from above. Though it had only happened once, he'd been far too intimately involved with it than he cared to remember. He would avoid a repeat incident, if he could.

Secondly, the wizard knew that navigation would be easier if he followed the wall of the chasm, rather than trying to work his way through the central section of the city. Even then, the thick smoke caused him difficulty in flying. He was surprised at how haze-choked the cavern had become. More than once, he nearly careened off a trench wall, still intact web street, or building. Nonetheless, he still considered the challenge of navigating through that to be far safer than having to maneuver through the center of Ched Nasad, where the sound of fighting was constant. Occasionally he heard explosions, loud pops, and howling winds in the distance as fierce magical battles raged. Arcane forces were being unleashed on gathering troops. There was no doubt about it—the entire city was engaged in a desperate struggle for control of the streets.

Mostly, the reverberations of conflict reached the mage's ears from his level or below. What had in all likelihood begun in the plaza outside of House Melarn had quickly spread, engulfing the citizens and visitors all across the city, on every level. The wizard wondered how many had actually managed to flee into the caverns surrounding the City of Shimmering Webs. Though the team from Menzoberranzan had been indisposed for much of the initial martial activity, he recalled that, since their escape from the collapse of House Melarn, they had seen surprisingly few ordinary folk in the streets. Of course, that was also because they'd spent most of their time high in the city, where only the nobles prowled. Farther down, in the lower sections, he imagined a much different scene. There, he supposed, the general rabble had gotten caught up in the fighting, much like the rebellion back home.

The uprising had taken a decidedly different twist than the insurrection in Menzoberranzan, though. The insurgents involved in the upheavals in Ched Nasad were the noble Houses themselves. Their own infighting was the flash point. Pharaun counted himself fortunate that the Houses of Menzoberranzan had proven less prone to petty backbiting. If they had, there might not be a city for him to return to. The mage grimaced, thinking of Gromph's attempts on Quenthel's life, and his own sister Greyanna's failed efforts to kill him.

There might not be anything left, he thought, before this is completely finished.

As he neared the section of the city where the inn was located, the wizard noticed that the damage was less severe there. In fact, the Flame and Serpent was thus far unscathed. Immediately he saw the reason why. A horde of mismatched drow and other creatures, probably residents of the inn, self-reliant mercenaries, and whatnot had formed a perimeter defense around the place. It didn't appear that they were under fire at the moment, but an intense battle must have raged there earlier, judging by the number of bodies present.

Not wanting to be either attacked or drawn into the midst of the siege, Pharaun elected to circle around to the back side of the inn and enter it that way. He recalled the window of the room he shared with Valas and Ryld, the one that looked out on the wall of the massive cavern that Ched Nasad called home, and he made for that. He approached from the roof and settled down between the wall of the building and the wall of the trench. It was just wide enough for him to levitate down between the two, and he hovered there while he contemplated how best to get through the opening without attracting attention.

He had just the spell, the Master of Sorcere realized, a minor incantation that would open the window from the inside, so that he wouldn't have to break it to get through. Reaching into his *piwafwi,* he fumbled around in three or four pockets before he found what he was looking for. He pulled out a brass key and tapped it softly against the window as he uttered the words that would complete the spell. The window opened without resistance, and Pharaun squirmed inside the room.

The wizard, the weapons master, and the scout had taken all of their belongings when they'd left the inn upon being summoned to attend the "party" in their honor. That seems almost a lifetime ago, Pharaun mused as he made his way out the door and down the hall to Quenthel's chambers.

Upon reaching the door, the mage hesitated, wondering if the high priestess had placed some sort of protective enchantment on it before leaving, but then he remembered that Ryld and Valas had invaded the room when they came seeking healing magic. Chuckling, he tried the door and found it locked.

Of course, Pharaun silently muttered. Leave it to Valas to put it back the way he found it.

Shrugging, the wizard dug around in the pockets of his *piwafwi* yet again, drawing forth a pinch of clay and a small vial of water. Sprinkling the water over the clay, he invoked the Weave and completed the spell. A portion of the wall next to the door began to sag, transforming from solid stone to thick, viscous mud. The wall oozed down into a puddle, and Pharaun stepped back to avoid soiling his boots. When the opening was wide enough, the Master of Sorcere nimbly leaped through into the room beyond, avoiding the mess he'd made.

Pharaun spied Quenthel's backpack, filled with extra supplies, on a table near the Reverie couch. Some of Faeryl's things, including the ambassador's haversack, were on the other table. The wizard hefted the high priestess's pack and grunted.

So, the mage thought with a wry grin, she finally figured out a way to make me carry her possessions.

He slung the backpack over his shoulder, grabbed up the second one, Faeryl's, and turned to go.

A crossbow bolt smacked into Pharaun's chest, somehow managing to slip through the part in the *piwafwi*'s fabric, and embedded itself in his shoulder. The Master of Sorcere grunted and stumbled back into the room, spinning away so that his back was to his assailant and he was more completely protected by the *piwafwi*. He looked down to see that it was a drow bolt, and he realized his magical invisibility had worn off.

Pharaun staggered over to the opposite side of the room, dropping the two satchels as he scrambled to find cover. There were really only two good places he could go: behind the Reverie couch or into an armoire. As he rushed past the armoire, he grabbed the door and yanked it open, then shoved it shut again as he slumped behind the Reverie couch. The door to the oversized cabinet slammed shut just as two pairs of boots darted into the room, which Pharaun observed from beneath the couch. The mage stayed low, on his knees, watching under the couch as the two pairs of boots spread apart, both slowly headed toward the armoire, their owners presumably covering the room.

"He went into the cabinet," one of the creatures said in the language of the drow.

The crossbow bolt set his shoulder throbbing, but Pharaun quietly watched for his assailants to appear. He blinked, unable to focus clearly, and he suddenly began to feel lightheaded. He kept thinking that if he could just cast a spell, this would all be over, but a decision about which one or how to go about doing it eluded him. The crossbow bolt wound had begun to burn, and Pharaun realized that he was growing weak. The bolt had been coated with poison. He would have to hurry to get back to the others before it overwhelmed him, and he only hoped they had a means of treating the toxin.

As his foes both came into Pharaun's line of view, crossbows held up and ready, he could see why they'd attacked him on sight. They were both dark elves, and they wore the livery of House Zauvirr. Mentally kicking himself for not considering the possibility that Ssipriina might send someone to their inn on the expectation that he or others in the group might return, Pharaun tried to phrase the arcane words of a spell, but they wouldn't come. The two drow were grinning as they sighted down their crossbows at him.

Pharaun closed his eyes, wondering if it would hurt much to die, and pondered whether or not he could work his rapier free, when he heard a noise. The expected twang of crossbows being fired it was not. Instead, he heard a woman's voice—a familiar voice—uttering a quick phrase. The wizard squinted, his vision blurry, as a spray of intertwined, multicolored beams of light cascaded over his two foes.

Both drow reeled backward from the sudden, bright assault, crying out and flinging up their hands to cover their eyes. The first one spasmed as crackles of electricity raked over his body from the yellow ray of light, while the second drow was engulfed in flames upon coming into contact with the red beam.

Pharaun watched as the two soldiers crumpled to the ground. Whether either or both of them were dead or not, he didn't know, nor did he care. He was growing intolerably weak from the effects of the poison.

"Hello, Pharaun," the voice purred.

With an effort, Pharaun opened his eyes again and looked up, realizing who it was.

"Aliisza," he slurred, relaxing as the alu came around the couch toward him. "How did you find—"

The fiend's slap across Pharaun's face stung immensely and he jerked, alert, his eyes watering.

"What the—" the wizard grunted, rubbing his cheek as Aliisza squatted down beside him, her hand upraised. "What's the matter with you?"

He again wondered if he could produce the rapier.

"How dare you!" the alu growled, one eyebrow arched, but without the accompanying smile. "How could you be interested in that trollop after sharing *my* bed?"

Pharaun blinked, thoroughly confused. Trollop?

"Who in the blazes are you talking about?" he demanded, feebly raising his good arm to ward off the impending slap.

"Don't you play dumb with me, you wretched excuse for a dark elf. You know the one I mean. The pretty you pulled from that collapsing house. I should have gouged her eyes out!"

"Oh, by the Dark Mother," Pharaun muttered, understanding at last. "It's not what you think. . . ."

"Ooh! You males *always* say that. According to your gender, it never is. I don't want to hear it."

Aliisza reached down, grabbed the wizard by both lapels of his *piwafwi,* and drew him up to her. She crushed his mouth to hers in a rough kiss, biting his lip so hard he was sure she drew blood. In fact, he decided, it felt not so much like a kiss as like the fiend was marking her territory.

"That's so you won't forget me so easily. If you stray, I'll know it. I'll smell her on you, and I will not be happy. I'm not through with you yet, wizard," Aliisza warned, looking him in the eyes.

She blinked, and that sardonic smile was back.

"Well, I guess I'd better get you to some help," she said lightly, hefting Pharaun up and slinging him over her shoulder, careful of his chest, where the crossbow bolt still protruded.

The wizard felt the utter fool, being toted like a sack of mushrooms, but he could hardly protest. His entire body felt . . . well, "fuzzy" was the best word he could think of to describe it.

"The satchels," he mumbled into the alu's shoulder. "Don't forget the satchels."

Scooping up both Quenthel's and Faeryl's bags, Aliisza carried Pharaun across the room, out the hole he'd made in the wall, down the hallway, and back into his own room. She set the wizard down on the Reverie couch. Taking the satchels, she moved to the window and leaned out, bracing her feet against the rock wall of the chasm. Pharaun watched helplessly as she tossed the packs onto the roof.

The alu returned and scooped the wizard up once more and hauled him out into the gap between the building and the wall, shoving him upward above her. He felt the bolt in his shoulder ram against the side of the inn, but the pain was strangely diminished. Still, it was forceful enough to make him grunt.

"By the Abyss, can't you help at all?" she puffed, working the mage to the roof.

Pharaun didn't answer. His face was going numb, and everything was fading to black.

Ryld was sitting on the roof of a building that bordered the alley, with his legs dangling over the side, his crossbow in his hands, watching parts of Ched Nasad burn. Finally having a chance to really study the layout of the city, he could see what was happening with greater clarity. The fighting had diminished in the highest reaches, though he could still hear the sounds of combat from a couple of streets over. It was mostly the lower sections of the city that seemed to be receiving the worst of it, those areas where the lesser races were most numerous. He supposed that the violence down there took the form a general rioting, just a byproduct of the tensions of the city coupled with the more severe military maneuvers that had played out higher up. Of course, he supposed, having a large chunk of the city fall from above wasn't going to help calm things.

Halisstra sat down beside the weapons master and stared forlornly out at her homeland.

"Valas has gone to see what chance we have of getting out through any of the city gates," she told Ryld. "I told him about one or two places where we might be able to depart unseen, and he's going to see if they're secure."

Ryld only nodded. If anyone could sneak through the city unchallenged, it was the Bregan D'aerthe scout. He doubted seriously if any exits had been left unguarded, though.

"How could this have happened?" Halisstra muttered softly. "So much destruction."

"We have grown complacent," the Master of Melee-Magthere answered. "The drow race has been squabbling in a controlled manner for so long, we never expected that our own little games would get out of hand. And they—" the weapons master gestured downward, in the direction of the slums—"just feed off of it, now."

"But the fire. How is it possible to burn down a city made of stone?"

"Alchemy, I suppose. We saw the same thing in Menzoberranzan. It's more devastating here, because your whole city is suspended on stone webbing. They were very clever to bring the firepots here."

"Of course," the drow maiden breathed. "Set the webs on fire, and everything attached to them falls to its destruction. Including House Melarn."

Ryld glanced over at the dark elf beside him. Her face was one of sorrow, and her red eyes glistened with uncharacteristic tears. It was not often that he saw a drow cry. It was considered a sign of weakness. He found it refreshingly honest in the priestess.

"I am sorry for your loss. Perhaps we will learn from this. If we survive."

Something caught Ryld's eye, and he had his crossbow up and was sighting down the shaft in an instant. A winged figure, bobbing and weaving haphazardly, emerged from the smoke, coming for their position. It was a drow, possibly, though it had wings, and it bore a rather large bundle. The warrior could tell something was wrong by the erratic way it was flying. Suddenly, he recognized it— the demon from Ammarindar!

He had his finger on the trigger, ready to fire a bolt through her heart, before he realized she was carrying Pharaun.

As the demon closed in on the edge of the building, she seemed to lose her balance, and Ryld literally had to reach out and grab her as she went by. All three of them tumbled to the stone in a heap at Jeggred's feet. The draegloth stepped between the beautiful creature and the rest of the team.

"You!" Quenthel hissed, her scourge raised, ready to strike. "What are you doing here?"

The fiend, whom Pharaun referred to as Aliisza, Ryld remembered, eyed both Jeggred and the high priestess warily as she panted where she'd fallen. She made no move to defend herself.

"Bringing your precious wizard back to you, drow," she muttered. "I know how fond you are of him."

"He's hurt," Ryld said, turning the mage over.

Everyone but Jeggred gathered around as the weapons master began to examine Pharaun. It didn't take him long to find the puncture wound in the wizard's shoulder, a portion of a crossbow bolt still lodged in it. Most of the shaft had snapped off during his crash landing.

"The bolt is poisoned," Quenthel said, standing over Pharaun's prone body. "Healing him won't do a bit of good unless we get the poison out of his blood first. If we don't, he'll die."

"I could have told you that," Aliisza said, sitting up, though she was still breathing heavily from her ordeal. "Here . . . he insisted we bring these."

She tossed two backpacks at Quenthel's feet.

"So, how do we remove the poison?" Ryld asked Quenthel, looking up from where he was tending to the Master of Sorcere. "Do any of you have the magic to do so?"

Quenthel shook her head.

"Yngoth can sense it in his body," she said, patting the whip that was once again hanging from her hip, "but my spells are, of course, lost."

Ryld looked at both Halisstra and Danifae.

"How about either of you?"

Both females shook their heads.

"I dabble in a bit of arcane magic," Halisstra confessed, "but I am not yet powerful enough to eliminate poison."

Jeggred continued his vigil over Aliisza but said, "Perhaps our good friend the ambassador had some means of aiding him."

The draegloth nudged the satchel at his feet.

"You'd better hope she did," Ryld muttered at the unconscious Pharaun, sliding the pack over toward Quenthel. "There's nothing else we can do for you, my friend."

Pharaun was sweating profusely. Ryld knew the wizard might be their single best chance to escape the city. If they lost him, they might very well be trapped, unless Valas could find a way out.

Quenthel began rummaging through Faeryl's things, flinging clothing and personal items to the side. As she dug her way toward the bottom, Ryld thought he heard the high priestess mutter something disparaging about the ambassador and a comment about her being a waste of space then her face brightened as she pulled a thick tube free.

"Ah *ha!*" she said triumphantly. "Let's hope these are spells."

She opened the tube, slid out a handful of parchment pages and unfurled them, scanning their contents quickly.

"Oh, how delightful," she said. "Faeryl, you clever girl, where in the Underdark did you steal these from?"

Both Halisstra and Danifae crowded around the Mistress of Arach-Tinilith, each of them trying to get a glimpse of what was on the pages. The weapons master could see looks of elation on their faces.

"Is there anything helpful?" Ryld demanded. "Something to neutralize the poison?"

"I don't know, yet," Quenthel snapped. "Give me a moment."

She continued to scan the pages, leafing through them rapidly.

"Several of these could prove quite helpful," she said, "but I don't see—oh, wait. Yes! Pharaun Mizzrym, you are in luck. Give me some room," she said, motioning for Ryld to move out of the way.

The weapons master did so, sliding off to the side as Quenthel knelt beside the wizard. Laying one hand atop the wound, the high priestess began chanting, reading through the words on the scroll in her hand. There was a tiny flash of light as the handwritten text vanished from the page, and a soft glow passed through Pharaun's body, emanating from the point where Quenthel's hand touched him.

Almost immediately, the Master of Sorcere's breathing slowed, and he seemed more relaxed. His eyes were still closed, but he was smiling.

"My thanks, Mistress Quenthel," he said, and he sounded about as sincere as Ryld had ever heard him. "I ran into a spot of trouble at the inn, you see. A couple of fellows in the employ of Matron Mother Zauvirr were decidedly unhappy that I paid the place a visit. They caught me off guard."

"I find that terribly difficult to believe," Ryld said, eyeing Aliisza, who was still sitting on the opposite side of Jeggred.

"Yes, well, I'm sure you could have given them a lesson or two on how to more accurately find the most vulnerable point in a wizard's defenses."

"All right," the high priestess said, standing again. "Get that out of his shoulder, and I can heal him."

She went over to her own pack, where she tucked the scrolls, back in their protective tube, into a pocket. She began fishing around in another section of the container and produced a wand, which Ryld recognized from before.

The weapons master turned his attention back to the broken end of the bolt. He checked to see if it was lodged against any bone, and when he was satisfied that it was not, he gave a fierce shove, pushing the head through Pharaun's shoulder and out the back side.

Pharaun arched his back and cried out in pain.

"Damn it, Master Argith," he muttered finally, breathing fast. "You certainly know how to welcome a friend back."

The wizard closed his eyes, still grimacing.

"I think the greeting was entirely appropriate for someone who managed to get himself shot," Ryld replied, once more making room for Quenthel to work her own magic.

The high priestess waved her wand over the freshly bleeding puncture and muttered a trigger word. The flesh that was exposed began to knit itself together, closing the hole and forming a pale gray scar on his jet black flesh. Pharaun sighed as Quenthel stood up once more.

"There," she said, returning the wand to her pack. "Now, try to avoid crossbow bolts. There's only so much of that to go around."

Ryld threw a glance at Halisstra and saw the drow priestess looking jealous as she watched Quenthel store away the wand.

To the victor goes the spoils, he thought grimly. You bowed your head to her and named her your mistress . . . don't expect any generosity in return.

Pharaun was sitting up, helped by Danifae. He looked around. When he spotted Aliisza, still being guarded by the draegloth, he grimaced and pulled his hand free from the battle captive's. Ryld glanced over and saw that the dark-haired beauty was frowning severely.

Uh oh, Ryld thought. This smacks of a jealous lover. Surely the wizard isn't that big a fool, to lie with a demon. . . .

Pharaun managed to get to his feet and move over to where the demon sat.

"It's all right," he said to Jeggred as he passed. "You can stand down. She's not going to bite."

Jeggred studiously ignored the wizard and maintained his position.

"Look, I owe you for this," he said, speaking low but not so quietly that Ryld couldn't hear the conversation.

To his utter surprise, the demoness grabbed hold of Pharaun, her hands to either side of his head, and kissed him savagely. The wizard didn't do anything to resist, though the warrior could see his fists clenching and unclenching at his sides.

"Remember what I said," Aliisza said, pressing her mouth to the mage's ear, but speaking loudly enough that everyone could hear. "I will know."

Ryld saw that she was staring right at Danifae as she said this. The battle captive caught the steely stare and turned away, a smile of amused disbelief on her face. Quenthel gave a disgusted growl in the back of her throat and spun on her heel to ignore the ridiculous display.

"Now, I've been too long in this city," Aliisza said. "I'll leave you all to whatever silly dark elf games you intend to play while the place falls down around you."

With that, she opened a bluish-white doorway, stepping through as Jeggred snarled and made a leap for her, but she was gone.

"By the Dark Mother, Pharaun," Quenthel snapped. "All of your talk about not tempting fate, and you're off dallying with that . . . that *thing?* You are such a male."

Pharaun shrugged at the accusations.

"Nothing happened," he said, rubbing his mouth thoughtfully. "I went to get your things, I got jumped, and she saved my life. That's the end of it."

"See that it is," Quenthel snarled.

Pharaun looked around, scratching his head.

"Where's Valas?" he asked, and Danifae explained the situation to him.

The wizard nodded and said, "Yes, the sooner we can get out of the city, the more quickly we can figure out how to get to his friend, the priest."

The Master of Sorcere raised a single eyebrow and glanced over at Quenthel.

"Assuming we've settled on that as our next course of action?" he asked her.

The high priestess gave him a single curt nod.

"Yes, you've convinced me," she said. "Once we're clear of Ched Nasad, we'll need to decide the best way to reach this priest. I assume you have some means of getting us to where we'll want to go?"

Pharaun nodded as he got slowly to his feet.

"I may, depending on where Valas tells us the fellow is, but I won't be doing it today," he added. "I have nearly depleted my assortment of spells. Without some rest and a chance to review my grimoires, I'm severely hampered."

"Then let's just concentrate on getting out of Ched Nasad and worry about that later," Quenthel said. "As soon as Valas returns, we'll see what he's discovered and make appropriate plans."

"The news isn't good," the scout said, appearing is if on cue. He climbed up and over the wall against which they'd been sitting. "Every major gate seems to be either heavily guarded or under attack, and the other places Halisstra mentioned are inaccessible at the moment. There's no way out of the city."

"Nonsense," Quenthel said firmly. "Pharaun, do you have any means at all of transporting us? Some spell that would open a gate? Anything?"

The wizard shook his head.

"Then we'll just have to clear a path through one of the gates. I'm sure that with the seven of us we can accomplish this."

"There is only one way to find out," the mage answered. He studied their position for a moment then turned to Valas. "We need to get up higher, above those duergar, don't you think?"

Valas nodded and said, "The fighting is still heavy over in that direction. If we can avoid that, all the better."

"Let's not dawdle any longer," Pharaun agreed. "We go up."

Quenthel nodded her assent to the plan, and everyone prepared to depart.

As Ryld assembled his gear, he realized that he was exhausted. Between his exploits with Valas at the taverns, fighting their way into and out of House Melarn, and dealing with both the duergar and the spiders, the warrior hadn't rested in over a day.

It has to be almost morning, he realized, *and we're not even close to being finished, yet. Let's hope we can find a relatively painless way to slip past the gate forces.*

The team set out, but they had to move in shifts, for Jeggred had to carry both Valas and Danifae to higher ground, and the draegloth, despite his immense strength, could only transport one of the dark elves at a time. Thus, half the group rose to the next web street overhead as Jeggred conveyed one drow, while the remainder waited with the other for the fiend to return.

The first team, consisting of Pharaun, Quenthel, and Jeggred carrying Danifae, alit atop a web street and discovered that it was actually being defended by drow troops. Several of the dark elves leveled hand crossbows at the four of them, and when they saw the draegloth, they nearly panicked.

"What in the Nine Hells is that?" one of the soldiers, an older male with plenty of battle scars, called out, pointing to Jeggred with his crossbow.

The fiend growled low, turning to face his would-be assailants, but Pharaun stepped between the draegloth and the others.

"Easy, there," the wizard said, his hands out, palms up in a placating manner. "We're just passing through. No need to get jumpy."

Beside him, Quenthel sniffed, but when the drow soldiers saw that she seemed unconcerned by the fiend's presence, they quieted down, returning their attention below them, where the fighting was still taking place. Jeggred departed to retrieve Valas.

Pharaun found a spot to take a seat and did so, reclining against a wall to rest for a few moments.

"Might as well get comfortable," he said to the two females with him. "Rest when you can."

Quenthel scowled but consented to sit across from the wizard, and Danifae settled down, too.

The trio's rest was short-lived, though, for soon, shouts emerged from farther along the street. All the drow around them grew restless as word spread that dark elves from an enemy House were heading their way.

A priestess of middling rank came stalking down the street, accompanied by a pair of male wizards. They were cajoling the troops to form up.

"On your feet! It's time. Get up, you worthless rothé, and fight! Fight for House Maerret!"

When she reached Pharaun and the others, she stopped and stared at them.

"What are you three doing here? You're not part of this unit. Who are you?"

Pharaun gave the priestess that same placating motion that he'd used earlier and said, "We're just passersby, not here to cause any trouble."

"Well, you'll join ranks, then. Get forward and help the other wizards."

"We thought we'd better serve the cause by helping to watch this end of road," Pharaun replied, smiling broadly. "You never know when those pesky grays will try to circumnavigate our flank and surprise us."

"Get on your feet, wizard, and go join the other spellcasters. And you two! You can help me rally the troops and keep order. Up off your hind ends—*now!*"

Pharaun could see that Quenthel was about to lash out at the priestess, so before she could cause a scene, he pulled the drow commander to the side.

"Listen," he said quietly. "We're actually working on a special assignment for Matron Mother Drisinil Melarn. We've got permission to avoid the fighting while we take care of a very important mission."

"Oh, is that so?" one of the male wizards replied coldly. "Well, Drisinil Melarn was my mother, and I happen to know that she was murdered by traitors before this civil war even started. Since you don't wear a House insignia, I'm guessing you're the spies who were accused of collaborating with her. Maybe it's time you died."

The Melarn wizard stepped back, reaching into his *piwafwi,* but before Pharaun could react, a voice drifted from behind him.

"Hello, Q'arlynd," Halisstra said as she and the others floated up over the side of the web street.

The Melarn wizard stopped, peering at the priestess for a moment. Then he broke into a broad grin.

"Dear sister," he said. "I thought you were dead."

"When the fighting got worse, several of the matron mothers, including Maerret, came to the Dangling Tower and asked us to aid them," Q'arlynd explained. "They said it was a full-scale civil war and the rebels were going to tear the city apart if we didn't stop them. Matron Mother Lirdnolu explained to me what had happened to House Melarn. I knew Mother was dead, and we'd heard that she was killed by Ssipriina Zauvirr with collaborators from the outside who wanted to see the downfall of Ched Nasad."

"And you thought I'd perished, too," Halisstra said, squatting down beside her brother.

"Yes, either at the same time Mother was murdered or in the fall of our House. Is it really gone?" the Melarn wizard asked.

Halisstra only nodded.

"By the Dark Mother," he breathed.

"Well, the family reunion is nice and all, but we still need to get out of this city," Pharaun said, standing. "What's the situation?

Where's the closest way out that we can get through?"

Q'arlynd shook his head and said, "There are none, so I've heard. All the gates have either been commandeered by rebel forces or hordes of escaped slaves or they've collapsed outright because of the fighting. This alchemical fire that burns through stone is wreaking havoc on—"

"Believe me, we know," the Master of Sorcere interrupted, "but your report doesn't leave us with many options. We've got to find a way to get free of the city."

Quenthel had just opened her mouth, most likely to command Pharaun to figure out a method of escaping Ched Nasad, the wizard imagined, when a commotion broke out from farther down the boulevard. Pharaun turned and looked just in time to see a jumble of dark elves stumbling to their feet in disarray. Many of them fell again just as quickly, cut down by a growing horde of gray dwarves who were emerging through a magical doorway hovering in the air only a couple of feet above the street. The duergar were streaming through as fast as they could, firing off crossbows at any drow targets they could find before casting the missile weapons aside and pulling out axes, hammers, and the occasional mace.

"Attack! We're under attack!" the cry went up as more drow surged to their feet, moving to stop the advance of the gray dwarves.

"Come on, you flat-footed, sorry excuses for soldiers—get up there and fight before they split us down the middle!" the battle priestess yelled, returning from the far end of the street and shoving troops forward as fast as she could get to them. "Wizard! Throw a spell! Drive them back. If they reach the square, we're done for."

Pharaun sighed and nodded, grabbing the battle priestess and spinning her around to face him. His smile was gone.

"Tell your troops to fall back to this point," he said.

"What? And let them come at us unopposed? I think not."

"Do it, or they will be trapped. Set up three positions of missile fire, here—" he pointed to several positions in the street—"there, and there."

The battle priestess looked at the mage as though he were crazy but finally nodded and shouted for an organized retreat.

Pharaun rolled his eyes at the battle priestess's short-sightedness and began organizing the drow soldiers himself, sorting them into groups of crossbowmen, stationing them where he'd pointed earlier. As more and more of the dark elves dropped back from the duergar, they fell in with the others already positioned. As a unit, they began to fire into the mass of milling gray dwarves, who were slaughtering the few remaining stragglers.

They're lost to us, the wizard said to himself.

He cast, and a great mass of webs appeared, spanning the width of the street, anchored to the pavement and the buildings on either side. A handful of the dark elves were caught in the sticky strands, and perhaps a dozen or so were trapped on the other side, but the gray dwarves were effectively sealed off from advancing, at least until they penetrated the webs or the spell wore off.

"Come on," Q'arlynd said, motioning upward as he began to levitate.

Pharaun followed the other wizard upward to a position where they could see over the top of his webs, down into the field of battle where the gray dwarves had quickly killed the few remaining drow who had been trapped with them. The duergar were milling about, seemingly unsure what to do. Halisstra's brother had components out, ready to cast a spell, and one look at the lump of bat guano in his hand told Pharaun what the wizard planned.

"Hold on," Pharaun said, laying a hand on Q'arlynd's arm. "They're waiting," he explained, pointing down at the duergar. "They want a shaman or something to come try to dispel the webs. He's probably the same one who opened the dimensional doorway."

Sure enough, a duergar dressed in robes and wearing several totems and other magical trinkets stepped through the glowing doorway. One of the duergar addressed him—Pharaun couldn't hear what was being said—and pointed to the webs. The shaman nodded and began to cast.

"Do it," Pharaun said.

Q'arlynd went into action, letting loose with his spell, aiming it directly at the shaman. It was a direct hit, and that entire side of the street was engulfed in a white-hot ball of fire that blossomed outward and vaporized an instant later. Charred and burning gray dwarves lay everywhere. A few moved, having survived, but they were few and far between. Most importantly, the dimensional pathway had been banished, winking out when the shaman who created it died.

The two wizards settled back to the ground again, noting that Q'arlynd's fiery ball of magic had ignited the webs, which were quickly burning away. Already, though, another gateway was forming, this one at the opposite end of the street. The battle priestess rallied her troops to deal with the new threat.

"You know you only delayed the inevitable," Quenthel said as Pharaun and Q'arlynd returned. "We're wasting time, here. We have to get out of the city."

"I know," the Master of Sorcere replied, "but it was fun."

"Look!" Danifae shouted, pointing toward the new gateway.

Duergar were streaming out, and drow were arriving from above and below, levitating from the web streets on the two adjacent levels.

"It's House Zauvirr troops," the battle captive explained. "They've got us pinned."

"Fall back," the battle priestess commanded, turning to point back the way the duergar had come, but as she began to direct her soldiers, she took a crossbow bolt in the ear. The missile passed through and protruded from the other side of her head, and she was already dead, motionless, as she fell to the pavement.

"We're surrounded!" Q'arlynd cried out. "Stand and fight!"

He produced a wand and waved it, conjuring a sudden and violent tempest of ice fragments the size of Pharaun's head. The chunks of ice pelted down on the front ranks of gray dwarves, beating them down and slicing them to ribbons amid cries of anguish.

In reply, the duergar began throwing more of the firepots into the ever-tightening mass of House Maerret drow, who were bunched together and made easy targets. More and more of the gray dwarves appeared, forming ranks, establishing a shield wall in front so that the back ranks would have protection as they fired crossbows and hurled firepots and spells.

Pharaun had no idea where any of his companions were. Every-one had been scattered in the initial panic of the attack. He had no concerns that they couldn't take care of themselves, at least for the moment, but the longer they remained there, the less their chances became of escaping at all. He spun in place, looking for a sign of any of them in the thickening smoke, when a creature materialized in front of the wizard, its back to him.

Pharaun's ability to note magical emanations made it clear to him that this creature had been summoned from somewhere, most likely the lower planes. It was a huge thing, vaguely humanoid, cov-ered with white fur and possessed of four arms. It had a sloping brow and a flattened nose, but the most terrifying aspect was its gaping mouth and fangs. The beast spun around, roaring in rage, and spot-ted the wizard. Its red eyes glittered in delight as it lunged forward, claws outstretched, ready to rend the Master of Sorcere.

Pharaun fumbled to free his rapier, but the fiendish creature was on him too fast, and he took a painful slash across the shoulder that knocked him sideways several feet. The wizard stumbled to the ground as the thing bounded forward again, pounding its chest with all four fists and roaring a challenge.

Goddess, Pharaun thought in a panic, scrambling backward and trying to activate his rapier.

From one side, a flash of movement caught the mage's eye, and Valas darted in behind the beast, raking both kukris along its ham-strings. The beast roared in pain but amazingly, it spun around before Valas could blend into the surroundings, slashing at the diminutive scout with outstretched claws.

Pharaun heard the other drow grunt and watched him go sprawl-ing from the force of the blow, but it bought him the time he needed to get his rapier free. He mentally commanded the thin blade to attack, and when it jabbed at the beast, which was looming over Valas, the creature snarled and spun back to see what had hurt it. Valas scrambled to his feet and faded from sight.

The fiendish thing growled and roared, swiping at the dancing rapier, but the blade was too quick, darting and weaving and getting several pokes in. Already, the white fur of the monster was tainted red from multiple wounds. This only seemed to be enraging the beast further, and Pharaun had to suppress a grin.

With the blade now protecting him from attack, the wizard could cast a spell. He gestured and uttered a few syllables, and instantly, he was surrounded by more than half a dozen exact duplicates of himself that flickered and spun about.

At the same time, a clay pot shattered right at the feet of the summoned creature, engulfing it in flames. It screamed in pain and flailed about, and Pharaun was forced to back a few steps to avoid it as it went running to escape its torment. Blinded by fire and pain, the fiendish creature charged over the side of the web street, vanishing into the void below.

Pharaun turned to assay the battle, his rapier still bobbing and weaving, waiting for a target, and the wizard nearly got his head taken off by a series of whirling blades. This spell he knew well enough, for it was a favorite of the priestesses, but he doubted that any of the drow had cast it. Two of the spinning blades tore through his *piwafwi*, nipping at his arm and creating quick, thin lines of blood. Instinctively, he dropped to the ground, avoiding the full brunt of the spell, though several of his duplicates vanished after being struck. The mage rolled out from beneath the spinning range of the spell and regained his feet.

Quenthel was nearby, a wand in one hand and her whip in the other. She was slashing at a duergar with her whip, and at the same time, Pharaun noted, she was directing a glowing, floating apparition of a hammer about with the wand. She swiped at the gray dwarf with her whip, and as he backed up to avoid the attack, she brought the hammer in from behind, slamming it into the back of his skull. The duergar jerked once, his eyes rolled up into his head, and he crumpled to the ground.

Ryld maneuvered into view, swinging Splitter all around himself. Pharaun could see that the Master of Melee-Magthere was engaged with three drow, and the way they were handling their own weapons, it appeared that Ryld had matched up with fellow weapons masters. The three opponents stalked around him, feinting and jabbing, trying to get the warrior to over-commit on defense, but Ryld maintained his position, flowing from one stance to the next. Pharaun could see that, despite the exhaustion that was apparent in Ryld's heavy breathing, there was also a gleam in the weapons master's eye. It was taking every ounce of concentration Ryld had, but he actually seemed to be enjoying the challenge.

Black, waving tentacles appeared among Ryld and his three adversaries, and Pharaun watched as two of the writhing appendages latched on to the Master of Melee-Magthere, while several more slithered around the legs and ankles of his foes. All four of the combatants were trapped, and yet none of them was willing to lower his guard in order to try to free himself.

Reacting quickly, Pharaun yanked his wand free of his *piwafwi* and triggered it, sending five screaming points of light into the first of the two tentacles that held Ryld down. The tentacle spasmed and vanished. With a quick spin of his greatsword, Ryld cut through the second black, shiny appendage, then leaped into the air as more of the writhing things reached for him. He levitated upward, out of range of the three weapons masters, who were struggling to free themselves. Before they could, though, a handful of duergar closed in, firing crossbows at the helpless drow, and the dark elves went down quickly.

Pharaun could see that House Maerret's position had been completely overrun. Duergar had closed in on one side, and drow on the other. The fight was simply a mad, whirling jumble of perhaps three dozen combatants fighting for their lives. What few remaining forces of House Maerret still survived were dropping quickly. Opponents closed in from all sides, and soon enough, Pharaun was reunited with his companions as the circle that surrounded them drew tighter and tighter.

"We're out of time," Quenthel said, still swinging her whip and directing magical hammers at her foes. "Do something now, wizard!"

"You!" came an angry shout from behind Pharaun. He turned to see who was making the commotion, and standing there, facing Quenthel, was Ssipriina Zauvirr, glaring at all of them. "You are the reason for all of this!" she screamed, raising her mace and pointing at them. "You should never have come to Ched Nasad!"

"Zauvirr!" came a second angry shout, a much more gruff voice, from the other side. Pharaun turned back the way he had originally been watching and spotted a large, well-armored duergar, one obviously of rank. "Foolish drow, I will see you dead!" the gray dwarf called.

"Betrayer!" Ssipriina spat back. "I should have known better than to trust you, Khorrl Xornbane. You can die with the meddlers. Kill them," she cried to her few remaining soldiers, who were massing in a line. "Kill them all!"

"Death to all drow!" Khorrl Xornbane roared, and motioned his handful of troops forward.

Pharaun's shoulders sagged.

We're never going to get out of here, he thought, swinging his magical rapier around.

Thick black smoke from the burning stone was blinding Ryld, making it hard to see more than a few feet in any direction. The battlefield had suddenly grown quiet. There were no more explosions, no flashing bursts from the firepots. Only the sound of steel on steel, but even that was greatly diminished.

He stepped forward to meet an onrushing contingent of gray dwarves. To his left, Halisstra also entered the fray, her heavy mace and an impressive mithral shield held ready. Quenthel took up a position on the warrior's other side, swinging her whip back and forth experimentally as she advanced.

The duergar, dozens of them, fanned out to meet the eclectic group, bloodlust plain in their eyes. Two came directly at Ryld, battle-axes held high. The weapons master parried the first swing at his shoulder and sidestepped a cut to the knees from his second foe. He brought the greatsword down atop the axe, snapping the haft cleanly, but then had to shift his weight almost off-balance to avoid a punching dagger to the ribs. Spinning, he kicked out with one booted foot, catching the gray dwarf square on the wrist and sending the dagger flying.

A third duergar loomed up behind Ryld, holding a length of chain that he spun in a circle over his head. Ryld saw that the foe was eyeing his legs, so when the attack came, he managed to leap high enough that the metal links missed him and went skittering across the pavement. In mid-leap, Ryld managed to turn completely around, flicking his blade across the head of the first gray dwarf's axe, unable to knock it completely loose, but nonetheless managing to force the combatant off-balance. As he landed, Ryld swung Splitter back around again, swiping at the chain-wielder's throat. The duergar jerked back from the attack, reeling in his chain for another attempt then stiffened in pain as the head of Danifae's morning star came down squarely on his skull in an enchanted shower of sparks. The creature slumped over as Danifae spun away to attack another foe.

Ryld maneuvered back around to face his original foe, who had regained his balance and had his axe level again. His companion, holding his injured wrist limply at his side, had fumbled a smaller hand axe free and was circling around Ryld, still trying to maneuver behind the weapons master. Ryld stepped back as though he were trying to avoid being surrounded, even as he casually blocked a couple of strokes from the battle-axe. Finally, when he saw the gray dwarf rear back for another, even more powerful cut, he planted his toe inside the coils of chain that the downed duergar had been swinging and flipped it up with his leg. As the chain sprayed out, it caught the humanoid squarely in the face. The duergar flinched, ruining his attack.

The Master of Melee-Magthere saw the hand axe coming toward his shoulder and twisted himself so that the blade just missed him then flicked Splitter back and up, slicing cleanly through the gray dwarf's arm at the elbow. Howling in agony, the duergar stumbled away, letting the momentum of the blow bear him out of harm's way. Ryld let the sword swing spin him completely around so that he planted his feet facing once more in the direction of the original enemy, who had disentangled himself from the chain and had flung it away.

Ryld shifted his greatsword a couple times, circling with the gray dwarf, the two of them warily sizing one another up. The weapons master stepped into a handful of slices and thrusts, flinging half-hearted attacks toward the dwarf that never really threatened it but allowed Ryld to see just how eager his opponent was to engage with him. The gray dwarf shied away from every cut and parry, and the Master of Melee-Magthere knew the duergar would break off the fight soon, assuming its companions dwindled to sufficiently small numbers around it.

Ryld stepped into an attack again, keeping his blade low and squarely in front of him, and the duergar trod backward another step. Then, as if out of nowhere, Valas appeared from the shadows, swinging one of his kukris low across the gray dwarf's hamstring. The duergar's knee buckled, and the scout came over the top with his other blade, stabbing it into the creature's chest. The duergar made a gurgling sound as he shivered and fell over.

The Master of Melee-Magthere shifted his attention elsewhere as soon as he saw the threat eliminated. He spied Jeggred ripping a drow to shreds. Only two others were visible, looking for a way to get inside the draegloth's reach, but Ryld doubted that would be the case for long. Another dark elf was fighting to keep Pharaun's rapier away from him, but Quenthel was closing on his flank, and the high priestess lashed out with her scourge, allowing the snake heads to sink their teeth deeply into the creature's neck. Jerking from the sudden sting of the bites, the drow was unable to maintain his attention on the rapier, which ran through his eye.

Another foe was squared off with Halisstra, who warded off a pair of stout blows with her mithral shield. On the third stroke from the dark elf across from her, she used the shield to deflect the strike and throw her opponent off-balance, then swung the heavy mace in her other hand upward in a vicious stroke, right into his chin. There was a loud, drumlike boom, a magical concussion that was obviously much louder than the simple impact of metal on bone, and the drow sank to the ground, his jaw shattered.

Breathing heavily, Ryld surveyed the battlefield. In addition to his six companions and Halisstra's brother, the only ones still standing were a small circle of perhaps a dozen exhausted drow and duergar who had ceased fighting for the moment and were watching as the duergar commander squared off with Ssipriina Zauvirr. The gray dwarf and the matron mother circled one another warily, as smoke wafted about, obscuring everything beyond the circle of Menzoberranyr and the three remaining members of House Melarn.

"Now is our chance," Pharaun said from next to the weapons master. "Let's go."

"No," Quenthel and Halisstra said together.

"Not until she goes down," the daughter of Drisinil Melarn added.

The Mistress of Arach-Tinilith nodded in agreement and said, "If she kills him, we're finishing her."

Pharaun groaned. "This is hardly the time for revenge, Mistresses."

Ssipriina feinted with her mace, and as the gray dwarf twisted out of the way of the attack, the drow palmed a wand and aimed it at her enemy. A thin ray of grayish light shot forth from the tip of the magical device, striking the duergar squarely in the chest. The gray dwarf clutched at his chest and cried out. He dropped to one knee with a groan, and Ssipriina loomed over him.

The duergar disappeared.

Snarling in rage at this trickery, the matron mother slammed her mace down where her foe had been, but she struck nothing but the pavement. Spinning, she swung back and forth wildly, trying to gain a lucky hit, but she found nothing.

The gray dwarf commander appeared again, leaping forward from one side as Ssipriina had turned her back to him. His axe was high, but his war cry gave the drow time to roll away from the worst of the attack. Instead of taking the blade of his weapon full on her skull, it raked across the back of her shoulder with a spurt of crimson.

The matron mother cried out, tumbling prone. She rolled to one side as Khorrl lifted his axe for another stroke. As she came around to face him, she fired off another beam with the wand.

With a grunt, Khorrl Xornbane dropped his axe and clutched his stomach, then crumpled to the ground, letting out a gurgling death sigh.

Quenthel and Halisstra both came at Ssipriina, who was trying to get to her feet, clutching her wounded shoulder with her good hand. Quenthel stepped to one side of the matron mother and struck down with her whip. The fangs of the snakes bit into the drow's flesh and she screeched in pain, then tried to spin around and aim the wand at the high priestess. Halisstra was ready for that, though, and she swung her mace down hard on Ssipriina's hand. The crunch of bone was unmistakable.

Around them all, the duergar and the drow began to fight again, and Ryld had to duck to avoid a sword swung at him by one of the dark elves. He sank to one knee and reversed Splitter, driving the point of the blade into his opponent's midsection. The drow threw up blood and sank to his knees, staring down at the sword in his gut. Impassively, Ryld planted his boot on the other drow's chest and yanked his greatsword free, turning back to see what was happening between the females as the body of his foe collapsed.

Quenthel had a hold of Ssipriina's hair, holding her head up. Both of the matron mother's arms were injured, and she could barely lift them to protect herself—and the poison was starting to take effect.

"Stop it!" Quenthel cried, yelling at the combatants around her. "Stop fighting, *now!*"

Slowly, the duergar and the drow began to back away, turning to look at Quenthel.

"Enough!" the Mistress of Arach-Tinilith said, her voice echoing through the haze. "This is pointless. The city is burning, and we must get out. If you stay here now and try to kill your enemies, you simply bring about your own death. That is not the drow way, and I cannot imagine it is the duergar way, either."

There were murmurs all around as the dark elves and the gray dwarves eyed each other hatefully, but Ryld saw more than a few shake their heads, agreeing with what Quenthel was saying.

"If you want any chance of living, then go your separate ways and get out of here, before the whole—"

The web street shook violently, tossing everyone about. Ryld, already on one knee, managed to maintain his balance. He peered around uncertainly. The whole length of the calcified webbing was unstable, listing sharply to one side. Ryld knew their time was up, and he began to levitate. Then he spotted what had created the upheaval as a second shock wave made the crumbling pavement shift again.

A giant spider had descended from overhead and was scurrying toward them. Behind it, a second spider was also drifting downward, playing out a length of web as it glided down.

Damnation, Ryld thought. There's just no end to this.

He peered around, looking for a direction to go to get clear of the approaching beasts.

Pharaun appeared beside the weapons master, hovering in the air and eyeing the advancing spiders.

"I think I've had quite enough of this," the wizard commented dryly, allowing his dancing rapier to disappear into his ring.

Ryld saw Quenthel and Halisstra, still standing over the slowly dying Ssipriina. He pointed them out to Pharaun.

"They don't know, yet," he said, dropping back down. "We've got to warn them!"

Once on his feet, the weapons master carefully managed to hold his balance as he rushed across the intervening space.

"Spiders!" he shouted as he neared them, pointing.

Quenthel looked up and her eyes grew wide. Jeggred appeared out of the haze of smoke next to her, his fur matted with blackening blood.

"We still don't know where to go," Pharaun said, a tinge of despair in his voice as he joined Ryld. "The best choice for now is simply over the side."

"Use your magic," Quenthel commanded. "Get us out of here!"

Pharaun spread his hands helplessly.

"Believe me, Mistress," he said, "if I had the means I would be using it. I've got nothing left. I can't conjure a gate just by willing it."

The first spider loomed closer, and Jeggred advanced toward it, determined to keep himself between the giant arachnid and his mistress. Valas slunk into the group, pulling Danifae along by the hand. The battle captive had a large cut across her forehead, and blood was dripping down into her eyes, making it difficult for her to see.

"Wait!" Ssipriina said, gasping for air as the poison closed her throat. "I know . . . of a way out. Save me . . . from . . . poison . . ."

"What?" Pharaun demanded. "Where? Get us there!"

"Say it, wretch," Quenthel commanded.

"Dangling . . . Tower," the dying matron mother replied. "Old, unused . . . dormant portal. Poison . . . please . . ."

Ignoring Ssipriina's pleas, Quenthel turned to Pharaun and asked, "Could you activate it?"

"I'll damn well try," Pharaun said. "Which way?"

"There . . ." Ssipriina whispered, looking up.

Ryld followed her gaze to a see a large, stalactite-shaped building hanging above them, an inverted tower like many of the estates back in Menzoberranzan. He groaned.

"We don't have enough time to get there!" Pharaun cried.

"Why not?" Q'arlynd Melarn said, floating up into the air to demonstrate. "We just levitate!"

"We can't all do that," Pharaun replied desperately. "As I've pointed out a time or two today already, I am fresh out of transportive spells."

"The battle captive gets left behind," Quenthel said bluntly. "I'm sorry, but that's the way it has to be."

Danifae sank to her knees, her head bowed. She seemed to accept her fate, but Ryld actually felt sorry for the drow. As if to punctuate the lack of time, the stone beneath them shifted again. Ryld left his feet to keep from losing his balance, and everyone else did, too, all except Valas and Danifae.

Q'arlynd shook his head.

"I didn't know," he said, shrugging. "Let's go."

"Wait!" Halisstra said. "I can get us all there," the priestess volunteered.

Pharaun and Quenthel both turned and looked at her. "You can?" the wizard asked.

"Yes," Halisstra said, nodding. "I dabble a bit in magic, myself. Different from your style, but some things are the same. Ryld says you're fond of using those dimensional doorways. I can do that."

Pharaun motioned for her to hurry.

"Open it into the main gallery," Q'arlynd shouted to Halisstra, pointing upward. "Where I took you that time?"

Another shock wave reverberated through the web street, causing it to buck wildly. Danifae and Valas both went sprawling, nearly being tossed over the side. The first spider was upon them, and Jeggred engaged it in a fight, levitating up to strike at its head. Ryld peered around wildly as the spider reared up and snapped at the draegloth, causing the web street to buck again.

The biggest rumble yet whipped through the thoroughfare, and the stone began to shift and crack.

"It's going to collapse!" Ryld shouted.

"Priestess, open your doorway!" Pharaun yelled as another roiling tremor dislodged the side of the street only a few feet away from them. "We're going through now!"

"No!" screamed Ssipriina, holding the wand she'd used to defeat Khorrl in both of her hands, her feet splayed out beside her, trying to maintain her balance.

She mumbled something and aimed the beam at Halisstra. The gray sliver of light struck the priestess in the leg and she buckled over in agony.

"You're . . . going to . . . die with me," the crazed matron mother said, turning the wand toward Quenthel. "No one . . . gets out . . . alive!"

Quenthel couldn't flee, as she was hovering in the air. She eyed the enraged drow across from her, licking her lips in desperation.

"I think not!" Halisstra shouted, standing straight again.

Before Ssipriina could trigger the wand again, the priestess spun around, swinging her mace with both hands. She struck the matron mother squarely in the face. There was a loud thunderclap, and Ssipriina Zauvirr was driven back a dozen feet, her face a ruined mess of pulpy flesh and bone.

"To the Abyss with you!" Halisstra screamed at Ssipriina Zauvirr's lifeless body.

Groaning and clutching at her leg, Halisstra wove a spell as the web street tilted again. She was singing, her voice quavering over the roar of battle. Ryld had never heard such a sound. She held a single, perfect note, and a bluish-white doorway opened in the air before her.

"Jeggred! Let's go!" Quenthel called, moving toward the doorway.

The draegloth dropped his attacks on the spider and scampered backward. When he reached the rest of them, he caught hold of

Valas, while Halisstra helped Q'arlynd get a hold of Danifae. Pharaun launched himself through the opening. Ryld followed the wizard to protect him from whatever might be on the other side, stepping through the magical frame just as the street gave way and tumbled into the darkness below him. He hoped the others were right behind him.

Chapter

TWENTY

The moment the doorway opened, Pharaun dived through it, hoping he was doing the right thing by trusting the children of House Melarn with his life. For all the wizard knew, she could have picked that moment to exact her revenge upon the Menzoberranyr for all the injustices they'd inflicted upon her family, her home, and herself. She certainly had a right to.

But the pathway didn't deposit the wizard into some scorching furnace or pit of doom. It was a poshly decorated hall, but unfortunately the mage found himself facing a huge, slavering lizard with incredibly sharp teeth. The being spotted him and advanced eagerly, eyeing the wizard as if he were its next meal.

Reacting quickly, the mage flung himself backward, out of the way of the thing, and willed a spell into being that created a series of floating balls of lightning. As the lizard darted toward him, Pharaun directed the balls to engage the creature, sparking as they did so. The beast jerked and backed away, but Pharaun was relentless, slamming all of the spheres of lightning into it. After the fourth one, the creature sprawled to the ground. It twitched a couple of times and lay still.

"What in the Abyss is that?" Ryld asked, popping through the portal with Splitter up and ready. "Are we in the right place?"

"Fortunately, yes," Pharaun replied, jumping up. A shiver through the building caused him to stumble forward. "Unfortunately, Halisstra, having never been here before, must not have known about the guard animals inside. Or else Q'arlynd forgot to warn us."

"By the Dark Mother!" Danifae said, spying the beast as she leaped through into the cell. She had her morning star up in an instant. "Is it dead?"

"I certainly hope so," Valas said, following close behind.

The scout had his kukris in his hands, and he was looking at the dead lizard. The hall shook again, and part of a wall collapsed, exposing the room to the city outside. Everyone splayed their legs out to try and maintain their balance.

One by one, the rest of the team passed through the portal to join them. Jeggred was the last one to clear the gate.

"The whole city's falling," the draegloth announced. Halisstra let the doorway wink out once he was safely through. "The falling stonework must be making the entire cavern quake with its force."

The fiend sounded too matter-of-fact for the wizard's taste.

Halisstra's brother was casting a spell, one Pharaun didn't recognize. He began to radiate an aura of divination magic—Pharaun's ring told him that much—as he looked around, almost as if he was sniffing something out.

"The dormant portal is this way," Q'arlynd said, leading the group out into a hallway. "Follow me."

The entourage followed the Melarn wizard through several passages, up a couple of staircases, and into a hallway that obviously hadn't been used in a long time. Several times during the journey, the structure shook, but they were deeper rumbles, vibrating through the whole of the Underdark.

"If this doesn't work . . ." Quenthel began.

"It'll work," Pharaun cut her off. "I'll need a couple of moments to study it, but it will work."

"You'd better hope so, wizard," the high priestess muttered.

Q'arlynd led them all to the end of the passage and stopped before an open doorway at the end of it.

"It's in there," he said, "but it's magically sealed and warded with protective glyphs. I have no way of getting through."

Pharaun knelt to study the opening. The barrier between the hallway and the larger room beyond was invisible but solid. Pharaun could see that it radiated some sort of magic and reported such.

"If I had the proper type of magic at my disposal," the Master of Sorcere said, "I'd be able to bring it down in mere seconds, but as it is, I can't do so until I've had a chance to rest and regroup."

"Do you have another magical doorway at your disposal?" Quenthel asked Halisstra.

The priestess shook her head miserably, reaching out to steady herself against a wall as another rumble rocked the room and everyone in it.

"Well, then, wizard, what are we going to do?" the Mistress of Arach-Tinilith asked. "We can't sit in here while you recharge your magical energies."

"Quite true," the mage replied. "Give me a moment."

"Mizzrym, we don't have a moment!"

As Pharaun studied their predicament, the building shook again, even more roughly. Everyone was pitched to the floor, and behind them a large portion of the ceiling collapsed, with shards of stone showering down.

"That is getting tiresome," Quenthel complained, regaining her feet with a horrid scowl on her face. "I will *not* die trapped in a cage like some animal. Not after all I've been through."

Growling deeply, Jeggred bounded across to the door and began to attack the invisible opening, raking his claws ineffectually against the barrier. A crackle of electrical energy raked over his body, but it didn't stop him from throwing himself at it again and again. His efforts were fruitless.

"Jeggred, stop it!" Quenthel said at last. "You're not helping."

With another deep-throated growl, the draegloth backed off.

"If we don't get through there," Danifae said to Pharaun, measuring each word for emphasis, "we're all going to be pulverized. Do something!"

"All right, all right," the mage replied, holding up a hand. "The problem is, we have no way to open the door from the inside. The magic that seals us out here keeps me from using even a simple spell. If I was over there, I could simply remove the barrier manually, but that's easier said than done. That's all. Such a simple trick, and yet impossible . . ."

He looked at them all miserably.

"Wait," Ryld said, stepping over near the wizard. "Move back."

Raising Splitter high over his head, the weapons master swung the blade down hard against the barrier. The enchanted weapon sliced into it with a flash of light, and Pharaun saw the magical emanations from the seal fade from view. The blade had dissipated the magic.

"Thank the Dark Mother," someone said as the entire group rushed into the chamber beyond.

"All right, wizard, lead us out of here," Quenthel said, sounding desperate, "and hurry!"

"We'll be departed in a moment," Pharaun said, gesturing for Q'arlynd to show him the way.

The Melarn wizard led the group into the large chamber, which looked like a library, though all the shelves were empty. Several statues lined the walls. Q'arlynd headed toward a spot on one wall, near the back of the room. It was an archway, but it led nowhere at the moment, filled instead with worked stone blocks. It did, however, glow with faint dweomers of transference.

"Here," he said.

"Excellent!" Pharaun replied, grinning as he studied the spot more closely. "Now, I'll just need a moment to—"

The mage's words were cut off by yet another tremor in the floor. This was followed by another, and another, again definitely different than the previous rumbling. Turning to look over his shoulder, Pharaun groaned. A massive statue of iron was striding slowly but inexorably toward them, and with each step the floor trembled under its weight.

"Lolth preserve us," Ryld said, dropping into a defensive crouch. "What is that?"

"It's a magical construct," Pharaun answered. "A golem. I can't do anything about it."

Ryld leaped forward to slice at the huge thing. His blade struck against the side of the construct and skittered off.

Pharaun shouted, "If it exhales, don't breathe the vapors!"

Jeggred snarled and leaped at the golem, slashing at it. In response, the huge construct swung one massive fist around and caught the draegloth squarely in the ribs, sending him flying across the room with a painful grunt. Jeggred was down on his hands and knees, shaking his head.

Ryld moved in again, wary of the huge sword in the golem's other hand. When the weapons master found an opening, he lunged forward, swiping at the metallic hide of the construct. Sparks flew as Splitter cut a deep furrow across the golem's flank. Ryld spun and ducked down, trying to stay behind the thing.

Another tremor rocked the chamber, and part of the ceiling collapsed behind the golem, sending bookshelves flying as shards of wood. Pharaun went down on one knee from the shaking, then looked up to see that part of the room on the far side had not just collapsed but had completely broken away and disappeared. The Dangling Tower was coming apart around them, just as House Melarn had done. Beyond the jagged edge of the room, Pharaun could see the smoky glow of the burning city. They were indeed running out of time.

"Forget the fight," Quenthel said, grabbing the wizard by the collar of his *piwafwi* and spinning him to face her. "Just get that portal open. *Now!*"

Pharaun nodded and turned away as Jeggred leaped back in beside Ryld. Valas, Halisstra, and Q'arlynd also circled the construct, each of them waiting until the thing turned its attention to another before sliding in to gain an attack. Ignoring the fight behind him, Pharaun concentrated on studying the magical glows from the portal. He needed a few moments to determine the key that would activate the thing.

"Hurry!" Quenthel said, watching him over his shoulder.

Pharaun gave the high priestess a very deliberate look.

"Don't rush me," he said flatly, and continued studying.

Behind the mage came a deep grunt, and Ryld slid up against the wall in a heap. The weapons master shook his head, apparently trying to clear the cobwebs, and regained his feet.

"Hurry," the weapons master hissed, "I don't know how long we can keep this thing off you."

Pharaun rolled his eyes and bent to his task once more. He tumbled onto his side as the floor bucked with another foundation-crumbling shudder.

"I've just about got it," the Master of Sorcere said, when half the wall next to the portal exploded in a shower of rock and dust.

Fragments of debris smacked into the wizard, knocking the breath from him as he went sprawling. He felt the floor shift, not just from buckling but because the whole building was tipping. He knew it was going to break away soon, and their chances for escaping the city would disappear with it.

The mage struggled up into a sitting position and looked around. What was left of the room was considerably smaller than before. The iron golem teetered near the edge of the floor, then took a step toward its nearest foe, causing the stone beneath its feet to groan. Everyone in the group lay sprawled, half buried in rubble and dust, and just beyond Valas, the floor was gone, replaced by the void of the city. The rock groaned and shifted again as the golem took a step toward the scout, and Valas rolled toward the opening.

"Jeggred," Pharaun yelled, "grab Valas!"

Even as the words left his mouth, Valas, who seemed considerably dazed, tumbled the rest of the way over and dropped over the edge, disappearing from sight.

The draegloth, who had been caught beneath a large section of collapsing rubble, let out a snarl of fury so unearthly that it chilled Pharaun's blood. Shoving his way out of the debris, the enraged fiend leaped across the distance and dived over the edge after the scout.

The golem swung its sword toward the demon, but it was too slow. With Jeggred out of sight, the golem focused its attention on its next victim. Q'arlynd Melarn lay facedown, unmoving, close to it. Nearby, Danifae was sprawled across the shattered remains of a bookcase, the wound on her forehead bleeding freely. The golem took another step, and Pharaun nearly fell as the stone floor popped and protested.

We're not going to make it, the mage thought, trying to figure out a way to distract the golem from killing the unconscious pair.

Out of the corner of his eye, Pharaun saw Ryld regain his feet.

"Help them!" the wizard shouted to his friend, pointing to Danifae and Q'arlynd.

The weapons master had a deep gash across his forehead, but his red eyes seemed clear, and when he spotted the forms of the battle captive and the Melarn mage, and the golem moving toward them, he nodded.

The room tilted over some more, and Pharaun slid across the floor a few feet. The blackness of the vast cavern of the city yawned before him. He ignored it and looked to Ryld.

The weapons master measured his distance from the golem, who had gotten close enough to Danifae that it raised its sword high, preparing to deliver a killing blow. Ryld sprang forward, charging as fast as he could, aided by the downhill slope of the floor. When he was within a few feet of the construct, he leaped into the air, extended both feet, and hit the golem with a pile-driving kick to its midsection. The force of the blow drove Ryld back up the slope of the floor, and the golem barely seemed to move.

But then Pharaun saw that it was teetering. The construct took a step back to steady itself, and had the floor been level, it probably would have worked, but the weight of the golem, coupled with the slope of the floor, caused it to overbalance. Another step backward brought the toppling construct near the edge of the floor, and the room shifted more, sinking and increasing the slope. Then, with one final off-balance step, the golem shifted forward again, falling up the slope rather than down. It dropped to one knee and reached out for Q'arlynd, who was shaking his head as he returned to consciousness.

The fractured stone could no longer hold the construct's weight, and it gave out beneath the golem. Even then, the construct latched on to the wizard, gripping him tightly. Q'arlynd screamed in agony. Ryld took two steps forward to save the wizard, but both Q'arlynd and the golem slowly, ponderously went over, slipping from sight.

Halisstra cried out, "*No!*" from the other side of the room.

She ran to the edge, but the weapons master grabbed her and held her back, shaking his head.

Disheartened, Pharaun turned back to the portal. He thought he'd it figured out and reached forward, ready to activate the magic of the portal, and stopped. Something felt . . . wrong. The room shifted over some more, and the wizard was forced to begin levitating to maintain his position. Behind him, he heard one of the females give a startled scream, but he ignored it. Peering at the magical emanations, he realized that he was seeing something illusory. He hadn't noticed it before, but understanding what to look for, it was much clearer.

"Pharaun," Quenthel yelled as everyone gathered around him, "if you can make that thing work, do it! The whole city is going down!"

Shaking his head at what he'd been about to do, the mage began to cast a spell, one that he'd not expected to need that day but was thankful for. He fished an ointment from one of his many pockets and dabbed a bit on each eyelid. Suddenly, everything about the archway became plain to his vision. He could see the runes that had been hidden from his view before, scribed into the stone around it. He cast a second spell, one to decipher the script, and found what he was looking for. The writing contained the trigger word.

"I've got it!" he shouted. "Get ready!"

Pharaun stepped back, uttered the triggering word aloud, and the portal shimmered to life, glowing with a deep purple hue. The whole thing took on a sense of depth, of distance. The stone in the center of the arch faded and was replaced by a shimmering curtain of light.

Pharaun turned back to his companions and shouted, "It's ready! Step through!"

Quenthel was the closest, but she hesitated.

"Where does it go?" she asked.

"I don't know," Pharaun admitted. "The script inscribed on the perimeter mentions something about a city, but I don't recognize the name. We'll find out on the other side."

Quenthel shook her head.

"No. Someone else must go through first."

Ryld, Halisstra, and Danifae were gathered around, with the weapons master helping to keep Danifae from sliding down the floor to her death. The rest of them were levitating.

Ryld pushed Danifae toward the opening and said, "I'm right behind you!"

The master of Melee-Magthere nudged the battle captive into the arch. Danifae cast one last, aggravated look over her shoulder, nodded, and leaned forward into the archway. In a flash, she was gone. Ryld lunged forward a heartbeat later, followed by Halisstra.

Pharaun looked at Quenthel.

"Well?" he said.

"You first," she replied, still gazing at the gate in trepidation.

"I can't," the Master of Sorcere explained. "I must go last. Because I opened it, the portal will shut behind me."

"What about Jeggred?"

"I will wait for them as long as I can," Pharaun said as another groan emanated from the stonework around them.

The remains of the building tilted some more, and Quenthel's eyes widened.

"There is no more time. Go through!" Pharaun said, and he pushed Quenthel toward the opening.

In a fury, the high priestess spun around, her hand reaching for the whip at her side. The five snakes were writhing madly, lashing at the mage even from where they hung, but the building lurched and tipped and Quenthel couldn't hold on. She stumbled against the wizard, and the snakes snapped ineffectually against his *piwafwi*.

Pharaun caught her and set her on her feet again.

"Please," he said to her. "We don't have time for this."

Quenthel's scowl faded slightly, and she looked at the wizard with a slight smirk.

"If I didn't know better, I would think you're getting soft, wizard."

With that, she backed into the archway and was gone.

Pharaun shook his head in wonder and turned to see if there was any sign of Jeggred and Valas. The floor was slanted at a fairly steep pitch, and the mage slid down its surface toward the edge to peer over the side. Below, he could see the two of them, rising as rapidly as Jeggred's levitation would allow. Chunks of stone and other debris was falling into the void beyond them, and Pharaun knocked a fragment loose from the edge of the crumbling floor. He cringed as he watched it tumble toward them, but it shot past, barely missing them.

Finally, almost excruciatingly slowly, the draegloth and his charge reached what was left of the structure. Together, the three of them worked their way toward the archway, which still glowed with an intense light.

"The others are waiting on the other side," Pharaun explained, motioning to the doorway. "I have to go last. Hurry!"

Without hesitating, Jeggred leaped through the archway and vanished. Valas scrambled to go after him just as there was one final, bone-rattling tremor, and the remains of the room began to free fall. Pharaun gave the scout a good shove and dived in after him.

The portal sealed up and its light faded. A heartbeat later, what was left of the Dangling Tower, including the wall where the portal had been anchored, shattered into a million fragments as it struck a web street below.

Aliisza cringed when she saw the fury in Kaanyr Vhok's eyes. He was displeased that she had neglected to keep him apprised of the situation in the drow city, and even her explanation of her troubles, the difficulties she had encountered with the drow, did little to soften his mood.

"So you say the entire city is ruined?" the cambion growled, pacing. "Brought down by a horde of miserable gray dwarves?"

"Not just gray dwarves, darling, but the drow themselves. They squabbled among themselves so much that they lost control. It destroyed them."

"How could this have happened? Not that I bear any regret at the fall of the overly proud dark elves, but they do not seem to be the type who would allow such a travesty to occur to their great city. The forces of the Underdark are clearly out of balance."

"I know," the alu-fiend said, moving close to her mate, "but there is a reason."

"You know what it is?"

"Yes, love, but your pacing is putting me on edge. Sit down, and I will tell you."

Kaanyr Vhok sighed, but turned and plopped himself down in his throne.

"All right," he said, patting his lap. "Tell me."

Aliisza sashayed over to Vhok and settled herself into his lap. She had missed him, she realized, more than she'd thought she would. She leaned around and began to nuzzle his ear.

"Mmm," he said, "I missed you," echoing her own thoughts. "But before we get to the 'welcome homes,' tell me what you found out."

Aliisza giggled as his fingers stroked her arm.

"They've lost contact with their goddess," she whispered, blowing the words softly into his ear.

"What?" the cambion rumbled, sitting up straight and nearly dumping the demon on the floor. "Are you serious?"

The alu-fiend folded her arms beneath her breasts in a huff.

"Of course I'm serious," she sniped. "Lolth has vanished from their sight, and they're trying to figure out why, but of course, them being—what did you call them? Oh, yes—'overly proud dark elves.' Them being overly proud and set in their ways, they warred with one another to the point of bringing about their own extinction."

"I see. Well, with Lolth out of the picture, I suppose if you wanted to gain a little retribution for some wrongs inflicted upon you in the past, now would be the time to do it," the cambion said, staring absently into the distance.

"So, are you thinking of exacting a little revenge?" Aliisza said, nuzzling against her lover's neck again.

"Maybe," Vhok replied. "We'll have to see. I guess it won't be against Ched Nasad, hmm?"

"Mmm," Aliisza purred, squirming, as Kaanyr Vhok's fingers began to roam over her body again. "I guess not."

All thoughts of the ruined City of Shimmering Webs left her then, for a good, long while.

High above the ruined City of Shimmering Webs, a single dark elf sat upon a perch of stone near the roof of the great cavern and watched. The smoke was heavy there, thick and acrid, but it didn't bother him. He stared down at the destruction and smiled.

He was not attractive, not by drow standards, certainly, and few of any other species would look on him and think him handsome in the least, but he didn't mind that either. What he sought was much more substantial than beauty.

They will be pleased, Zammzt thought, watching as fires slowly burned away, as whole sections of the city crumbled and collapsed, dropping into the murky depths of the cavern below. It is a good first step. There is still much to be done, but it is a good first step.

Shaking himself out of his reverie, the drow stood and stretched.

I must go, he thought, somewhat regretfully.

He was proud of what he'd wrought, and he wished to stay and observe it a bit longer, but the others would be waiting.

Sighing, he turned his sweeping gaze over the ruins of Ched Nasad one last time, then stepped into the darkest recesses of the shadows and vanished.